THE DAY AFTER
WORLD WAR III

Edward Zuckerman

THE DAY AFTER WORLD WAR III

THE VIKING PRESS   NEW YORK

To Rochelle and Louis Zuckerman

Portions of this book appeared originally, in different form,
in *Esquire, Harper's Magazine, The New York Times, Penthouse,*
and The Alicia Patterson Foundation *Reporter.*

Library of Congress Catalog Card Number 83-040230
ISBN 0-670-25880-6

Grateful acknowledgment is made to Tom Lehrer
for permission to reprint four lines from his song
"We Will All Go Together When We Go. . . ."
Copyright © 1958 by Tom Lehrer. All rights reserved.

Printed in the United States of America
Set in Times Roman

Contents

CHAPTER ONE: **"Present Address: Mortuary #10"**   **1**

CHAPTER TWO: **Fermi's Bet**   **15**

CHAPTER THREE: **"The Good News Is You'll Be President"**   **44**

CHAPTER FOUR: **"All This from One Bomb"**   **67**

CHAPTER FIVE: **"This Area *Will* Be Evacuated"**   **97**

CHAPTER SIX: **"The Number-One Myth of the Nuclear Age"**   **125**

CHAPTER SEVEN: **The Long Nuclear War**   **149**

CHAPTER EIGHT: **"We Sound a Little Crazy"**   **176**

CHAPTER NINE: **Continuity of Government**   **211**

CHAPTER TEN: **"Comrade, What Is This?"**   **239**

CHAPTER ELEVEN: **Open for Business**   **273**

CHAPTER TWELVE: **The Day After World War III**   **295**

CHAPTER THIRTEEN: **The Day Before World War IV**   **331**

Sources   **343**

Index   **391**

THE DAY AFTER
WORLD WAR III

ONE

"Present Address: Mortuary #10"

On the day after the outbreak of nuclear war, the president of the United States, circling high above the fallout in his fortified 747, will issue an order freezing wages, prices, and rents. The purpose of the order, according to current government planning documents, "will be to restrain inflationary pressures . . . during the postattack recovery period." The only products exempted from the price freeze will be those intended for military use. Presumably, this will encourage the production of goods necessary for successful prosecution of the war.

The general freeze order is part of Federal Emergency Plan D, a classified collection of "Presidential Emergency Action Documents" that have been drawn up and set aside for use after a nuclear war. As one official of the Federal Emergency Management Agency (FEMA) has pointed out, in the aftermath of a nuclear attack the president "won't have a big staff there to say to, 'Go prepare me a legal document with all the necessary details,' so these have been done ahead of time."

All government planning for the "postattack" period includes declarations of support for traditional American democratic practices, so Plan D is accompanied by a parallel set of documents designed not for presidential proclamation but as draft legislation to be submitted to Congress—if Congress can be found. This set, also classified, is called "Documents for Contingencies (Other Than a Plan D Situation) Which Justify Application of Emergency Measures on a National Scale." For short, they are known as the "Other Than D" documents.

The Other Than D documents include a draft bill authorizing the Internal Revenue Service to waive interest penalties against taxpayers who, after a nuclear attack, file late returns "due to reasonable cause and not due to willful neglect." Another draft bill authorizes the secretary of the treasury to modify the size, design, or composition of United States coins as he deems necessary during the post-nuclear-attack period. A third draft bill is a declaration of war.

In case the war in question has destroyed the Congress, the Presidential Plan D documents include a proclamation that a state of war exists (only Congress can *declare* war). "Legally, a lot of things [including emergency powers] depend on that," the FEMA official explained.

So the proclamation has already been drafted, with a few blanks left to be filled in later—like the date, and the name of the enemy.

Some of the finer points of the post-nuclear-war federal tax system were worked out at a government-wide postattack exercise in 1980. The economists who devised it, laboring at their temporary desks inside a hollowed-out mountain in northern Virginia, found the subject tricky. Postattack tax policy has always been considered a difficult subject by government planners, partly because it is linked to the touchy question of war-loss sharing. Official government policy is to "support the equitable sharing of war losses throughout the economy . . . not to guarantee individuals against war losses, but to assure the maintenance of a 'going concern' economy." Exactly what that policy means, however, is a matter of some debate.

As long ago as 1963, a Treasury Department report on the subject found that "our files are already fat with indemnification histories." The basic issue, it said, is whether you want to distribute surviving assets equally among surviving people, which would involve a transfer of wealth through the tax system, or if you want to reserve surviving resources for purposes that "will contribute most

2

to the mobilization effort." Even if you decide you do want to tax those with surviving wealth to reimburse the newly poor for their losses, another study noted a few years later, it will not be a simple matter to measure wealth in the postattack world. "Consider a firm whose principal assets consist of a professional football team valued, preattack, at $15 million," the study said. "Suppose that the players survived the attack and that all debts of the team were fully paid up. Any plan to levy . . . a net-worth tax postattack must face up to the fact that this firm's relative net worth in real terms is certainly not going to be the same as preattack."

Even if that football team's value is drastically reduced by the war—its quarterback is caught standing under the stadium, say, and the stadium is caught standing under a hydrogen bomb—a post-attack tax proposal endorsed by the Internal Revenue Service in 1977 would not allow the team's owners any tax deduction for their loss. No deductions should be allowed for war losses, the proposal said, because the tax rate would have to be raised too high to compensate for all those deductions. The proposal did, however, support handing out tax-free cash grants to war survivors. In 1980, at the postattack exercise called REX-80 ALPHA, a young Treasury Department planner named Gary Robbins and his colleagues came up with something else.

"You have to protect the banking system," Robbins explained, "the ones who have made loans on real assets. You want to reestablish the productive base of the United States. You want to give entrepreneurs enough money to start their businesses somewhere else. If you had seventeen Rembrandts, that's nice, but you won't be reimbursed for them, because they don't add much to your productivity. But a house is part of the productive structure, because if you don't have a place to live you can't go to work.

"In the exercise we were told that two trillion dollars' worth of property was destroyed. We assumed that ninety percent of the people who owned that property and of the banks who lent money on it were within the radius of destruction themselves. That left two hundred billion dollars to be compensated.

"The owners of the destroyed property can't pay off the mortgages, but, if they default, the banking system collapses. So the federal government is going to have to buy the destroyed assets. It can't pay in full now. It will have to accept the mortgages and pay them off over time. The titles transfer to the federal government, which eventually can sell the property and recoup some of the losses. If the property is paid up, the government will pay the owner over time, and he can use the proceeds to rebuild."

And how is the government going to finance its purchase of all that destroyed property?

That which originally belonged to the states will be bought back from the federal government by the states, "using the proceeds of accounts of deceased at financial institutions transferred to the States under the rule of escheat," said a memo prepared by Robbins and his colleagues after the exercise. The government's purchase of the rest of the property will be financed by federal taxes, the planners decided. That there would be people left to pay taxes was assumed in the exercise scenario, which stipulated that nuclear weapons fell on only about 25 percent of the country.

"The pattern of the attack ran along the East Coast—they hit New York and Washington—and then through Georgia and out to the missile installations in the West," Robbins said. "The results were interesting. The attack destroyed the entire capability of the United States to print money, and we were told there were no currency reserves. It was a frightening situation. East–West transportation was cut off. Communications were wiped out. And the explosions' electromagnetic pulse wiped out computer memories. In that situation, our current tax policy is absolutely meaningless. Employers have no records, so they can't fill out W-2 forms. Bank records are gone. Paper backup records are no good. You can't process them fast enough.

"Now you need a different kind of tax policy. You have to forgive all current taxes. If the attack happens on July 1, say, some people have paid withholding and some people have paid nothing, but you have to forgive and forget on both sides. It's not fair to some people, but it's too hard to figure out. Then you probably want to put on something like a sales tax. That's the simplest one to administer. Stores are already familiar with the system, and you don't want to have to train them at this point. The rate would probably be close to thirty percent—that equals the current government take plus enough extra money to finance the war-loss sharing—with absolutely no exceptions. If state and local governments were exempted, a black market would appear immediately."

And how would all this be communicated to the surviving population?

"I'm not exactly certain," Robbins said. "Normal communications wouldn't work. You'd probably post it somewhere."

But Robbins hadn't reckoned with the planners at the U.S. Postal Service.

As soon as possible after a nuclear attack on the United States, the following message, which has already been recorded, will be broadcast over surviving radio stations to surviving radios:

> This is the United States Emergency Broadcast System with a message about emergency mail service and how it will help to reunite separated families.
>
> If because of the emergency you become separated from or do not know the whereabouts of family members, relatives, employers, employees, or government agencies . . . the Postal Service will provide the principal, and perhaps the only, means available for reestablishing such contacts.
>
> Welfare offices and post offices . . . which are still functioning after an attack will furnish persons whose regular post offices or home addresses are no longer usable with two types of important cards with instructions for filling them out. One is called a Safety Notification Card; the other an Emergency Change of Address Card.
>
> The Safety Notification Card should be completed and mailed promptly to the last known address of those whom it is important for you to contact. . . . The Emergency Change of Address Card should be addressed to the Postmaster at the post office where you normally received your mail at the time of the attack, even though that post office is known to be out of operation. . . .

If that post office *is* out of operation, the Emergency Change of Address Card will be sent to a special "Emergency Postal Concentration Center" (PCC) that will be set up to process and forward mail to people whose old addresses no longer exist. Sites for PCCs have already been selected in "areas of maximum safety," according to the Postal Service's *Emergency Planning Manual*. The manual, revised in 1981, contains detailed instructions on how to test Emergency Change of Address Cards for dangerous radioactivity before processing them ("to enhance the safety of postal employees"), explains how the cards should be alphabetized and filed ("sort according to the first letter of the last name"), and suggests that all postmasters stockpile a plastic letter tray (stock item 1262, now obsolete), which is perfect for stacking incoming Emergency Change of Address Cards, a large number of which are expected.

Other "Postmaster General Standby Emergency Actions" that will go into effect after a nuclear attack authorize local postmasters to burn stamps to prevent their "falling into enemy hands," restrict postattack mail to first-class letters, and place an immediate ban on the issuance of money orders for payment in the country that attacked the United States. Although the times are expected to be depressing—"the objectives of the [Emergency Change of Address Card] program are essentially of a welfare or morale nature," the manual observes—one Standby Emergency Action will be good news for people who have to use the cards: they will go postage-free.

Every post office in the United States has already been provided with a supply of the cards, along with detailed instructions on how they are to be filled out. "It is essential that Forms 809 [the Emergency Change of Address Card] be executed correctly in order to be effective for mail directory purposes," the manual warns. Every displaced person must fill one out, the manual says, including escaped mental patients and convicts. ("A single Form 809 completed in the name of the institution would suffice for all those continuing to receive mail in its care.") To make sure there are no mistakes in following the directions, the manual provides a selection of properly completed sample cards. They tell a very sad story.

The first card is filled out by a Mr. William Thomas Butler. His "pre-emergency" address, he records, was 2501 Upton Street, Washington, D.C. His new address is Box 21, Rural Route #2, Leesburg, Virginia. The card does not relate how Butler made it safely from Washington to Leesburg. But that is not important. He is alive, and his mail will be forwarded.

6

The next card in the series is filled out by Butler's wife, who is also in Leesburg. In accordance with a Postal Service recommendation, Mrs. Butler has actually filled out two cards, one as Mrs. William Thomas Butler and one as Mrs. Mary Alice Butler. This will minimize the possibility of her missing any of her mail.

A third card is filled out by the Butlers' daughter Agnes, who is also safe in Leesburg. And the family has also addressed a sample Form 810 (Safety Notification Card) to a family friend. It informs her of the family's new address and assures her that William, Mary, and Agnes are safe. But it adds, rather ominously, "Whereabouts of Mabel Jane not known."

Unhappily, readers of the Postal Service manual know exactly where Mabel Jane (the second Butler daughter) is. A sample Emergency Change of Address Card has been filled out for her, too. Her pre-emergency address, like the others, is recorded as Upton Street in Washington. But her present address is not Leesburg. It is " 'Deceased,' Mortuary #10, Falls Church, Virginia."

It is important to fill out cards for the dead, the postal manual explains, so that letters for those persons can be returned to sender from the PCC (marked "deceased per notice dated————") or, if they lack return addresses, be filed with the Dead Mail.

The fate of Mabel Jane's mail is thus made clear; it is not so certain, however, what will happen to her remains.

The postattack responsibilities of every federal agency are carefully spelled out in Executive Order 11490. The Department of the Treasury, for example, is charged with establishing "tax and debt policies." The Postal Service is mandated to forward mail. And the Department of Health and Human Services, which includes the Public Health Service, is charged with planning for "sanitary aspects of disposal of the dead." This was a responsibility that the government once took very seriously. A 1956 manual on "Mortuary Services in Civil Defense" explains, "Disposal of bodies as nearly as possible in accordance with normal customs and religious rites will be a major contribution to morale, but such methods may be impossible. Embalming, use of caskets, lying in state, and individual religious ceremonies may have to be omitted." It advises that even formal identification of the dead may have to be forgone. "Ten thousand unidentified bodies would require over 5.5 acres of space

7

... for adequate display. A person would walk 5 miles between the rows of bodies before all were seen and for each 25,000 identifiable bodies probably 10,000 would be unrecognizable because of disfigurement by injury or fire." Even preliminary identification of each body from its personal effects would be difficult. "Ten identification teams (30 men) working steadily should be able to handle an average of about 100 bodies an hour or 800 bodies per 8-hour shift. . . . If the season, climate, and weather are advantageous, the local civil defense mortuary services will have not more than a week at most before postmortem changes will make processing of bodies extremely unpleasant." Therefore, "A method of rapid, mechanical grave digging and filling will be needed. . . . If conditions permit, mechanically dug continuous trenches offer the best solution to the burial problem. If the machines available are capable only of digging narrow trenches, bodies can be placed head to foot instead of side to side."

Unlike the Treasury and Postal Service, the Department of Health and Human Services has not kept its mortuary literature up to date, possibly because there is nothing else to be said on the subject. "If we're involved in a small war," Public Health Service Emergency Coordinator Harold Gracey said in 1981, "we'd just go with an extension of the present system. If we had one hundred million dead, it would be more of a dump-truck operation.

"When I got this job," he added, "my predecessor told me, 'They'll try to shove off planning for sanitary disposal of the dead on you. Tell 'em we'll just dig trenches with bulldozers. We'll bury them, but afterwards we won't be able to say exactly what happened to Aunt Susie.' "

As displaced persons, the surviving Butlers will have the advantage of being first in line for postattack housing managed by the Department of Housing and Urban Development. (Second in line will be workers in essential industries, and third will be those who work in the management of postattack housing.) Rents will be set at levels corresponding to those for similar housing in the neighborhood, but no one will be evicted for not paying his rent if "in the judgment of the Housing Manager or Managing Agent, the failure to pay is due to causes beyond the control of the occupant." The Butlers and their fellow displaced persons may be put up in requisitioned tents, hastily constructed barracks, or even privately owned homes "whose owners have disappeared or are unable to function," but if the owners of such homes show up again, the new tenants will have to move out within thirty days.

All of this is spelled out in HUD's *Emergency Housing Management Manual*, published in 1980 "to provide guidelines ... in the management of emergency housing in the event of an attack on the United States." The agency realizes, of course, that much postattack housing will not be luxurious. Provision has been made to repair damaged housing (federal aid for such repairs may be obtained by submitting Form EHR-1 in triplicate), but HUD notes that survivors of a nuclear war will be expected to tolerate windows that are "boarded up or covered with paper, board, plastic, or other material." HUD stipulates, however, that electric wiring must be inspected "even though electric current is temporarily not available." And no housing shall be repaired unless it is "free of radioactive contamination."

Radioactivity is not expected to be too much of a problem by the postattack planners at the Department of Agriculture, at least not if the attack happens to come at the right time of year. "If you get the attack in June," says Harold Gay of the Agriculture Stabilization and Conservation Service, "you'll have a hell of a loss of yield of the corn crop, because radioactivity attacks the living organism of the young plant. But if you get the attack in August, if it's safe enough to get out in the fields and run your picker, the [radioactive] dust'll fly right off the plants. . . .

"Just because you have fallout on a crop doesn't mean it's not safe to eat. Fallout is dust. It can be removed by normal washing, peeling, and so on. If it's mixed in with the actual food product, then you would store it. Radioactivity decays. Milk, for example, is very susceptible to radioactivity. You can't hold the milk until the radioactivity decays, but you can process it into cheese and store the cheese."

Postattack planners do recognize that not all nuclear war survivors will have the patience to wait for radioactive Velveeta to become edible. "You're going to get a run on goods," acknowledges

9

one FEMA official. "You're going to get some very irrational behavior in the marketplace." And so you're also going to get rationing.

The Department of Agriculture has already prepared a series of "Defense Food Orders" and placed them in the Code of Emergency Federal Regulations, a compilation of federal rules that will go into effect after an enemy attack. Defense Food Order No. 2 spells out the National Emergency Maximum Food Distribution Allowance for postattack diets. Food dealers will be allowed to stock only enough meat, for example, to provide each of their surviving customers with three pounds a week. If there's a bone in the meat, the customer can have four pounds. If there's no meat, the customer can substitute thirty-six eggs or eight-and-one-quarter pounds of potatoes. If there are no eggs or potatoes, the customer can have three pounds of dry peas or six pounds of canned pork and beans. If all foods are available, the customer will simply get his three pounds of meat, along with six eggs, four pounds of cereal products, two pounds of frozen vegetables, one-half pound of fats and oils, two pounds of potatoes, and one-half pound of sweets.

"That's about two thousand to twenty-five hundred calories per person per day," Gay points out, "about two-thirds of normal caloric input right now, if you could have something from every grouping." ("A daily intake of 2200 calories would probably be adequate for a month or more," another postattack food expert asserted in 1967, "or perhaps even beneficial in view of the estimates that twenty percent of all adults and . . . children are obese.")

The actual mechanics of consumer rationing will, according to the plan, be devised at the local level. Local ration boards "composed of prominent citizens" should be promptly created, FEMA advises. Teachers and PTA groups should be considered for running consumer registration centers. Ration cards should be printed, using "light cardboard or heavy stock paper." (Printer-ready ration-card mats were distributed to the states during the 1960s in folders labeled "Information Herein Applies Only in Event of Nuclear Attack," but that printing technology is now obsolete and most of the old mats are unaccounted for.)

To conserve as many farm resources as possible, rationing will not be confined to food for people. The distribution of seed and farm-equipment repair parts will also be controlled, and farm animals will be put on rationed diets. (Lactating sows will be allowed twelve pounds of feed a day, laying chickens one-fifth of a pound. If there's not enough feed for both, the chickens will take precedence over the sows. Fatally irradiated animals will be allowed no feed at all.) And Defense Food Order No. 5 limits the use of fertilizer following "a surprise enemy attack upon the United States" to essential crops, specified to include all food grains, vegetables, fruits, fiber crops, oil crops—and tobacco, which seems to be a case of post-attack planners working at cross-purposes. "The long-term effect" of a nuclear attack on the United States, postattack health researcher Dr. Conrad Chester told a congressional committee in 1976, "could be an increase of thirty percent in cancer incidence in some parts of the country. While this increase is undesirable, it does not threaten national survival. It could be cancelled out by neglecting to rebuild the cigarette industry."

If the cigarette industry is rebuilt anyway, it will have to compete with other, more crucial industries for scarce postattack resources. (To guide postattack decision-makers, a list of six thousand manufacturing plants "considered to be of exceptional importance to national security" has been classified Secret and distributed in sealed envelopes to federal offices around the country.) The ultimate authority for deciding who gets what will be the Office of Defense Resources, an organization that will be created, according to the circumstances, either by a Plan D presidential proclamation or an Other Than D act of legislation. All major federal agencies will have both resource-claimant and -supply roles. The Department of Agriculture, for example, will be the resource agency for food, because it presumably will be controlling farming, while it will be a claimant agency for labor, because the farms it controls will need labor to produce. If a dispute arises—say Agriculture needs workers to harvest corn and the Public Health Service needs people to bury the dead but the Department of Labor doesn't have enough workers on hand for both—then the Office of Defense Resources will step in and make the decision.

One of the toughest resources to handle will in fact be labor. "Individual and small group foraging and hoarding of found supplies consume available resources and do nothing to bring about future resupply," one civil defense manual observes. "Means must be found for satisfying the survivors' basic needs while, at the same time, motivating and directing the efforts of survivors in other critical recovery activities." The actual means for directing survivors into useful activities are only hinted at in unclassified postattack planning documents. But the *Civil Emergency Preparedness Handbook* of the Department of Labor's Employment and Training Administration does state that, following a nuclear attack, "previously prepared mobilization plans . . . would be implemented. These plans include workforce registration." Additional measures that "will be undertaken only as a last resort when voluntary actions prove insufficient" include "mandatory controls in the area of workforce mobilization." Such measures may include the "requirement that certain workers provide their services to meet essential survival needs."

The planning for medical workers is more straightforward. "In the event of a nuclear attack on the United States," another Labor Department manual says, "many physicians, dentists, veterinarians, podiatrists, and optometrists would suspend private practice and become salaried employees of emergency treatment centers." Several physicians' groups opposed to the nuclear arms race have in recent years argued at great length that it is hopeless to plan for any meaningful medical care after a nuclear attack, but the planners are not discouraged. "We have a zillion allergy doctors out there," says one FEMA official. "Their work can be redirected."

One provision for immediate postattack medical care has been made in the National Defense Stockpile of Strategic and Critical Items. The stockpile contains fifteen billion dollars' worth of sixty-one essential items ranging from aluminum to zinc. The stockpile goal for each item is the amount that would be needed by the United States during a three-year conventional war or the amount that would be needed during a nuclear war, whichever is greater. "Only in the case of opium did the nuclear war goal (75,000 pounds) exceed the conventional war goal (70,000 pounds)," a stockpile official told a congressional committee in 1976. In 1980, the requirement was refigured, and the opium goal was raised to 130,000 pounds. Seventy-one thousand pounds are currently on hand.

The purpose of the stockpile, and all the other planning, will be full national recovery, which is not seen as too difficult a task. A 1972 government-wide study conducted for the Joint Chiefs of Staff, based on a "computer-processed simulation" of a 1971 nuclear war involving a 6800-megaton attack on the United States, concluded that the nation "could survive, continue the conflict and recover." Six years after the war, the study said, the economy would have recovered to such an extent that survivors "would have approximated a 1965 per capita standard of living, except for automobile production." By the seventh year, a 1970 standard of living would have been achieved, it said. It did not say whether new Thunderbirds would be available by then. (Other studies have pointed out the paradox inherent in measuring the per capita standard of living. The more people are killed, the better it is. "Return to preattack GNP per capita has been used in other studies as a reasonable recovery goal," a 1979 study said. "But would we have achieved recovery if there were ten survivors living at this level?")

To hasten recovery, standby postattack federal personnel rules establish a forty-eight-hour work week for all government workers except those who are dead. ("Employees reported as dead should be carried on administrative leave until the reported date of death," the applicable regulation states.) Government construction contracts will be allowed to go to other than low bidders "where a showing is made that the national interest is [thus] best served." And all workers, government or private, who are engaged in "essential activity considered vital . . . in support of the national emergency" will be given priority for seats on civilian airlines. Applicants for such priority will have to fill out forms, in triplicate, with their names, sponsoring organizations, occupations, destinations, and the weight of their excess baggage. If accepted, they will be granted "urgent," "essential," or "important" priority. The plan specifies, however, that no one will be guaranteed a seat in first class.

"You can have all the plans you want," said Senator Patrick Leahy (D-Vermont) at a Senate committee hearing in 1982, "and I think it's going to be an illusion for us." He was addressing General Louis Giuffrida, director of the Federal Emergency Management Agency, which is responsible for American civil defense and coordinating all postattack planning. "You're going to delude this country into thinking that somehow we can survive a nuclear war."

"Is it better," asked Giuffrida, "to have a realistic, long-term plan to address this kind of emergency, and then use every effort we have to preclude ever having to implement it, or to have no plan at all? I agree that the ideal alternative would be to immediately abolish nuke [*sic*] weapons. Failing to do that, it seems to me that this is a morally prudent action to take."

"Have you ever seen the movie *Dr. Strangelove*?" asked Leahy. "As you work with these plans do you ever get a Strangelovian feeling at all?"

"I didn't think the movie was very good," said Giuffrida.

"I'm not surprised," said Leahy.

TWO

Fermi's Bet

On an overcast night in the New Mexico desert in the summer of 1945, as a small army of American scientists prepared to explode the world's first atomic bomb at dawn, the brilliant physicist Enrico Fermi offered to take bets on whether the nuclear chain reaction that created the bomb's blast would ignite the earth's atmosphere and, if so, whether it would destroy the entire planet or merely the state of New Mexico. This annoyed Major General Leslie Groves. Groves had been commanding the effort to produce the atomic bomb since 1942, when he was just finishing supervising the con- struction of the Pentagon. He had authorized the spending of more than two billion dollars on the atom bomb project, and he had hired more than 120,000 people to work in the secret scientific laboratory at Los Alamos, at huge factories for the production of radioactive fuel in Tennessee and Washington (the Tennessee development had become the state's fifth largest city), and at thirty-four other instal- lations in sixteen states. In May 1945, two months before the bomb was ready to be tested, Germany, whose supposed lead in atomic research had led to the crash American effort, had quit the war. Groves had proceeded to rush along the bomb's final testing. He was concerned, some scientists surmised, that Japan, too, might sur- render before the bomb could be used. He was certainly concerned that the bomb might be a dud. (Earlier in the year he had warned aides that, if the bomb fizzled, each of them could "look forward to a lifetime of testifying before congressional investigating committees.") On the eve of the bomb's first test, he had no patience for idle speculation about the destruction of the earth.

And Fermi's speculation was, on the face of it, not entirely serious. "The bet as a bet was in itself an idiocy," recalls the physicist Edward Teller. "If he won his bet, how would he be paid off?" Teller had spent the war at Los Alamos and he had studied the question of possible ignition of the atmosphere. "We proved without a shadow of a doubt—well, very little doubt—that it would not ignite. But Fermi believed in surprises. We had a long talk and I asked him, 'How could it happen?' He had no concrete suggestions. He only said, 'Maybe there's something we have not thought of.' "

Eventually, Groves forgave Fermi for his troubling wager. "I realized that his talk had served to smooth down the frayed nerves and ease the tension of the people at the base camp," Groves concluded. During the long final countdown in the desert that night, punctuated by thunderstorms that threatened to delay the test, Groves found predictions of the imminent end of the world relaxing.

America's work on the atomic bomb during World War II was shrouded in secrecy. Newspapers were asked not to print, in any context, phrases such as "atomic energy," and they did not. (Decoy words like "yttrium" were included on the banned list so that the list itself would not be a clear clue about the work on the bomb.) But the idea that atomic energy would soon be tapped, and that the results would be sensational, had been in the air since the turn of the century. Experiments with radium, uranium, and thorium in the last years of the nineteenth century had shown that these elements spontaneously and mysteriously emitted radiation. The amount of energy in the radiation was of no practical use—"if all the radium in America were turned over to the popcorn man on the corner it would not suffice to continuously pop his corn," one scientist observed—but it still seemed vast, for it appeared to be coming from nowhere. The radiating substances were not visibly burning or exploding; they were just sitting there quietly and, somehow, producing energy.

What was happening, the English physicist Ernest Rutherford

16

and chemist Frederick Soddy had theorized in 1903, was that the atoms of these elements, which were among the heaviest known, were unstable and that, from time to time, one would break up with a tiny subatomic explosion. The reason that the radiating element did not appear to be changing was that it was changing so slowly. Rutherford and Soddy were correct; it was subsequently established that it takes more than four and half trillion years for *half* the atoms in a sample of the most common type of uranium to disintegrate naturally.

The amount of energy produced in these disintegrations was enormous relative to the size of the atoms involved, but atoms are so small, and so few were decaying at any given moment, that the energy didn't amount to much. "We cannot yet artificially accelerate or influence the rate of disintegration of an element," Soddy lamented in a 1908 lecture, "and therefore the energy in uranium, which requires a thousand million years to be evolved, is practically valueless." Nevertheless, Soddy referred to the energy locked in the heavy atoms as the "hidden treasure-house of Nature" and he was not above dramatizing its potential. "This bottle contains about one pound of uranium oxide," he said, waving a small vial in front of his listeners at the University of Glasgow. "Its value is about £1. Is it not wonderful to reflect that in this little bottle there lies asleep and waiting to be evolved the energy of at least one hundred and sixty tons of coal? The energy in a ton of uranium would be sufficient to light London for a year. . . . It can scarcely be doubted that one day we shall come to break down and build up elements in the laboratory . . . and the pulses of the world will then throb with a new source of strength."

Soddy's enthusiastic prediction of the marvelous atomic future was only one of the first in a long, long chain. An early popularizer of the idea was Sir Oliver Lodge, an English physicist best known for his work on electricity. In two lectures in 1919, Lodge proclaimed that the energy locked in atoms might help mankind through what appeared to be an approaching energy crisis as known coal reserves were depleted. Atomic energy would improve the conditions of factory life, Lodge said, because it would produce no smoke or ash, and there would be no coal dust in the air. On the other hand, he acknowledged, there might be an occasional explosion resulting from the liberation of energy a bit more rapidly than was desired. In any case, he said, the potential was terrific. The energy latent in the piece of chalk he was using to illustrate his lecture to the Royal Society of Arts in London could lift a hundred thousand tons some three thousand feet, he said. (In fact, this was a vast underestimation.) Lodge calculated elsewhere that the energy in a single ounce of matter could raise all the German ships sunk in the Scapa Flow (where the surrendered German fleet had been scuttled by its crews that June) and pile them on top of the Scottish Highlands. Popular magazines soon began to play this game, weighing in with more practical suggestions. "In the little finger of every human being there is said to be enough energy to run all the railway trains in the United States for a few minutes," one journal reported in 1920. Using what became by far the most popular example of this genre, the *Literary Digest* quoted one professor a few years late as saying that the energy locked in a penknife—"if it could be released"—could "send the largest ocean liner across the Atlantic."

The theoretical basis of these predictions had been established in 1905 in one of the scientific papers written by Albert Einstein when he was not occupied with his chores as a technical expert (third class) in the Swiss patent office. "$E=mc^2$," Einstein wrote: energy is equal to mass multiplied by the square of the speed of light. When the nucleus of an atom breaks up, a small amount of its mass is converted to energy. The mass in question may be unimaginably small—perhaps a few octillionths of a gram—but the speed of light is unimaginably large, so a little mass can create a big kick. In the first decades of this century, however, no one knew how to induce a single nucleus to break up, let alone how to get a penknife to give up its grip on solidity and drive a ship.

A step forward was taken in 1919 by Rutherford at the University of Manchester. There he exposed a target of nitrogen to the radiation of a sample of radium. Some of the nitrogen atoms absorbed the radiating particles and ejected one of their own. The ejection occurred in a tiny burst of energy, but what was compelling was that the nitrogen was no longer nitrogen; the subatomic exchange of particles had transformed it into oxygen.

Now this was news. From ancient times to the Middle Ages, al-

18

chemists had attempted to transmute base metals into gold. By 1903, this had not been a respectable pursuit for at least two centuries. But the theory of radioactivity put forward by Rutherford and Soddy predicted that unstable elements would emit particles until they achieved a stable state, at which point they would have become other elements. (The end product of uranium decay, for example, is lead.) "Don't call it *transmutation*," Rutherford is reported to have said to Soddy. "They'll have our heads off as alchemists."

Rutherford and Soddy recognized, however, that transmutation and the release of atomic energy were in fact inextricably linked. "Transmutation of the elements carries with it the power to unlock the internal energy of matter," Soddy said in his 1908 lecture, but he turned the alchemists' traditional quest on its head. "If it were possible artificially to disintegrate an element with a heavier atom than gold and produce gold from it, so great an amount of energy would probably be evolved that the gold in comparison would be of little account. The energy would be far more valuable than the gold."

Both the energy *and* the gold looked promising to some. In a 1927 magazine article headlined "Six Ways to Make a Billion Dollars," one Henry Smyth Williams reported that "the newest discoveries in physics make it clear that the creation of gold by transmutation is theoretically possible, even probable." All an enterprising reader had to do, Williams wrote, was to come up with the correct process and a billion dollars would be his. The inventor would not even have to bother carting his gold to the bank, Williams pointed out. "It will quite suffice to have discovered a method by which it *can* be manufactured . . . and any European government will gladly give you a billion for your secret." Williams was savvy enough to realize that a process for manufacturing cheap gold would devalue *all* gold, but, he counseled, "you will have had your billion, and will have converted it into real property, long before the smash comes."

In case the manufacture of gold turned out to be too difficult, Williams also offered his readers the chance to discover a way to tap atomic energy. Rutherford's 1919 transformation of nitrogen to oxygen had expended more energy than it had created, but Williams was still optimistic. "Get a glass of water," he told his readers, "and put it in front of you . . . In each molecule of water in this tumbler, two hydrogen atoms are held captive by a big oxygen atom. If you will liberate these captives, and permit them to join, four by four, to form helium atoms . . . there will be no trouble at all about forming a syndicate to give you a billion for your process . . . For from each group of hydrogen atoms harnessed four by four, you will get a *trillion* times the energy that was ever obtained from a like mass of matter." (Williams was just a bit ahead of his time here. The conversion of hydrogen to helium is in fact what powers the sun—and the hydrogen bomb.)

"The terms of the problem are clear enough," Williams encouraged his readers in parting. "The conditions are well understood. It is now a mechanical rather than a mathematical problem. Why is not *your* chance to solve it as good as the next man's?"

With billions at stake, why not indeed? Or so must have reasoned Willi von Unruh, an engineer of Leipzig, who in 1920 constructed a large wooden box, filled it with what one contemporary account described as "curious machinery," and announced that it could break up atoms and release their stupendous energy. He summoned German scientists to witness five bright electric lamps burn with the power provided by his invention. When the scientists asked to examine the box, he declined. He had, after all, to protect his secret. An English investor traveled to Germany to offer von Unruh one million pounds for the British, French, and American rights to his invention, provided that it first be verified by independent scientists. By that time, however, von Unruh was already in jail for fraud.

But the glowing predictions continued, with only the more responsible commentators pointing out that they were purely theoretical: "By breaking up the atom . . . and harnessing the pent up power in it . . . each person could release from among his ordinary possessions enough motive energy to make him his own millionaire. In his cigarette case he could store enough force to carry him in an airplane around the world" (*The New York Times*, 1920).

In 1932, the game received fresh impetus from two landmark discoveries at Cambridge's Cavendish Laboratory. First John Cockcroft and E.T.S. Walton rammed artificially accelerated protons into the nuclei of lithium atoms and split them into pairs of helium nuclei. Almost simultaneously, James Chadwick discovered the neutron, a subatomic particle with no electric charge. While positively charged protons had to be accelerated to very high energies to overcome the repelling positive charges of the nuclei they were aimed at, the neutron could slip in with much less resistance. The atom appeared to be under effective siege and many proclaimed that the prize of its energy was now within reach. Rutherford, who had in a way started it all, was moved by all the speculation to complain that "anyone who says that, with the means at present at our disposal and with our present knowledge, we can utilize atomic energy is talking moonshine." A *Scientific American* editorialist commended Rutherford for his common sense and added, "Perhaps this will at least partially cool the ardor of irresponsible writers who have . . . for the past decade or two told their impressionable readers that the time may come when the atoms contained in a mere thimbleful of matter will drive a liner across the Atlantic and back." To have found such "irresponsible" predictions about powerful thimblefuls, the indignant editorialist need only have looked at a recent issue of his own magazine. "We have gone far enough to think of an engine which will harness the energy released in atom building . . . ," an editor had written. "Perhaps some powerhouse engineer of the remote future will simply pour a few thimblefuls of sand into a disintegrating chamber. Perhaps he will actually change cheap metal into gold in the process of furnishing a city with light. Who knows?"

It was realized early on, of course, that if atoms contained enough energy to raise the German fleet from the bottom of the Scapa Flow to the top of the Scottish Highlands, they also contained enough energy to send the German fleet in the opposite direction. If the energy in a thimbleful of matter could light a city or power an airplane or drive the *Queen Mary*, it could also, if released all at once, make one hell of a bang.

The consequences of this were obvious to some. In 1921, when Germany's struggles to pay its World War I reparations were in the news, an American magazine commented: "If some German scientist should happen to discover a way artificially to break up the atom, and if this new-found power were to be employed by the Teutons to destroy their conquerors, there would be a new set of victors and a new treaty to fulfill." The implications of such a discovery had been considered by Sir Oliver Lodge in a 1919 lecture in which he expressed the hope, according to one report, "that the human race would not discover how to use this energy until it had brains and morality enough to use it properly, for, if the discovery were made before its time, and by the wrong people, this very planet would be unsafe." But not everyone was concerned, and the credibility of Lodge's warning was not enhanced by his widely publicized interest in investigating mental telepathy with the dead. "These apprehensions [about potential misuse of atomic energy] somehow are remindful of Sir Oliver's excursions into the Land of Spirits . . . ," *The New York Times* editorialized. "Of course, atomic energy is real, and its amount he does not exaggerate, but—well, why did not Sir Oliver permit its exploitation for destructive purposes to remain in the very competent hands of H. G. Wells?"

The *Times* was referring to *The World Set Free*, a 1914 novel by Wells that had been inspired by the work of Frederick Soddy. Wells had read of the 1908 lecture at which Soddy had waved his small bottle of uranium oxide and proclaimed its equivalence to one hundred and sixty tons of coal, and he placed a similar lecture at the start of his novel. If a way could be found to speed up radioactive decay, Wells's lecturer declares, the energy made available would be "so potent that a man might carry in his hand the energy to light a city for a year, fight a fleet of battleships or drive one of our giant liners across the Atlantic . . . I see the desert continents transformed, the poles no longer wildernesses of ice, the whole world once more Eden." In 1933 (in the time scale of the novel), a way to disintegrate the atom is discovered, and the rest of the book is a working-out of that discovery's consequences, Edenic and otherwise.

The immediate consequences are negligible. The discoverer of the process considers entrusting his discovery to "some secret association of wise men" but does not. Journalists speculate about the manufacture of gold. Twenty years pass before atomic power plants begin to produce electricity on a commercial scale. In 1954 atomic engines for cars are introduced.

In the late 1950s, following a worldwide depression (coal miners are thrown out of work, which causes the entire preatomic-energy economy to collapse), war breaks out. The Central European powers attack the Slav Confederacy, and England and France side with the Slavs. The Germans drop an atomic bomb on Paris; the French drop an atomic bomb on Berlin; the Germans drop atomic bombs on the Dutch dikes. The narrative continues:

> The whole world was flaring then into a monstrous phase of destruction. Power after power about the armed globe sought to anticipate attack by aggression. They went to war in a delirium of panic, in order to use their bombs first. China and Japan had assailed Russia and destroyed Moscow, the United States had attacked Japan. . . . By the spring of 1959 from nearly two hundred centres . . . roared the unquenchable crimson conflagrations of the atomic bombs. . . . Most of the capital cities of the world were burning; millions of people had already perished, and over great areas government was at an end. Humanity has been compared by one contemporary writer to a sleeper who handles matches in his sleep and wakes to find himself in flames.

The World Set Free ends happily, with the war concluded, a benevolent world government established, and a new civilization constructed outside the destroyed, and still radiating, cities of the old. But the book's description of the destructive potential of atomic power (including "puffs of luminous radio-active vapour drifting sometimes scores of miles from the bomb centre and killing and scorching all they overtook") were long remembered by many readers.

One of those readers was Leo Szilard, a Hungarian-born physicist who had moved to Berlin in 1919 and had studied under Einstein and other great physicists of the age at the university there. After receiving his doctorate, he continued to work in theoretical physics and also, with Einstein, developed and patented a pump for a household refrigerator. In 1932 he read *The World Set Free*.

"The book made a very great impression on me," Szilard said later, "but I didn't regard it as anything but fiction." Within a few months, Hitler came to power, and Szilard, who was Jewish and who always had a knack for predicting the future course of events, took to living with two suitcases permanently packed. A few days after the Reichstag fire, he left for England. He was living in London in September 1933 when he read of the speech in which Rutherford had denounced as "moonshine" predictions that atomic energy would soon be available. "This sort of set me pondering as I was walking the streets of London," Szilard said later, "and I remember that I stopped for a red light at the intersection of Southampton Row. As I was waiting for the light to change . . . it suddenly occurred to me that if we could find an element which is split by neutrons and which would emit *two* neutrons when it absorbed *one* neutron, such an element, if assembled in sufficiently large mass, could sustain a nuclear chain reaction. . . . It might become possible to set up a nuclear chain reaction, liberate energy on an industrial scale, and construct atomic bombs." Six months later, Szilard applied for a patent describing such a chain reaction and the "critical mass" of radioactive material that would be necessary to sustain it. "Knowing what this would mean—and I knew it because I had read H. G. Wells—I did not want this patent to become public," Szilard said. "The only way to keep it from becoming public was to assign it to the government." The War Office wasn't interested in Szilard's idea, so he gave it to the British Admiralty.

Szilard did not pursue his idea immediately. To carry out the work, he tried to obtain £2,000 with the help of Chaim Weizmann, a noted chemist who later became the first president of Israel. Weizmann attempted to raise the money but failed. Szilard spent much of the next several months dreaming of experiments while soaking in the bathtub at the Strand Palace Hotel. "There is no place as good to think as a bathtub," he explained.

Eventually, Szilard did get to work. Other physicists in Britain, Germany, Italy, France, and the United States were working too. In Rome, Enrico Fermi was firing neutrons at the nuclei of a variety of elements, including uranium, and inducing them to decay. Energy was created in these experiments (and in similar experiments elsewhere), but as a rule more energy was expended in firing the neutrons than was created when the particles struck the nuclei. Far from being a source of fantastic power, experiments in induced radioactivity were actually great *consumers* of power. The problem was compounded by the fact that most of the particles fired at an experimental target passed right through it without hitting anything, so the energy expended in firing them was totally wasted. It was, Einstein said, like "shooting birds in the dark in a country where there are only a few birds."

But the concept of the chain reaction could change everything. If, as Szilard speculated, there was an element that could be split by a neutron and, in the course of splitting, would emit *two* neutrons, then the reaction would power itself. An experimenter need not, at great cost of energy, pump millions of neutrons into a target. A *single* neutron, striking home, would create more neutrons, which, upon striking other nuclei, would create more neutrons, and so on until the entire mass of the target element was exploding. The problem remained that many of the neutrons created would fly right through the target without striking anything; the "critical mass" of an element would be an amount large enough so that the odds would favor a neutron's striking a nucleus before it flew out of the mass. Using Einstein's metaphor, a bullet fired randomly in the midst of a handful of birds probably won't hit one before it passes beyond them into the empty sky, but a bullet fired randomly in the midst of a great cloud of birds probably will.

The question of whether a chain reaction was feasible assumed new urgency in the winter of 1939, when word came from Berlin that two German scientists had split the nuclei of uranium atoms with neutrons. Uranium was the heaviest element then known. Its "fission," as the splitting was called, created more energy than that of any lighter element; one scientist computed that the energy from the fission of a single atom "could make a visible grain of sand make a visible jump." Multiplied by the number of atoms in even a tiny mass of uranium, that amounted to the potential for a mighty explosion.

In splitting, did the uranium atoms emit neutrons? If they did, then a uranium chain reaction was possible and so was a uranium explosion. "All the things which H. G. Wells predicted appeared suddenly real to me," reflected Szilard, who was by then in New York. Fermi, also a refugee in New York, was not as concerned, predicting only a "remote possibility"—perhaps a 10 percent chance—that uranium fission would create the crucial neutrons. Their colleague Isidor Rabi reacted to Fermi's prediction, Szilard said later, by saying, "Ten percent is not a remote possibility if it means that we may die of it. If I have pneumonia and the doctor tells me that there is a remote possibility that I might die, and it's ten percent, I get excited about it."

Szilard set out to perform the crucial experiment. He borrowed $2,000 from a friend to rent a gram of radium and obtain other necessary apparatus, and he asked for and received permission to do the work at Columbia University. On March 3, 1939, he recalled later, "everything was ready and all we had to do was to turn a switch, lean back, and watch the screen of a television tube. If flashes of light appeared on the screen, that would mean that neutrons were emitted in the fission process of uranium and this in turn would mean that the large-scale liberation of atomic energy was just around the corner. We turned the switch and saw the flashes. We watched them for a little while and then we switched everything off and went home. That night there was very little doubt in my mind that the world was headed for grief."

Szilard immediately thought about his discovery in the context of the German threat. War seemed imminent, there was the potential for a powerful weapon in this work, and it was a pair of German scientists who had broken things open. Szilard launched a one-man campaign to convince researchers in the United States, Britain, and France to keep the results of their experiments on uranium fission secret. But a French team that found neutron emission at about the same time Szilard did rejected his plea for secrecy and the campaign failed.

Several months later, Szilard and Eugene Wigner, another Hungarian-born physicist now living in America, began to worry that the United States might not have a sufficient supply of uranium should war break out and a race to develop an atomic bomb ensue. They knew that uranium was mined in the Belgian Congo and feared that the Belgians, unaware of its value, might sell the ore to Germany. Szilard recalled that Einstein was a close friend of the Queen Mother of Belgium and thought he might write to her. So Szilard and Wigner drove out to Long Island, where Einstein was spending the summer, and put it to him. Einstein said he would rather write to a member of the Belgian Cabinet he knew than to the Queen Mother. Wigner suggested that any such letter ought to be shown to the U.S. State Department first. It was so agreed, but at this point Szilard had second thoughts about the way they were proceeding and consulted friends with more experience in the ways of governments. It was finally decided that Einstein should write directly to President Franklin Roosevelt, and Szilard and Einstein sat down to draft the letter. They produced a long draft and a short draft. "We did not know just how many words one could put in a letter which a President is supposed to read," Szilard said later. "How many pages does the fission of uranium rate?"

Ultimately, the longer version was sent (and has since become famous). It suggested that the United States might want to give attention to "the problem of securing a supply of uranium ore." It explained that in the "last four months it has been made probable—through the work of Joliot in France as well as Fermi and Szilard in America—that it may become possible to set up a nuclear chain reaction in a large mass of uranium by which vast amounts of power . . . would be generated."

It continued: "This new phenomenon would also lead to the construction of bombs, and it is conceivable—though much less certain—that extremely powerful bombs of a new type may thus be constructed. A single bomb of this type, carried by boat and exploded in a port, might very well destroy the whole port together with some of the surrounding territory . . . I understand that Germany has actually stopped the sale of uranium from the Czechoslovakian mines which she has taken over . . . Yours very truly, A. Einstein."

The letter was delivered to President Roosevelt on October 11, 1939. He turned it over to his secretary, General Edwin Watson, with the words, "This requires action."

The possibility that the chain reaction that set off an atomic bomb would spread to ignite the atmosphere and destroy the world was first considered by the scientists working on the American bomb at a meeting in Berkeley in the summer of 1942. Edward Teller, yet another Hungarian-born physicist, arrived at the meeting with an idea, suggested to him by Fermi, for skipping beyond the atomic bomb to a "super" bomb many times more powerful. It had recently been determined that the enormous energies of the stars were created by nuclear reactions that included the fusion of hydrogen atoms into helium. This process could take place only at tremendously high temperatures, which did not exist on earth—at least not yet. An atomic bomb, Teller calculated, would produce enough energy to set off the fusion of hydrogen. Surrounded by a hydrogen jacket, an atomic bomb could thus act as the trigger for the bigger "super." Teller's calculations raised another unsettling possibility, however; the energy set free by an atomic bomb might ignite not only hydrogen but also the nitrogen that makes up 80 percent of the earth's atmosphere.

The idea that the release of atomic energy could produce a global cataclysm, like the related ideas that atomic energy could lead to powerful weapons or create an Eden on earth, had been extant for several decades. In 1924, the British physicist F. W. Aston, noting that the transformation of hydrogen to helium would result in the conversion of mass to energy, wrote that this would open possibilities "greater ... than any suggested before by science in the whole history of the human race." He continued: "Should the research worker of the future discover some means of releasing this energy in a form which could be employed, the human race will have at its command powers beyond the dreams of scientific fiction; but the remote possibility must always be considered that the energy once liberated will be completely uncontrollable and by its intense violence detonate all neighbouring substances. In this event the whole of the hydrogen on the earth might be transformed at once and the success of the experiment published at large to the universe as a new star."

Speculation about uncontrollable explosions had renewed after the possibility of a uranium chain reaction was established in 1939. There might be a "catch" to performing such an experiment, *Newsweek* reported. "Neutrons would smash atoms, producing more neutrons to smash more atoms, and if the process continued it might grow to uncontrollable proportions like a snowball rolling downhill. The result might be an explosion that would make the forces of T.N.T. or high-power bombs seem like firecrackers." *Time* reported local concern that New York City was in danger of disappearing into a one-hundred-mile-wide crater because of "some well-intentioned physicists at Columbia University who were cracking uranium atoms with neutrons as contentedly as small boys crack nuts." A careless or unlucky experimenter, the eminent physicist Niels Bohr told a scientific congress, might blow up his entire laboratory and a good chunk of the surrounding countryside as well.

Others were less concerned, partly because it was soon discovered that only one rare type of uranium, U-235, was readily fissionable and that it was extremely difficult to separate U-235 from the far more common U-238. "The electric power alone required to produce a pound of Uranium 235 would cost more than the budget allows for a . . . year of Federal expenditures," said *The New York Times* (as things turned out, incorrectly). Additional calming news came when preliminary experiments seemed to show that a chain reaction, once started, would grow so energetic that newly created generations of neutrons would be flung out of the mass of uranium before they could hit anything, and so the chain reaction would eventually sputter out. "Readers made insomnious by 'newspaper talk' of terrific atomic war weapons held in reserve by dictators may now get sleep," concluded *Scientific American* in a 1940 article headlined "Don't Worry—It Can't Happen."

But, at the 1942 Berkeley meeting, it appeared that "terrific atomic war weapons" could be created fairly easily and that far worse things could happen as well. Accounts differ as to how concerned the assembled scientists were by the possibility that a chain reaction might spread to the atmosphere. In his memoirs, Arthur Holly Compton, the University of Chicago physicist who was then coordinating atomic research for the government, recalled that he received an urgent telephone call that summer from J. Robert Oppenheimer, who was running the Berkeley meeting. Compton and his family had driven to northern Michigan for a vacation at their summer cottage. "As our car pulled into the local store where the keys were kept, the phone was ringing. . . . Oppenheimer and his group had found something very disturbing. How soon could he see me? I gave him directions and told him I would meet him at the train the following morning.

"I'll never forget that morning. I drove Oppenheimer from the railroad station down to the beach looking out over the peaceful lake. There I listened to his story. What his team had found was the possibility of nuclear fusion—the principle of the hydrogen bomb.

... To set off such a reaction would require a very high temperature. But might not the enormously high temperature of an atomic bomb be just what was needed to explode hydrogen? And if hydrogen, what about the hydrogen of sea water? Might the explosion of an atomic bomb set off an explosion of the ocean itself?

"Nor was this all. The nitrogen in the air is also unstable, though in less degree. Might it not be set off by an atomic explosion in the atmosphere?

"These questions could not be passed over lightly ... This would be the ultimate catastrophe. Better to accept the slavery of the Nazis than to run a chance of drawing the final curtain on mankind!"

Other accounts given by scientists who were at the Berkeley meeting are less dramatic. (And some doubt must be cast on the details of Compton's account by the fact that he has Oppenheimer traveling two thousand miles overnight on a train.)

"Certainly Oppie was not that agitated at the study group itself," recalls Emil Konopinski, a now-retired professor of physics at Indiana University who was the youngest man at the Berkeley meeting and, as such, had been stuck with the job of taking notes. "I was so busily putting down the ideas that we were manufacturing in our discussions that I missed just who brought it up first, but either Hans [Bethe] or Teller ... I think it was Teller who first speculated that the atmosphere might just possibly be detonated by some mad scientist who set out to set off the largest possible bomb."

"It was a side issue," recalls Bethe, now retired from teaching at Cornell. "We probably spent a couple of hours on it during the Berkeley meeting, and the Berkeley meeting lasted several months." Bethe had been primarily responsible for explaining the nuclear reactions that take place in the sun (for which he later won the Nobel Prize) and so he was asked to check the mathematical possibilities of catastrophe. "I did some calculations—sort of back of the envelope—in which I concluded there was no chance," Bethe recalls. The study group moved on to other topics.

The next two and a half years were an exciting time in applied nuclear physics. Under the command of General Groves, the Manhattan Project, as the American bomb effort was called, constructed immense plants for the separation of U-235 and the manufacture of plutonium, a man-made element heavier than uranium that was determined to be a second source of power for atomic bombs. Under the direction of Oppenheimer, the Los Alamos Scientific Laboratory was established on a remote New Mexico plateau and a quorum of the world's leading physicists gathered there to design the new weapon. The project was intellectually stimulating, the company was inspiring, and, for added motivation, the fear lingered that German scientists might produce an atomic bomb first. By the winter of 1944–45, two promising designs for the bomb were well in hand at Los Alamos and delivery of the fuel to power them was only months away. It was time to reconsider the question of whether the earth's days were numbered.

The question had never gone away, because the possibility of igniting the atmosphere was evident to any competent nuclear physicist and newcomers to the project kept stumbling upon it. "Every theorist who joined the project did the problem for himself," says Philip Morrison of the Massachusetts Institute of Technology, who was at Los Alamos during the war. "I spent half a day on it myself in 1943." All concluded that the atmosphere was safe (and the possibility of igniting the oceans was easier to eliminate), but in early 1945 it was decided to lay the question to rest once and for all. "We thought it was important to check on it," says Emil Konopinski. "After all, it's our only earth."

The task fell to the research group, headed by Teller, that was concentrating on the "super." Teller took an interest in it himself— "It was a very wonderful exercise," he says—but the bulk of the work was passed on to his deputy, Emil Konopinski. "The signal was to get cracking on it," Konopinski recalls, "to concentrate on it, and so I proceeded. Teller was probably the most fantastic idea man on the whole project. . . . I was the pinner-downer."

And so early in 1945, working in an office in the "T Building," a hurriedly constructed wooden structure that looked more like a barracks than a laboratory, Konopinski sat down to calculate the odds that the upcoming test of the first atomic bomb would blow up the world. He had the assistance of Cloyd Marvin, Jr., a former physics student now in Army uniform. "He punched the calculations into a Marchant calculating machine, which is what we had then," Konopinski recalls. "He didn't understand the calculations

but could be trusted to put the numbers in and add and subtract . . .
He was a nice rosy-cheeked boy." Konopinski himself was constantly being interrupted by experimenters on other projects wanting to discuss their results. And so the work proceeded.

One of the first questions Konopinski faced had to do with the
"nitrogen-nitrogen cross section." That was the probability that,
under the influence of a nearby atomic explosion, nitrogen nuclei
would fuse. A large cross section would mean fusion was likely. And
fusion would create energy, which would create more fusion, which
would create more energy as the inexorable momentum of a chain
reaction took hold.

Konopinski and the others in Teller's group had already studied the identical problem with respect to isotopes of hydrogen, to see
if a chain reaction in that element would take off, and if it was thus
possible to build a hydrogen bomb. They had concluded that it was.
"We were able to prove that if an A-bomb worked, then an H-bomb
would also," says Konopinski.

With that exercise behind him, the approach to the nitrogen
question was clear. "It was so much like designing a hydrogen
bomb," says Konopinski, "with the problem of detonating hydrogen
in the one and the problem of detonating nitrogen in the other. . . . It
became duck soup to take a look at this problem." There was one fly
in the duck soup: "We didn't know most of the numbers."

While the fusion cross section of hydrogen had been established, the fusion cross section of nitrogen was still unknown. It was
evident, however, that the nitrogen cross section would be smaller
than the hydrogen cross section, and thus nitrogen would be less
likely to ignite. "What you have to do [to create fusion] is make
these positively charged nuclei approach each other closely enough
to smash each other," explains Konopinski. "Positive charges repel
each other, so it has to be done against electrostatic repulsion." Nitrogen nuclei carry larger charges than hydrogen nuclei, so they
would have a more difficult time overcoming that repulsion.

To be on the safe side, Konopinski assumed that the fusion
cross section of nitrogen was the same as its geometric cross section.
That is, he assumed that every time two nitrogen nuclei collided,
they would fuse, even though it was known that most times they
would not. This assumption made the calculations very conserva-

tive; it also made the calculations possible in the first place, because the geometric cross section of nitrogen was known. Konopinski put it at about two "barns."*

This gave Konopinski a rough (and overstated) estimate of how much energy would be created in the atmosphere by fusing nitrogen nuclei following an atomic explosion. He next took into account the portion of that energy that would uselessly radiate away from the scene of the explosion instead of remaining available to create more fusion. If the amount of energy lost exceeded the amount created, a chain reaction was impossible. If the amount of energy created exceeded the amount lost, a chain reaction was inevitable. "The temperature, if such exists, at which the energy production rate equals the radiative loss rate will be the temperature of ignition," Konopinski noted in the paper that was the product of his investigation. Titled "Ignition of the Atmosphere with Nuclear Bombs," it was signed by Konopinski, Teller, and Marvin, and was classified Secret until 1973.

To be on the safe side, Konopinski had already overstated the amount of energy likely to be created. Now, to be on the safe side again, he understated the amount that would be lost. "We made the worst-case assumption about the production process and then neglected to take into account various loss processes," he says. Even with those distorted figures, the paper concluded that, "whatever the temperature to which a section of the atmosphere may be heated [by a nuclear weapon]," no chain reaction "is likely to be started." It explained, "The energy loss to radiation always overcompensates the gains due to the reactions. . . . The only disquieting feature is that the 'safety factor,' i.e., the ratio of losses to gains of energy, decreases rapidly with initial temperature, and descends to a value of only about 1.6 just beyond a 10-MeV temperature."

Sitting in his office in Bloomington, Indiana, almost four dec-

---

* A barn is a unit of measurement equal to one-septillionth of a square centimeter. "It's a facetious word that has taken hold," Konopinski explains. "It was started at Cornell while I was there. A man by the name of Charlie Baker was measuring cross sections for nuclear physics processes that were possible with the little cyclotron that was available at the time, and he came upon one that was surprisingly large, and he said, 'Why, that's as big as a barn.' So they decided to name a cross section of that size a 'barn.' It was much easier than saying 'ten to the minus twenty-four square centimeters.' "

ades after writing those words, Konopinski found them not disquieting in the least. "We don't know how to produce ten MeV temperatures," he said. "The temperatures achieved in present nuclear weapon designs are about the same as they are at the center of the sun. That's about one-sixtieth MeV. We took the curves up to these ridiculous temperatures simply because we were thinking someday some mad scientist is going to make a temperature six hundred times as great as the temperature at the center of the sun. Nobody had any idea of how to produce such a temperature. What was interesting to us was that even if we went to infinite temperature there was still a safety factor."

But the paper did allow for miscalculation. "In spite of the considerable magnitude of these safety factors it is not inconceivable," it said, "that our estimates are greatly in error and thermonuclear reaction may actually start to propagate."

But even if that happened, it said, the loss of energy through radiation would quench the reaction before it spread more than a hundred meters or so through the atmosphere.

On the other hand, it continued, following even a promptly quenched reaction, "the resultant earth-shock and the radioactive contamination of the atmosphere might become catastrophic on a world-wide scale."

The bottom line was this: It was "unreasonable to expect" that the nitrogen in the atmosphere could be ignited. "However, the complexity of the argument and the absence of satisfactory experimental foundations makes further work on the subject highly desirable."

With the possibility of an atomic bomb detonating the earth's atmosphere thus ruled out (more or less), it was still apparent that an atomic bomb would be a weapon unlike any other. The discovery of a way to separate U-235, *The New York Times* had reported in 1940, before wartime secrecy took the subject out of the newspapers, bears "tremendous implications . . . on the possible outcome of the European war . . . If one pound of U-235 exploded . . . the pressure produced would be on the order of 100,000,000,000 atmospheres . . .

about 1,000,000 times the pressure produced by TNT or nitroglycerin."

As always, a few were slow to see the possibilities. The scientist who had isolated the U-235 said "hardly enough to spring a mousetrap" had been produced so far and he saw no way to produce enough in time to have an impact on the war. Two months later, taking a firm step in a ridiculous direction, "U-235 gave its world premiere public performance as a usable source of power," the *Times* reported, "when the splitting of one of its atoms turned on radio station WBZ's new 50,000-watt, air-cooled transmitter." Meanwhile, a member of a British committee looking into atomic power suggested that it might be used to produce a powerful searchlight. A German committee discussed atomic-powered cars. And, at the first meeting of the American committee established by President Roosevelt after he received Einstein's letter, the U.S. Army representative lectured the scientists present about their naiveté in believing that a new explosive could make a significant military contribution; everyone knew that it was troop morale, not weapons, that won wars.

Even then-Colonel Leslie Groves was unenthusiastic when he was offered a "very important assignment" in the fall of 1942. "If you do the job right," he was told, "it will win the war." Groves's spirits fell as he realized what the job was. "Oh, that thing," he said, before accepting command of the project that would build the atomic bomb.

But the confident attitude of Groves's superior—"it will win the war"—spread through the military and scientific establishments as the project unfolded and the implications of the bomb's vast power became clear. "One B-29 bomber could accomplish with such a bomb the same damage against weak industrial and civilian targets as 100 to 1,000 [conventionally armed] B-29 bombers," two scientific advisors reported to Secretary of War Henry Stimson in 1944. And if the hydrogen bomb was developed, they said, "one such super-super bomb would be equivalent in blast damage to 1,000 raids of 1,000 B-29 Fortresses delivering their load of high explosive on one target. One must consider the possibility of delivering either the [atomic] bombs at present contemplated or the super-super bomb on an enemy target by means of a robot plane or guided missile. . . . That such a situation presents a new challenge to the world is evident."

The nature of that challenge was spelled out more precisely when Stimson briefed Harry Truman on the atomic bomb project shortly after the death of President Roosevelt in April 1945. Truman had assumed the presidency without knowledge of the atomic bomb. As chairman of a Senate committee on the war effort, he had once dispatched investigators to several Manhattan Project installations, but Stimson, without explaining why, had asked him to withdraw his men. Truman patriotically complied.

Now, as president, Truman was visited again by Stimson. This time, the secretary of war told him that the United States was within four months of constructing "the most terrible weapon ever known in human history." Stimson added that other nations were likely to develop this weapon and warned, "The world in its present state of moral advancement compared with its technical development would be eventually at the mercy of such a weapon. In other words, modern civilization might be completely destroyed."

The next day, James Byrnes, who had been Roosevelt's director of war mobilization and would be Truman's secretary of state, called on the new president and told him that the atomic explosive was "great enough to destroy the whole world."

The same tenor was maintained a few weeks later when Secretary Stimson convened a meeting of the "Interim Committee" chosen to consider the future of atomic weapons. "This project should not be considered simply in terms of military weapons," Stimson told the committee, "but as a new relationship of man to the universe." The most immediate relationship to be addressed, however, was that of the atomic bomb to Japan. Germany had already surrendered, and Japan was clearly on the road to defeat. The committee concluded that its surrender should be hastened by dropping an atomic bomb, without warning, in an effort "to make a profound psychological impression on as many of the inhabitants as possible." The ideal target, committee members agreed, would be a vital war plant "employing a large number of workers and closely surrounded by workers' houses."

The question of whether the bomb should be dropped at all was not discussed. "At no time, from 1941 to 1945, did I ever hear it suggested by the President, or by any other responsible member of the government, that atomic energy should not be used in the war . . . ," Stimson wrote later. "The possible atomic weapon was considered to be a new and tremendously powerful explosive, as legitimate as any other of the deadly explosive weapons of modern war."

At least one responsible member of the government, however, eventually recorded his opposition to using the bomb. "My own feeling was that in being the first to use it," wrote Admiral William Leahy, who served as Roosevelt's and then Truman's chief of staff, "we had adopted an ethical standard common to the barbarians of the Dark Ages. I was not taught to make war in that fashion." While it is not recorded that Leahy made his views known at the time, his failure to do so may have resulted from his often-expressed opinion that the bomb "sounds like a professor's dream to me." (After sitting in with Truman at a briefing on the Manhattan Project in April 1945, he told the president, "That is the biggest fool thing we have ever done. The bomb will never go off, and I speak as an expert in explosives.")

Another professional warrior, General Dwight Eisenhower, commander of the Allied forces in Europe, did make his opposition to using the bomb known to Secretary Stimson in July. "During his recitation of the relevant facts," Eisenhower wrote later of a meeting where Stimson told him about plans for the bomb, "I had been conscious of a feeling of depression and so I voiced to him my grave misgivings, first on the basis of my belief that Japan was already defeated and that dropping the bomb was completely unnecessary, and secondly because I thought that our country should avoid shocking world opinion. . . . The Secretary was deeply perturbed by my attitude, almost angrily refuting the reasons I gave for my quick conclusions."

The only organized questioning of American plans for the bomb came from some of the people who had built it. Many of the Manhattan Project scientists had been motivated by the fear that Germany would create an atomic bomb first. Yet when Germany surrendered, and that threat ceased to exist, the American bomb project kept rolling along. In June 1945, a committee of scientists working for the Manhattan Project at the University of Chicago began a report to Secretary Stimson by explaining that they felt compelled to take a stand "because the success which we have achieved in the development of nuclear power is fraught with infinitely greater dangers than were all the inventions of the past." The report (which came to be known as the Franck Report, after committee chairman James Franck) predicted that other nations could soon produce atomic weapons and warned against the dangers of a nuclear arms race. To best forestall the mistrust that would fuel an arms race, the report proposed "a demonstration of the new weapon ... before the eyes of representatives of all the United Nations, on the desert or a barren island ... After such a demonstration the weapon might perhaps be used against Japan if the sanction of the United Nations (and if public opinion at home) were obtained, perhaps after a preliminary ultimatum to Japan to surrender or at least to evacuate certain regions as an alternative to their total destruction. This may sound fantastic, but in nuclear weapons we have something entirely new in order of magnitude of destructive power, and if we want to capitalize fully on the advantage their possession gives us, we must use new and imaginative methods."

Not surprisingly, perennial maverick Leo Szilard was a member of the committee that drafted the report. General Groves already considered Szilard a "pain in the neck" and not without reason. Szilard had protested several times during the war when he thought the bomb work was going too slowly or was being mismanaged. In the spring of 1945, Szilard had decided that immediate planning for postwar nuclear arms control was essential, and, to press his case, he attempted to arrange a meeting first with Roosevelt and then with Truman. Truman passed him off to James Byrnes, his prospective secretary of state, and Szilard, with two other scientists, traveled to meet Byrnes in May at his home in Spartanburg, South Carolina. Byrnes found Szilard abrasive. "His general demeanor and his desire to participate in policy-making made an unfavorable impression on me," he said. Szilard found Byrnes's attitudes appalling. For one thing, when Szilard expressed concern about a future nuclear arms race with Russia, Byrnes replied, "General Groves tells me there is no uranium in Russia." Byrnes also said, Szilard later recounted, that in its postwar behavior in Europe, "Russia might be more manageable if impressed by American military might, and that a demonstration of the bomb might impress Russia." As Szilard, deeply depressed, left Byrnes's house, he reflected, somewhat immodestly, "how much better off the world might be had I been born in America and become influential in American politics, and had Byrnes been born in Hungary and studied physics."

Back in Chicago, Szilard drafted and circulated a petition to President Truman asking that Japan be given a chance to surrender before the bomb was used and that, in any case, Truman consider the "moral responsibilities" involved in "opening the door to an era of devastation on an unimaginable scale." Sixty-nine scientists signed. Szilard sent copies of the petition to a colleague in Los Alamos but was not optimistic about its success there. "Of course, you will find only a few people on your project who are willing to sign such a petition," he wrote in his covering letter, "and I am sure you will find many boys confused as to what kind of thing a moral issue is."

One person at Los Alamos whom Szilard thought might help with the petition was Edward Teller. Teller declined, although he said, in a letter to Szilard, that he was not untroubled about using the bomb. "First of all let me say that I have no hope of clearing my conscience," he wrote. "The things we are working on are so terrible that no amount of protesting or fiddling with politics will save our souls. . . . But I am not really convinced of your objections. I do not feel that there is any chance to outlaw any one weapon. If we have a slim chance of survival, it lies in the possibility to get rid of wars. . . . Our only hope is in getting the facts of our results before the people. This might help to convince everybody that the next war would be fatal. For this purpose actual combat-use might even be the best thing."

This ironic argument—that the terrible power of the bomb did not mean that it should not be used but that it *should* be used, not to win the present war but to prevent the next one—carried a lot of weight among the atomic scientists. "The view was that this was going to change war forever," says Philip Morrison, who spent the war at Los Alamos and has been involved with organizations opposing the nuclear arms race ever since. "To some extent that was responsible for what you could say was the enthusiasm for using the bomb at Los Alamos. People felt that it must be brought into the public domain." If people saw what the bomb could do, it was reasoned, they would not allow circumstances to arise in which it would be used again. "In this war the atomic bomb was only a signal to the world," Morrison says. "The real problem was the next war." (The next war that Morrison himself was concerned about at the time was one against a resurgent Japan.)

This argument had appealed at one time even to Szilard. The postwar public would not tolerate the infringements on national sovereignty necessary for strict nuclear arms control "unless high efficiency atomic bombs have actually been used in this war and the fact of their destructive power has deeply penetrated the mind of the public," Szilard wrote in 1944. And the argument arose again when Arthur Compton delivered the Franck Report to the office of Secretary Stimson. In an accompanying letter, Compton told Stimson that the report failed to take into account "that if the bomb were not used in the present war the world would have no adequate warning as to what was to be expected if war should break out again."

A few days later, a scientific advisory panel to Stimson's Interim Committee, consisting of Compton, Oppenheimer, Fermi, and Ernest Lawrence, recommended that Russia, France, and China be informed of America's nuclear weapons progress and invited to make "suggestions as to how we can cooperate in making this development contribute to improved international relations." But it went on to conclude, rejecting the Franck Report and other appeals, that "we can propose no technical demonstration likely to bring an end to the war; we see no acceptable alternative to direct military use."

Target selection proceeded. A "Target Committee" consisting of scientists (including Oppenheimer), military weapons experts, and meteorologists had been set up in April to decide which Japanese cities should be struck by atomic bombs. Cities that had not been much damaged by the conventional air raids then pounding Japan were preferred; the absence of previous damage would make it easier for American scientists to measure the effects of the new weapon and would produce the greatest possible psychological effect upon the Japanese. (The committee also wanted to make "the initial use sufficiently spectacular for the importance of the weapon

to be internationally recognized when publicity on it is released.")
Kyoto, the ancient capital of Japan, seemed ideal. "Kyoto has the
advantage," the committee reported, "of the people being more
highly intelligent and hence better able to appreciate the significance of the weapon." Nonetheless, Secretary Stimson vetoed the
selection of Kyoto, partly because of the cultural and artistic significance of its temples and palaces and partly because "the bitterness
which would be caused by such a wanton act might make it impossible during the long postwar period to reconcile the Japanese to us
in that area rather than to the Russians." Apparently no such bitterness was feared as a reaction to the loss of the four cities finally included on the target list: Niigata, Kokura, Nagasaki, and
Hiroshima.

Meanwhile, on the South Pacific isle of Tinian, part of a U.S.
Army air base had been turned over to personnel from Los Alamos
who would prepare and see off the bombs for the target cities.

And at a remote spot in the New Mexico desert 150 miles south
of Los Alamos, scientists, soldiers and technicians were gathering to
prepare for a test of the world's first atomic bomb, code-named
"Trinity." William Laurence, a *New York Times* reporter working
as a consultant to the Manhattan Project, told his editor in a letter to
get ready for some big news. "When it breaks it will be an eighth-
day wonder," Laurence wrote, "a sort of Second Coming of Christ
yarn. It will need about 20 columns on the day it breaks."

Among those gathered at the Trinity site, in a stretch of desert
the Spanish had called *Jornada del Muerto*—the Dead Man's
Trail—there was still some uncertainty about the extent of the
power they were about to unleash. Several press releases had been
prepared for possible distribution after the blast. The one to be used
if the test was a success explained the huge explosion in the desert as
the accidental detonation of an ammunition dump. Another, to be
used if the test was too successful, announced that J. Robert Oppenheimer and other scientists had been killed in a freak accident.

On July 15, 1945, the day before the "gadget," as the scientists
called it, was to blow, test director Kenneth Bainbridge was furious
to hear scientists again discussing the possibility that the bomb

might detonate the atmosphere, especially because they were doing so in front of soldiers ignorant of nuclear physics (and the calculations of Emil Konopinski). Some soldiers were already speculating that the blast might knock the earth off its axis or alter its orbit around the sun. Some scientists with doubts of their own asked Oppenheimer if he was sure he wanted to view the test from a shelter only ten thousand yards from ground zero. Enrico Fermi offered his bet about the destruction of the world.

The bomb exploded at 5:29:45 a.m. on July 16, 1945. Scientists at their vantage points saw a light brighter than any ever seen on earth. Then there was a mighty fireball, then the shock wave, then the noise. Sixty miles away, an observer noted that it was bright enough to read a newspaper. Fifty miles away, a blind girl riding in a car turned to the driver and said, "What's that?" In the shelter ten thousand yards south of ground zero, Brigadier General Thomas Farrell, Groves's deputy, exclaimed, "The longhairs have let it get away from them!"

But they hadn't. The bomb, fueled by a core of plutonium the size of a grapefruit, exploded with the force of nineteen thousand tons of TNT. The world did not end.

"The effects could well be called unprecedented, magnificent, beautiful, stupendous and terrifying," General Farrell reported in a memo that was rushed to President Truman. "No man-made phenomenon of such tremendous power had ever occurred before. The lighting effects beggared description. The whole country was lighted by a searing light with the intensity many times that of the midday sun. It was golden, purple, violet, gray and blue. It lighted every peak, crevasse and ridge of the nearby mountain range with a clarity and beauty that cannot be described but must be seen to be imagined. It was that beauty the great poets dream about but describe most poorly and inadequately. Thirty seconds after the explosion came first, the air blast pressing hard against the people and things, to be followed almost immediately by the strong, sustained, awesome roar which warned of doomsday and made us feel that we puny things were blasphemous to dare tamper with the forces heretofore reserved to The Almighty."

Chemist George Kistiakowsky, who led the team that designed the Trinity weapon, said the next day, "I am sure that at the end of the world—in the last millisecond of the earth's existence—the last human will see what we saw."

Others reacted with simple exultation—the gadget worked.

On August 6, 1945, an American B-29, accompanied by two observer planes carrying measuring instruments and a scientist filming the occasion with a home movie camera, dropped the world's second atomic bomb on Hiroshima. The world didn't end then either. According to low early estimates, seventy-eight thousand people were killed, somewhat fewer than had died in the conventional fire-bombing of Tokyo by U.S. warplanes five months before. But hundreds of planes had dropped thousands of bombs over Tokyo. Hiroshima was destroyed by one bomb dropped by one plane.

President Truman was eating lunch on a naval vessel crossing the Atlantic Ocean when he got the news. He shook the captain's hand and said, "This is the greatest thing in history." An official announcement was issued in Truman's name; it said the new bomb harnessed "the basic power of the universe."

Three days later, a B-29 carrying the world's third (and, at that moment, last) atomic bomb took off to drop it on Kokura. Kokura was covered by haze, so the bomb was dropped on Nagasaki instead. Forty thousand people were reported killed or missing. "I realize the tragic significance of the atomic bomb," President Truman announced that day. "No one can foresee what another war would mean to our own cities and to our own people. What we are doing to Japan now—even with the new atomic bomb—is only a small fraction of what would happen to the world in a third world war."

On September 2, 1945, accepting the surrender of Japan aboard the battleship *Missouri* in Tokyo Bay, General Douglas MacArthur expressed "profound concern, both for our future security and the survival of civilization." Scientific advances in weaponry, he said, had "now reached a point which revises the traditional concept of war. . . . We have had our last chance. If we do not now devise some greater and more equitable system [for preserving peace] Armageddon will be at our door."

Two weeks later, a draft study by the U.S. Army Air Forces concluded that, "to insure our national security," the United States ought to arm itself as soon as possible with 466 atomic bombs.

THREE

"The Good News Is You'll Be President"

If the Soviet Union ever launches its nuclear-armed missiles against the United States, the infrared radiation of the missiles' booster rockets will be spotted within seconds by three American satellites hovering 22,300 miles above the Soviet missile fields along the Trans-Siberian Railway and the Atlantic and Pacific patrol areas of Soviet missile-launching submarines. Signals from the satellites will flash to the Combat Operations Center of the North American Aerospace Defense Command (NORAD) in a complex of fifteen windowless steel buildings inside Cheyenne Mountain, Colorado. The same signals will be received at Strategic Air Command (SAC) headquarters near Omaha, at the National Military Command Center in the Pentagon, and at the Alternate National Military Command Center underground near Fort Ritchie, Maryland. The senior controller in SAC's subbasement war room will order the "alert crews" always standing by at SAC air bases to race to the cockpits of their nuclear-armed bombers and supporting tankers— already lined up for quick escape from their airfields—and to start the engines. But, for the moment, no planes will take off and no irrevocable action of any kind will take place. The four command posts that have received the satellite data will convene a "missile display conference." Such conferences are not uncommon, as a variety of atmospheric and benign terrestrial events, such as forest fires, may look to the warning satellites like the launching of a nuclear-armed missile. In the first six months of 1980, no fewer than sixty-nine missile display conferences were convened in response to events that resembled missile launches. None of them were attacks on the United States.

To avoid overreacting to false alarms, the American missile warning centers rely on "dual phenomenology." A real missile attack will be detected by two independent warning systems that are not susceptible to the same errors. A minute or two after the warning satellites have sounded their alarm, missiles that were launched from submarines off American shores will be spotted by PAVE PAWS radars in Massachusetts and California, each of which can detect an object the size of a basketball in flight twelve hundred miles away. (The Perimeter Acquisition Radar Attack Characterization System—PARCS—in Concrete, North Dakota, will provide radar coverage of submarine launches in the Arctic Ocean.) Several minutes later, Ballistic Missile Early Warning System (BMEWS) radars in Alaska, Greenland, and England will spot the missiles launched from the Soviet Union. By this time, the commander in chief of NORAD, sitting before screens displaying "TOT MISL" (total number of missiles fired) and "TTG" (time to go before first detonation), will have concluded that there may be a threat to North America, and the missile display conference will have become a "threat assessment conference." The commanding officers of the four command centers on the warning circuit, including, at the Pentagon, the chairman of the Joint Chiefs of Staff, will get together on a conference telephone line. Between October 3, 1979, and June 3, 1980, four threat assessment conferences were convened. On October 3, a radar at Mt. Hebo, Washington (since replaced by the PAVE PAWS in California), observed a piece of an old rocket falling through low earth orbit and reported it as a submarine-launched missile. On November 9, 1979, exercise data designed to simulate a Soviet attack were fed accidentally into the NORAD computer. On March 15, 1980, four intermediate-range Russian missiles were launched from a submarine near the Kuril Islands during a training exercise and one of them appeared to be heading toward the United States. On June 3, 1980, a faulty computer chip caused display screens at SAC and the National Military Command Center (but not at NORAD) to display a massive Soviet attack.*

---

* The June 3 incident generated widespread publicity and a Senate investigation, resulting in the (unusual) release of false alert data for 1979 and 1980. A Senate report

45

In an actual Soviet attack, those participating in the threat assessment conference will find that the data from the satellites and the radars verify each other, that all four command posts are receiving the same information, and that the unfolding attack pattern makes some kind of sense—unless the attack has been preceded by an attack on the warning system itself. Some American military officials and defense consultants have expressed concern that the Russians may be developing weapons capable of blinding or destroying American missile warning satellites. (The Soviets have tested an exploding "killer satellite" that destroys other satellites in low earth orbit, but that is more than twenty thousand miles beneath the orbits of the missile warning satellites. The United States, meanwhile, is testing an airplane-launched rocket to destroy Russian satellites in low earth orbit and is experimenting with more exotic antisatellite laser weapons.) To defend against any future Soviet antisatellite breakthrough, the United States has begun development of a new generation of warning satellites designed, according to the Pentagon, "to operate reliably after an initial Soviet attack." Survivability measures under consideration include the launching of numerous nonfunctioning decoy satellites, the launching of "dark" (dormant) satellites that would be switched on only after functioning satellites were destroyed, the positioning of replacement satellites on American missiles ready for quick launch after functioning satellites were destroyed, and equipping satellites in orbit with the ability to detect attackers, maneuver away, and dispense chaff.

More immediate efforts are going into increasing the security of the handful of satellite ground stations and communications links without which even perfectly functioning warning satellites can not get their messages to earthbound command centers. "It is a little bit of a paradox to me as to how we are worried so much about the antisatellite capability of the Soviets," said Senator Sam Nunn dur-

___

concluded that the United States was never "close to unleashing nuclear war" as a result of the June 3 false alarm, but it said "there seemed to be an air of confusion following the determination that the data were erroneous." The report questioned the practice of training command post personnel to respond to every situation by following the instructions on an appropriate checklist: "Is it possible to develop checklists to cover every possible scenario and is the training given to the controllers adequate to give them a balance between reliance on checklist and application of sound judgment?"

ing a 1981 hearing. ". . . All they need to do is get a Piper Cub, two people, and a couple of hand grenades and knock out the ground station." Congress has now approved funds to develop mobile satellite ground terminals concealed on ordinary-looking military vans that will stay on the move during crises to complicate attempts at sabotage.

The greatest concern of warning system planners is that during a Soviet attack our generals in their command centers will sit pondering screens displaying information that is hopelessly incomplete or confusing. "We cannot assume that the enemy, if he actually plans to attack, will necessarily do us the favor of furnishing warning that is unambiguous," Secretary of Defense Caspar Weinberger wrote in 1982. "It seems likely that skillful deception could deprive us of clear warning."

Of course, ambiguous warning data will become conclusive if IONDS (Integrated Operational Nuclear Detonation Detection System) sensors scheduled to be deployed on American satellites later in this decade detect one or more nuclear detonations within the United States—or if one of the command centers participating in the threat assessment conference suddenly disappears.

Even before such drastic confirmation, our generals will be aided in their evaluation of ambiguous warning data by their knowledge of other recent events. Have reconnaissance satellites spotted unusual levels of activity at Soviet missile bases that might indicate preparations to launch? Has the network of microphones our Navy has laced through the world's oceans detected more than the usual complement of Russian missile-launching submarines off our Atlantic and Pacific coasts? Have the submarines moved closer to shore than their usual patrol routes? Has the Soviet premier vowed to destroy the United States?

Most to the point, are the United States and Soviet Union already at war somewhere in the world? Of all the scenarios for global nuclear war rehearsed by the Pentagon, almost none anticipate a "BOOB" (bolt out of the blue) missile surprise. That a massive Russian attack will come *this* afternoon, unexpected, for no apparent reason, seems far less likely than that an attack on the American heartland will occur only after the shedding of blood by Russian and American troops somewhere else. And it will seem even more

likely following the use elsewhere of relatively small "tactical" nuclear weapons—which is, in a way, already part of the plan.

The first use of tactical nuclear weapons against an overwhelming conventional Russian attack has been established American policy since 1953. In that era, the United States had imposing
nuclear superiority over the Soviet Union, and the United States
and its North Atlantic Treaty Organization allies were not enthusiastic about an expensive buildup of conventional forces to face Soviet conventional forces in Europe. Tactical nuclear weapons looked
like a cheap way to maintain the military balance.* In 1953, the
American "atomic cannon," an eighty-five-ton artillery piece
mounted on an unwieldy truck, was deployed in West Germany,
and it was soon followed by an imaginative assortment of nuclear
artillery shells, nuclear land mines, nuclear bombs for land- and
carrier-based airplanes, nuclear missiles, nuclear antisubmarine
depth charges, nuclear antiaircraft guns, and even, for a while, a nuclear bazooka called the Davy Crockett that was two feet long and
weighed less than fifty pounds. "Where these things are used on
strictly military targets and for strictly military purposes, I see no
reason why they shouldn't be used just exactly as you would use a
bullet or anything else," President Dwight Eisenhower said in 1955.
The deputy supreme commander of NATO elaborated: "I want to
make it absolutely clear that we . . . are basing all our operational
planning on using atomic and thermonuclear weapons in our own
defense. With us it is no longer: 'They may possibly be used.' It is
very definitely: 'They will be used, if we are attacked.' "

---

* American nuclear weapons are roughly divided into three categories: "strategic,"
"theater" or "intermediate-range," and "tactical." Strategic weapons are intercontinental ballistic missiles based in the United States, bombs on long-range bombers
based in the United States, and missiles on American submarines, all of which are targeted against the Soviet Union and its allies. Theater or intermediate-range weapons
are missiles and aircraft based in the European "theater" that can fly hundreds of
miles to strike the Soviet Union and its allies. Tactical weapons are short-range (in
some cases less than ten miles) weapons intended for use against enemy forces on or
near a battlefield. The categories are, in some cases, arbitrary and debatable. The Soviet Union has protested that "theater" nuclear missiles and aircraft capable of striking Moscow are indistinguishable from "strategic" nuclear missiles and aircraft
capable of striking Moscow. Moscow doesn't care whether the weapon that destroys it
begins its flight in West Germany or North Dakota.

In 1982, NATO Commander General Bernard Rogers worried that this was not the best of all possible policies. "We have mortgaged our defense to a nuclear response," he said, "and I don't like that." Nevertheless, the United States maintains about six thousand tactical nuclear weapons in Europe, about seven hundred in South Korea, and thousands more on American ships around the world and in storage in the United States. Among them are nuclear shells for 8-inch and 155-millimeter howitzers, nuclear warheads for the Lance and Honest John missiles, plane-dropped bombs, and "atomic demolition munitions," nuclear land mines designed to obstruct enemy forces by blowing mountainsides into passes, destroying bridges, and starting forest fires. The "neutron bomb" (actually a small hydrogen bomb designed to maximize deadly neutron radiation at the expense of some blast and heat energy) now being produced in the United States for possible deployment overseas is being manufactured in the form of eight-inch artillery shells and warheads for the Lance missile.

The tactical nuclear weapons already in Europe, Secretary of State Alexander Haig said in 1982, "are a concrete manifestation of NATO's willingness to resort to nuclear weapons if necessary to preserve the freedom and independence of its members." Haig was speaking in opposition to a proposal by four prominent former American officials that the United States pledge never to be the first to use nuclear weapons, a pledge the Soviet Union has taken. (One of the four was former Secretary of Defense Robert McNamara, who assured a congressional committee in 1964, "We have stated many, many times—I have stated on several different occasions . . . that we will use whatever weapons are necessary to protect our interests, including nuclear weapons.")

"Western proponents of a 'no first use' policy [do not] acknowledge the consequences for the Western alliance of an American decision not to pose and accept the risk of nuclear war in defense of Europe," Haig said in 1982. "A 'no first use' policy would be the end of flexible response and thus of the very credibility of the Western strategy of deterrence."

"Flexible response" means that America and its allies will attempt first to defeat a conventional Russian attack with conventional forces and, if that fails, will resort to tactical nuclear weapons.

(Or worse. "First use could conceivably, let me underscore conceivably, involve what we define as strategic forces and possibly, possibly, underscore possibly, involve selective strike at the Soviet Union," Secretary of Defense James Schlesinger told reporters in 1975.) "The first use of U.S. tactical nuclear weapons would probably be in a defensive mode based on prepared defense plans," says the U.S. Army Field Manual 100-5, *Operations*. "Later use could include nuclear support for offensive operations to destroy the enemy or regain lost territory." The manual refers to this as "the present concept of conventional-nuclear war," in which nuclear weapons will play a major role. "With nuclear strikes, *either side could deliver instantaneously crippling combat power*. Depending on the deception, surprise, target acquisition, and boldness of the user, such weapons could change the course of battle very quickly."

Historically, most of the scenarios for such a battle have been set in Western Europe, which the Russians are always presumed to be ready to invade. But the nuclear weapons also stand ready in Korea, and, following the Russian invasion of Afghanistan in 1979, the Pentagon carefully hinted that tactical nuclear weapons might be used to oppose a further Soviet move toward the Persian Gulf. "We are thinking about theater nuclear options in other areas than NATO," an unnamed senior Defense official told the press at a special Pentagon briefing.

Early in his administration, President Ronald Reagan told a group of newspaper editors, "I could see where you could have the exchange of tactical [nuclear] weapons against troops in the field without it bringing either one of the major powers to pushing the button." This created a public outcry in Europe but Reagan had, in fact, merely restated decades-old American, and NATO, doctrine. "The ultimate objective of the employment of nuclear weapons is to terminate a conflict at the lowest level of hostilities on terms acceptable to the United States and its allies," says Army Field Manual 101-31-1, *Nuclear Weapons Employment Doctrine and Procedures*. In other words, tactical nuclear weapons will be used to prevent the use of strategic nuclear weapons, to end the war by escalating it and thus prevent further escalation. Field Manual 101-31-1 explains: "Since the national purpose of employment is to terminate a conflict, the employment of nuclear weapons should serve to demonstrate to enemy leaders that potential losses outweigh gains if a conflict is continued or escalated. To accomplish this end, nuclear weapons could be used to positively and dramatically alter the course of battle and preclude the enemy from achieving his objectives. Depending on enemy response to initial nuclear deployment, additional employment of nuclear weapons may be required or directed. In all cases, follow-on strikes should support the basic purpose of decisively terminating a conflict at the lowest level of violence consistent with national and allied goals."

The manuals do not make clear why enemy leaders will quit the fight rather than use *their* tactical nuclear weapons against our tactical nuclear weapons, perhaps preemptively. (Another field manual, *Operations for Nuclear Capable Units*, does caution that "special ammunition supply points" should not be distinguishable from nonnuclear ammunition depots to external observers, and it prescribes procedures for the emergency destruction of nuclear weapons in positions that are about to be overrun.) It is made very clear, however, how American commanders will decide to use nuclear weapons, how they will select nuclear targets, and even how they will time their attacks—all in the interest of ending the war.*

To begin, every American corps and division is charged with developing, in peacetime, tentative nuclear strike plans based on "assumed penetrations into the proposed corps defensive area." Should war come, these plans will be amended "based on actual threat." Targets for nuclear strikes may include enemy nuclear forces, tanks, conventional artillery, headquarters, bridges, and reserves. If the selected target is a concentration of advancing enemy troops, the American strike will be designed to cover 30 to 40 percent of the target area with sufficient radiation to give enemy soldiers doses of at least eight thousand rads,† enough to cause "immediate permanent incapacitation" (IP). Failing that, doses of

---

* FM 101-31-1 also strikes a blow against sexism on the nuclear battlefield. "Due to its stated purpose," it notes, "throughout this manual the word 'he' is intended to include both the masculine and feminine genders and exceptions have been noted."
† A rad is a unit of absorbed radiation equal to one hundred ergs per gram of body tissue.

three thousand rads will produce "immediate transient incapacitation" (IT), and that will be good enough. "An active soldier suddenly exposed to 3,000 rads . . .," explains Field Manual 100-5, "may recover to some degree in about 45 minutes, but due to vomiting, diarrhea, and other radiation sickness symptoms, he would be only partially effective until he dies within a week." The radiation goal for defensive units, which are harder to defeat, will be to cover 40 to 60 percent of the area with IP, IT, or at least "LL" (latent lethality) doses. Commanders are also advised not to neglect the potency of other nuclear weapons effects and combinations thereof: "A soldier suffering from burns from thermal radiation, ear drum damage from overpressure, cuts and broken bones from flying objects, and vomiting from radiation sickness is not likely to be very effective in any capacity."

Once the corps commander has selected his targets, he will request permission to fire an appropriate "package" of tactical nuclear weapons. "At any given time, corps should have a preplanned nuclear weapon package to support each probable tactical contingency," instructs FM 100-5. It describes one hypothetical package as containing two atomic demolition munitions, ten nuclear missiles, five aircraft-delivered bombs, and thirty nuclear cannon shells. Since only the president of the United States can authorize the use of such a package, commanders are advised to submit their requests early enough "to minimize personnel and material vulnerability" while they are waiting for an answer. A "request sequence" chart in FM 100-5 allows fourteen hours for a request for permission to use a package to go from corps level up to CENTAG (Central Army Group), AFCENT (Allied Forces Central Europe), SHAPE (Supreme Headquarters Allied Powers in Europe), and finally the president, and for presidential approval to work its way back down the chain. The chart allows three hours for the president to make up his mind. (America's allies France and Britain have their own nuclear weapons and their own procedures for authorizing their use.)

Once permission is granted, nearby friendly units will be notified of the impending nuclear strikes "as rapidly as possible" and "aimpoints may be adjusted to incorporate the latest intelligence." Deciding exactly where to aim the nuclear artillery shells and other weapons in the package will be a very tricky matter, because the location of the target will not be the only consideration. Field Manual 101-31-1 contains a number of sample targeting problems of the type "target analysts" in the field will face. One of them concerns a hypothetical short-range cannon firing a one-kiloton nuclear shell (equivalent to one thousand tons of TNT) at an enemy position seven thousand meters away. The precise center of the target is known, but the shell cannot simply be aimed there, because there is a concentration of friendly troops twelve hundred meters south of the enemy. It happens that the friendly troops cannot be warned of the blast in advance, so it is assumed they will be standing in the open at the moment of detonation, with bare skin exposed to the heat. The target analyst must see that they suffer no more than "negligible risk," which is defined as the likelihood that they will suffer no more than 1 percent casualties and 2.5 percent "nuisance effects . . . such as eardrum rupture, first degree burns, and vomiting from radiation." And the problem includes a second "limiting requirement." Three hundred meters east of the target center two roads intersect in a woods. The intersection is of military importance and must be kept clear; the trees around it, which are deciduous, must not be blown down by the nuclear blast.

So the problem stands: find the aimpoint that is as close as possible to the target center without exposing unwarned friendly troops twelve hundred meters south to more than "negligible risk" or blowing down deciduous trees three hundred meters east.

The solution (according to Field Manual 101-31-1):

The target analyst consults the "safety distance table" provided for the one-kiloton short-range cannon. (Such tables for actual nuclear weapons are contained in a classified manual carried by troops in the field.) By looking in the proper column, he sees that, at a range of seven thousand meters, the "minimum safe distance" (MSD) for negligible risk to unwarned troops is fourteen hundred meters. (For "moderate risk"—2.5 percent casualties and 5 percent "nuisance effects"—the MSD is thirteen hundred meters. "Moderate risk should not be exceeded," the manual warns, "if troops are expected to operate at full efficiency after a friendly burst.")

Continuing, the target analyst consults another column on the table to see that "forest blowdown" for deciduous trees will occur at six hundred meters. (For coniferous trees it will occur at five hundred meters.)

The analyst will therefore take out his map of the battlefield, draw a line fourteen hundred meters north of the line of the friendly troops, and then draw an arc of radius six hundred meters around the woodsy crossroads. The intersection of the line and the arc is the point at which he will aim. It turns out to be about three hundred meters northwest of the target center, close enough to damage the enemy but far enough to spare the friendly troops and the trees.

Problem solved.

As it happens, however, this particular problem does not involve another important targeting consideration—the avoidance of "collateral damage" to civilians. This is expected to be an especially important factor in Europe, because, as several military analysts have pointed out, "the towns in West Germany are only two kilotons apart." Most scenarios project millions of NATO civilian casualties in a tactical nuclear war. Undeterred, Field Manual 101-31-1 establishes the "degree of acceptable risk" to civilians as "normally a 5-percent incidence of casualties at the edge of populated areas unless otherwise specified by the corps commander or higher authority." To help calculate when that risk level will be reached, target analysts are provided with "collateral damage avoidance tables." But FM 101-31-1 also notes that "the balance between military effectiveness and collateral damage" must be considered. If necessary, those firing the weapons can request that collateral damage "limiting requirements be exceeded."

The final constraining factor on the use of a tactical nuclear weapons package, once approved, will be time. The order authorizing the package's use will specify a "timeframe" of several hours during which it is to be fired. The corps commander may fire the first weapon in the package at any point in the timeframe, but, once the first weapon is fired, all the rest must be fired "in the shortest possible time." The purpose of concentrating the nuclear firepower will be "to convey to the enemy that we are using nuclear weapons in a limited manner." Presumably, a sudden nuclear barrage in a single geographic area will be interpreted by the enemy as "limited" and not part of a general nuclear counterattack.

If the enemy doesn't seem to be getting the message, he can always be telephoned. Field Manual 100-5 notes, in fact, that the use of a nuclear package will be timed "to insure full integration with . . . diplomatic actions." And FM 100-31-1 says a tactical nuclear barrage will be counted as successful only if "the resultant force ratios are such that the enemy forces are halted and can be controlled by conventional means throughout a sufficient pause for political channels to be utilized to terminate the conflict."

So the war will be over. Or possibly not. The manuals recognize that the enemy may not fold so easily. "Tentative plans should be formulated for subsequent packages to counter such situations as an enemy reinforcement and continuation of conventional efforts or an enemy nuclear response in the battle area or theater. . . . Intelligence collection efforts must be intensified to detect failure of the initial pulse to terminate the conflict."

While battlefield commanders are peering over the radioactive hills to see if the enemy is coming back for more (assuming that they have not been reduced themselves to "immediate permanent incapacitation" by the enemy's weapons), the generals at NORAD and the other command centers on the missile warning circuit will be looking at their display screens with special intensity, wondering if the Russians intend to reply to our package with a mighty package of their own. Missile launch officers on American submarines and in launch control centers beneath the Western plains will be studying their operations manuals. SAC bombers at coastal airfields will disperse to fields inland, buying themselves a few more minutes to escape should a Russian missile attack come from submarines offshore. Predesignated Alternate Reconstitution Base (ARB) teams will leave every SAC base for remote and presumably safe areas, taking with them everything they will need to service returning bombers if their bases are destroyed and alternates must be set up at civilian airports or on straight sections of interstate highways.

In Washington, the Central Locator System will be operating at top speed. Designed by the Federal Emergency Management Agency and administered by the White House, the Central Locator System keeps track of the locations of the president and his sixteen legally designated successors, from the vice president to the secretary of education. Its purpose is to make it easy to find a new and legal president if we lose the one we have. "In peacetime," says FEMA's Keith Peterson, "all the locator system can tell you is if a given successor is in town or out of town." But, even in peacetime, the system is used to prevent all the successors from gathering with the president where a single bomb or other disaster could eliminate them all. On the occasion of President Ronald Reagan's first State of the Union message, for example, it was discovered that all the successors were in town and planning to attend, so low man on the totem pole T. H. Bell, the secretary of education, was ordered to stay home. "The good news," White House Chief of Staff James Baker told Bell, "is that if the Capitol is subjected to a nuclear attack you'll be president of the United States. The bad news is that you don't get to go and hear the speech."

"During a period of increasing tension," says FEMA's Peterson, "we can escalate the reporting requirements so that we know if a successor is in his office, his house, or his car, or even know when he goes down the hall." (Following the attempted assassination of President Reagan in March 1981, Speaker of the House Thomas O'Neill, who is second in line to the presidency, reported that he received a phone call from FEMA within minutes asking where he was and if he was safe.)

The reason for keeping close tabs on presidential successors during a crisis, of course, is that if a crisis develops into a missile attack, no spare minutes will be available to start searching shopping malls for the vice president.

If the warning satellites detect flashes in the Soviet missile fields, and the radars detect blips to match the flashes, and the missile display conference of the warning centers becomes a threat assessment conference, and the generals conclude that yes, there is a threat—and all of that is done in five minutes—there will be twenty-five minutes left before the Soviet intercontinental ballistic missiles from Central Asia begin exploding on their American targets. The missiles launched from Russian submarines will be less than ten minutes away.

At SAC bases the bombers will move out for self-preservation in well-rehearsed Minimum Interval Take Offs (MITOs), one lumbering B-52 after another blasting off the runway with less than twelve seconds between them. In Washington, the Central Locator System will be quickly consulted and Air Force helicopters will swoop down to pick up the presidential successors and bear them away to safe havens to wait out the attack. At Andrews Air Force base near Washington, the National Emergency Airborne Command Post, a specially equipped 747 sitting on permanent alert for the president or his successor in a nuclear war, will prepare to take off. (In 1983 SAC announced that the president's plane would soon be reassigned from Andrews, which is uncomfortably close to Soviet missile-launching submarines in the Atlantic, to Grissom Air Force Base in Indiana.) At the White House, an operator on the military switchboard will hit a button setting off an alarm in the bomb shelter beneath the East Wing. A military aide stationed there will dash to the president's side with the "football," a black briefcase containing descriptions of and authorization codes for the president's nuclear retaliatory options. The president will be on the telephone with the commanders at the Pentagon, NORAD, and SAC in the ultimate stage of the warning chain—a "missile attack conference"—during which he may make the most important decisions ever made by a president of the United States. If the Soviet attack includes submarine-launched missiles aimed at Washington, the president at this point will have less than five minutes to live.

"I don't mean to introduce an element of levity to the situation," Representative Melvin Evans said during a 1980 congressional hearing on the warning system, "but as a practicing physician who has been on call at night, sometimes it takes me a couple of minutes to clear my mind, and here we have a president who might be asleep, and we are asking everything to be taken care of in [words censored from the hearing transcript for security reasons]. It seems to me a little bit unrealistic."

"Because we must have, and do have, positive human control," replied Gerald Dinneen, assistant secretary of defense for communications, command, control and intelligence, "and that positive human control ultimately rests in the president, that is, of course, one of the awesome responsibilities that he takes on."

That responsibility may fall on the shoulders of a president who is worse than groggy. He may just have returned from a cocktail party, or have taken a sleeping pill. He may not be in the White House at all. He may be riding a horse in California or floating down a river in a rubber raft. (When Jimmy Carter floated down the Salmon River in Idaho in 1978, the football was carried on a nearby raft.) The president may be visiting a foreign country, even one that is a potential enemy. (When Richard Nixon visited China in 1972, two National Emergency Airborne Command Post aircraft flew continuously along the Chinese coast—"to conduct communications training," the Air Force said.) Someone around the president may be forgetful. (When Gerald Ford deplaned in Paris in November 1975, the football was inadvertently left behind in a safe on Air Force One.) The president may just have been shot. (When Ronald Reagan was stripped of his clothing at George Washington University Hospital following the attempt on his life, FBI agents seized all his belongings, including a secret code card in his wallet that he would use to establish his identity to military commanders if he were caught away from secure communications facilities during an attack. Reagan's military aide demanded the card back, but the FBI agents refused, saying it might be needed for evidence.)

In anticipation of such emergencies, recent presidents, who are empowered to delegate their military authority, have established secret nuclear chains of command, generally beginning with the vice president. But a further obstacle to rapid convening of a missile attack conference was revealed in the memoirs of Bill Gulley, a former director of the White House Military Office, which is responsible for safeguarding the president and keeping him in touch with military forces during an attack. For more than a decade, Gulley said, the secret "White House Emergency Procedures" (WHEP) manual existed in two different, conflicting versions. This was discovered when Donald Rumsfeld, secretary of defense under Gerald Ford, went to the National Military Command Center in the Pentagon to test the emergency system. According to the Pentagon WHEP, a phone in the NMCC was supposed to be a direct line to the president. Rumsfeld picked it up and found himself speaking not to Gerald Ford but to a White House military operator who kept Rumsfeld on the line for either three or ten minutes (depending on whether you believe the operator or Rumsfeld) while, in accordance with the White House version of WHEP, the operator tried to find the director of the Military Office to ask for approval to put the call through to the president. A "personally ambitious" Military Office director under President John Kennedy, Gulley explained, wrote himself this important (and time-consuming) role in the White House manual. Knowing it would not be accepted by the Pentagon, he excised it from the Pentagon's copy. "In all those years," said Gulley, "no one had bothered to test the system without alerting everybody ahead of time, and we were darn lucky no foreign power tested it for us."

Now the system has been corrected, and it is expected that the president will be found promptly and put on the telephone with the football by his side. The innocuous-looking black briefcase with a combination lock contains four items. There is a procedures manual for the Emergency Broadcast System, which the president is supposed to use to address the American people after a nuclear attack. There is a card with identification codes (like the one seized by the FBI). There is a list of secret "Presidential Emergency Facilities," where the president can go to wait out a nuclear war. And there is the "Black Book," a looseleaf notebook containing descriptions of Soviet nuclear weapons and likely attack patterns and a menu, printed in red, of American retaliatory options.*

Up to this moment, no nuclear retaliation will have been launched. SAC's bombers will be flying not directly to their targets but to "positive control" points outside the airspace of the Soviet Union, where they will circle and wait for orders, and they will still be hours away even from those points. The submarine- and land-based missile launch crews will just be tensing up. Only the president, if he is alive, awake, and in communication, can authorize the use of nuclear weapons and he will not yet have spoken.†

---

* Harvard law professor Roger Fisher has suggested that the codes authorizing American nuclear retaliation be implanted in a capsule inside the chest of the president's aide. "The [aide] would carry with him a big, heavy butcher knife as he accompanied the President. If ever the President wanted to fire nuclear weapons, the only way he could do so would be for him first, with his own hands, to kill one human being . . . When I first suggested this to friends in the Pentagon they said, 'My God, that's terrible. Having to kill someone would distort the President's judgment. He might never push the button.'"

† This presidential authority made some officials nervous during the last White House days of Richard Nixon. "I can go into my office and pick up the telephone and in twenty-five minutes seventy million people will be dead," Nixon had remarked to a

One option the president will have will be to do nothing, at least for the moment, and that is in fact the option that is favored. It is a popular misconception that the president will automatically order a nuclear counterattack under the shadow of incoming missiles. On the contrary, great care and many billions of dollars have been spent to construct American nuclear weapons systems that will survive a nuclear attack and give the president the luxury of determining his response after the shape of battle is clear. "It has been and continues to be the policy of the Defense Department to design strategic offensive systems in such a way that they can either ride out an attack before being launched, or if launched on warning, can be reliably recalled, as in the case of U.S. bombers," an administration official told a congressional committee in 1976. Secretary of Defense Caspar Weinberger reaffirmed this policy in his 1982 report to Congress: "U.S. forces will be capable under all conditions of war initiation to survive a Soviet first strike and retaliate in a way that permits the United States to achieve its objectives." In pursuit of this goal, and because new, more accurate Soviet missiles are supposedly capable of destroying American Minuteman missiles in their hardened silos, the Carter and Reagan administrations have pushed for the deployment of the new MX missile in a succession of Rube Goldbergesque basing schemes, all designed to enhance survivability. If American strategy called for launching American missiles as soon as an incoming attack was confirmed, it wouldn't matter if American missiles were survivable or not. They would be gone by the time Russian missiles landed on their empty silos.

This "launch under attack" option has often been considered by military planners, but it has never been embraced. For one thing, it is dangerous, because a false alarm could trigger a real response. (In 1960, American radar signals reflected off the moon and "all hell broke loose" at NORAD, according to Senator Charles Percy, who happened to be touring the facility that day. "They were absolutely convinced there were missiles coming at us.") Another reason not to launch under attack is that it is unnecessary; thousands of American

---

group of visiting congressmen in November 1973. The following summer, when Nixon's resignation was imminent, Secretary of Defense James Schlesinger deferred all trips and ordered the armed forces to accept no commands from the White House without his concurrence.

nuclear weapons on bombers and in submarines would survive any conceivable Soviet strike. Finally, even if it were safe and necessary, it would still be awfully hard to do. "I got involved in launch under attack during the Ford Administration," recalls Daniel Payton, the deputy director for nuclear technology at the Air Force Weapons Laboratory in New Mexico. "It came up in testimony to Congress that maybe the Russians were planning on it, and it began to be looked at enthusiastically in some circles in the Air Force. Suddenly an emergency study was called for, called a Warning Attack Assessment Study. One thing it focussed on was, do you have enough time? We looked at the time line and the decision process and the decision meetings that are part of it and asked, how much time does the president have to respond? If you're going to have launch under attack, you'd better have your response predetermined and not even have any options. People don't want that. But how can you decide how to retaliate on ten minutes' information? I convinced myself and, I think, most of the Air Force and Department of Defense officials that it's not technically feasible to do launch on attack assessment.

"Still," adds Payton, "it has a lot of closet advocates. Hawks like it because it's sort of macho. Doves like it because you can do it without spending money. You really have to fight hard to get people to think seriously about it."

All advocates of launch under attack point out that it would be a powerful disincentive to a Russian first strike against American missile fields, and, for that reason, the option has always been officially left open. "Let me put it this way," then–Secretary of Defense Harold Brown told a congressional committee in 1980. "The Soviets should not be able to count, and I think aren't able to count, on our not doing it, but we surely should not count on being able to." When Secretary of Defense Caspar Weinberger was pressed on the issue by a reporter in 1981, he demurred that "what our policy is in connection with a nuclear attack on the United States [is] nothing I would want to discuss or disclose publicly ahead of time."

Whatever the president's intention, one of the first things he will hear in his conference telephone call with the generals will be an assessment of the incoming attack. The BMEWS radars in Greenland, Britain, and Alaska, and the PARCS radar in North

Dakota are programmed to provide a count of incoming missiles and estimates of where they will land. Whether the president intends to retaliate now or later, an attack consisting of a dozen missiles headed for missile silos in Wyoming will provoke a different response than will an attack by a thousand missiles against targets all over the country. An attack consisting of even a single missile, if that missile is heading toward Washington, will prompt the president's first decision—not how to respond to the attack but whether or not to get the hell out of the White House.

The president will have several options, most of which involve the National Emergency Airborne Command Post (NEACP, pronounced "Kneecap"), which is the designation given to whichever one of a small fleet of specially modified 747s is standing on alert that day. Until 1974, the president's getaway plane was a modified 707, which was so small, former secretary of defense Melvin Laird once complained to a congressional committee, that "before a person can go to the back of the plane, everyone has to move out of his chair." Clearly, that would have been an awkward way to run a nuclear war, so Congress approved development of the E-4A, the first 747 to fill the NEACP role. Three E-4As were in service by 1975, and Jimmy Carter flew in one on a trip from Plains to Washington. It was a "very sobering" flight, he said. In 1980, a new, improved model E-4B was delivered (all the E-4As are also being remodeled into E-4Bs), and Ronald Reagan flew in it back to Washington after a Texas turkey shoot in 1981. "It gives me a sense of confidence," he said.

The E-4B will seat ninety-four during a nuclear war, including a battle staff of fifteen and an Air Force crew of twenty-seven. The president's private quarters, furnished with bunk beds and decorated in gold, are located in the area occupied by first-class passengers on a commercial 747. Behind the presidential quarters is a conference room with nine seats around a rectangular table. The president will sit at its head, next to a secure red phone and facing a wall of display screens upon which the progress of the war will be traced. Farther back are a larger briefing room, the battle staff compartment, and an elaborate communications section through which the president will communicate to dispersed American forces via a variety of radio frequencies and routes. Trailing behind the plane will be a five-mile-long wire antenna for very-low-frequency radio contact with American missile-launching submarines.

When an incoming attack is detected, the NEACP will prepare for immediate takeoff, and the president will have the option of helicoptering from the White House and climbing aboard. It is supposed to be possible to do this within the available warning time, but when Carter national security advisor Zbigniew Brzezinski sprang a surprise test on the system in 1977, he was still coptering over Maryland long after that part of Maryland would have ceased to exist in a real war. "The people who run the system weren't notified there'd be a test," William Baird, FEMA's assistant associate director for national security plans and preparedness, explained later. "And they had no indication it was the real thing." That is, no radar or satellite warning had sent the system into a higher state than day-to-day alert. "And Brzezinski didn't use the right code words."

In a real attack, it is officially expected that the NEACP will be ready and waiting. If there's not enough time for the president to get to it before Russian missiles do, the plane will take off and circle until a rendezvous with the president can be arranged at an undamaged airfield.

Or the president can elect not to go airborne at all and head instead for a secret underground "Presidential Emergency Facility." There are nine such facilities within twenty-five minutes' helicopter flying time of the White House, by Bill Gulley's account, and more than seventy-five scattered around the country in case the president is out of town when an attack comes. "Actually," said William Baird, "there are many more than eighty sites where the president could be dropped off. The president has choices. He can go up. He can go down. Or he might want to stay right in the White House, as the act of a leader."

Or the president might already *be* airborne at the time of an attack, having taken to the skies as a precautionary measure during the preceding crisis, although, as Baird implied, that would hardly be considered the act of an inspirational leader. ("I am sure that in England during World War II, when Churchill was standing there trying to encourage his people to resist, it would have been a strange sight if he had taken off in a plane instead," former senator William Fulbright said of the NEACP.)

More likely, in a major international crisis the president will send the vice president up in the NEACP, or at least on an extended speaking tour of rural Oregon. During "Ivy League," a nuclear war exercise conducted in the spring of 1982, the vice president, played by former CIA chief Richard Helms, took off in the NEACP after, according to the exercise scenario, U.S. forces were attacked in Europe, South Korea, and Southwest Asia; Soviet tactical nuclear weapons were used against an American ship in the North Atlantic; and the United States launched tactical nuclear counterattacks. While the "vice president" took to the skies, Secretary of the Interior James Watt and Secretary of Commerce Malcolm Baldrige, playing themselves, were dispatched to underground federal facilities in Massachusetts and Texas. The president, played by former Secretary of State William Rogers, stayed in the White House (where a bomb shelter, complete with a paneled presidential office and accommodations for twenty-four staff members, was built during the Truman administration). On the fourth day of the crisis the Soviets launched a massive nuclear attack against the United States, and the "president" was "killed."

The possibility that the real president will die early in a real nuclear war is considered a strong one. Most of the planning literature about nuclear war therefore refers not to "the President" but to "the National Command Authorities" (NCA), defined (by the Department of Defense *Dictionary of Military and Associated Terms*) as "the President and the Secretary of Defense or their duly deputized alternates or successors." It is always "the NCA," not "the President," who will select the retaliatory option, authorize the use of nuclear weapons, or sit on the gold-upholstered sofa in the private "NCA quarters" aboard the NEACP.

If the president is killed, the Central Locator System will be put to its ultimate test—to establish quickly and authoritatively who is the new president/NCA. "It is essential . . . that the legitimacy of the new President be established with high reliability," notes a 1980 study conducted for the Federal Emergency Management Agency on "continuity of government." "We need only note in support of this proposition that the law provides that if a successor is sworn in and then a higher ranking successor is found indeed to have sur-vived but to have been out of communication, he cannot retrieve the office from the sworn successor." It would indeed be a messy affair if the Speaker of the House crawled out of some rubble somewhere and found that the secretary of energy was already running the country, but for a long time this problem was neglected. "One of the things we discovered is that there was no authentication system," FEMA Director Louis Giuffrida told a meeting of the American Civil Defense Association in 1981. "So that if a successor got on the horn and said, 'I'm *the* successor,' and somebody said, 'Prove it,' [no one could]. So we're working on that, and FEMA will be the auth-enticating mechanism to say, 'Yeah, this guy's for real. The Presi-dent's gone and we don't know where the Vice President is . . . and this is the man.' "

Once that is established, the NEACP will swoop down to pick up the new president and continue on its meandering flight above the destruction. It will meander to evade enemy detection; beyond that, its flight plan is a well-kept secret. One logical route for it would be straight out of the United States to the territory of an un-attacked ally in the fallout-free Southern Hemisphere. (During the "Ivy League" exercise, a White House abroad was set up in an American embassy in Europe to simulate what would happen if a presidential successor was consulting with allies there when the at-tack came.) If the NEACP remains airborne for safety, above the United States or anywhere else, it will be periodically refueled by surviving tankers from surviving airfields until, after seventy-two hours, it needs an oil change. Then it will land, to replenish its oil and take off again, or to drop off the NCA at an undamaged Presi-dential Emergency Facility, or simply to sit on a runway somewhere and function as a ground command post.

"We remain concerned, however, about the ability of airborne command posts to operate beyond the first few days of a nuclear war," Secretary of Defense Caspar Weinberger said in his 1982 re-port to Congress. "We will therefore develop and deploy terrestrial mobile command centers (MCCs) that could supplement or take over the key functions of airborne command posts if they could no longer operate effectively." These MCCs might be disguised as ordinary moving vans, traveling the nation's highways in a random pattern during an international crisis.

It's hard to imagine that the other truckers at Rosie's Café won't spot something funny about the short-haired drivers in the shiny black shoes. But they will provide another option for the president of the United States on the day after the start of World War III.

FOUR

"All This from One Bomb"

Thirty-one days after the world's second atomic bomb exploded over Hiroshima, a small team of American physicists and physicians preceded American occupation troops into the city. Among them was physicist Philip Morrison, who had worked on the Manhattan Project at Los Alamos, had personally carried the plutonium core for the world's first atomic bomb to the Trinity test site, and had lately been working on Tinian Island in the Pacific assembling the bombs that were dropped on Hiroshima and Nagasaki. Morrison was apprehensive about his visit to Hiroshima. "I thought it was quite dangerous for us to go there," he recalls. "I thought we would be marked targets. But there was not even any resentment, except for this one man." The one man was Dr. Masao Tsuzuki, a Japanese radiologist who had once done research at the University of Pennsylvania. Morrison and his colleagues met Tsuzuki in Tokyo while they were en route to Hiroshima, and he showed them a paper he had done in Pennsylvania describing the deaths by hemorrhaging and other ailments of animals exposed to heavy doses of X rays in laboratory experiments. "Ah, but the *Americans*—they are wonderful," Tsuzuki told Morrison. "It has remained for them to conduct the *human* experiment."

The purpose of the scientists' mission to Japan, according to a Top Secret memo from General Leslie Groves, commander of the Manhattan Project, was "to make absolutely certain that there can be no possible ill effects to American troops from radioactive materials at either Hiroshima or Nagasaki as well as to ascertain the extent of all damage at these two places. Although we felt that Japanese casualties from radioactivity were unlikely it is most important, for the future of the atomic bomb work as well as for historical reasons, that we determine the facts."

Manhattan Project scientists had long been aware that atomic bomb blasts could produce radioactive particles with lingering dangerous effects, and both the Hiroshima and Nagasaki bombs had deliberately been fused to explode more than sixteen hundred feet above the ground to minimize those effects. But the first full Japanese report on the atomic bombings, issued two weeks after the attacks, said that many people were still dying from the "uncanny effects" of the bombs. "Even those who received minor burns and looked quite healthy at first weakened after a few days for some unknown reason," the report said. The Japanese also claimed that rescue workers at Hiroshima were made ill by the bomb even though they had entered the city *after* the blast. And in New York, Harold Jacobson, an American scientist who had had a minor connection with the Manhattan Project, wrote a widely circulated article in which he asserted that radioactivity would make Hiroshima uninhabitable for seventy years.

The U.S. Army was prepared to acknowledge that its atomic bombs sent out deadly bursts of radiation at the moment of explosion. It noted, however, that most people receiving lethal doses of radioactivity would be dead of burns or of being buried beneath shattered buildings long before they could exhibit any symptoms of radiation poisoning. The radiation effects would be critical only among the relatively few victims who were within a thousand yards of an explosion but escaped immediate death because they happened to be shielded from the bomb's heat by something too strong to be knocked over by its blast (or too light to kill them when it was knocked over), Philip Morrison explained to a Senate committee a few months later. "Many literally crawled out of the wreck of their homes relatively uninjured," Morrison said. "But they died anyway. They died from a further effect ... of radiumlike rays emitted in great number from the bomb at the instant of the explosion. This radiation affects the blood-forming tissues in the bone marrow. ... The blood does not coagulate, but oozes in many spots through the unbroken skin, and internally seeps into the cavities of the body."

"You mean the skin would be absolutely normal and yet the blood would be coming through?" asked the committee chairman.

"Yes," said Morrison. "There might be a slight burn on the skin, but it was not essential. The white corpuscles which fight infection disappear. Infection prospers and the patient dies, usually two or three weeks after the exposure. I am not a medical man, but like all nuclear physicists I have studied this disease a little. It is a hazard of our profession. With the atomic bomb, it became epidemic."

This epidemic the Army acknowledged, but it remained extremely sensitive about any suggestion that some residue of the explosions was dangerous to those entering the areas later. Such suggestions called into question American respect for the rules of warfare, including the prohibition on the use of poison gas (to which Japanese broadcasts in the days before surrender had compared the atomic bomb), and might even produce public revulsion that could jeopardize, in Groves's phrase, "the future of the atomic bomb work." Reporter Daniel Lang observed that the Army "felt called upon to prove as soon as possible that the new bombs were entitled to the same degree of respect accorded by the civilized world to rockets, mines, incendiaries, and sixteen-inch shells." Old-fashioned bombs dropped on Tokyo had killed as many people as the atomic bomb dropped on Hiroshima, and nobody had raised any fuss about that. The question of lingering radioactivity seemed to make the difference.

In New York, Dr. Jacobson was promptly visited by agents of the FBI and other government authorities. After several hours of questioning, he issued a statement saying that his article about contamination at Hiroshima had not relied on confidential information, that he was now "surprised and pleased to learn" that there was only a small amount of lingering radioactivity at the Trinity test site, that he had learned that "eminent and qualified scientists" disagreed with some of his opinions about Hiroshima, and that he was ill and upset about the whole thing. Meanwhile, J. Robert Oppenheimer, the scientific director of Los Alamos, broke a security news blackout to say "there is every reason to believe that there was no appreciable radioactivity on the ground at Hiroshima and what little there was decayed very rapidly." In New Mexico, General Groves himself led reporters on a tour of the Trinity site to demonstrate that little radio-activity remained there and thus, *The New York Times* reported, "gave the most effective answer . . . to Japanese propaganda."

In Japan, the findings of the American scientific mission supported the American position. After spending a night in honeymoon cottages at a resort outside Hiroshima, the scientists spread out through the city with Geiger counters and detected little residual radioactivity. The city was safe to live in. Those who had died, and would die, from the bomb were victims of its immediate radiation effects, and of its heat (tens of millions of degrees), and of being battered to death by the bomb's shock wave, and of having buildings fall over on them, and of the fires that sprang up in the bomb's immediate aftermath. And that was plenty. (In Nagasaki, an American soldier accompanying the scientists recoiled in confusion when he was told he was standing on a corpse. "I looked down," he wrote later. "My feet were in a circle of fine white ash, not thick enough to feel through my boot soles.")

"There was one more novelty," Philip Morrison told the Senate committee. "A Japanese official stood in the rubble and said to us: 'All this from one bomb; it is unendurable.' We learned what he meant. The cities of all Japan had been put to flame by the great flights of B-29s from the Marianas. But at least there was warning, and a sense of temporary safety. If the people in Kōbe went through a night of inferno, you, living in Nagoya, were going to be all right that night. The thousand-bomber raids were not concealed; they even formed a pattern of action which the war-wise Japanese could count on. But every hour of every day above any Japanese city there might be one American plane. And one bomber could now destroy a city."

A few days after the bombing of Hiroshima, *The New Yorker* published, "for the benefit of future social historians," a collection of the world's first jokes about the atomic bomb. "One Broadway hot-spot wag observed that the Japanese were suffering from atomic ache," the magazine reported. A radio-show "jokespert" proposed that the bomb be called "an aerial atomizer." That was as good as they got.

Several weeks later, a humorist writing in *The New York Times* suggested that atomic bombs could be put to good use removing balky ice trays from the refrigerator. "With quite sizable atomic bombs," he wrote, "there is a fantastic possibility that even the windows of non-air-conditioned suburban trains can be manipulated."

In Los Angeles, only days after the news of Hiroshima, the Metro-Goldwyn-Mayer studio trotted out before photographers an unknown starlet in a two-piece bathing suit and announced that she was the "Anatomic Bomb." "Starlet Linda Christian brings the new atomic age to Hollywood," *Life* reported. "So far she has been in no pictures, the publicity role of the Anatomic Bomb being her first important assignment."

Others were less lighthearted. The Vatican City newspaper recalled in an editorial the day after Hiroshima that Leonardo da Vinci had designed a submarine and then destroyed the plans because "he feared that man would not apply it to . . . constructive uses of civilization but to its ruin." The paper implied that the same ought to have been done with the atomic bomb. In New York, on the day Nagasaki was bombed, the president of the Federal Council of Churches of Christ in America and John Foster Dulles, chairman of the council's Commission on a Just and Durable Peace, urged a temporary halt in the atomic bombings. "If we, a professedly Christian nation, feel morally free to . . . wreak upon our enemy mass destruction such as men have never before imagined . . .," they said, "atomic weapons will be looked upon as a normal part of the arsenal of war and the stage will be set for the sudden and final destruction of mankind." A few days after the war's end, thirty-four American clergymen condemned the atomic bombings as a "colossal crime" and appealed to President Truman to discontinue the bomb's production. The use of the bomb, they said, "will have to receive judgment before God."

Truman had made his own divine reference on the day Nagasaki was bombed: "We thank God that it [the atomic bomb] has come to us, instead of to our enemies; and we pray that He may guide us to use it in His ways and for His purposes." The connection between the atomic bomb and God was a common one. "Atomic Power," one of the first popular songs about the bomb, written by cowboy singer Fred Kirby in August 1945, included the lines:

Hiroshima, Nagasaki, paid a big price for their sin.
When scorched from the face of earth, their battle could not win . . .
Take warning, my dear brother, be careful how you plan.
You're working with the power of God's own holy hand.

The song was recorded by more than half a dozen groups, and Kirby rode in Truman's 1949 inaugural parade.

The Anatomic Bomb aside, it was clear that America's new weapon marked a revolution in warfare. "What I am trying to tell you," General Henry H. Arnold, commander of the Army Air Forces, said at a press conference on August 17, "is that this thing is so terrible in its aspects that there may not be any more wars." Improved atomic bombs, he said, would soon be mounted on huge bombers and guided missiles which could reach and obliterate any place on earth except "a small section of the Antarctic continent" that happened to be out of range. A joint statement by President Truman and the prime ministers of Great Britain and Canada, issued in November, said that no nation could maintain a monopoly on the atomic bomb and that "there can be no adequate military defense" against it. An Illinois congressman warned that the A-bomb had made large American cities "the most dangerous spots on the face of the earth" and said it might be necessary to disperse American industry, evacuate and scatter the population of American cities, and commandeer abandoned mines to shelter people and factories. By 1946, the federal Army and Navy Munitions Board was surveying caves.

Meanwhile, the proof provided in Japan that atomic energy could be tapped led to a resurgence of predictions of atomic utopia. At the French Foreign Office, "where they had long been racking their brains over the future of the Ruhr, the Saar and the Rhineland, officials concluded that they might as well go fishing," *The New York Times* reported two days after the bombing of Hiroshima. "Why acquire gray hairs over the Ruhr and the Saar if . . . coal is to become useless and abundant heat and energy are to be derived from systematically disintegrated atoms?" In a book rushed out before the end of 1945, the science editor of the Scripps-Howard newspapers predicted the world would soon see automobiles fueled for a year by atomic pellets the size of vitamin pills, houses heated for an entire winter by the same atomic pellets, atomic planes large enough to carry thousands of passengers nonstop from New York to Australia, atom-powered outdoor air conditioning, atomically illuminated indoor farming, and atomic rockets to the moon—all unfolding in an era of "universal and perpetual peace" created by atomic abundance and the fear of atomic war.

The revolutionary nature of atomic war came up again at the Senate hearing in which Philip Morrison painted his grim picture of Hiroshima. "What relation," asked the committee chairman, "has a ten-million-man Army, every one of them able to shoot the eye out of a squirrel at a thousand yards . . . to the ability or the power compressed in these bombs as a matter of defense?"

"If you have," Morrison replied, "as you will have in a future war, one thousand or five thousand long-range rockets striking our industrial areas, each one loaded with enough atomic explosive to destroy any city district . . . you will lose, as I think has been said before, something like one-third of your population in the first day of the war. . . . Against such an attack a conventional army is of no value."

The Army, naturally, had a different view; it had gone on record the day after the bombing of Hiroshima that its new weapon in no way meant there was any reason for cuts in the Army's previously announced manpower goals. Other narrow interests reacted to the bomb in other narrow ways. One senator interrupted Morrison's testimony several times to ask about the usefulness of lead in protecting people from the effects of atomic bombs. "What does the person wear if he goes into one of these infected areas?" the senator asked. "I don't quite understand," said Morrison. "There is nothing you wear for protection." Persevering, the senator said he'd heard that a special tank that approached the Trinity test site right after the blast had been lined with lead. "When the men get out of that tank," he asked, "what do they wear?" Still mystified, Morrison replied, "They didn't get out. They would have been fried if they had gotten out." But more questions about lead ensued, until Morrison finally caught on that the senator was from a state where one important industry was the mining of lead. Morrison allowed then that a man could be protected from a bomb's radiation if he wore a fifty-ton lead suit, and the questioning was allowed to get back on course.

In 1976, Pentagon consultant T. K. Jones, who upon the advent of the Reagan administration would be appointed deputy undersecretary of defense, submitted a report to a congressional committee that called into question the devastation of Hiroshima. The report was illustrated by a number of photographs taken in Hiroshima shortly after the atomic bombing. "In viewing Figure 2," Jones wrote, "one gets the impression of vast and total destruction. The devastation is complete, reaching as far as the eye can see. In Figure 3, the grotesquely twisted dead tree in the foreground symbolizes the awesome, life-destroying powers of the blast. It also diverts attention from the surviving buildings in the center of the photo. Figures 4, 5 and 6 again show terrible destruction, but the presence of surviving buildings is increasingly prominent." Jones's point was that too much attention had been given to what had been knocked down at Hiroshima and not enough attention given to what had been left standing. "If we fix on the impressions of Figures 1 and 2," he wrote, "we can convince ourselves that nuclear war would be the end of all mankind. If we examine carefully that which has survived nuclear detonations, it is possible to construct a program for national survival of a nuclear war."

Jones's attack on what he considered the wrong lessons of Hiroshima was only one round in a debate that began at the end of the war and continues to this day. Jones's point had in fact been answered thirty-one years before it was made, in Philip Morrison's 1945 testimony to the U.S. Senate's Special Committee on Atomic Energy. "A good deal of comment has been attracted by the ferroconcrete structures whose walls still stand," Morrison said. "These are very strong buildings. But they too are useless. I have been in these buildings. The window casements are gone, the interior walls are down, the roofs are collapsed, the furniture battered, plumbing fixtures and heavy machinery overturned. A great blast wind followed the shock and ripped through the buildings, destroying their interiors. Most of them burned. Brick buildings, and even steel-frame buildings with brick walls, are extremely vulnerable."

The 1945 counterpart of T. K. Jones was Major Alexander P. de Seversky, a former commander of the Czar's Baltic naval fighter plane force. De Seversky toured Europe as a consultant to the American secretary of war after the collapse of Germany and told reporters at the time (June 1945) that "any talk of a practical application" of atomic power for bombs was "just propaganda." After the defeat of Japan, de Seversky, unembarrassed, toured Hiroshima and Nagasaki and reported, first to the War Department and then in a *Reader's Digest* article titled "Atomic Bomb Hysteria," that the effects of the atomic bombing "had been wildly exaggerated. If dropped on New York or Chicago, one of those bombs would have done no more damage than a ten-ton blockbuster." He acknowledged that future atomic bombs might be more powerful, but asserted that Hiroshima and Nagasaki were "highly flimsy and inflammable" cities, and that, in any case, many of their buildings, and even flagpoles, had been left standing. (Morrison pointed out that, directly beneath an atomic bomb exploded in the air, as those in Japan had been, the blast wave would come straight down, leaving poles intact while people were burned alive.) "Humankind has stampeded into a state of near hysteria at the first exhibits of atomic destruction," de Seversky concluded. "Fantasy is running wild."

Other authorities replied that the only fantasy was de Seversky's. General Thomas Farrell, who had led the American scientists to Japan, said that one atomic bomb "could blow the Empire State Building to hell." Rather than being equivalent to a single blockbuster, he said, an atomic bomb dropped on New York would do as much damage as at least eighty blockbusters. Farrell had said earlier that eight Hiroshima-type atomic bombs could destroy New York; de Seversky said it would take hundreds.

That the new weapon possessed unprecedented power was continually stressed by those who had built it and did not want to see it used again. Hundreds of Manhattan Project scientists organized themselves into the Federation of Atomic Scientists (which grew into the Federation of American Scientists) to lobby Congress and educate the American public about the bomb. The scientists opposed military control of, and secrecy in, atomic research, and they warned that the American monopoly on atomic weapons would inevitably be short-lived. (The greatest "secret" about the bomb, they said, was that it could be built, and that secret was out.) Therefore, the scientists argued, the weapon had to be put under effective international control; the alternative specter of many nuclear-armed nations was too awful, because—and this was the heart of their message—there was no effective defense against the atomic bomb. "Even leadership in an atomic armament race will in no way assure our safety against sudden attack by an aggressor, who might easily have enough bombs to destroy every one of our major cities in a single day," a committee of scientists declared in October 1945.

To get their message out, the scientists buttonholed congressmen, held press conferences, wrote magazine articles, and took advantage of every public forum they were offered, no matter how unlikely.* One senator complained that, "instead of entering the political arena," the scientists ought to go back to their laboratories and invent a defense against the atomic bomb. "If there is no defense, they should be developing one," he said. "That is their job." But they saw their job as something else. "We have turned ourselves into twenty-five hundred Jeremiahs," a scientist explained. "You have to shake [people] by the shoulders." Scientists at Los Alamos took to mailing pieces of fused glass created from sand by the Trinity bomb to American mayors as reminders that their cities would be destroyed in the first hours of an atomic war. (Souvenir hunters besieged Los Alamos for more fused glass and supplies were soon exhausted.) Fifteen scientists collaborated on a book called *One World or None*, which included a detailed description by Philip Morrison of what would happen if a single atomic bomb were dropped on New York City. (Describing the effects of a single bomb on New York would become, thirty-five years later, a standard of

---

* A few years later, physicist Samuel Goudsmit described to a reporter his appearance on the "Tex and Jinx" television show: "It was quite a production. Boy Scouts were on the program. So was the pilot who dropped the bomb on Hiroshima. He said that war was hell. I was introduced to Johnny, the Philip Morris midget. A United Nations chorus of twenty-five voices sang 'Rock of Ages,' and there were two ducks, one of them radioactive, in the cast."

anti-nuclear-arms-race meetings and literature.) "If we do not learn to live together ...," Morrison concluded, "the cities of men on earth will perish."

The scientists' campaign was well advanced by the spring of 1946, when attention began to focus on the Pacific atoll of Bikini, where the American armed forces proposed to detonate a series of atomic bombs above and beneath a fleet of captured and obsolete warships. American military officials persuaded Bikini's credulous native inhabitants to leave their home by telling them they were like "the Children of Israel whom the Lord had saved from their enemy and led into the Promised Land," and asking, "Would you be willing to sacrifice your island for the welfare of all men?" (And giving them little chance to say no.) Meanwhile, it appeared that the scientists' campaign to emphasize the power of the atom might have succeeded too well. Some people expressed fear that the underwater blast scheduled for Bikini would blow a hole in the bottom of the ocean and let all the water drain out. Others worried that the explosion would turn the oceans to gas. A professor emeritus of physics at Yale agreed that the underwater bomb might blast a hole in the ocean floor, with the result, he said, that cold sea water would mix with molten rock, generating tremendous explosions and mile-high waves that could swamp all Pacific islands and the western coast of the United States. Moreover, he said, that tumult might displace so much matter from the South Seas to northern latitudes that the rotation of the earth on its axis would speed up, shortening the day and quickening the "tempo of many human activities, if any still persisted."

Such predictions were not regarded happily by the Federation of American Scientists, which was devoted to the argument that the atomic bomb was awfully powerful, but not *that* powerful. Exaggerated predictions, the FAS feared, could lead the public to underestimate the power of the bomb when they were not fulfilled. The scientists were already aware and concerned that exploding a bomb over dispersed and floating ships would inevitably produce less spectacular results than exploding a bomb over a city crowded with rigid structures. Their concern was validated when the first Bikini test, an airburst detonated on July 1, 1946, sent only two of seventy-three target ships to the bottom. (Three that were damaged sank later.) An invited Russian observer on a nearby naval vessel pointed to the mushroom cloud and said, "Not so much." And the American public agreed. "On returning from Bikini," William Laurence reported in *The New York Times*, "one is amazed to find the profound change in the public attitude toward the problem of the bomb. Before Bikini the world stood in awe of this new cosmic force.... Since Bikini this feeling of awe has largely evaporated." The second blast at Bikini, an underwater burst that threw up a spectacular half-mile-wide pillar of radioactive water a mile into the air, brought back some of that awe. But much public attention remained on a young pig. To test the effects of radiation, hundreds of pigs, mice, guinea pigs, and goats, and thousands of rats had been made passengers on the target ships before the first Bikini blast, and one piglet (number 311) became a popular heroine when she swam from the doomed Japanese cruiser *Sakawa* to safety. A few weeks later, "the celebrated swimming pig of Bikini Lagoon" was invited to be a "distinguished guest" at a festival in Harlingen, Texas. Admiral Chester Nimitz replied that the pig couldn't come.

Still, no one was about to mistake the atomic bomb for a firecracker. The U.S. Strategic Bombing Survey, after extensive studies of Japan, reported that 70,000 to 80,000 people were killed or missing after the bombing of Hiroshima while 83,600 were killed or missing after the bombing of Tokyo a few months earlier. The key difference was the number of planes involved. These figures assumed new import in September 1949, when the American public learned that America's atomic monopoly was at an end. "We have evidence that within recent weeks an atomic explosion occurred in the USSR," President Truman announced. "Ever since atomic energy was first released by man, the eventual development of this new force by other nations was to be expected. This probability has always been taken into account by us." General Omar Bradley, chairman of the Joint Chiefs of Staff, was as cool as Truman. *Pravda* reported that the Russian bomb had given Bradley insomnia; the general replied that he was still getting six hours of sleep every night and that it was sound.

But not everyone was so relaxed. A senator from Michigan urged that the Defense Department immediately disperse from its central headquarters buildings in Washington. Otherwise, he said, "we would be a sucker for a solar plexus atomic blow which could knock our country out of an atomic war a few minutes after such a war started." A member of the Joint Congressional Atomic Committee proposed that the government establish an alternate capital, perhaps underground, as a defense measure. Over the next few months, a lot of individuals decided that, whether or not dispersal was a good idea for the government, it was a good idea for them. Washington realtors advertised "Small Farms—Out Beyond Range of Atomic Bombs," and a boom in rural real estate was reported around big cities all over the country.

Meanwhile, a few atomic scientists were lobbying to answer the Russian atomic bomb with a new bomb so powerful it *would* make the atomic bomb look like a firecracker. This was the hydrogen bomb, or "super," which Edward Teller had proposed to the scientists meeting at Berkeley in the summer of 1942. Sitting in that meeting as the super was discussed, Emil Konopinski recalls, "I felt, Geez, this is getting *bad*." Atomic bombs derive their power from splitting uranium or plutonium nuclei; hydrogen bombs mimic the process that powers the sun, fusing, at enormously high temperatures, hydrogen atoms into helium and radiating vast energy as they do. Atom for atom, fusion generates more energy than fission. Moreover, there is an upper limit to the size of an atomic bomb, because as soon as you assemble a critical mass of uranium or plutonium it will ignite whether you want it to or not, but there is no limit to the size of a hydrogen bomb. The high temperature needed to ignite it can be reached only by using an atomic bomb as a trigger. Before firing that trigger, you can load the bomb with all the hydrogen fuel in the world if you want to.

In the autumn of 1949, the hydrogen bomb remained only a theoretical possibility, but Edward Teller, Ernest Lawrence of the University of California, and a few other physicists took the case of the super to Washington and found a receptive audience in key congressional leaders and members of the Atomic Energy Commission, which had taken over atomic-weapons work from the Manhattan Project. "Two experienced promoters have been at work ...," J. Robert Oppenheimer wrote to a friend in October. "The project has long been dear to Teller's heart; and Ernest has convinced himself that we must learn from Operation Joe [the Russian bomb, named for Stalin] that the Russians will soon do the Super and that we had better beat them to it." Oppenheimer, who opposed building the new weapon, continued, "I am not sure the miserable thing will work, nor that it can be gotten to a target except by ox cart . . . What does worry me is that this appears to have caught the imagination, both of the Congressional and of military people, as the answer to the problem posed by the Russian advance. . . . That we become committed to it as the way to save the country and the peace appears to me full of danger."

On October 29, the AEC's General Advisory Committee, chaired by Oppenheimer, met to consider whether or not there ought to be a crash program to develop the hydrogen bomb. Unanimously, it voted no. Its decision was based partly on strategic reasons—in the entire Soviet Union there were only two targets (Moscow and Leningrad) big enough to merit being targeted with hydrogen bombs, it concluded, and they could be destroyed just as well with several atomic bombs—but its reasoning was also political and moral. "We all hope that by one means or another, the development of these weapons can be avoided . . .," its report said. "In determining not to proceed to develop the Superbomb, we see a unique opportunity of providing by example some limitations on the totality of war, and thus eliminating the fear and raising the hopes of mankind." In a separate report, committee members Enrico Fermi and Isidor Rabi wrote, "The fact that no limits exist to the destructiveness of this weapon makes its very existence and the knowledge of its construction a danger to humanity as a whole. It is necessarily an evil thing, considered in any light."

A bare majority of the AEC agreed with its advisory panel and voted not to rush ahead with the bomb, but supporters of the new weapon rallied and the political climate of the time was on their side. (Five years later, when Oppenheimer was ignominiously declared a security risk, his opposition to the hydrogen bomb was made part of the evidence against him.) On January 31, 1950, President Truman announced that the hydrogen bomb project would go ahead.

Scientists opposed to the new weapon promptly took their arguments to the public. "A hydrogen bomb, if it can be made, would be capable of developing a power 1,000 times greater than the present atomic bomb," twelve prominent atomic scientists declared. "New York, or any other of the greatest cities of the world, could be destroyed by a single hydrogen bomb. . . . This bomb is no longer a weapon of war, but a means of extermination of whole populations. Its use would be a betrayal of all standards of morality and of Christian civilization itself."

Albert Einstein went further. With a successful hydrogen bomb, he said, "radioactive poisoning of the atmosphere and hence annihilation of any life on earth has been brought within the range of technical possibilities." On a network radio program, Hans Bethe and Leo Szilard, who had become a professor at the University of Chicago, explained how that could be done. The most efficient way, Szilard said, would be to coat a hydrogen bomb with an element that would be made highly radioactive by the burst of neutrons produced by hydrogen fusion. "Assuming that we have a radioactive element that will last for five years," Szilard said, "we just let it go into the air. During the following years it will gradually settle out and cover the whole earth with dust. I have asked myself: 'How many neutrons, or how much heavy hydrogen, do we have to detonate to kill everybody on earth by this particular method?' Well, I come out with about fifty tons of neutrons being needed to kill everybody, which means about five hundred tons of heavy hydrogen."*

Among those who objected to such gloomy prophecies was Dwight Eisenhower, then president of Columbia University, who told a convention of student journalists, "Don't get the idea that someone is going to come over here and drop a bomb on Mississippi and that the United States is going to disappear. . . . Don't let them make pessimists and defeatists out of you." Worse than pessimists, pointed out former AEC chairman David Lilienthal, were Communists. "Oracles of annihilation," he said, were encouraging "hope-

---

* Szilard's calculations were studied in detail by James Arnold of the University of Chicago, who concluded it would cost more than $40 billion to build a bomb big enough to exterminate all life and even then, owing to idiosyncrasies of wind and rain, you couldn't count on the deadly radioactivity spreading to every corner of the earth. So some people would survive. "It is possible, however," Arnold added, "that the vast majority of the race can be killed off in this way. . . . Moreover, it is apparent that advances are to be expected, and a repetition of this discussion 10 years from today may give very different results."

lessness, futility and confusion" among the American people, and that played "right into the hands of destructive Communist forces." Such oracles apparently included not only Albert Einstein and Leo Szilard, but also singer Sam Hinton and the Western-style group called Sons of the Pioneers. In August 1950, their recordings of "Old Man Atom," a talking blues that warned that "all men may be cremated equal" and that people had to choose between "peace in the world or the world in pieces," were withdrawn by RCA Victor and Columbia Records after something called the Joint Committee Against Communism complained that the song followed the Communist Party's "peace line." The song's composer protested that he thought viewing atomic war as disastrous was the policy of the U.S. government, but to no avail.

The United States detonated the world's first full-scale thermonuclear (hydrogen) explosion on the Pacific island of Elugelab in the fall of 1952. The "device" (it was too unwieldy to be called a bomb) recalled Oppenheimer's warning that a hydrogen weapon might have to be delivered to its target in an ox cart; it weighed sixty-five tons and included a refrigeration plant. But it demonstrated that man could recreate on earth the energy processes of the sun. By 1954, the United States had tested a hydrogen bomb small enough to be carried on an airplane—and so had the Soviet Union. Lewis Strauss, chairman of the Atomic Energy Commission, attracted a great deal of attention when he confirmed at a press conference what scientific critics had long said about the power of the new weapon: "It can be made to be as large as you wish . . . large enough to take out a city."

"How big a city?" asked Strauss's questioner.

"Any city."

"Any city? New York?"

"The metropolitan area, yes."

Immediately after the press conference, Strauss explained that by "the metropolitan area" he meant central Manhattan, not the metropolitan area. And Val Peterson, head of the Federal Civil Defense Administration, warned people not to run amuck if a hydrogen bomb fell on their city. "They should find shelter immediately, keep calm, and not panic . . . ," he said. "Personally, at the Las Vegas tests, I found a slit-trench offered good protection." Peterson acknowledged, however, that a Russian attack on the United States would kill at least twenty million people and that the only certain way to save your life if a hydrogen bomb exploded over your city was "not to be in the city."

None of this was calming news, and it was compounded when the FBI warned all local police forces to be on the lookout for enemy saboteurs smuggling compact atomic bombs into the United States in suitcases. "The suitcases would be heavy, but no heavier than many a sailor's sea bag . . .," reported *U.S. News & World Report*. "Russians . . . have easy access to the U.S. They have a Communist fifth column already set up and functioning. They have, in addition, access to U.S. ports through Communist ships' crews of many nations." To combat this menace, the magazine reported, police all over the country were alertly watching for "exceptionally heavy luggage." A few months later (in July 1954), the Eisenhower administration proposed a bill authorizing rewards of up to half a million dollars for anyone who turned in an enemy agent with an atomic bomb in his sea bag. The Justice Department said the rewards would probably be tax-free.

But by then the American public had something else to worry about.

Until 1954, few Americans had ever heard of radioactive fallout. People knew that nuclear weapons could blow them up or burn them up or even zap them with deadly radiation, but to fall victim to any of those things you had to be somewhere in the vicinity of the bomb itself. Then people learned that the bomb could kill at a distance. You didn't have to see it explode or hear it explode; you could be so far away from it that you didn't even *know* it had exploded. And it could kill you all the same.

"I was the first guy who ever gave Eisenhower a full briefing on the fallout threat," recalls Jack Greene, then director of the Radiological Defense Division of the Federal Civil Defense Administration. "I still remember it. We were in the Indian Treaty Room in the old State Department building. But it didn't get across. Eisenhower listened and then he said, 'Gee, that's important, isn't it? Is everybody ready for lunch?' "

But Eisenhower would soon have to face up to fallout, and it would be a major public issue for the rest of his presidency, an issue born in the explosion of a hydrogen bomb by the United States on the Pacific island of Namu in the Bikini atoll on March 1, 1954. This was the test following which AEC Chairman Lewis Strauss attracted the attention of the nation by declaring that a hydrogen bomb could destroy any city. It was also the first nuclear explosion since Nagasaki to kill a human being.

The bomb, known as shot Bravo of the CASTLE test series, exploded at 6:45 a.m. and it was spectacular. Scientists had expected a blast of about eight megatons (equal to eight million tons of TNT); they got fifteen. More important, however, was an unexpected shift in the wind. Within a few hours, radioactive gray ash and other particles were falling on American servicemen and scientists, and natives of the Marshall Islands. While American sailors washed down their ships, Marshallese and Americans were evacuated from the islands of Rongelap, Rongerik, Alinginae, and Utirik. The natives were "well and happy," AEC Chairman Strauss reported. (One of them promptly gave birth to a baby girl, who was named after Strauss's wife; Strauss gave the family ten pigs to provide for the child's dowry.) Meanwhile, unknown to the American authorities, the gray ash was also falling on the *Fukuryu Maru* (the *Lucky Dragon*), a Japanese fishing boat eighty-five miles east of Bikini—outside the zone that had been declared dangerous and off-limits before the test.

When the boat returned to Japan two weeks later, most of its crew were sick. Japanese doctors recognized the fever, bleeding gums, and nausea as symptoms of radiation poisoning, and the story broke big in Japan, which was, of course, sensitive to the hazards of nuclear weapons. The tuna in the *Lucky Dragon*'s hold were found to be radioactive, and a tuna scare swept the country. Government inspectors worked their way through fish markets with Geiger counters, and housewives took tuna from their kitchens and buried it. On September 24, Aikichi Kuboyama, radioman of the *Lucky Dragon*, died in Tokyo. Some American officials declared that, while Kuboyama had had radiation sickness, he had actually died of jaundice. The Japanese angrily rejected that explanation and so, formally, did the U.S. government, which apologized and gave Kuboyama's widow a check for twenty-eight hundred dollars.

The radioactive fallout that killed Kuboyama (and that, Strauss's claim notwithstanding, made many Marshall Islanders ill) had been created when the Bravo bomb exploded just seven feet above the surface of a coral reef, low enough to dig out a gigantic crater. When a nuclear weapon explodes, the nuclear reactions taking place in and near the weapon produce radioactive isotopes. If the weapon explodes without touching the ground (as did the bombs at Hiroshima and Nagasaki), the radioactive isotopes, which are created atom by atom, literally float away on the wind. Because they are so light, they fall to earth only over a period of years—a little here and a little a thousand miles away. This is known as global fallout, as opposed to local fallout, and it does not concentrate in the area of the bomb blast.

When a nuclear weapon explodes on or near the ground, however, vast quantities of dirt and other matter are scooped up into the fireball. The radioactive products of the explosion mix with the relatively heavy dirt and ash particles. These too are blown on the wind, but they fall to earth fairly rapidly and create a major radiation hazard at the site of the explosion and for a few hundred miles downwind. The Bravo blast produced local fallout that was dangerous over an area of seven thousand square miles—almost as large as the state of New Jersey.

Leo Szilard, Hans Bethe, and other scientists had warned years before that hydrogen bombs could create dangerous fallout—perhaps dangerous enough to kill all mankind—and now their warnings had been at least partially realized. That fallout from bombs like the one that killed Kuboyama could kill millions of people was soon common knowledge. In 1956, General James Gavin told a Senate committee that an American nuclear attack against the Soviet Union would kill "on the order of several hundred million" people, many of them from fallout and not all of them Russians. "If the wind blew to the southeast," Gavin said, "they [casualties] would . . . extend into the Japanese and perhaps down into the Philippine area. If the wind blew the other way they would extend well back up into Western Europe." This was not good news for the NATO alliance. In 1957, a civil defense meteorologist testified that by 1960 the Soviet Union could launch an attack on the United

States that would kill eighty-two million Americans, of burns, of blast, and of fallout.

Still, that was not everyone in the world. The limiting factor on the lethality of fallout is the "half-life" of its radioactive components. The half-life of any radioactive element measures both the rate at which it radiates dangerous particles and the length of time it will do so. An element with a long half-life will radiate for many years but at a relatively low rate. An element with a short half-life will be much more intensely radioactive but will cease radiating entirely relatively soon. The fallout from a typical hydrogen bomb contains hundreds of different radioactive isotopes, with half-lives ranging from a fraction of a second to millions of years. Their combined radioactivity is intense but relatively short-lived; it decays to a sublethal level within weeks of the bomb's explosion. That's long enough to kill anyone unprotected within a few hundred miles downwind of the explosion, but too short to kill everyone on earth, unless enough hydrogen bombs are exploded to make sure that everyone on earth is directly downwind of at least one.

It is possible, however, to manufacture a hydrogen bomb with vastly more dangerous fallout. One way to do so would be to coat the bomb with cobalt, which would be transformed by the bomb's detonation into the radioactive isotope cobalt-60. Cobalt-60 has a half-life of five years, short enough to be intensely radioactive yet long enough to remain lethal while it is spread over most of the earth by the gradual process of global fallout. This "cobalt bomb" was the weapon Leo Szilard had described in 1950 as one that could destroy all human life. (Asked who would use such a weapon, Szilard had replied, "Suppose we are at the point of winning [a] war against Russia, maybe after a struggle which lasts ten years. Russia's rulers then can say: 'You come no further . . . or else we detonate our H-bombs and kill everybody.' Facing such a threat, I don't think we can go forward.")

In 1954, following the irradiation of the *Lucky Dragon*, Assistant Secretary of Defense Donald Quarles confirmed that a cobalt bomb could be built. He added, however, that it was "not feasible" to use it as a weapon in a war, for obvious reasons.

But it was not the doomsday cobalt bomb nor even the prospect of massive fallout from ordinary hydrogen bombs blanketing the

earth after a nuclear war that became the main nuclear issue of the
1950s. The issue was instead the much lower—but already present—level of fallout produced by nuclear weapons tests. The Russians detonated at least half a dozen nuclear weapons in the
atmosphere between 1949 and 1954. The British, starting in 1952,
had detonated at least three weapons in Australia. And the United
States had tested at least twelve bombs in the South Pacific and, beginning in 1951, thirty-one at the Nevada test site eighty miles
northwest of Las Vegas. After some initial trepidation, Las Vegans
had relaxed about the nuclear explosions. Local residents woke their
children up at dawn to witness the flash of the atomic bombs, and
gamblers gathered in casino cocktail lounges to drink and await the
blasts. "Some fellow who'd been sitting around with his girl all night
would suddenly look at his watch and say, 'Guess it's time for the
bomb,' " one bartender recalled. "They'd grab their drinks and dash
out, and then the rest of the crowd would follow them. After the
damn thing went off, they'd all disappear, but by that time we'd
have done more business than if we had television." After the experience of the *Lucky Dragon*, some trepidation returned.

From 1954 to 1963, the issue of banning the testing of nuclear
weapons was on the public agenda in the United States. Democratic
candidate Adlai Stevenson brought it into his 1956 presidential
campaign against Dwight Eisenhower, declaring that the radioactive "poisoning of the atmosphere" was calling into question "the
actual survival of the human race." (With somewhat less scientific
justification, Stevenson's running mate, Estes Kefauver, warned that
large hydrogen bomb explosions could "blow the earth off its axis
by sixteen degrees, which would affect the seasons.") Stevenson
called for an international agreement to ban hydrogen bomb tests
and denounced the "madness" of the nuclear arms race. If the Russians caught up with us, he asked, "what does Mr. Eisenhower propose then? That we go ahead with the development of the cobalt
bomb to try to gain another advantage?"

Vice President Richard Nixon replied that Stevenson's proposal was "not only naive but dangerous to our national security."
And Eisenhower himself, whose administration was engaged in fit-
ful nuclear-arms-control negotiations with the Russians, responded
to Stevenson at some length. He said that continued nuclear weap-

ons testing was necessary to maintain American strength, that Russia might cheat on a test ban unless rigorous inspection procedures could be negotiated, and that, in any case, "the continuance of the present rate of H-bomb testing—by the most sober and responsible scientific judgment—does not imperil the health of humanity."

Both sides in the test ban debate, of course, cited scientific evidence. It was well established that the high-energy rays emitted from radioactive elements can wreak havoc with cells in the human body. Acute doses (such as those received by the Hiroshima victims and the *Lucky Dragon* crewmen) were known to cause immediate sickness and death and, among survivors, a variety of long-term effects, including leukemia and other cancers, thyroid disease, and genetic damage. The same long-term effects can be produced by an accumulation of low radiation doses from fallout, but it was not clear how much fallout was required to produce which effects. And testing advocates argued that there is a "threshold" radiation dose, below which no ill effects at all are created.

From the beginning of the fallout debate, the Atomic Energy Commission declared repeatedly that test fallout was no hazard to human health. When a prominent geneticist declared that fallout from the Bravo test alone would cause birth defects in eighteen hundred children around the world, an AEC scientist replied that such predictions were "comparable to contending that meteors from outer space are a major threat to safety on our highways and threaten the survival of all motorists." The AEC was naturally pleased when, in 1957, three Columbia University scientists, having studied bones from corpses on five continents, reported that they contained very little strontium-90, a fallout component that enters the food chain and concentrates in human bones. (Fighting bone with bone, nuclear testing opponents launched a campaign to collect fifty thousand baby teeth for strontium-90 checkups.) The AEC was so devoted to minimizing the dangers of test fallout that it even passed up chances to score Cold War propaganda points. When fallout from Russian nuclear tests caused concern in Europe and Japan, the AEC announced that there was nothing to worry about.

Meanwhile, opponents of nuclear testing were declaring that there was a great deal to worry about. Linus Pauling, who had won the Nobel Prize for chemistry and would later win the Nobel Peace

Prize for his anti-test crusade, warned that "there exists a real possibility that the lives of 100,000 people now living are sacrificed by each bomb test." In England, chemist Frederick Soddy, whose 1908 lecture on the marvels of atomic energy had inspired H. G. Wells's 1914 novel that had inspired Leo Szilard's conceptual breakthroughs in the 1930s, said that nuclear weapons tests were "fouling the air with radioactivity" and that it was "nonsense to say it is harmless." Back in the United States, the newly founded National Committee for a Sane Nuclear Policy (SANE) bought newspaper ads demanding, "We must stop the contamination of the air, the milk children drink, the food we eat."

Such test ban proponents were attacked not only for their scientific reasoning but for their politics. Pauling's name "has often been linked with Communist-front groups," *Newsweek* reported. "When the U.S. or Britain sets off a nuclear bomb, you hear loud cries of protest and warnings of grave danger to mankind," said a bold-face paragraph in *U.S. News & World Report.* "Let Soviet Russia explode a similar bomb, however, and you hear few protests. This is what Western officials find as they study the record. The conclusion that they reach is this: Much of the clamor about the danger of fallout is inspired by Communists."

At least some of the clamor, however, came from normally conservative Western ranchers. Following a series of eleven nuclear explosions at the Nevada test site in 1953, 1,420 sheep grazing downwind of the test site and 2,970 of their new lambs died. "The ewes had scabs on their noses, ears and mouths where they had eaten," one rancher recalled later. "The lambs were small, deformed; some were even born with no wool." Eleven ranchers sued the U.S. government for damages. The government denied that fallout had anything to do with the dead sheep, and the ranchers' case was thrown out of court in 1956. In 1982, the same judge who had ruled against the ranchers twenty-six years earlier ordered a new trial, saying the government had "perpetrated a fraud upon the court" by withholding evidence and presenting witnesses who made "intentionally false or deceptive" statements during the original proceedings.

All through the 1950s, while the AEC was exploding some one hundred nuclear weapons in the atmosphere in Nevada, it continually assured local residents that there was no fallout danger while doing little to be sure that was the case. The first fallout-detection system used in Nevada employed hastily converted vacuum cleaners. When the AEC worried that milk produced near St. George, Utah, might be contaminated, it arranged to purchase milk for testing surreptitiously and made no public announcement. Years later, after the leukemia and thyroid cancer rate had risen in southwestern Utah and other areas downwind of the tests (and hundreds of lawsuits had been filed against the government), a congressional committee concluded that residents of the area had been made "guinea pigs in a deadly experiment." At the very least, the committee said, "the government owed these people a responsibility to inform them of the exact time and place of each test and the necessary precautions that should have been taken to protect their health and safety."* The AEC's attitude toward the Nevada test site's downwind neighbors can be inferred from the minutes of a 1955 Commission meeting at which Chairman Lewis Strauss informed his colleagues that a Nevada state legislator had proposed a bill asking the AEC to leave the state, and that both Las Vegas newspapers had attacked the bill as "nonsense."

"This is a sensible view," said Commissioner Willard Libby. "People have got to learn to live with the facts of life, and part of the facts of life are fallout."

Strauss agreed. "It is certainly all right, they say, if you don't live next door to it."

Throughout the decade, Strauss maintained that the "vague, unproven danger" of fallout from nuclear tests was minuscule compared with "the more immediate and infinitely greater dangers of defeat and perhaps of obliteration" posed by nuclear war; by continuing to develop and test nuclear weapons, Strauss argued, the United States was deterring the Soviet Union from ever starting a nuclear war. (Some anti-arms-race scientists agreed that nuclear war

---

* Although local residents were not informed of all tests in advance, the Eastman Kodak Company in Rochester, New York, was. Following the 1945 Trinity test, fallout in the Midwest had contaminated strawboard used to package Kodak film, and the packaging fogged the film. Kodak detected more fallout following the first test in Nevada in 1951. The company considered suing the government, and the AEC responded by offering to provide Kodak with advance information on all Nevada tests so the company could protect its products.

was a far greater threat than the sometimes-exaggerated effects of fallout, but they disagreed that safety lay in developing more weapons.) The cost of continued testing, one AEC report said, was "well within tolerable limits" —only 196 additional leukemia deaths and 800 additional birth defects each year in the United States. Meanwhile, the AEC was dealing with fallout by experimenting with anti-radiation pills for humans and anti-radiation fertilizers for crops. In 1958, the Army Quartermaster General reported excitedly that preliminary animal experiments showed that eating "cabbage and broccoli may be the means of doubling the capacity of man to withstand" fallout radiation. In 1981, state officials in Tennessee actually distributed potassium iodide pills, which slow down the absorption of radioactive substances by the thyroid gland, to people living near the Sequoyah nuclear power plant, for use in case of an accident. But little more was ever heard of anti-fallout vegetables.

One of the most prominent proponents of the linked views that national security required nuclear testing and that, in any case, test fallout was nothing to worry about was Edward Teller. After lobbying successfully for the hydrogen bomb program, Teller had made major theoretical contributions to the bomb's development and had become popularly known as "the father of the hydrogen bomb." Now, in articles, books, and public appearances, he attacked the test ban advocates on several grounds.

First, Teller argued (as did the AEC) that nuclear test fallout was insignificant compared to the natural background radiation all people are exposed to from cosmic rays and radioactive elements occurring in soil, water, rocks, and other natural objects. "Brick contains more natural radioactivity than wood," Teller wrote in *The Legacy of Hiroshima*. "A person living in a brick house . . . is exposing himself to . . . perhaps as much as ten times the amount of the current dose from radioactive fallout. If fallout really is dangerous, we should tear down all of our brick houses. I would hate to do this, because I live in a brick house myself."

Other anti-radiation measures proposed by Teller for those who believed small doses were dangerous included the evacuation of Denver (because of its high elevation, it receives a lot of cosmic radiation) and the destruction of all watches with luminous dials. (Test ban advocates replied that much human damage from fallout comes from radioactive particles that have been ingested and that most people don't eat their watches.) As for radiation-induced birth defects, Teller pointed out that such defects are also caused by increasing the temperature of the reproductive organs. "Our custom of dressing men in trousers causes at least a hundred times as many mutations as present fallout levels, but alarmists who say that continued nuclear testing will affect unborn generations have not allowed their concern to urge men into kilts." Anyway, asked Teller, what's wrong with mutations? "Without such abnormal births and such mutations, the human race would not have evolved and we would not be here. Deploring the mutations that may be caused by fallout is somewhat like adopting the policies of the Daughters of the American Revolution, who approve of a past revolution but condemn future reforms."*

In the political arena, Teller (along with the Pentagon) argued that the Soviet Union could not be trusted to observe a test ban treaty. In 1958, Soviet and Western scientists meeting in Geneva concluded that it was technically possible to detect nuclear explosions from inspection stations hundreds of miles away and thus to monitor a test ban agreement. A few months later, however, a new scientific study suggested by Teller found that underground nuclear tests could be effectively hidden if conducted in large caverns. Scien-

---

* Later, during the debate about the safety of nuclear power plants, Teller's biographers report he enjoyed pointing out that the human body contains the radioactive isotope potassium-40 and telling this story: "One young employee of the AEC asked a friend of mine a question: From what do you get more radiation—from leaning up against a reactor for a full year or from sleeping each night with your wife? My friend did not know the answer. The young man from the AEC made some calculations and sent around a notice which said: 'I have calculated that, and actually you get a little more radiation if you lean up for a full year against the Dresden III reactor than from your habit of sleeping each night with your wife. I am not going to initiate a campaign for a regulation that all married couples must sleep in twin beds. However, I must warn, from the point of view of the radiation hazard, that if you sleep each night with *two* girls you will get more radiation than from leaning up for a full year against the Dresden III reactor." Years later, nuclear power critic John Gofman felt compelled to answer this attack. He wrote: "Those who belittle the hazard from radiation by telling us that our spouses irradiate us in bed . . . really do not understand their physics very well. Since only 11 per cent of [potassium-40] decays with a gamma-ray emission . . . and only a small part of any gamma rays emitted from one person can possibly reach another, the dose from another person's gamma rays is *minuscule* compared to the dose from our *own* [potassium-40] beta-particle emissions."

tists favoring a test ban eventually confirmed the new findings. "I had the doubtful honor of presenting the theory of the big hole to the Russians in Geneva in November, 1959," Hans Bethe wrote later. "I felt deeply embarrassed in so doing, because it implied that we considered the Russians capable of cheating on a massive scale. I think that they would have been quite justified if they had considered this an insult and had walked out of the negotiations in disgust."

Edward Teller was not embarrassed. "Past experience suggests that any international agreement to stop tests may well be followed immediately by secret and successful tests behind the Iron Curtain," he wrote in a feature article in *Life*.

Finally, Teller argued that continued testing was necessary not only to develop new weapons that would preserve American strength but also to develop one particular new weapon that would make a nuclear war, should one come, much less fearsome. This was the "clean" hydrogen bomb, a bomb that (by reducing its fission component) would produce practically no fallout. The argument for the clean bomb (which emerged again years later as the "neutron bomb," a relatively low-fallout, low-blast battlefield nuclear weapon) was very neat. Its development would supposedly eliminate the very menace that was leading people to call for an end to nuclear testing, but it could be developed only by nuclear testing. So if you opposed nuclear testing (because of fallout), you had to support nuclear testing (to develop the weapon that would end fallout).

Teller, along with Ernest Lawrence and two other scientists, presented the doctrine of the clean bomb at a hearing of the Joint Congressional Committee on Atomic Energy in June 1957, just when East–West negotiators in London were making progress toward a test ban agreement. The committee hearing was closed, but Senator Henry Jackson announced the good news about the clean bomb to the press. Four days later, the scientists met with President Eisenhower and told him the good news personally. Two days after that, at a presidential press conference, Eisenhower told the country: "They [Teller and Lawrence] tell me that already they are producing bombs that have 96 percent [less] fallout than was the case in our original ones, or what we call dirty bombs. . . . They say, 'Give us four or five years to test each step of our development, and we will produce an absolutely clean bomb.' "

"Mr. President," a reporter asked, "is there any possibility that Russia may learn how to make these clean bombs, and do we have assurance they would use them on us?"

"You know," replied Eisenhower, "I don't know of any better question, because I asked it myself . . . I would hope that they would learn how to use clean bombs and would use them." (At his White House meeting with the scientists, Eisenhower had asked about sharing the clean-bomb secret with the Russians so that a Russian attack on the United States, if one ever came, would be less terrible; the scientists replied that it would be impossible to separate the clean-bomb secret from secrets the Russians should *not* be given.)

The clean-bomb balloon was punctured when Soviet leader Nikita Khrushchev said that Eisenhower was talking "stupidities." "How can you have a clean bomb to do dirty things?" Khrushchev asked. Teller and his colleagues persevered. To stop nuclear testing before the clean bomb was developed, they said, would be "a crime against humanity."

But public opinion was set against them. A Gallup Poll in the spring of 1957 had found that 63 percent of the population supported an international halt to hydrogen bomb tests. Later that year the most influential novel about nuclear war ever published appeared. Nevil Shute's *On the Beach*, the melodramatic story of the last days of the last survivors of a nuclear war, knocked *Peyton Place* out of its spot as number-one best-seller, was serialized in forty newspapers, was made into a popular movie starring Gregory Peck and Ava Gardner, and is still in print today. The plot of *On the Beach* relies on the widespread use of cobalt bombs in its fictional nuclear war (which begins with an Albanian attack on Italy). As the story opens, the bombs' deadly fallout has already killed everybody north of the equator and is inexorably heading south. "I won't take it," protests madcap bachelorette Moira Davidson, one of the small group of Australians on whom the book is centered. "It's not fair. No one in the Southern Hemisphere ever dropped a bomb. . . . Why should we have to die because other countries nine or ten thousand miles away from us wanted to have a war? . . . It's not that I'm afraid of dying, Dwight. We've all got to do that sometime. It's all the things I'm going to have to miss. . . . All of my life I've wanted to see the Rue de Rivoli . . . and I'm never going to see it. Because there isn't any Paris now, or London, or New York."

Moira's companion, Dwight Towers, the commander of an American submarine that has taken refuge in Australia, attempts to comfort her: "The Rue de Rivoli may still be there, with things in the shopwindows and everything. . . . It's just that folks don't live there anymore."

But Moira is not comforted. "I'll never have a family . . . ," she mutters (drunkenly). "Even if you took me to bed tonight, I'd never have a family, because there wouldn't be time." In the end, Dwight does not take Moira to bed. He takes his submarine out into the Indian Ocean and sinks it, and himself. Moira, watching from a cliff, washes down with brandy two suicide pills distributed (free of charge) by the Australian government. Everyone else dies too. *Everyone.* A history of the final war, inscribed on glass bricks, is placed on the tallest peak in Australia, waiting to be read by any new intelligent life-form that might someday appear on the scene.

Edward Teller hated *On the Beach*. "Considered coldly and factually, Shute's story has no relation to any possible future event," he wrote in a chapter of *The Legacy of Hiroshima* called "Off the Beach." Cobalt bombs did not exist, Teller said, and, as Assistant Secretary of Defense Quarles had pointed out in 1954, they would hardly be considered practical weapons if they did. But the novel's emotional end-of-the-world imagery had made its mark. "When I was fourteen I read *On the Beach*, and I remember wondering, 'Where are the statesmen who will prevent all this?' " Helen Caldicott told an interviewer in 1982. "I've been wondering that ever since." Caldicott, herself a native Australian, grew up to become president of Physicians for Social Responsibility, an organization active and effective in the American anti-nuclear-weapons movement of the early 1980s.

In 1959, two years after *On the Beach* and one year after the United States, the Soviet Union, and Great Britain began a temporary moratorium on all nuclear weapons tests, fallout (from premoratorium explosions) provoked a major public scare when rising levels of strontium-90 were found in milk and parents became exercised over the threat to the health of their children. Evidence of the dangers of fallout kept mounting, and public sentiment remained so strong that, in 1961, when the Russians resumed atmospheric nuclear testing and President John Kennedy replied that the United States would resume testing too, Kennedy hastened to add that the American tests would only take place "underground, with no fallout." The same public pressure that was thus appeased was appeased again, and for good, in 1963, when the United States, the Soviet Union, and Great Britain, citing their desire "to put an end to the contamination of man's environment by radioactive substances," finally signed and ratified a treaty banning all nuclear tests in the atmosphere, under water, and in outer space.

This marked the end of the nuclear test ban movement—but not of nuclear tests. The 1963 treaty prohibited testing above the surface of the earth, but not beneath it. The air would be clean, but the tests would continue. "They managed to blunt the treaty's arms control effect by making it a strictly environmental sanction," says Philip Morrison. "We were caught napping by that one." The underground testing allowed by the treaty has proven perfectly adequate for the development of generation after generation of new nuclear weapons. The testing continues to this day.

FIVE

"This Area *Will* Be Evacuated"

If a nuclear attack on the United States ever appears imminent, the Plattsburgh, New York, police department will assign two patrolmen to direct traffic at the corner of Broad and Cornelia. That was one of the decisions made at a series of meetings held in the Emergency Operating Center beneath Plattsburgh police headquarters to plan the evacuation of Plattsburgh, site of a Strategic Air Command base, during a major confrontation between the United States and the Soviet Union. Such an evacuation is expected to cause traffic problems, so two hours were set aside to consider them.

It was Plattsburgh Police Sergeant George Rabideau who said, "You'll need at least two men there," when the intersection of Broad and Cornelia was pointed out on a map. Rabideau was sitting across from a captain representing Plattsburgh Air Force Base and a very bored-looking young man from the Clinton County Highway Department.

New York State civil-defense planner Joseph Hein, at the head of the table, pointed out a number of other intersections likely to be congested on the eve of a nuclear war. He calculated that to keep traffic moving will require two shifts of twenty policemen each, which will strain the resources of the forty-five-man Plattsburgh department.

"Couldn't we use school crossing guards?" suggested the Air Force captain.

"They're too old," said Rabideau. "They couldn't take it. It's hard on the body to direct traffic."

Plattsburgh's part-time civil-defense director, a professional insurance salesman, suggested that civil-defense volunteers be trained for the task.

Rabideau approved. "That will leave us free to cover car accidents," he said, "or fires, or fights between individuals. People will be emotional. I don't know if they're going to be hysterical, but they're definitely going to be emotional."

Indeed they are. The Plattsburgh evacuation plan is part of the national civil-defense program called Crisis Relocation Planning, under which the residents of areas considered to be likely targets for nuclear attack will move to low-risk "host areas" during a period of extreme international tension, such as that which might accompany tactical nuclear warfare between American and Russian forces on a foreign battlefield. On the theory that "there is nothing quite so helpful as being, say, ten miles or more away from a nuclear weapon when it goes off," plans are being made now to move 150 million residents of 400 "risk areas" to several thousand small towns throughout the country.* The Federal Emergency Management Agency, which is supervising the planning, predicts that 65 percent of the risk-area population can be evacuated in one day, and more than 95 percent in three days. "No one is in a position to provide an iron-clad guarantee that this kind of time would be available," FEMA acknowledges. "But it is the judgment of the Department of Defense that if the U.S. should ever suffer a nuclear attack, it is much more likely that this would follow a period of intense international tension than occur as a 'bolt from the blue.' "

Crisis Relocation Planning has therefore been designed not merely to save lives if an attack occurs but to play an important role in managing that intense preattack crisis. "Civil defense . . . is an essential ingredient of our nuclear deterrent forces," President Ronald Reagan decreed in a 1982 National Security Decision Directive. As "an element of the strategic balance," the directive says, one of the purposes of civil defense is to "assist in maintaining perceptions that

---

* Risk areas are defined as those in which nuclear weapons are based, those containing other important military facilities or war industries, and cities with populations of more than fifty thousand. Risk area selection was, however, based on unclassified information, so secret installations of military importance, of which the Soviets may well be aware, are not included on the risk area list.

this balance is favorable to the U.S." It will thus "reduce the possibility that the U.S. could be coerced in time of crisis."

So if the Russians ever, say, invade Iran, and the United States replies by dispatching the Rapid Deployment Force, and the Russians reply by increasing the alert status of their intercontinental nuclear forces, and the United States wants to resist the "coercion" implicit in that move by reducing the potential American death toll of a Soviet attack (or by letting the Russians know we're getting ready to reduce it), residents of Plattsburgh will find on their doorsteps, perhaps as a supplement to their local newspaper, a large-format brochure headlined EVACUATION INSTRUCTIONS.

"This area *will* be evacuated," says the brochure, which has already been prepared. "If a nuclear attack occurs, [this area] would be subject to the greatest danger. All persons living in this risk area must evacuate, when ordered, to lower risk portions of Clinton County called 'host areas.' " Printed on the back page of the brochure are seven large letters—A to G—one for each Plattsburgh neighborhood and its designated host area. Plattsburgh residents are instructed to cut out the letters assigned to their neighborhoods and attach them "to the lower left-hand (Driver's Side) corner of your car windshield," so that emergency personnel, including the two policemen at the corner of Broad and Cornelia, will be able to tell at a glance if a given carload of evacuees is driving in the right direction.

If for some reason the brochures are not delivered, Plattsburgh residents will be able to find detailed evacuation instructions in their local telephone directory, where, as part of a pilot public information program, FEMA has taken out a four-page ad. The phone book specifies, among other things, that if you live in the town of Plattsburgh, "north of Saranac River *not* including Cumberland Head," you are in evacuation group C. After placing that letter against your windshield, you will drive north on the Old Military Turnpike to the town of Ellenburg, where you will be received at the Northern Adirondack Central Junior-Senior High School. "When you arrive at the reception center," the phone book instructs, "stay in your car—you will be given a number. When your number is called go inside the reception center where you will be registered and directed to a lodging facility." (A similar Boston-area evacuation brochure, also already prepared, includes a questionnaire to be filled out "in duplicate before arriving in host area." It asks for evacuees' names, ages, sexes, occupations, and Social Security numbers, and leaves room for reception workers to fill in the evacuees' fallout shelter assignments.)

The instructions include a list of things to take along on the evacuation, among them sleeping bags, canned food, radios, toothpaste, extra socks, shovels, toilet paper, credit cards, and your will. (For the youngsters, FEMA is testing a coloring book with a page headed, "Color what you would need in a shelter." Kids are supposed to color in the canned beans and the candle, not the cake or the fish.) The evacuation brochure includes a one-page primer on the effects of nuclear explosions and three pages of instructions for building several types of fallout shelters, ranging from a relatively comfortable basement shelter to one built by digging a ditch under your car and then loading the car with dirt. You sit in the ditch.

During an intense international crisis, while 150 million residents of Plattsburgh and other risk areas are pondering this advice, gathering up their radios and shovels—and waiting—they will be able to pass the time by turning on their television sets and watching *Protection in the Nuclear Age*, a twenty-five-minute animated civil defense film that has been produced (in English and Spanish versions and with captions for the deaf) for showing on just such an occasion. The film opens with a drawing of the planet earth floating peacefully in space as an announcer intones, "We live in a world of tension and conflict. And peace, even where it does exist, does so without guarantees for tomorrow." The view zooms in toward the North American continent. "We must therefore face the hard reality that someday a nuclear attack against the United States might occur. And—equally important—we must also realize that horrifying as that prospect may seem, destructive as such an attack might be, we *can* survive. It would not mean the end of the world, the end of our nation. And you can greatly improve your own chances of survival if you'll remember these facts—about Protection in the Nuclear Age."

Copies of this, the last film millions of Americans may ever see, have already been distributed to local civil-defense officials, some of whom have in turn already passed copies on to their local television stations.

"Defense Department studies show," the film's narrator says, "that, even under the heaviest possible attack, less than five percent of our entire land area would be affected by blast and heat from nuclear weapons. Of course, that five percent contains a large percentage of our population."

Red flashes erupt over small target areas on a map of the United States.

"But, even in these high-risk areas, if there's sufficient time to permit evacuation, many millions of lives could be saved."

Pink radioactive clouds drift out of the red flashes.

"The other ninety-five percent of our land would escape untouched. Except possibly by radioactive fallout."

The pink fallout spreads across the map.

"Now, here are things you need to know."

The film proceeds to describe warning sirens, the effects of nuclear weapons, fallout shelter construction, the practicability of evacuation ("after all, we relocate millions of workers from our big cities every evening rush hour"), and other emergency measures. All of them are acted out by animated stick figures. When evacuation is described, a stick-figure family packs up its car and drives past stick-figure policemen to a relocation center, where it is greeted by a stick-figure hostess. Stick figures were selected for the film after many old civil-defense films had to be withdrawn from circulation partly because the old-fashioned clothing on their live actors started to look funny. "Stick figures don't get obsolete as fashion changes," explains an employee of the FEMA audiovisual department.

Protection in the Nuclear Age concludes with a pep talk: "The greatest danger is hopelessness, the fear that nuclear attack would mean the end of our world, so why not just give up, lie down, and die? That idea could bring senseless and useless death to many—for protection *is* possible."

A similar pep talk concludes a series of fifteen camera-ready newspaper articles that have been distributed by FEMA to five thousand local civil-defense officials to pass on to local publications in a crisis. The articles include detailed information about constructing fallout shelters, administering first aid, extinguishing flaming curtains ignited by a nuclear explosion ("*prompt* action could save the lives of everyone in the building"), protecting cattle from fallout, and saving industrial equipment from blast damage by covering it with dirt. The fifteenth article is headlined, "Would Survivors of Nuclear Attack Envy the Dead? . . . Experts Say No."

"The newspaper articles would be supplemented by the twenty-five-minute television film . . .," FEMA has explained. "The cost of such materials is very low, and we estimate that the emergency information newspaper articles and television films could add survivors amounting to perhaps 8 to 12 percent of the U.S. population."

And so, merely by watching the film and reading the articles as the United States and Soviet Union head toward nuclear war, the anxious residents of Plattsburgh and other risk areas will be saving no less than eighteen million of their own lives. Or so FEMA figures. The possibility will remain, of course, that the Russians, seeing this material being distributed in the United States, might conclude that the Americans are getting ready to launch a nuclear war and decide that they (the Russians) had better strike first. This irony—that the dissemination of information to save lives in a war might ignite the war—has been taken into consideration by FEMA. It is the reason that the newspaper columns and television film have been predistributed to thousands of *local* civil-defense officials. "One advantage of predistribution," explains FEMA spokesman Russell Clanahan, "is that giving the columns to newspapers will be purely a local decision. We don't have to appear to be escalating the crisis by issuing orders from Washington."

If distributing civil-defense information in a crisis alarms the Russians, then actually ordering the evacuation of hundreds of American cities will terrify them—possibly into launching a preemptive nuclear strike. "If the relocation were executed in the absence of a major move by the other side, it could trigger an unwelcome Soviet response and escalate the crisis," concluded a study of "the potential effect of crisis relocation on crisis stability" sponsored by the Defense Civil Preparedness Agency (a predecessor to FEMA). The report did not worry too much about this scenario, however, because it assumed that the United States would most

102

likely order its cities evacuated only as a countermove to a Russian evacuation of *their* cities or some other provocative first step by the Russians. "Different individual Presidents would undoubtedly have different 'evacuation thresholds' for deciding whether a given move were hostile enough to warrant unilateral U.S. relocation," the study noted. "Most respondents [experts interviewed by the study's authors] felt that a Soviet invasion of Western Europe accompanied by use of theater-nuclear weapons was above their 'evacuation threshold.' "

One guess about what might actually precede the call to evacuate has been hazarded by Massachusetts civil-defense officials, who have prepared a recording, for use in exercises, with the type of announcement that may someday be directed to 150 million nerve-wracked risk-area residents:

> This is President Reagan. You, as well as I, have been carefully following the international events of the past few weeks. As you know, we have been airlifting supplies to West Berlin since the road corridors through East Germany have been closed by the Soviet bloc. Ground and air warfare continues in the Middle East. Three of our supply aircraft have been shot down this morning. Our protest to the Soviet Union has gone unanswered. The major Russian cities have been ordered evacuated. As a strategic response, I am now ordering the use of our Crisis Relocation Plan, which was distributed nationwide on Monday and Tuesday. An effective relocation of our population to safer areas could demonstrate to the Soviets our national resolve and buy time for further negotiations. If they should launch a limited or general nuclear strike, the relocation would result in survival of most of our people. The nation is not—I repeat not—under attack. But we believe a serious possibility of attack does exist. Following the Crisis Relocation Plan can reduce the possibility of attack. If, God forbid, an attack should be launched, the plan could save millions of lives. We ask you to tune to your local TV station or stay tuned to this radio broadcast and carefully follow instructions. We will continue to work for peace and to pray for peace. God bless you.

This is a point that no president will ever want to reach. The mere existence of the evacuation plans is supposed to have a deterrent effect on the Soviets—in the words of Reagan's National Security Decision Directive, to "enhance deterrence and stability in conjunction with our strategic offensive and other strategic defensive forces." If the plans in themselves deter insufficiently (and their deterrent effect rests on the Russians' believing that we believe that the plans really can save tens of millions of lives), a prudent president might decide they are too provocative to implement under any circumstances. FEMA claims that a well-planned and supported evacuation will insure the survival of more than 80 percent of the American people (including about two-thirds of the evacuees) even in a massive nuclear war, but even FEMA recognizes that you will insure the survival of 100 percent by not having the war.

All of this will be on the minds of 150 million risk-area residents as they wait, their cars packed for evacuation, listening to their radios to hear the president say yea or nay. Some of them will have their own "evacuation thresholds." Hearing rumors of war or news of foreign battles, they will head for the hills on their own. (The need to bring order to such "spontaneous evacuation" is one of FEMA's arguments for evacuation planning.) All will surely sense that a centrally ordered national evacuation will bring international tension to a head. As Herman Kahn, the think-tank nuclear war strategist, told the authors of the DCPA report on crisis relocation and crisis stability: "Crisis relocation by both sides ... would sharply increase the probability that the crisis would be resolved quickly, one way or the other."

One way will be a visit to the country; the other will be nuclear war.

Following the call to begin crisis relocation, to match a Soviet evacuation or some other Soviet move with the evacuation of four hundred American cities, 80 to 85 percent of the residents of those cities will get into their cars or make their way to public transportation to begin the trip out of town, turning back for one last look at the homes they have been told are in the crosshairs of Russian nuclear weapons. The other 15 to 20 percent, FEMA estimates, won't go. They will listen to the president, say good-bye to their neighbors, go back in their houses, and lock the doors. A study conducted for the Defense Civil Preparedness Agency as it was developing crisis relocation planning predicted that those who will insist on staying put "might include disproportionate numbers of the sick, the disabled and handicapped, people with mental problems, alcoholics, drug addicts, and some of the elderly lonely," as well as "professional thieves and burglars" and "some political terrorists." Also likely to stay home, the study predicted, will be "the small proportion of our people who are convinced that no survival in nuclear war is possible . . . and those who feel that even were they to survive an attack, the post-attack world would be unlivable or they would not want to live in it." Finally, there will be those who are convinced that the president has "miscalculated the risks."

"If they don't want to evacuate, that's fine," said Richard Herskowitz, the chief civil-defense planner for New York State, as he drove back to his underground Albany office following the meeting at which traffic control for the evacuation of Plattsburgh was discussed. "That will make it easier for everybody else in the host areas."

Among those who will stay behind with the drug addicts, terrorists, and doomsayers, Herskowitz expects, will be pet lovers; their animals will not be welcome during the evacuation. "We've had a lot of concern about pets at our seminars," Herskowitz said. "We advise people to leave their pets in the basement with a couple of weeks' worth of food. If you come back, your pet is still there. If the area's blasted, he had an easy death."

Many of those who *will* want to evacuate, meanwhile, will not have an easy time of it. The residents of Plattsburgh (population 25,-000) will endure a few red lights as they head down Cornelia Street, but what about the residents of New York City? "Nobody's suggesting you could move New York City in fifteen minutes," FEMA director Louis Giuffrida has said. "That's stupid. But we could do New York if we had a plan in place; we could do New York in five days, a week."

Most New Yorkers are skeptical—"Christ Almighty! It took me twenty-five minutes to get through the Brooklyn–Battery Tunnel this morning because there was a little snow," was the reaction of one former chief of the city's Office of Civil Preparedness. In 1982, the New York City Council voted overwhelmingly to join a number of other cities around the country that have refused to have anything to do with crisis relocation planning. Replying to the skeptics, FEMA cites a feasibility study of evacuating New York which concluded that 11.33 million people in the metropolitan area could be evacuated in 3.3 days, using cars, trucks, buses, trains, planes, and boats. This could be done, the study said, by sending 75,000 residents of Manhattan up the Hudson River to Saratoga County on three round trips of five Staten Island ferries. Meanwhile, 300,000 additional Manhattanites would travel by subway to the rail freight yards in Hoboken, where they would board boxcars and ride to Cayuga County; 614,600 people in the Bronx would drive north on Interstate 87 to Ulster County; 43,200 residents of Queens would fly from LaGuardia Airport to Bradford, Pennsylvania, in an airlift "with characteristics similar to the Eastern Airlines shuttle." And so on.*

To avoid highway congestion during an evacuation of New York, the study envisions dividing the city into small districts and assigning car owners in each district specific evacuation times. To pass instructions on to small groups by radio, the plan proposes addressing them by a combination of their ZIP codes, two digits of their license plates, and birth dates. "The objective," it says, "should be to address instructions and messages to a few hundred people at a time." A resulting broadcast would sound like this: "Group 10020AZ14, start driving up Broadway at four a.m."

The study assumes that each host area will receive five times its own population in New York City evacuees. (Nationwide, the actual ratio of relocatees to host-area residents will range from two to one to five to one.) This will, of course, cause additional problems, not the least of which will be cultural. The sudden news, for example, that half a million black and Hispanic residents of the Bronx are heading for rural Ulster County is likely to create tremors in Ulster

---

* In 1981, the New York City Transit Authority solicited bids for equipment to protect the city's subways from being knocked out by "electromagnetic pulse," a nuclear-weapon effect which can destroy electrical systems hundreds of miles away from a nuclear explosion. Such protection would be essential if the subways were to be used in evacuating New York after a nuclear attack on another part of the country, such as the midwestern missile fields. A Brooklyn state senator, however, brought the Transit Authority plan to public attention and attacked it as a waste of money. "The Transit Authority can't keep the trains rolling during an average rush hour," he said. "Why is it worrying about a nuclear attack?" The plan was abandoned the next day.

County. "How are you going to keep those people there from shooting the people coming in?" a reporter asked Bardyl Tirana, then director of the DCPA, in 1978. Replied Tirana: "That's tough."

"Since you've studied the problem," the reporter offered, "you no doubt have an answer to this."

Replied Tirana: "Don't assume that."

(Such fears are not groundless. In 1961, when evacuation planning was not part of federal civil defense, a Las Vegas official proposed organizing a five-thousand-man militia to deal with nuclear war refugees from California pouring into Nevada "like a swarm of locusts." In 1980, FEMA ordered a special study "to examine the question of whether or not Blacks and other minorities might experience special problems in the event that nuclear war became likely and the President ordered a massive population relocation." It concluded that they would.)

In general, however, the planners predict that host-area residents will be hospitable to the strangers arriving in their towns. "Seventy-three percent of the people surveyed in host areas have indicated they would be willing to take in one or more families in the event of a relocation effort," FEMA says, "and local governments are urged to encourage such assistance." The Plattsburgh evacuation instructions encourage such assistance in a paragraph addressed to host-area residents: "Your neighbors who have evacuated their homes need your help, particularly those families with little children. Volunteer now to bring a family to live with you. . . . You may be saving their lives." A phone number will be provided for those willing to take in a relocatee.

But the planners are not relying on anybody to call. Host-area plans are designed to accommodate *all* relocatees in public and commercial buildings. To figure who will fit where, college architecture and engineering students employed by FEMA have been fanning out through the nation's designated host areas every summer, surveying every nonresidential building in sight. Each building is photographed. Then a form is filled out with the building's name, address, age, size, latitude and longitude, distance from soil that is readily available to be piled up around the building to shield it from fallout, and other relevant data. With this information in hand— more than one million host-area buildings have been surveyed so far—comprehensive host-area plans are devised. The plan for No-gales, Arizona (to which some residents of Tucson will evacuate), specifies, for example, that 200 evacuees will live at Kino Cleaners at 226 Arroyo Boulevard and will eat at the McDonald's at 205 Crawford Street: If war breaks out and bombs fall, they will be joined at Kino Cleaners by 342 of the 530 people living at Elks Lodge #1397, because Kino Cleaners can be more easily converted into a fallout shelter (by packing dirt around it) than can the Elks Lodge.

The present owners and occupants of buildings that will house relocatees have not been troubled with prior notification of any of these plans. A couple of years after the Nogales plan was written, a reporter tried to telephone Kino Cleaners. It took several phone calls to reach the right building, because Kino Cleaners had been converted to a True Value hardware store, but owner Ed Baez was finally contacted and told of the plan to house two hundred refugees in his store.

"Oh?" he said. "That's news to me."

He was told 542 people will live in his store after a nuclear attack.

"Jiminy Christmas!" he exclaimed. "I guess they could live here. It wouldn't be too comfortable. They'd have to stand in line to use the johns. There's only two."

(While he had no objection to housing nuclear war refugees in his store, Baez added, as for himself he'd probably just head over the hills into Mexico.)

The manager of the McDonald's on Crawford Street hasn't been notified yet either to expect a few hundred extra customers on the eve of a nuclear war, but FEMA has begun contacting wholesale food distributors about special arrangements for crisis relocation. "Sixty major food distributors have told FEMA that, with only twenty-five-percent manning, they can reroute food from risk to host areas," says John Dickey of FEMA's Emergency Management Program Office. And more direct measures are envisioned. "One thing that was raised at an exercise we had," says Wyoming civil-defense director Bill Reiling, "was what authority the governor has over interstate commerce. If a food truck is stopped by the crisis, we might have to take it and give the driver a receipt."

Consumer rationing will be imposed in the host areas and so, probably, will a price freeze. Withdrawals from bank accounts will be limited until the crisis is over, but host-area banks will be expected to cash out-of-town checks. One "planning assumption" for crisis relocation is that the federal government will pick up the tab for feeding, housing, and transporting evacuees as well as reimbursing the owners of food trucks seized by local civil-defense officials. Wyoming authorities have already anticipated a formal announcement of this policy by preparing a sample news release for host areas: "The Chairman of the Board of the County Commissioners announced that the Federal Government will accept responsibility for all expenses incurred as a result of Crisis Relocation activities which exceed normal local government or private sector expenditures. All department heads of government agencies and owners/managers of private businesses must maintain complete and accurate records to justify claims submitted after the Crisis Relocation emergency." ("This is an optional release which should reduce anxiety," the Wyoming civil-defense guide advises, "particularly on the part of small businesses and marginal government agencies which probably would not be able to re-open if federal assistance was not available.")

If the federal government does adopt such a policy, it will put an additional strain on a national economy already crippled by the movement of 150 million people away from their homes. FEMA expects crisis relocation to cost the country about two billion dollars a day. To prevent the economy from collapsing, key workers in risk areas will be evacuated to relatively nearby host areas from which they can commute to their regular jobs. Such key workers will include police and firemen guarding the abandoned cities, food industry workers needed to provide food for the relocated population, and defense-industry workers gearing up for the anticipated war that provoked crisis relocation in the first place. Exactly how key workers will be prevailed upon to enter areas they have been told are subject to imminent nuclear attack is not clear. "If things got pretty tough, they could say the hell with running the wholesale food business and get out," acknowledges one crisis relocation planner. "But, if key workers got a half-hour warning of an attack, they could get in their cars and get pretty far away. They wouldn't have to worry about the speed limit." (FEMA has also begun designing and testing blast shelters for key workers caught in town when nuclear war begins.) Similar questions have been raised about people like the bus drivers who are supposed to drive people out of town when the evacuation begins and then return for another couple of runs. "As for the likelihood of police officers, truck drivers, and others carrying out their assigned jobs in a crisis relocation emergency," FEMA says, "there can be no absolute certainty. But in peacetime disasters, most people who have a job to do get it done."*

FEMA's optimism extends to every aspect of crisis relocation. Will there be hopeless traffic jams on the highways? "Prepositioned bulldozers" will push disabled vehicles off the roads, says a FEMA official. Will people panic? Riot? Loot? "While no one can guarantee perfect behavior in such an unprecedented situation as crisis relocation," FEMA says, "the judgment of those who have studied peacetime and wartime evacuations is that constructive and law-abiding behavior would be predominantly, indeed overwhelmingly, the case." Will evacuees be able to settle into host areas in a calm and orderly way? Wyoming civil-defense officials have already prepared this news release for relocatees: "Assistance will be needed in food preparation, babysitting, recreational activities, communications, office work and a concentrated effort toward improving fallout shelters. Watch the bulletin board for details on how you can help."

A fuller description of host-area life is provided in a FEMA publication in which a fictional participant describes a fictional crisis relocation: "When Hamburg fell during the last week in July almost everyone knew that the CRP would soon be implemented. . . . We left our home at 7 p.m. on August 1 and arrived at our off ramp in Fremont at 9:45. . . . The community life was unusual from the

---

* Exhibiting somewhat less confidence, the Nuclear Regulatory Commission threatened in 1983 to shut down the Indian Point, New York, nuclear power plants partly because of the "questionable availability" of drivers for buses needed to evacuate residents near the plants in case of accident. In hearings on the evacuation plan, bus drivers had testified that they would not enter a radiation zone without monitoring equipment; some said they would walk off their jobs to get their own families out of the area. Ultimately, the commission allowed the plants to stay open, after utility officials began giving a course on radiation to area bus drivers so they could make "informed decisions" on whether to volunteer to drive during an emergency.

beginning. In the first place most stores, food, hardware, etc., and services such as doctors, dentists, laundries were open at least 16 hours a day (and 24 hours, in some cases), and 7 days a week . . . Doctors among the refugees shared offices with the local doctors, as did dentists. Retailers were able to handle the increased load by the extra daily hours and the weekends. The greater the efficiency of these operations, the more labor would there be available for shelter and other preparations as well as for work in the key industrial and commercial firms involved in military requirements, and in stock-piling."

Shelter preparation will in fact be the top priority of the evacuees. They will spend their days piling up dirt around and on top of the True Value hardware stores, schools, churches, and other buildings where they have taken up residence. "Fallout protection," FEMA says, "is dirt cheap. . . . One fallout-protected space can be developed by moving (on the average) about one cubic yard of earth (about 70 to 100 buckets)." Key workers commuting daily back to risk areas will not be available to help with this effort, but the host-area work force will be augmented by convicts guilty of minor crimes, who will be released from host-area prisons to make room for felons from risk-area prisons. All of this shoveling will be rather difficult in much of the country if the nuclear crisis should happen to take place in winter, but FEMA promises that construction equipment will be assigned to assist. FEMA is also developing plans to supply the shelters with sanitation and ventilation supplies.

The digging will continue until the crisis relocation ends. "It is assumed the evacuation period would last from one to two weeks," FEMA says, "though a longer period should not be discounted."

The crisis relocation will end, of course, in one of two ways, with "de-relocation" or worse. Wyoming civil-defense officials are already prepared for either eventuality with two alternate public announcements:

1. "The Governor has announced that improvements in diplomatic negotiations has *[sic]* greatly reduced the possibility of an attack on the United States and that it should be safe for the relocated residents of———County to return to their homes. Highway control procedures are currently being set up to keep traffic congestion to a minimum. . . ."

111

2. "A state of war now exists between the United States and
————. Nuclear detonations have been reported in————states
and we can expect attacks in our area at any time. . . ."

Most Americans, relocated or not, will not have to wait for a
postattack news release to learn that crisis relocation has failed as a
deterrent and nuclear war has begun. Many will figure it out for
themselves in the instant before they are burned or battered to
death. To get the news out to others a little sooner than that, FEMA
maintains a National Warning Center in the Combat Operations
Center of NORAD headquarters inside Cheyenne Mountain in Colorado. There, where military controllers constantly monitor satellite and radar data for signs of enemy attack, two FEMA warning
officers are also on duty twenty-four hours a day. Upon detection
of an attack, while NORAD is conferring with other military commands and the president, the FEMA warning officers will swing into
action.

"Alternate National Warning Center, I have an emergency
message," one of them will announce over the National Warning
System, a nationwide party line leased from AT&T.

"Authenticate," a warning officer at the alternate center (underground in Olney, Maryland) will demand. Nobody wants a false
alarm (or a false termination of a real alarm) from an impostor to
get out on the system.

"I authenticate," the first warning officer will reply, consulting
his secret authentication documents for the correct response. Then
(in accordance with the *Procedures Manual for National & Regional
Warning Centers*) he will ring the bell on the national party line for
exactly seven seconds.

Bells will ring on dedicated phones at ten regional FEMA offices, other underground FEMA facilities, four hundred other federal civilian and military installations, and more than two thousand
city, county, and state "warning points," most of them local police
and fire dispatching centers.

"Attention all stations," the FEMA warning officer will announce. "This is the National Warning Center. Emergency. This is
an Attack Warning. Repeat. This is an Attack Warning. Declaration

112

time————Zulu [Greenwich Time]. Alternate Warning Center acknowledge."

The alternate center will do so, and the Colorado center will call the roll of the FEMA regional offices. The regional offices will call the roll of state warning points. Meanwhile, the national warning officer will dial another number on his console to reach the national wire services and broadcast networks. "Attention news agencies," he will announce. "This is the National Warning Center. Emergency. An Attack Warning has been declared. . . ."

The president, if he is not too busy racing for his plane, may elect at this time to activate the Emergency Broadcast System (which replaced CONELRAD in 1963) and deliver a personal message to the American people. The National Oceanic and Atmospheric Administration will be broadcasting the attack warning over its FM Weather Radio System. The Coast Guard will be broadcasting it to ships at sea. The Federal Aviation Administration will be putting it out over its national teletypewriter network (and ordering all commercial airplanes to land).

In Maryland, the Alternate National Warning Center will activate the Washington Area Warning System, a network of outdoor sirens and bells and lights in federal government buildings. All over the country, city and county warning points will turn on their sirens, and Americans will hear a three- to five-minute wavering tone.

Some Americans will, anyway.

"We feel we can get the warning to the state and local levels," says Russ Lawler, who works in the area of warning for FEMA. "The weakness in the system is getting it to the individual."

If the enemy attack comes at 3 a.m., most Americans will be sleeping. Even if it comes at noon, very few Americans will happen to be hanging out in their local police dispatch rooms, or listening to the NOAA Weather Radio, or working in an FAA control tower.

"We ask local emergency operating centers, 'Can you receive attack warning in two minutes?,' 'Can you receive it on a twenty-four-hour basis?,' and 'What percent of the local population can you reach via public warning?' " says Joseph Mealy, chief of emergency management systems support for FEMA. "The numbers don't read too good. In theory, forty percent of the population can hear the sirens. I don't believe it."

The government has been trying for decades to find a way to overcome this problem. In the early 1960s, a device called NEAR (National Emergency Alarm Repeater) was designed. It was a small black box that individuals would stick into home electrical outlets. In an attack, civil-defense officials would send a signal over the nation's electric lines that would cause the NEAR to buzz and flash. A 1964 survey found that most Americans would welcome having a NEAR in their homes.

"We tested it in Michigan," says Mealy. "It didn't work."

In the late 1960s and early 1970s, the government developed DIDS (Decision Information Distribution System). DIDS was to consist of a nationwide network of low-frequency radio transmitters that, in an attack, would broadcast a signal that could automatically turn on sirens, other alarm systems, and even home television sets that had been fitted with inexpensive receivers. "The technology is there," says Mealy, who has a television set in his office that is fitted with a DIDS receiver. "The signal can turn it on and make it go to high volume. A device to retrofit a home TV would cost about thirty dollars. To install it as you manufacture the TV would only cost ten or twelve dollars." A 1972 survey found that 69 percent of all Americans would be willing to pay fifteen dollars for such a device, and a prototype transmitter was built in Maryland. "We had this thing ready and field-tested," says Mealy.

It has been mothballed. "The unfortunate thing that happened," Mealy explains, "was the downfall of Nixon with some of the things he did. After that, there was no way we were going to tell John Q. Public that we were going to put something in his home TV that was controlled by the government."

In 1982, FEMA Director Louis Giuffrida said he was still dissatisfied with the present system, mainly because the leased telephone line it runs on is unlikely to survive a nuclear attack. (In fact, it was never meant to survive a nuclear attack; its purpose is to get its message out *before* the missiles fall.) FEMA intends, Giuffrida said, to "replace the old system with a new one which will survive a nuclear attack and provide an operational capability throughout the emergency. . . . As equipment and funds become available, we will introduce satellite communications, low-frequency radio, and meteor-burst technology to provide an element of redundancy in the system."

Even now, with a nonsurvivable system that most people can't hear, Joseph Mealy is confident that the system will work if a war begins during crisis relocation. "In an international crisis, saber-rattling, or ground war in Europe, or initial use of tactical nuclear weapons, the American public will not be too hard to warn," he says. FEMA literature suggests that, in a crisis, neighborhood radio watches be established, with neighbors taking turns staying awake and listening for news. "And then there's the old neighborhood door-knocking routine," says Mealy. "It's human nature. When you get bad news, the first thing you want to do is verify it with someone else."

And then?

When you hear the warning siren, FEMA says, you should dash to a fallout shelter and take a radio with you. "It is possible— but extremely unlikely," the literature says, "that your first warning of an enemy attack might be the flash of a nuclear explosion in the sky some distance away. . . . If there should be a nuclear flash— especially if you are outdoors and feel warmth at the same time— take cover *instantly* in the best place you can find. By getting inside or under something within a few *seconds*, you might avoid being seriously burned by the heat or injured by the blast wave of the nuclear explosion." The best way to lie, FEMA says, is "on your side in a curled-up position," with your arms wrapped around your head. "This would give you some additional protection."

Of course, if you are too close to an exploding nuclear weapon, you will be killed no matter what you do with your arms. Asked what the National Warning System will do for civilians in target areas who will have no time to get away, the vice-commander of NORAD told reporters in 1981: "I guess they'll die all tensed up."

Even those who do reach shelters may never be seen again. A shelter in the basement of a twenty-two-story office building, FEMA figures indicate, will be buried beneath thirty-three feet of debris after a nearby blast. Such considerations led New York City's top civil-defense official to propose a few years ago that the city's sirens be disconnected. They were costing six thousand dollars a month in phone bills to maintain, he said, half of them didn't work, and: "A Russian submarine forty miles off New York can lob missiles at New York City that from launch to detonation will take seven seconds. In that time, the military command has to discern the attack at its headquarters in Colorado, and then notify Albany, and they notify us, and we have to notify fifty-six precincts to turn on the sirens, and the people who hear them will run into buildings and be turned to sand in a few seconds anyway."

Those who are not turned to sand, advises the narrator of the film *Protection in the Nuclear Age*, should not panic: "If your home is in an area where the heat wave has started small fires, use the next few minutes to put them out. Prevent them from growing into big ones. Then shut off your main water valve and other utilities. You'll have at least thirty minutes to do all this—and then find shelter— before radioactive fallout starts coming down."

Finding shelter, of course, will be the most important next step. Blast survivors might find a shelter marked with one of the familiar black-and-yellow signs left over from the ambitious, and now abandoned, shelter-marking program of the early 1960s. "There are more than 227,000 of these shelters coast-to-coast," says the narrator of the film, "enough to shield our whole population if they were perfectly distributed. Unfortunately, they're not." (In fact, more than two-thirds of them are in risk areas and thus unlikely to survive blast damage themselves.)

"Even if you're unable to reach a shelter," the film consoles, "you can still improvise some protection. Set up a strong table or workbench in the corner [of your basement] that's most below ground level—and away from windows. Cover the top with as much heavy materials as it will safely hold—doors, bricks, flagstones, books. Wall it in with heavy bookcases, chests of drawers. Then fill the drawers with earth or sand for added shielding. . . .

"Or you can dig an L-shaped trench in your yard, about four feet deep and three feet wide. Make the longer side of the L big enough to accommodate your family—the shorter leg will serve as the entrance. Shore up the sides of the trench for safety. Cover it with house doors or heavy timbers, then pile two feet of earth on top for protection."

Detailed plans for this "door-over-trench expedient fallout shelter," as well as the similar "car-over-trench" and other models, will be distributed during crisis relocation, on the theory that, if an attack comes, many Americans will have time to dig holes in the ground big enough for their families before dangerous fallout reaches them. FEMA knows such shelters can be built quickly because in 1977 its predecessor, the DCPA, sponsored a test in which average families were paid a fee to build the shelters from the plans. "They were also paid a bonus of $5.00 for every person-hour they could reduce from the anticipated construction time," the study report adds. "The bonus was used to simulate the stress situation that would exist in an actual emergency."

It is debatable whether a race to finish digging a fallout shelter to earn an extra ten or twenty dollars is as stressful as a race to finish digging a fallout shelter before fallout arrives and you die, but the test did establish that some average American families could build door-over-trench shelters in a day or less. A fatherless black Michigan family consisting of a mother, three sons, and a daughter dug theirs in thirty-one person-hours, earning a twenty-seven-dollar bonus. Two people in Colorado built a car-over-trench shelter in only four person-hours. "If a cross-section of American families will build shelters to earn some money," FEMA concluded, "it's likely that a substantial number of crisis evacuees would work hard to develop fallout shelters that could save their lives."

And so, if all goes well, and the ground's not frozen solid, within a few hours after a nuclear attack, previously unprepared Americans will be sitting in ditches under cars and doors; if all has gone well with the relocatees, they will be sitting more comfortably in church and school basements surrounded by the extra dirt they piled up during the relocation period. Even then, however, the shelterees will not be guaranteed immunity against fallout sickness or death. An especially heavy attack upwind, or just a bad break on wind direction, may bring enough fallout to overwhelm the defenses of dirt-covered churches, not to mention car-covered ditches. (Even if all goes as expected, two federal civil-defense researchers not affiliated with FEMA found in a 1981 study, sixteen of the forty-nine American counties likely to suffer the highest levels of fallout after a large Soviet attack have not been designated risk areas; shelterees in those counties will have a very hot time of it.)

Whether or not they are receiving lethal doses of radiation is something the shelterees will want to know. But that will not be easy. People who start vomiting in their shelters may be exhibiting the first symptom of fatal radiation poisoning, they may be exhibiting the first symptom of mild radiation poisoning, or they may only be nervous and upset. Symptoms specific to radiation sickness, such as loss of hair, will not become apparent until it is too late to take measures to avoid the radiation that caused it.

FEMA is working on this problem now, hiring and training state Radiological Defense Officers, maintaining 237,000 sets of radiation meters deployed in the early 1960s (one-third of which are defective), and manufacturing new radiological defense kits for shelters. Each kit will include one ratemeter (to measure the rate at which radiation is entering the shelter), two dosimeters (to measure cumulative radiation doses), and one charger (to charge the dosimeters). FEMA's goal is to produce seven million kits. FEMA is also working on plans to get the kits to the shelters in time of need.*

If the kits don't arrive in time, and shelter residents are out of communication with anyone informed about fallout levels, the shelterees will have to guess, or improvise. FEMA literature suggests that a white plate or cloth be placed outside the shelter. Fallout particles will show up against the white background. "A flashlight beam will illuminate fallout as it descends at night," FEMA adds. People entering the shelter after fallout has begun to descend should remove or shake off their outer clothing. "Later they can be visually inspected for radioactive particles. Use combs and brushes to re-

---

* Radiation meters will play an important role in preserving fallout shelter morale, Herman Kahn observed in his 1960 book, *On Thermonuclear War*. As a result of "anxiety, unfamiliar environment, strange foods, minimum toilet facilities, inadequate shelters and the like . . . some high percentage of the population is going to be nauseated, and nausea is very contagious," he wrote. "It would not be surprising if almost everybody vomits. Almost everyone is likely to think he has received too much radiation. Morale may be so affected that many survivors may refuse to participate in constructive activities. . . . The situation would be quite different if radiation meters were distributed. Assume now that a man gets sick from a cause other than radiation. Not believing this, his morale begins to drop. You look at his meter and say, 'You have received only ten roentgens, why are you vomiting? Pull yourself together and get to work.' "

move particles, or brush them off, and then sweep these small amounts of fallout out of the shelter."

Then shut the door.

While tens of millions of American shelterees are waiting to emerge into the outside world—a wait, FEMA says, that will not exceed two weeks in host-area shelters—they will spend their sleeping hours laid out head to foot. "A head-to-toe arrangement, as shown in the following diagram," says the comprehensive FEMA guide, *How to Manage Congregate Lodging Facilities and Fallout Shelters*, "is the best position for sleep, in that it decreases the spread of respiratory ailments." But respiratory ailments will not be the only concern when the lights go out. Unmarried men and women will be separated from each other; if everyone is sleeping in one room, family groups will sleep in the middle, with the unmarried men on one side and the unmarried women on the other. "High social standards, particularly for sexual behavior, should be maintained in the sleeping area," the guide specifies. "Management should try to identify *potential* problems and keep them from becoming *actual* problems."

A great deal of responsibility for all sorts of problems will fall on the shoulders of fallout shelter management, and so FEMA has prepared *How to Manage Congregate Lodging Facilities and Fallout Shelters* as a practical guide for people trained as shelter leaders, perhaps during the crisis relocation period. "It is . . . quite feasible to take someone with a strong management background and in a short time give him the technical information required to manage a shelter effectively," says another FEMA publication, the *Attack Environment Manual*. Maturity, leadership experience, and courage are among the qualities that will make a good shelter manager, it says, and it offers a short test—"Rate Yourself as a Potential Shelter Leader"—for curious readers. Excellent physical health earns ten points on the test, as does having been a successful sales manager. Military officers who have led men in combat are awarded eight points, as are high school teachers. Mountain climbers, cave explorers, clergymen, and PTA presidents rate six points. Simply believing that you can manage a shelter effectively earns you five points.

119

"What's that?" the test concludes. "You say you're a middle-aged spinster who teaches English at the high school, scuba dives on weekends, and thinks managing a shelter would be a blast? You'd make a good choice. Take me to your shelter, leader!!"*

In case of a shortage of pretrained managers, or if managers can't make it to every shelter, FEMA has prepared a short version of the shelter management guide that will simply be left in designated shelters to be picked up by the first person to run in. A notice is printed on the cover of the booklet: "The safety and well-being of the people in this shelter depend on capable leadership. If a civil defense manager is not present, anyone seeing this handbook who has leadership experience can and should TAKE CHARGE IMMEDIATELY."

Once the shelter manager has taken charge, he (or she) will supervise the entrance of shelter residents, see that they fill out registration forms, confiscate their weapons, and, if possible, collect their perishable food, radios, drugs, and liquor. The manager will then appoint assistants and deputies and organize the shelterees into work teams devoted to radiological defense, supplies, technical maintenance, health, fire control, safety and rescue, communications, administration, water, training and education, security, night watch, psychological first aid, shelter upgrading, recreation, religion, food, sanitation, and ventilation. (Faced with the "threat" of "an emergent leader who has assumed control before Manager and trained staff entered shelter," the guide advises that the manager give the upstart a position in the shelter hierarchy.) The shelter will also be organized into community "units" of seven to twelve friends and/or family members; the units will combine into "sections" of forty to sixty people; the sections will be parts of "divisions" of two hundred to four hundred people; and, if the shelter is really big, the divisions will be organized into "squadrons" of one thousand to fifteen hundred. "Such living groups will provide individuals with the reassurance they receive from group membership," the shelter man-

* In its newer literature, FEMA is resolutely nonsexist. "In the following pages," notes *How To Manage Congregate Lodging Facilities and Fallout Shelters*, "the manager and staff are often referred to as 'he,' which term is intended only as a space-saving convenience, with no implications whatsoever of any sexual discrimination. In the event of nuclear disaster, women will be playing major roles as Managers and other key staff in helping our nation survive and recover."

agement guide says, "and (2) will help you run the shelter more effectively."

Even so, it is expected that there will be problems. "Managing a [fallout shelter] is similar in many ways to running a hotel," the guide says. But it points out some differences as well. For example: "If you lack enough medical resources, including drugs, to meet the needs of your total population, and you are unable to increase your supplies, you must decide which patients will receive the scarce drugs, and in what order of priority. . . . It may be necessary to let some people die."

Other problems may arise from the fact that standard fallout shelter designs provide just ten square feet per person. In such close quarters, heat stroke and carbon dioxide poisoning can be fatal unless adequate ventilation is supplied. If nuclear attack has knocked out electrical equipment, shelters will be pitch black. Civil-defense officials have run a shelter living test in which volunteers spent twenty-four hours in the dark and they "apparently adjusted very well," FEMA reports, but a shortage of batteries or generators in a shelter will still make life difficult.

Water will be drinkable after an attack, FEMA says; fallout-contaminated water can be filtered. But there is likely to be a scarcity of water in the shelter, and foraging trips outside during days of heavy fallout will be dangerous. When fallout levels dip to where there is no threat of immediate incapacitation, foragers will be risking getting cancer later. Long-term cancer deaths can, however, be reduced, two federal civil-defense researchers suggested in 1981, by selecting foragers from among the older shelterees. "Older people will come to the end of their natural life spans before reaching the end of the risk [of fallout-induced cancer] . . .," the researchers wrote, "thus, the same exposure may produce fewer total excess cancers in this group than within a younger segment of the population."

It will not be necessary to risk the life of anyone, old or young, to go out searching for food, FEMA shelter literature advises: "Healthy individuals should be physically able to survive a several-week shelter stay without any food. If shelterees are expected to participate in postshelter recovery operations, however, they will require food during the confinement period. Moreover, food has tremendous emotional significance and failure to provide what is commonly perceived as a basic need can make the keeping of people in shelter very difficult." As for other basic needs, regulation shelters will be equipped with one portable sanitation kit (a barrel with a plastic liner and a toilet seat) for each fifty shelterees. "To increase toilet area cleanliness," says the shelter management guide, "it will be necessary for both men and women to perform all toilet functions sitting down. . . . It may be necessary to schedule toilet use at peak hours (early morning, late evening) and you must remember that any illness causing diarrhea or vomiting will increase toilet use."

People will adjust surprisingly well to most odors in the shelter, the guide assures, but one odor that may cause problems will be that of dead bodies. "Death in a Fallout Shelter causes three management problems," the manual advises, "(1) Health (the body might contain disease-producing organisms); (2) Emotional impact of death on your population; (3) Legal problems." The trained manager will see that people who die are really dead ("those who have not been medically trained must use great caution in pronouncing death"), then record the death, wrap the corpse in a sheet or blanket, "quickly remove it from your main area, out of sight of the population," and bury it outside "as soon as external radiation levels allow a short trip."* Finally, the manager or "a member of the religious activities team" will "conduct a simple service" and "provide emotional support to family members."

Bereaved family members will not be the only ones needing emotional support. "Maintaining the morale of people confined in close quarters and possibly in semi-darkness for two weeks will not be easy," notes the management guide, "especially if they are worried about the effect of an enemy attack on our nation and their own ways of life." But the well-trained shelter manager will try to keep spirits up. At least one interdenominational religious service will be conducted on the first day in the shelter, with more to follow. Group

---

* While waiting for radiation levels to dip, former federal civil-defense researcher Cresson Kearny has observed, "the sickly-sweet stink of a decaying human body is [likely to be] greatly disturbing. Some civil defense workers have theorized that the best way to take care of a corpse in a shelter until the fallout dose-rate outdoors is low enough to allow burial is to seal it in a large plastic bag. A simple test with a dead dog proved this idea impractical: gas pressure caused the bag to burst."

singing will be encouraged, as will board games. "Improvising checkerboards and pieces, cards, etc., is an important part of your recreational program," the guide says, "and is a team effort that will bring people together." The checkerboards and cards may be made by shelterees during arts and crafts sessions. ("Arts and crafts products can be shown and admired," says the manual.) Special emphasis will be placed on news briefings about the world outside (if any information is getting in): "It is vital . . . that you [the manager] take steps to give your population factual, official information and move swiftly to counter and stifle rumors that will weaken their motivation to adjust and to prepare themselves for the day when they will emerge from the fallout shelter to an uncertain future."

This will be the manager's greatest challenge—to dispel negative thinking among the shelter population. "Some of your population may be upset by the danger in which they think they are placed as the result of the attack or attack threat which forced the move to Fallout Shelters. They may be even more worried than before about the safety of family and friends with whom they have not been able to make contact. They may believe that the attack means the end of their way of life and are afraid of being killed or having to live under impossible conditions."

If these doubts and pressures lead any of the shelterees to commit antisocial or criminal acts, they will be disciplined or confined. (Mock trials and/or expulsion from the shelter, which could be fatal, are specifically not recommended, however.)

For the rest, "discussion groups" and "training-education classes" will be organized. These will teach "survival techniques for the post shelter world." It is also probable, says the shelter manual, that surviving government officials "will at some point provide you with an outline of recovery information which our government wants you to discuss with your population." Despite their importance, such classes will have to be kept short. "Under the stress of a nuclear attack, people will not be able to concentrate easily for extended periods of time." The best time for such sessions will be shortly after meals or coffee breaks, "when your population is most alert."

These sessions will be one of the most important parts of the weeks underground, as they will reach out to those who have concluded that nuclear war leaves them nothing to look forward to. "Such training will shift thinking positively toward the future," promises the shelter management guide. "The best lesson that your population can learn in the Fallout Shelter is to know they can survive and to believe in a future in which our society can be rebuilt."

SIX

"The Number-One Myth of the Nuclear Age"

There is a connection between the fact that Walmer E. (Jerry) Strope dislikes *On the Beach* and the fact that he once sat in a hole in the ground and waited for an atomic bomb to explode less than a mile away. "It was," Strope recalls with a tinge of pride, "the closest manned station to a shot that I know of." The "shot," called "Diablo," was a seventeen-kiloton atomic weapon perched on a five-hundred-foot tower in the Nevada desert in the summer of 1957, when American military scientists were exploding nuclear weapons in the open air at the rate of more than one a week. They were testing the weapons themselves, and the effects of the weapons on blast and fallout shelters, and, in Strope's case, the effects of the weapon on human beings in the shelters.

Strope, then a civil-defense researcher for the Navy, was a little upset the day before the shot to find that construction workers had not buried the shelter he was going to be sitting in—an arched, corrugated-steel structure—quite as deep as it was supposed to be. Nevertheless, he and seventeen other volunteers climbed in at midnight to begin their wait. They sat on the floor, back to back, away from the walls, as the final countdown began just before dawn. They could hear it on a public-address system wired into their shelter. Five, four, three, two, one. Zero.

Nothing happened. While scientists on the surface tried to figure out what had gone wrong, concluded that Diablo was not about to go off at any moment, and, finally, recruited a brave soul to drive over to the tower and disconnect the wires, Strope and his colleagues waited underground. They were finally let out of the shelter late that night.

Two months later they were back—in the shelter, on the floor, back to back, away from the walls. The countdown went to zero, and this time Diablo exploded. "We started counting," Strope recalls. "At four the blast wave came. It sounded exactly like you were inside a garbage can and somebody slammed the cover. Suddenly dust was very visible. The blast wave bounced it up. We got a double pulse on our buttocks and our feet. The first was the direct ground shock. The second was where the ground shock hit the underlying rock and bounced back up. . . .

"It was," Strope concludes, "very interesting."

A quarter of a century later, Strope is still a civil-defense researcher (although he now works for the government on a consulting basis). He also writes a column for the *Journal of Civil Defense*, the official publication of the American Civil Defense Association, in which he displays little patience with those who deny that protection is possible in a nuclear war. In 1982, when an M.I.T. scientist reported that a nuclear attack on the United States would leave "few survivors," Strope replied scornfully that, among "professionals," the scientist's credibility had sunk "to the level of the lady [Dr. Helen Caldicott] who leads the socially responsible doctors [Physicians for Social Responsibility] who, if she is being quoted correctly, believes that the fictional events of *On the Beach* are scientifically valid."

The professionals Strope invoked are civil-defense researchers and civil-defense and nuclear-war planners and strategists who earn their livings by thinking about what they believe is only naively regarded as "the unthinkable." ("Nuclear war is very thinkable," Strope told a congressional committee in 1976. "I have thought about it for twenty-five years, and have never had any problem thinking about it.") Few of these professionals have, like Strope, ever been close enough to an exploding nuclear weapon to hear it crashing down on them like a giant garbage can lid, but most of them share his impatience with those who believe that civil defense is futile and that nuclear war would be the end of human civilization or worse.

When a reporter asked Zbigniew Brzezinski, while he was President Carter's national security advisor, whether he would be able to urge the president to retaliate against a Russian nuclear attack with an American nuclear attack, "even though that might make the chance of the regeneration of human society that much more difficult, even impossible," Brzezinski replied, "Well, first of all, that really is baloney ..." ("The fact of the matter is. ... ," Brzezinski explained, "that if we used all our nuclear weapons and the Russians used all of their nuclear weapons, about ten percent of humanity would be killed. ... It's not the end of humanity. It's not the destruction of humanity.")

The civil-defense professionals are alternately dismayed and mystified by the widespread public acceptance of this "baloney." In 1976, a pro-civil-defense congressman named Donald Mitchell went so far as to conduct an inquiry to find out where it was coming from. At a hearing on civil defense, he asked in frustration, "Don't you think the majority of people believe you can't survive [a nuclear war]? Someone is teaching us this. Who is teaching that?"

The witness to whom Mitchell first addressed the question, T. K. Jones, agreed that "someone" was teaching that "foolishness," but he named no names. (He did, however, mention and commend an acquaintance who was giving translations of Russian civil-defense manuals to his friends as Christmas presents. "What greater gift can you give to people who are really your friends than the gift of telling them how to survive if the country gets into a war?" Jones asked.)

Other witnesses at the hearing were more willing to finger villains. "Some people in the forefront of disarmament movements and so forth," offered Walmer Strope, "have felt a psychological need for believing that this was the ultimate weapon and that a nuclear war would be an unmitigated catastrophe. It's probably the number-one myth of the nuclear age."

Federal civil-defense researcher Dr. Conrad Chester singled out *On the Beach* as a source of this "myth" and then added some very specific information about the origin of the related "myth of overkill ... the frequently heard statement that the world's nuclear arsenal can kill everyone 'twelve times over' or 'seventeen times over':

As nearly as we can tell, this myth originated in an article in the *Bulletin of Atomic Scientists* in which the casualties per kiloton in Hiroshima and Nagasaki were multiplied by the number of kilotons in the world's arsenal. This misleading calculation implies that some means can be devised to collect the entire target population into the same density as existed in Hiroshima and Nagasaki, and keep them in a completely unwarned and hence vulnerable posture. A statement of identical validity is that the world's inventory of small arms ammunition, or, for that matter, kitchen knives, can kill the human population several times over."

Witness Paul Nitze, later appointed chief negotiator on theater nuclear weapons by President Reagan, agreed with Chester about the "myth of overkill," only Nitze attributed it to "a professor at Columbia University" who did not "really understand much about the defense problems." (By the professor's reasoning, Nitze said, there is also a "vast overkill" of rifle bullets in the world.) But Nitze found other, more prominent, parties at fault as well in propagating such "myths," namely, "every President and . . . every Secretary of State" of the United States. "It has been a politically popular thing to say," Nitze complained, "that both sides have the ability to destroy the other; that nuclear war is unthinkable."

The other witnesses at the hearing had to agree that their rhetorical opponents were not merely uninformed professors and psychologically deficient disarmament proponents; the record of presidential statements is clear. "The atomic armaments race . . . overshadows not only the peace but the very life of the world," Dwight Eisenhower told the United Nations in 1953. "Man holds in his mortal hands the power to abolish . . . all forms of human life," John Kennedy said at his inauguration in 1961. "The survivors [of a nuclear war], if any, would live in despair amid the poisoned ruins of a civilization that had committed suicide," Jimmy Carter said in his farewell address in 1981. (Only after prolonged controversy about his administration's attitude toward nuclear war did Ronald Reagan make a statement approximating these. "There can be only one policy for preserving our precious civilization in this modern age," he told the Japanese parliament in 1983. "A nuclear war can never be won and must never be fought.")

With authorities like these to rely on, along with the historical records of Hiroshima and Nagasaki, the documented dangers of fallout, and the relentless growth of nuclear arsenals, the popular media have long carried messages that dismay the civil-defense professionals. Science fiction books and movies portray postnuclear war landscapes populated only by tiny bands of human survivors and mutant creatures spawned by radioactive fallout. Cartoonists draw the postnuclear-war last man and woman on earth discussing their sexual possibilities. A popular video game called "Missile Command" requires the player to defend his nation's cities against incoming nuclear weapons; inevitably all are destroyed and the screen displays a final huge explosion with the legend THE END. Less than a year after Walmer Strope walked away unscathed from Shot Diablo, the satirist Tom Lehrer sang:

> We will all go together when we go,
> Every Hottentot and every Eskimo.
> When the air becomes uranious,
> We will all go simultaneous. . . .

Not a word about the protection offered by fallout shelters or crisis evacuation.

More that thirty years of this kind of negative information about nuclear war have left civil-defense boosters feeling frustrated and unfairly put-upon and, in the case of Congressman Mitchell at least, searching for a lively popular medium in which to get the civil-defense message across in rebuttal. "You can inform people in a couple of different ways," Mitchell said at the 1976 hearing, "and I feel we've got to get their attention. . . . What is the novel—I suppose a movie's been made of it—that starts the day after the bomb is dropped?"

That was *On the Beach*, a witness replied, and it probably wasn't the kind of thing Mitchell was looking for. "They have fearful scenes in that," he explained. "At the conclusion everybody dies."

"That's not going to serve our purposes then," Mitchell said.

"Hardly," said the witness.

"We'll have to have a sequel there to amend it," Mitchell suggested.

"Yes," agreed the witness, "so that everybody lives."

• • •

Even before the world's first atomic bomb exploded in the summer of 1945, those familiar with its power warned that the only effective civil defense against such weapons would be the complete redesign of the American nation. "If the race for nuclear armaments is allowed to develop," Manhattan Project scientists warned in the Franck Report in June 1945, "the only apparent way in which our country can be protected from the paralyzing effects of a sudden attack is by dispersal of those industries which are essential for our war effort and dispersal of the populations of our major metropolitan cities." It would be prudent, Leo Szilard wrote a few weeks after the atomic bombing of Japan, to undertake a ten-year plan for the relocation of thirty to seventy million urban Americans. Large cities could continue to exist, Szilard said, "but they might have to be built in certain shapes," perhaps rectangles one mile wide and fifty miles long. (Compact circular cities could be too easily destroyed by a handful of bombs.)

The scientists' warnings were as much arguments for arms control as for civil defense, but the 1946 report of the U.S. Strategic Bombing Survey on the lessons of Hiroshima and Nagasaki urged the same course. "Though a reshaping and partial dispersal of the national centers of activity are drastic and difficult measures, they represent a social and military ideal," the report said. A few years later, the Truman administration issued Defense Mobilization Order 1, which made it official American policy "to encourage and, when appropriate, to require that new facilities and major expansions of existing facilities important to national security be located, in so far as practicable, so as to reduce the risk of damage in the event of attack." The stated overall goal of DMO-1 was to "make urban areas less attractive targets" through industrial dispersion. DMO-1 remains in effect today.

American cities *did* disperse after World War II, but the growth of the suburbs probably owed less to fear of atomic attack than to the desire for a backyard. ("When you read how the big New York department stores . . . are burgeoning forth into large numbers of suburban branch stores, a person's first impulse is to say it must be the A bomb. . . . ," noted *The New York Times* in 1946, "[but] the idea is not to make life safer for American shoppers by keeping as many as possible away from New York, but to make life pleasanter for them by sparing them the trip into town.") Early postwar civil-defense activity did not even include shelter construction (although the U.S. Strategic Bombing Survey had noted that well-built shelters survived the atomic bombings in Japan) let alone moving Detroit.

American interest in civil defense increased after the Soviet Union exploded an atomic bomb in 1949. Congress passed the Federal Civil Defense Act of 1950, establishing federal civil-defense bureaucracies and authorities. "We must organize ourselves in every city, factory, office and home . . . ," President Truman told a 1951 civil-defense conference. "We have two immediate jobs. One is to teach all our people how to protect themselves in the event of enemy attack. The other is to organize millions of volunteers as active members of the United States Civil Defense Corps." Recruiting began promptly, with a goal of 17.5 million volunteers. By December 1951, 1.5 million had signed up, including ten thousand New York City cabdrivers who joined a civil-defense Emergency Taxi Corps. Special efforts were undertaken to recruit ministers; religious leaders were told at a Washington conference that "we have to face the possibility of helping 200,000 to 300,000 people die within two or three minutes." In Chicago, local officials announced plans for every Chicagoan to wear a dog tag inscribed with his or her name, address, and blood type to help identify lost children and the seriously injured after an atomic attack.

For the fiscal year 1951, the Truman administration asked Congress for $403 million for civil defense, but civil defense had its critics then as now. Congress appropriated $32 million, inaugurating a pattern of administration request followed by congressional opposition followed by administration retreat that would be repeated for thirty years. In 1952 Truman asked for $537 million. He got $77 million. "We are not trying to neglect civil defense . . . ," explained Congressman Jamie Whitten, "but . . . you cannot build enough holes in the ground with all the money in the federal treasury, including the federal debt, to be perfectly safe from the atomic bomb."

The Federal Civil Defense Administration, great-grandfather

of today's Federal Emergency Management Agency, wasn't so sure about that. "We can go underground and build shelters of reinforced concrete with air conditioning and sanitation facilities that can withstand any weapon man could devise," FCDA director Val Peterson said after the Soviet Union exploded its first hydrogen bomb. Peterson acknowledged, however, that the cost of such shelters—"many billions of dollars"—was prohibitive. Undismayed, the FCDA proceeded with the testing of more modest shelters at the Nevada weapons test range. "The family-type shelter which we tested in March at Yucca Flat would give a reasonable amount of protection from an H-bomb in a home ten miles from the center of the city," Peterson said in 1953.

Two years later, the FCDA testing program reached its zenith with the construction of a mock American city—the FCDA called it Survival City, the press dubbed it Doom Town—at the Nevada test site. The town included industrial buildings, gas lines, a working electrical system, a radio station, and ten full-sized houses inhabited by mannequins. The houses were equipped with modern appliances and well stocked with food, all provided by manufacturers wanting to test the effects of nuclear war on their products.

On May 5, a twenty-nine-kiloton atomic bomb was exploded less than a mile from Survival City. "Civil defense rescue teams worked briskly to free trapped families," *The Las Vegas Review Journal* reported the next day. "Along Doomsday Drive, a dirt road 4,700 feet from the blast . . . a mannequin mother died horribly in her one-story house of precast concrete slabs. Portions of her plaster and paint body were found in three different areas. . . . In the one-story masonry brick house . . . Civil Defense monitors said that kitchen cabinets stocked high with groceries withstood the blast. But a simulated mother was blown to bits in the act of feeding her infant baby food." On the brighter side, canned food left in shallow trenches less than a quarter mile from the blast was tested and found to have retained all its niacin and riboflavin. Power lines a mile from the blast were knocked down but the Survival City radio station was left in working order. Bomb shelters beneath the destroyed houses on Doomsday Drive were unscathed, as were civil-defense officials and reporters who observed the explosion. "I had a trench full of civilians with me at the ten-thousand-foot mark," recalls Harold Goodwin, who was test operations director for the FCDA, "including a bunch of crazy photographers who wanted to jump up and take pictures of the bomb. We had to grab them by the seat of the pants so they wouldn't be burned. We wanted to prove you could survive being near a blast. We all had a good time. The fallout went the other way."

Despite these findings, civil-defense planners recognized that the best place to be during a nuclear attack was out of town. In an era before missiles, when nuclear bombs could only be delivered by airplanes after flights of thousands of miles, it was reckoned that residents of target cities would be able to flee between the time enemy bombers were spotted and the time they arrived. Civil-defense evacuation was one justification for creating the multi-billion-dollar interstate highway system (officially the "National System of Interstate and Defense Highways"). Evacuation route signs were posted on some highways, and a series of actual evacuations was carried out to test the concept. In one drill, 200,000 people were evacuated from downtown Portland, Oregon.

In June 1955, President Dwight Eisenhower fled Washington in a speeding Cadillac, leading fifteen thousand government employees in a mass exodus to secret rural relocation sites. Three hours later, Washington was "destroyed" in a mock air raid. Nationwide, "Operation Alert 1955" was front-page news as sixty-one American cities were "attacked" by Russian bombers and missiles, causing mock casualties of more than eight million dead and another six million injured. Air raid sirens sounded in most of the target cities, and pedestrians and drivers were ordered to take shelter. In New York City, where 2,991,285 people were "killed" by a five-megaton hydrogen missile warhead landing in Brooklyn, city buses stopped in their tracks as the sirens sounded; passengers were ordered off and handed "raid checks" that would allow them to reboard without paying another fare when the all-clear signal sounded ten minutes later. (Twenty-nine pacifists, some of them carrying signs saying END WAR—THE ONLY DEFENSE AGAINST ATOMIC WEAPONS, refused to take cover and were arrested, as were a laborer in Manhattan, and a salesman in Brooklyn who refused to leave his truck.) Meanwhile, the president appeared at a relocation site identified by the press (which was there) only as being in "a mountainous wooded area within 300 miles of Washington." The president sat on a metal folding chair in a tent and conferred with Cabinet officers and other officials. He then spoke to the nation in a speech carried live by the radio and television networks. "We are here," he explained, "to determine whether or not the government is prepared in time of emergency to continue the function of government so that there will be no interruption in the business that must be carried out."

Such operations, complete with federal government relocation, civil-defense exercises, and air raid drills, were conducted annually for several years. (During Operation Alert 1957, Dwight Eisenhower became the first American president to fly in a helicopter.) Two developments of the mid-1950s, however, forced civil-defense planners to alter the assumptions that underlay the evacuation strategy. First, growing appreciation of the dangers of fallout led to the conclusion that simply getting away from target areas was not enough; airborne radiation could follow you. Then, advances in Soviet rocketry, dramatized by the launching of *Sputnik* in 1957, meant that Soviet hydrogen bombs could be delivered by missiles as well as planes; attack warning time would be cut from hours to minutes; there would not be time to flee. In 1956, with these developments in mind, federal civil-defense officials proposed a national system of blast and fallout shelters. The projected cost was more than $20 billion.

President Eisenhower was taken aback by the proposal—the *total* federal budget in 1956 was only $66 billion—and he appointed a blue-ribbon panel that came to be known as the Gaither Committee to undertake an exhaustive study of the problem of protecting civilians in a nuclear war. The committee recommended a nationwide fallout-shelter program costing $22.5 billion. "This seems the only feasible protection for millions of people who will be increasingly exposed to the hazards of radiation . . . ," the committee's report said. "We are convinced that with proper planning the post-attack environment can permit people to come out of the shelters and survive."

Eisenhower was still reluctant. He refused to release the Gaither Report to Congress or the public (it remained classified Top

Secret until 1973), and its conclusions were contested by prominent members of his administration. Secretary of State John Foster Dulles opposed the shelter program with a perennial anti-civil-defense argument—that American security was best served not by attempting to reduce the damage that would be caused by a nuclear attack but by maintaining the power to retaliate devastatingly against any attacker and thus discourage an attack from being launched in the first place. In his memoirs, Eisenhower recorded how the shelter proposal was disposed of at a White House meeting:

> Former Governor Leo A. Hoegh of Iowa, now Civil Defense Administrator, argued that $22.5 billion for fallout shelters would be a good investment—one which might save fifty million American lives. But Foster Dulles disagreed, emphatically. "If a wave of a hand could create those shelters," he said, "we'd of course be better off with them than without them. But it's hard to sustain simultaneously an offensive and defensive mood in a population. For our security, we have been relying above all on our capacity for retaliation. From this policy we should not deviate now. To do so would imply we are turning to a 'fortress America' concept."
>
> "You *are* a militant Presbyterian, aren't you?" I remarked. A little laughter around the table helped to lighten the air.

When the laughter ceased, Eisenhower vetoed the shelter plan.

More modest civil-defense efforts continued, as did protests from civil-defense enthusiasts that they were not enough. One of the most vigorous enthusiasts was New York Governor Nelson Rockefeller. (Indian Prime Minister Jawaharlal Nehru, who presumably had other things on his mind, once emerged from a meeting with the governor and told reporters, "Governor Rockefeller is a very strange man. All he wants to talk about is bomb shelters.") In 1959, Rockefeller proposed legislation to require every homeowner in New York to build a basement fallout shelter. To promote the scheme, Rockefeller sat in a mock shelter in the window of a Manhattan bank. The state legislature killed the plan anyway.

The man Rockefeller credited with convincing him of the virtues of civil defense was Edward Teller, who advocated fallout shelters and more. Instead of merely building shelters in institutions like schools and hospitals, Teller asked, why not build the schools and

135

hospitals underground to begin with? "The builders of new warehouses, bowling alleys, theaters, parking garages, or supermarkets might find it to their advantage to build underground if the government offered appropriate subsidies," Teller advised. (An additional advantage for students in underground schools, he wrote, would be that room would be left on the surface for "a really adequate outdoor playground.") Teller also saw important cultural advantages in his plan: "I would propose that our museums and libraries be built underground and equipped as community shelters. In case of attack, such shelters would save many lives while preserving some of the chief reasons for living."

Teller carried his arguments to the new administration of John F. Kennedy in 1961 and succeeded in appalling at least one presidential advisor. "I must say I am horrified by the thought of digging deeper as the megatonnage gets bigger, which is the notion of civil defense that Dr. Teller spelled out to me after your meeting with him the other evening," McGeorge Bundy wrote in a memo to the president in December. "He thinks it can be done for $50 billion spent over a period of years. This is a position from which you will wish to be disassociated."

Kennedy did not want to go as far as Teller suggested, to be sure, but the new president had already established himself as the greatest supporter of civil defense ever to sit in the White House. Never before and never since (with the possible exception of Ronald Reagan) has a president taken civil defense so seriously nor, more significantly, spent so much money on it.

Kennedy, who had come into office vowing to "pay any price, bear any burden, meet any hardship, support any friend, oppose any foe to assure the survival and the success of liberty," appealed to Congress for a major civil-defense program (and for increased military aid to South Vietnam) in May 1961. Kennedy explicitly rejected one argument that would be put forward twenty years later by the designers of crisis relocation—that civil defense could be an element of the strategic balance. "We will deter an enemy from making a nuclear attack only if our retaliatory power is so strong and so invulnerable that he knows he would be destroyed by our response," Kennedy said. "If we have that strength, civil defense is not needed to deter an attack. If we should ever lack it, civil defense would not be an adequate substitute." Kennedy added, however, that civil defense could provide valuable "survival insurance" in case of nuclear war resulting from error or miscalculation. He announced that he would triple the civil-defense budget to provide funds for identifying existing structures suitable as fallout shelters, constructing new shelters, and stocking shelters with essential survival supplies.

Over the next few months, tensions with the Soviet Union flared over the issue of Berlin. Recently declassified documents indicate that Kennedy and his aides believed war was an imminent possibility and looked to civil defense to blunt its effects. "I think we should ask the Civil Defense people to come next week with an emergency program," Kennedy wrote to Bundy on July 5. "What could we do in the next six months that would improve the population's chances of surviving if a war should break out?" On August 29, two weeks after the sudden erection of the Berlin Wall, Kennedy wrote the secretary of defense, "I would appreciate receiving a weekly report on what progress we are making on Civil Defense. Do you think it would be useful for me to write a letter to every home owner in the United States giving them instructions as to what can be done on their own to provide greater security for their family?"

Kennedy did not write that letter, but he did the next best thing. A signed message from the president, addressed to "my fellow Americans," was reproduced as the introduction to a special section on fallout shelters in a September issue of *Life* magazine. "I urge you to read and consider seriously the contents of this issue of *Life* . . . ," the message said. "In these dangerous days . . . we must prepare for all eventualities. The ability to survive coupled with the will to do so therefore are essential to our country."

A headline next to the president's message said fallout shelters could guarantee the survival of 97 percent of all Americans in a nuclear war, and promised "you could be among the 97% to survive if you follow advice on these pages." The magazine offered sketches of basement shelters, words of praise for citizens who were building them, a catalog of shelter supplies (including a $21.95 "plastic suit to protect your skin and clothing from radioactive dust"), and a photo of a Texas bobby-soxer relaxing in her family's backyard shelter, chatting on the phone and sipping a Coke.

The press, the president, and international tension together fueled a fallout shelter boom that, briefly, swept the country. Shelter construction companies and sales lots popped up all over. "My best salesmen are named Khrushchev and Kennedy," one shelter manufacturer reported happily. The Westinghouse Corporation introduced a flat, glowing simulated window to furnish and illuminate the shelters of those who might otherwise suffer from claustrophobia. (Asked what shelter life would be like, civil-defense booster Herman Kahn told *Newsweek*, "Well, you're sipping a drink, munching on something tasteless, and it's dark and crowded—a Greenwich Village night club.") Television actress Barbara Hale (Perry Mason's Della Street) was hired to model a fallout shelter suit designed, according to its manufacturer, to be warm, comfortable, and stain-resistant ("since laundering facilities may not be available in most shelters"). A Beverly Hills pet shop introduced a shelter survival kit for dogs, made up of flea spray and other canine essentials. For humans on a budget, former Atomic Energy Commissioner Dr. Willard Libby demonstrated a "poor man's shelter" of sandbags and railroad ties that he built in his backyard for thirty dollars. (Libby's shelter was destroyed a few weeks later by a brush fire, prompting Leo Szilard to remark, "This proves not only that there is a God but that he has a sense of humor.") For those to whom price was no object, Hammacher Schlemmer advertised a super-deluxe "professionally planned, custom-made safety shelter" that could double, in the absence of nuclear war, as a "Family-Library-Music room . . . that is a beautiful addition to any family's plan for pleasant living." Optional accessories included a compact bath ($499.50) and a two-week food supply ($2.50); delivery was free within fifty miles of New York.*

Through all of this, theologians were widely quoted in the press debating whether shooting a desperate neighbor who tried to force

---

* Reacting to the craze a bit belatedly, the Federal Trade Commission in 1967 issued standards for advertising fallout shelters that prohibited "scare tactics, such as the employment of horror pictures calculated to arouse unduly the emotions of prospective shelter buyers."

his way into your family's overcrowded shelter would be the Christian thing to do. Another man of the cloth, the Reverend Jim Jones, read an article in *Esquire* listing "nine places to hide" from the effects of a nuclear war and promptly moved his congregation to Belo Horizonte, Brazil. (Years later, still worried about nuclear war, he and his People's Temple followers would end up in Jonestown, Guyana.) The other safe places recommended by *Esquire* included Guadalajara, Mexico ("dry, mild and healthy"); Mendoza, Argentina ("fabulously underdeveloped"); Tananarive, Madagascar ("open-minded about white men"); Christchurch, New Zealand; and, *On the Beach* notwithstanding, Melbourne, Australia.

In December 1961, the Department of Defense, to which Kennedy had transferred responsibility for civil-defense operations, began the National Fallout Shelter Survey, which would eventually identify more than 250,000 basements, corridors, caves, and other areas theoretically capable of sheltering 238 million people from at least some of the fallout produced by a nuclear attack. Many shelters were stocked with water cans, food, drugs, and other supplies; all were identified with the yellow-and-black signs still visible along many American streets. This government emphasis on public shelters, along with popular skepticism and confusion, led to the ruin of the private shelter industry by the spring of 1962. Over the next two years, the federal government program faltered as well. Dovish public opposition developed, questions were raised about the true life-saving potential of fallout shelters, and cost-cutting congressmen laced into the administration's requests for civil-defense appropriations. Under attack, the administration failed to hold its ground. "The Kennedy Administration's schizophrenia over civil defense was quite evident at [a] Hyannis Port meeting in November, 1961, at which the major decision was taken to shelter the entire population," recalled Steuart Pittman, appointed by Kennedy as the nation's first (and last) assistant secretary of defense for civil defense. Most of the president's advisors opposed the decision, Pittman wrote, and the president stuck to it only because he had promised the program in May. "It is not surprising then that the priority started dropping sharply almost immediately after the decision was made," Pittman said. For fiscal year 1962, Congress had appropriated $294 million for civil defense (still a record); in fiscal year 1963, Kennedy asked for $757 million but Congress appropriated only $128 million. Enthusiasm for civil defense receded still further following the Cuban missile crisis—during which the Soviet Union backed away from confrontation in the face of overwhelming American nuclear superiority—and the signing of the 1963 limited test-ban treaty. During consideration of the budget for 1964, President Lyndon Johnson failed to lobby for funds for the construction of new fallout shelters. The funds were cut; Pittman resigned. Civil defense was on the back burner once again.

After the heady days of 1961, the years that followed were frustrating ones for the civil-defense professionals. The civil-defense budget continued to decline (although it never dipped below $69 million), and the civil-defense bureaucracy was subjected to a seemingly endless series of reorganizations. The Office of the Assistant Secretary of Defense for Civil Defense became the Office of Civil Defense in the Department of the Army, which became the Defense Civil Preparedness Agency, which eventually became part of the Federal Emergency Management Agency. Military attention concentrated on the war in Vietnam, and the war in Vietnam proved you could battle Communism without any serious worry about risking nuclear attack. While fallout shelter signs remained in place, the shelter stocking program was abandoned. Shelter medical supplies, which included phenobarbital, were either removed by local authorities or, in the words of a New York City civil-defense official, "destocked by looters." Some shelter "survival ration crackers," steadily turning rancid, were removed and sent by CARE to starving people in Africa and Bangladesh. The crackers in New York City shelters were sold for one dollar a ton to an upstate farmer who used them to feed his pigs.* When people thought about nuclear war, if they ever did, they thought of it as an event in which they would die and so,

---

* A recent tasting of circa-1962 shelter food revealed that the crackers are still chewable but have a terrible aftertaste. Red hard candies included in shelter supplies tasted stale but otherwise okay, hard candy apparently being impervious to the vicissitudes of time.

probably, would most everybody else. A parody civil-defense poster of the 1970s contained these instructions:

> Upon the first warning:
> Stay clear of all windows . . .
> Loosen necktie, unbutton coat and any other restrictive clothing.
> Remove glasses, empty pockets of all sharp objects such as pens, pencils, etc.
> Immediately upon seeing the brilliant flash of nuclear explosion, bend over and place your head firmly between your legs.
> Then kiss your ass goodbye.

Through all this, the civil-defense professionals had at least one comfort—their research program. Millions of dollars were spent each year on studies farmed out to independent contractors (who included former federal civil-defense employees). The studies proved that nuclear war could be survived if civil-defense precautions were taken, and then they proved it again . . . and again. By 1980, FEMA was able to state that "some 369 reports on postattack recovery are available in FEMA's research library. . . . In years of research no insuperable barrier to recovery has been found."

In fact, there are *thousands* of reports occupying hundreds of feet of shelf space in the FEMA library, with more coming in all the time. (The 1984 FEMA research budget is $5.6 million.) There are reports on every imaginable aspect of nuclear war survival and recovery, from a study of the "consumability of animals exposed to radiation in a postattack situation" (it found that "thorough cooking would be mandatory"), to a study of the effect of nuclear war on the American rubber industry (it concluded that shortages of truck engine hoses would be a worse problem after a nuclear war than shortages of truck engine belts), to a study of the effect of fallout on radishes.

One active area of research, especially during the 1960s, was fallout shelter life, a field previously dominated by enthusiastic amateurs. (In 1959, Mr. and Mrs. Melvin Mininson of Miami spent their two-week honeymoon in an eight-by-fourteen-foot fallout shelter and reported upon emerging, "It was Heaven.") Walmer Strope conducted the first carefully monitored 100-person shelter living test in 1959. In a 1960 experiment, 93 California convicts spent five days in a buried Quonset hut and received one day off their sentences for each day underground. "By 1968," the Defense Civil Preparedness Agency reported, "nearly 7,000 volunteers had participated in over 22,000 man-days of shelter living in occupancy tests ranging from family size to over 1,000 people and for periods ranging from one to 14 days. . . . One of the first questions asked was whether American citizens (men, women, and children) could or would endure the confinement of a shelter for a period as long as two weeks. The answer obtained in early experiments was an emphatic 'Yes.' " The DCPA acknowledged, however, that these early successes owed something to the fact that the first test shelters were equipped with "bunks, prepared foods, furniture, good sanitary facilities, and the like." When shelters were made less comfortable, the DCPA said, "a significant proportion of volunteers decided to leave during the experiment." One result of all this research was the establishment of ten square feet per person as the national shelter standard. This is only half the space per person in a crowded jail cell, one DCPA publication said, but it is six times the space per person in the Black Hole of Calcutta. (And, Walmer Strope pointed out in 1982, in the Black Hole of Calcutta "lack of ventilation was the cause of casualties, not lack of space.")

Another popular endeavor among those working with civil-defense research money has been the design of econometric models of the post-nuclear-war U.S. economy. A 1978 RAND Corporation study (done for the Defense Nuclear Agency, one of several other government agencies commissioning this type of work) offered this description of the relationship between maximum industrial output and available capital and labor after a nuclear attack:

$$X^k = a[\alpha K^k + (1 - \alpha) L^k]$$

(X is maximum output, K is available capital, L is labor, a and α are constants, $k = 1 - \frac{1}{\sigma}$ and σ is the "elasticity of substitution.")

By 1973, the DCPA was able to draw on its research to report in its *Attack Environment Manual* that "major studies are highly affirmative as to whether the surviving physical and human resources are sufficient to permit a meaningful recovery." Industrial equipment can be protected from blast by sandbagging and other means, the manual said, and prompt postattack measures can prevent the "corrosion and rusting of neglected assets [that] caused much damage at Hiroshima and Nagasaki." The manual drew on a 1967 study to recommend that organic waste, including rotted food and human and animal corpses, be collected as rapidly as possible during the first month after nuclear war survivors emerge from their shelters. In the second month, it said, garbage collection should "return to normal."

Civil-defense studies of a purely technical nature, such as *Dynamic Analysis of Reinforced Concrete Floor Systems*, may be unassailable, but those that leap from conclusions about postattack concrete floors to conclusions that anything can "return to normal" two months after a nuclear attack embody nontechnical assumptions that are only rarely acknowledged. A 1980 study for FEMA on post-nuclear-war "survival, reconstitution and recovery" was more candid than most when it stated that "studies such as the current one must proceed from the position that the view from the right [that nuclear war survival is possible] may be correct, as otherwise there would be nothing to evaluate." So they do, and a multi-million-dollar consulting industry carries on.

The uniformly optimistic views of the civil-defense research consultants overwhelm the occasional negative finding. A 1969 study of fallout shelters in New Orleans reported that, even if all space and ventilation criteria were met, "heat casualties would probably occur after 24 hours." When the study was listed in the annual summary of DCPA research, it was with the comment that "the criteria used in this analysis are regarded by many as being overly severe." The consistent upbeat tone of the research is a product also of the inbred nature of the researchers. A handful of research groups get contract after contract, and some studies are based almost entirely on reviewing other studies and interviewing their authors. One such work is the 1979 report *Recovery from Nuclear Attack and Research and Action Programs to Enhance Recovery Prospects*. Written by a former DCPA director of postattack research (and two other consultants), it noted that there is some "uncertainty" about the long-term effects of a nuclear war on the global environment, but it concluded confidently:

No weight of nuclear attack which is at all probable could induce gross changes in the balance of nature that approach in type or degree the ones that human civilization has already inflicted on the environment. These include cutting most of the original forests, tilling the prairies, irrigating the deserts, damming and polluting the streams, eliminating certain species and introducing others, overgrazing hillsides, flooding valleys, and even preventing forest fires.

The report (which thus stopped just short of accusing Smokey the Bear of being more dangerous than nuclear war) did acknowledge that post-nuclear-war research, "unfortunately," cannot be verified "by reference to experimental data." Therefore, it said, researchers must sometimes rely on their "judgment and even intuition." The report was seventy-three pages long and cost American taxpayers $81,871. It is often cited by FEMA officials as an authoritative source.

The current civil-defense concept of crisis relocation—a hybrid of 1950s evacuation planning and 1960s fallout shelters, justified by the new assumption that several days will be available to evacuate before an attack—inspired a fresh spate of research reports in the 1970s. "Program D [crisis relocation] appears to provide the most effective option for saving at least 1/2 to 2/3 of the American people, given at least a one-week surge period, within a reasonable funding constraint of about three times the present U.S. level of expenditure for civil defense," a key 1978 study reported. Later that year, Walmer Strope, working for a consulting firm called SRI International, wrote with a colleague the feasibility study of evacuating New York that concluded the metropolitan area could be evacuated in 3.3 days. More studies followed.

In selling crisis relocation planning to the Carter administration, which finally bought it, the civil-defense professionals had allies more powerful, however, than themselves and their research library. Foreign policy hawks within and without the administration, who were lobbying against ratification of the SALT II arms control treaty and urging the development of new nuclear weapons systems, cast their glance at civil defense and saw yet another military shortcoming. Soviet evacuation planning and other civil-defense preparations, they asserted, were vastly superior to those of the United States. The resulting "civil-defense gap," they said, was a dangerous strategic imbalance. The Coalition for Peace Through Strength, several of whose members would later work in the Reagan administration, charged that the SALT II treaty constituted an "act of phased surrender" to the Soviet Union and that inadequate American civil defense would hasten that surrender. The Soviet Union, the Coalition said, could go so far as to launch a nuclear attack at American military targets, killing millions of American civilians, and the United States would not be able to launch a retaliatory second strike because of the civil-defense gap. "The Soviets might lose no more than 4 percent of their population [in an American retaliatory strike] because of their active civil defense," the Coalition said. "It is most unlikely that any U.S. President would retaliate after a Soviet first strike if the Soviet response would kill 100 million to 150 million Americans."

A similar argument was advanced by conservatives within the Carter administration, including Samuel Huntington, a Harvard professor and coordinator of security planning for Carter's National Security Council. "An American President would not be in an enviable bargaining position in a crisis if his ICBM force was vulnerable to a Soviet first strike [which officials of both the Carter and Reagan administrations have asserted is the case], if Soviet leadership and population were substantially protected against a U.S. second strike, and if U.S. leadership and population were highly vulnerable to a Soviet third strike . . . ," Huntington told a Senate committee. "If the Soviets attacked our ICBM force . . . we could well be deterred from then striking against Soviet cities because the Soviets then could in turn retaliate and utterly devastate American cities."

This alarmist thesis—that without effective American civil defense the Soviet Union would not be deterred from launching a first strike because the United States *would* be deterred from launching a second strike because it was too vulnerable to a Soviet third strike— did not go unchallenged. The Arms Control and Disarmament Agency, an arm of the State Department, published a study concluding that, while Soviet fatalities might be lower than American fatalities in a nuclear exchange, an American second strike would still substantially destroy the Soviet Union. "The Soviets can not be judged as so blind and so reckless as to assume that any present or prospective shelter program or any fond hopes of speedy evacuation to safe zones may make it possible for them to utilize strategic nuclear war as a means of achieving political objectives . . . ," former ACDA director and SALT II negotiator Paul Warnke told the Senate committee. "No rational leadership could subject its country to the unexampled destruction that would be punishment for the monstrous crime of initiating a strategic nuclear war."

As the civil-defense debate was carried on within the Carter administration—and it was—the actual effectiveness of civil defense (which all those research studies had so carefully demonstrated over all those years) came to assume a secondary role. In supporting an increase in civil-defense expenditures, Secretary of Defense Harold Brown said, "While I do not believe that the [Soviet civil-defense] effort significantly enhances the prospects for Soviet society as a whole following any full-scale nuclear exchange, it has obviously had an effect on international perceptions. . . . For that reason alone, I believe at least modest efforts on our part could have a high payoff." In September 1978, this view carried the day; Carter signed Presidential Directive 41 on civil defense. It stated: "Civil defense, as an element of the strategic balance, should assist in maintaining perceptions of that balance favorable to the U.S." Actually protecting people in a nuclear war was not overlooked entirely—civil defense could "provide some increase" in survivors, PD-41 said—but the emphasis was, once again, on "perceptions." It did not matter as much whether civil defense would save American lives as whether the Soviet Union believed it would, or whether the Soviet Union believed that *we* believed it would. For if we believed it, then we would not be reluctant to answer a Soviet first strike with an American second strike (because we would not expect to be overly vulnerable to a Soviet third strike); if the Russians believed that we believed it, then they would be deterred from launching their first strike, because they would expect us to answer with a second strike, because . . . etc. Or so the hawks argued, and Carter bought in.

This role for civil defense had been explicitly rejected in years past by John Foster Dulles, John F. Kennedy, and others. Now it was accepted by the Carter administration. "I do not think CRP [Crisis Relocation Planning] is, in its first instance, done to save lives once a war breaks out," said Carter's DCPA director, Bardyl Tirana.

"It is done to help prevent a war from breaking out in the first place ... I would hope that the existence of the plan itself would diminish or eradicate any possibility of the Soviet Union ever using its capability [to evacuate] or thinking that the use of its capability might be of some advantage." Just as the existence of American nuclear weapons deters the Soviet Union from using its nuclear weapons, so the existence of American crisis relocation plans would deter the Soviet Union from implementing its own crisis relocation plans. And if the Soviet Union never evacuated, we would never evacuate. ("I would never contemplate our evacuation unless we knew that people were walking out of Moscow and Leningrad," Tirana said.) So, if we had crisis relocation plans, we would never need to use them. We would only need them if we didn't have them. And we didn't have them. So we needed them.

Crisis Relocation Planning had actually begun on a small scale in 1974. Shortly after Carter signed PD-41, news stories appeared saying that he would be asking for $2 billion to pay for full-scale CRP. The figure was based on DCPA estimates of what it would cost over a seven-year period to develop effective crisis relocation plans and continue funding other civil-defense activities at the then-current rate of about $100 million a year.

In a period of austerity, the $2 billion figure was a political embarrassment. Editorialists and political cartoonists attacked the plan ("one of the worst ideas ever tossed into public discussion," said *The Washington Post*). Carter felt the heat, and backed off, as presidents had backed off on civil-defense proposals for thirty years. "The press reports about a two-billion-dollar civil defense program have been completely erroneous," Carter said at a November press conference, "and I have never been able to find where the origin of that story might have derived." Several weeks later, a Defense Department budget request for $145 million for civil defense in fiscal year 1980 (up from $98 million in 1979) was cut to $108.6 million.

CRP did proceed, but it proceeded slowly, its future not yet assured. A portent of its future, however, appeared in a syndicated political column a few days before Carter's press conference. "Even in the highest policy making positions in this country, there persists the erroneous belief that a nuclear attack would be so devastating as to make civil defense efforts meaningless ... ," the columnist charged.

147

"A renewed emphasis on civil defense preparedness is necessary. It should be an integral part of our national security."

The columnist was not a newspaperman by profession but had begun writing the column during a lull in his chosen career. His name was Ronald Reagan.

SEVEN

The Long Nuclear War

Major William Stalcup of the U.S. Air Force carries a TI-59 programmable pocket calculator with him as he goes about his work. You can buy a TI-59 for less than two hundred dollars and use it to calculate your taxes or solve a complicated engineering problem. Twelve hours after the outbreak of nuclear war between the United States and Soviet Union, Major Stalcup will use his to figure out ways to carry on the nuclear battle.

"Some of our bombers may have hit their targets and reached a safe recovery base and still have some weapons," Stalcup explains. "Or maybe they can be reloaded. I'll use the TI-59 to figure whether it's feasible for them to reach new targets. Then we can come up with a plan."

Stalcup will be doing this only if he happens to be on duty when the war begins. If not, he will probably be dead, killed in his home near Strategic Air Command headquarters in an Omaha suburb by the first wave of incoming Russian missiles.

If he is on duty, however, he will be safe above the attack. Stalcup works, as an operations planner, aboard SAC's "Looking Glass" plane. Every minute of every day since February 3, 1961, there has been a Looking Glass plane flying over the Midwest (usually somewhere between Minneapolis and Kansas City), carrying a SAC general and an eleven-person battle staff (women are included), ready to seize command of SAC's nuclear-armed missiles and bombers should a sudden Russian attack destroy SAC command posts on the ground. Before each flight, an intelligence officer briefs the general who will be aboard on the current locations of the president and vice president, whom the general will be attempting to contact should nuclear war break out during his eight-hour shift. Two armed Looking Glass officers carry nuclear authenticator codes onto the plane shortly before takeoff and place them in a double-padlocked steel box next to the general's swivel seat in the battle staff compartment. During the flight, the general sometimes sleeps in a bunk at the rear of the plane.

At the first sign of enemy attack, the Looking Glass will be joined aloft by the rest of what SAC calls the Post Attack Command Control System—two auxiliary Looking Glass planes, two communications planes to relay messages between the Looking Glass and the president's National Emergency Airborne Command Post, and three Airborne Launch Control Center aircraft to circle over American missile fields and launch the missiles by remote control if the ground launch crews are dead.

The first purpose of the Post Attack Command Control System will be to guarantee that American nuclear forces get their orders for prompt retaliation no matter what ground command posts have been destroyed. The second will be, in the words of SAC's commanding general, to help "control our forces and manage them effectively during protracted [nuclear] conflict."

Major Stalcup will begin by trying to find out what forces we have left.

"We'll conduct a launch poll," he says. "We'll be trying to determine what assets [missiles and bombers] got off the ground, what assets are on the ground, and what assets"—Stalcup makes a joke—"are *in* the ground." Looking Glass intelligence officers will meanwhile be "prioritizing" unhit enemy targets. Stalcup will be punching numbers into his pocket calculator.

"We'll be trying to determine how things have gone and trying to determine where to go from there," says Major Norwood Jennings, another Looking Glass operations planner. "How do we manage what we have left to manage our relation to the Soviets? Now that the initial plans have been executed, it's free play from here on."

While the Looking Glass battle staff is working this out, the plane's flight crew will be flying by instruments—even if the sun is shining and the weather is fine. The crew members' view of the sky will be blocked by aluminized fabric curtains they will place over the cockpit windows (the only windows in the plane) when the war begins. Their eyes will need that protection from the blinding light of hydrogen bombs exploding below.

Odds are that the first nuclear shot of the war will be fired by a relatively small tactical nuclear weapon. Almost all the scenarios rehearsed by the Pentagon involve a period of rising tension somewhere in the world, conventional battles, and, only then, nuclear escalation. In the "Ivy League" nuclear war exercise conducted by the Reagan administration in 1982, the mock conflict began with Soviet attacks on American troops in Europe, South Korea, and Southwest Asia. The first nuclear explosion was that of a Russian tactical nuclear weapon fired at an American ship in the North Atlantic. American tactical nuclear weapons were then loosed in Europe.

In a real war, if Russia sees no need to bring out its nuclear artillery, the United States will. It has been American and NATO doctrine for thirty years to use tactical nuclear weapons to turn back a winning conventional Russian attack. The first shot may be an eight-inch nuclear shell fired by an Army commander against Warsaw Pact tanks, or a nuclear depth charge dropped from an American helicopter hovering over a Russian submarine, or a nuclear bomb dropped by an American carrier-based airplane on a Russian supply depot. Or the first shot might be fired at nothing specific at all. "There are contingency plans in the NATO doctrine to fire a nuclear weapon for demonstrative purposes, to demonstrate to the other side that it is exceeding the limits of toleration in the conventional area," Secretary of State Alexander Haig told a Senate committee in 1981. Such a blast would be exploded high in the air, or at sea, or in some remote area, other officials explained, to produce maximum effect and minimum damage and to make the Russians think twice about continuing a conventional attack.* Wherever the war's first tactical nuclear weapon is fired, Secretary of Defense Harold Brown said in 1980, there is "a high probability that it could cause a pause; it could tell somebody that this is much more serious and you had better stop." On the other hand, Brown added, "At least as likely, in my judgment, is that that is the first step in a series of escalating steps that lead to the destruction of both countries."

American forces will be ready for the next step. By the time a crisis reaches the point where any nuclear weapons are fired, America's "triad" of intercontinental nuclear forces will be on full alert. Sixty feet beneath the flatlands of the upper Midwest, two hundred young Air Force officers will be standing by, as always, in one hundred Minuteman missile launch control centers.† The two-man crews work twenty-four-hour shifts. In peacetime, only one of each pair is required to be awake. Many of the men, who wear blue uniforms with jaunty yellow ascots, while away their hours underground studying for Master's degrees in business administration. The ten missiles under their control rest underground in silos nearby, each silo no nearer than three miles to any other silo or launch control center. Maintenance crews enter the silos periodically to service the missiles (and to peel manufacturers' decals— "Aerojet General," "Thiokol"—off their sides to take home for souvenirs). Air Force Security Police patrol the missile fields, responding to electronic alarms received by the missile launch crews in their capsules. The Security Police are trained to slip a secret "duress word" of the day into their reports back to the launch control centers if they are kidnapped by terrorists or the like, but the alarms are almost always false. "One crew noticed that the intrusion alarm came in around 7 p.m. every Saturday night from the same silo," a

---

* The day after Haig mentioned the demonstration blast, Secretary of Defense Caspar Weinberger denied that any such plan existed. Asked who was right, Weinberger or Haig, a State Department spokesman said, "Both are right. Secretary Haig was correct in noting that demonstrative use is an option that has been considered by NATO. Secretary Weinberger was correct that this option has never been translated into a military plan." Other, less diplomatically couched, evidence indicates that Haig—who is, after all, a former supreme commander of NATO—was more correct than Weinberger.

† Elsewhere, a diminishing number of other crews tend older Titan missiles. The Titans, one of which blew up in its silo in Arkansas in 1980, are now being deactivated.

former missile crewman recalls. "It turned out the guards had met a couple of girls from a nearby farm town and told them to throw a beer can onto the silo to set off the alarm so they could come out and spend some time with them."

In the prewar crisis, base security will be tighter, and nonessential maintenance will be curtailed, but overall not much in the missile fields will be different. (Ninety-eight percent of the missiles are *always* ready to be launched within thirty seconds.) The missile crewmen will put away their MBA textbooks; they will be sleeping less.

Visible changes within America's fleet of missile-launching submarines will be subtle as well. It is the object of the submarines, even in peacetime, to disappear. For seventy days at a time, the new Tridents (a few days less for the older Poseidons) cruise beneath the world's oceans, never breaking the surface. (A surfacing submarine just might be spotted by Soviet reconnaissance forces, and, if war should break out soon afterward, would be easier to find again than a submarine that had never been spotted at all.) Two-thirds of America's thirty-five or so missile-launching submarines (a new Trident is being added to the fleet every year) are always on patrol. Every submarine has two complete and separate crews; while one crew is cruising, the other is in training or on leave. To preserve their invisibility, and thus their invulnerability, cruising subs generate as little radio traffic as possible while receiving a constant stream of exercise war orders, intelligence information, warnings of navigation hazards, weather reports, and, when traffic permits, messages to crew members from their families, and the news. The submarines carry all the food, fresh air, and fuel they need for seventy days and more. Each also carries, President Jimmy Carter pointed out in 1979, "enough warheads to destroy every large and medium-size city in the Soviet Union."

In the prewar crisis, the submarines will strive to remain, as always, invisible. There will be no obvious change in the radio message traffic to them. (Even in peacetime, all messages are in code and broadcasting is continuous, so the tempo of the message traffic can never provide a clue to the Russians about changing operations.) Submarines at sea will remain longer at sea; those in port will depart ahead of schedule. And surveillance of Russian missile-launching submarines will be stepped up. The United States has a formidable technological lead in this area; American microphones on the ocean floor pick up the muffled sounds of most Russian submarines soon after they leave port, and they are tracked by American and NATO ships and planes for the duration of their cruises. In the crisis, antisubmarine aircraft will increase the surveillance, dropping additional microphone buoys in areas where Russian submarines are known or suspected to be. If war appears imminent, there will be strong incentive to attack the Russian submarines preemptively, saving dozens or hundreds of American targets from being struck by the submarines' missiles if war does come. But destroying the submarines will, of course, spark the war.

The detection of more Russian submarines than usual off the American coasts, or detecting them closer to shore than usual, will trigger protective measures at the SAC airfields where some 300 nuclear-armed B-52 and FB-111 bombers and 650 supporting tankers are based. In peacetime, 30 percent of the bombers and tankers are kept poised to attack, loaded with nuclear weapons and fuel and parked in guarded runway parking spots that have been carefully surveyed to one hundredth of a minute of latitude and longitude for the benefit of the planes' navigational systems. The crews of the planes standing on alert spend a week at a time in isolated alert facilities on the bases. They are briefed on the latest intelligence about the antiaircraft defenses and radars that will be hunting for them as they fly into the Soviet Union, and then they wait. While Minuteman missiles in their underground silos are primarily threatened by land-based Russian ICBMs, which are thirty flight-minutes away, bombers are vulnerable to less accurate submarine-launched missiles, which can reach coastal air bases in fewer than ten minutes. So, even in peacetime, the crews on alert practice racing to their cockpits once or twice a week. Whether they are studying radar maps of their targets, playing video games, showering, or sleeping, they must be prepared to be on their way in seconds. They are allowed to leave the alert facility for the base movie theater, but they sit in special alert seats at the rear of the auditorium. Their own blue trucks wait outside to rush them to their aircraft, and signs are posted on intersecting base roads warning drivers to yield to the alert crews. When the alarm sounds, they dash. Only when they get to the cockpits of their planes does a coded radio message tell them if this is just another drill or if they are on their way to bomb Russia.

In the prewar crisis, more planes and crews will go on alert. Bombers from coastal bases closest to patrolling Russian submarines will disperse to other bases, and civilian airports, inland. The alert crews will spend their weeks in the cockpits of their planes; if the situation is tense enough, the engines will be running. Alternate Reconstitution Base teams will pack up and leave every base, heading for remote areas that are not expected to be Russian targets and taking with them everything they will need to service returning bombers if their home bases are destroyed.

Increasing the number of planes on alert and sending some to dispersal bases will not only enable more planes to escape should attack come but will also send a signal of American preparedness and resolve in the preattack crisis. (It may backfire, however, if the crisis is a long one. "How long the [bomber] force could remain ready during a period of national crisis or chaos is unknown . . . ," the General Accounting Office reported in 1981. "A sustained alert of the full force could stress maintenance and logistics capabilities.") Even greater resolve will be demonstrated by the final step on the alert ladder—airborne alert. From 1957 to 1968, there were always nuclear-armed bombers in the air, just as a Looking Glass is always in the air today. Now bombers on day-to-day alert stay on the ground, saving fuel and aircraft wear, and eliminating the possibility of embarrassing and dangerous accidents. (During the 1960s, B-52s carrying nuclear weapons crashed in North Carolina, Spain, Greenland, and elsewhere.) At the peak of the prewar crisis, nuclear-armed bombers will take off. They will fly toward, but not to, the Soviet Union. "This procedure," the Air Force says, "enables SAC to deploy a portion of its bombers as a show of force in times of international tensions."

"It shows the Russians we mean business," explained Captain Frank Grindel as he sat at the controls of a KC-135 tanker flying near Greenland on a long August afternoon in 1982. Grindel and his plane were taking part in a mock airborne alert during the annual exercise called Global Shield in which SAC practices fighting a nuclear war. "We're exercising the war plan," Grindel said. "We're proving that the war plan can be done."

On the ground a few hours earlier, Grindel and other tanker crewmen (and one crewwoman) had been briefed on their mission in the alert facility at Loring Air Force Base in Limestone, Maine. Global Shield at that point had been going on for almost a week. The mock international crisis that precipitated it was heating up. An unspecified number of SAC aircraft and three thousand SAC personnel had actually dispersed from their usual bases to other airfields and civilian airports. Now seventy SAC bombers had taken off on simulated airborne alert. Grindel's KC-135 and three other Loring tankers would fly to the northeast and rendezvous with two B-52s from Barksdale Air Force Base, Louisiana, that were flying their airborne alert on the Atlantic North orbit.

"Your recall word is 'pillow' for abort," the Loring briefer said. He told the crews which radio frequencies to use during their flights and which to avoid. Low frequencies were plugged up because of solar flares, he said. And all frequencies were under assault by a "Red Team" simulating the activities of wartime Russian (and fifth-column) jammers and spoofers. "They're trying to create confusion," said the briefer. "Use your 2001 [radio] to make sure you're not getting bogus instructions. They're not going to have a foreign accent; they're just Joe American like you and me. The base radio has had people singing 'Ninety-Nine Bottles of Beer on the Wall.' "

There was some laughter in the briefing room at that. The briefer cut it short with a reminder about the real Red Team: "This exercise gives our enemies a good chance to observe us. There's a Soviet ship twenty-five miles off Portsmouth, New Hampshire, and two other Warsaw Pact ships in the area, so keep communications to the bare minimum."

Forty-five minutes later, the four tankers were airborne. Sergeant Gary Hunt, the boom operator on Grindel's plane, walked back from the cockpit and fitted green thermal radiation barriers over the tanker's doors. During a real crisis mission, he said, when Russian nuclear weapons might be exploding nearby, he and the rest of the crew would be wearing gold goggles during the daylight hours. "I have to keep my eyes from getting burned out so I can handle the refueling," he explained. At night, when it was too dark for goggles, they would wear single eye patches. "If you get flash effects, you'll lose one eye," Hunt said, "but you'll still have one that's operable."

The plane was somewhere between Greenland and Labrador when the B-52s appeared, way off to the south. Slowly, one came up behind and below the tanker. Hunt lay flat on his stomach on a platform in the rear of the plane, operating the ruddevator fins on the refueling boom as the bomber edged forward at 350 miles per hour. When it was just a few yards away, the boom slipped into a hole behind the B-52 cockpit, and the two planes flew in tandem for fifteen minutes while ten thousand gallons of jet fuel poured from one to the other. The bomber took more fuel from a second tanker, and the KC-135s headed back to Loring.

Early the next morning, it became apparent that, as a show of force, the airborne alert had failed. Just before 7:00 a.m., the Loring base sirens sounded, sending nonessential personnel into fallout shelters. An incoming enemy attack had been spotted. Three alert B-52s and three tankers took off in a Minimum Interval Take Off, just twelve seconds separating them as they lumbered down the runway and away. They escaped safely.

A few minutes later, imaginary incoming Russian missiles arrived, and Loring Air Force Base was wiped out. Global Shield moved into its final phase. Full-scale nuclear war had begun.

The only people at Loring who were not "dead" were members of the Alternate Reconstitution Base team who, after a brief trip off the base to a holding point in the Maine woods, had returned to Loring. They were pretending it was the Bangor airport, which according to the exercise scenario had survived the Russian attack. Two ARB weather forecasters set up their operation in the base public affairs office. An airman unpacked the kit containing a thermometer, anemometer, and other instruments that he will unpack at some surviving airstrip on the morning after the outbreak of nuclear war. "We should be able to get National Weather Service data at the reconstitution base," said the weather officer, a young woman in fatigues.

And if the Bangor airport, after a real war, is in no condition to receive them?

"We'll just go wherever PACCS [the Post Attack Command Control System] tells us. It's our job to regenerate the force."

The message from the president of the United States (or the surviving National Command Authority) to launch American nuclear forces against the Soviet Union will come into the hardened command center beneath SAC headquarters near Omaha—if it has not already been destroyed—over the gold telephone of the Joint Chiefs of Staff Alerting Network. There is a JCSAN phone in the office of the commander in chief of SAC, one in his home, and one on his desk on the balcony overlooking the underground command post. The SAC commander (if he has not already fled to the air in the auxiliary Looking Glass plane that is always standing by for him) will take the message on the balcony and pass it on to the senior controller in the command post below (who, for safety's sake, has a JCSAN phone on his desk as well). The command post floor—half the size of a football field—will already be tense, with officers looking up from their desks and their phones to the six large screens that dominate the underground. The status of SAC forces will be displayed there as the crisis unfolds—to begin, which bombers are sitting on which runways, then how long their engines have been running, then which have taken off in anticipation of attack, and finally which bases are known to have been destroyed. Three clocks on the wall count time from "A Hour," "P Hour," and "L Hour." "They're phases within a scenario," explains a SAC officer whose job includes leading press tours of the command post. "If I go off duty and you come on and it's P-plus-twenty-three hours, you can find out what's going on if I forget to tell you by looking at the checklist. It's all on checklists." But planning for P-plus-twenty-three hours in the SAC command post may be overly optimistic. Behind its walls of thick reinforced concrete, the command post can be sealed off totally from the outside world with its own wells, ventilation, power, and enough stockpiled rations to feed eight hundred people for two weeks. But it will not survive a direct hit by a nuclear weapon, and, when the order to attack comes in, one may be only minutes away.

As soon as he gets the message to strike, the senior controller on the command post floor will pick up a red telephone of the Primary Alerting System from the console in front of him. As he lifts it, a warbling alarm will sound and a rotating red beacon will begin to flash. The same alarm will sound in every missile launch control center and bomber and missile command post, and the crews working there will hear the senior controller carefully pronounce the series of phonetic letters and numbers that carry the Emergency Action Message to launch a nuclear attack: "Romeo, Delta, One, Tango, Four. . . ." The scattered SAC forces will acknowledge receipt of the message by hitting switches that will extinguish, one at a time, little red lights on a panel next to the controller's red phone.

To improve the chances of the message getting through in an environment that may be disrupted by exploding hydrogen bombs, the controller's voice will be carried to every receiving station via two separated telephone lines. The same message will be transmitted by teletype, so a printed copy of the attack order will appear in every command post a few seconds after it has been heard. To reach bombers that have already taken off to fly to their "positive control" points and await further orders, the message will be relayed by the high-frequency "Giant Talk" radio system. Since high-frequency radio is not reliable in the Arctic, the message will also be relayed by the ultra-high-frequency "Green Pine" stations arrayed from Alaska to Iceland. For additional redundancy, the message will be sent via low-frequency and very-low-frequency radio, via satellite relay, and by other means as well.

"The joke is," says a former missile crewman, "that if a rat crawls out of the toilet with the proper message in his mouth, you're supposed to launch."

Rats do not enter into the official planning, but the commercial telephone system does: it is considered a possible last-ditch means of getting the attack message out. So is individual initiative. If a missile launch crew gets the message and suspects that other crews have not, it is the crewmen's responsibility "to spread the word by *whatever means necessary*," according to one missile base officer. The ultimate method of spreading the word is the Emergency Rocket Communications System (ERCS), made up of about a dozen Minuteman II missiles in silos at Whiteman Air Force Base in Missouri. Instead of nuclear weapons, each of these missiles carries in its tip a tape recorder and a radio transmitter. The order to attack will be dictated into one or more of the recorders, those missiles will launch, and, as their payloads ascend and then fall back to earth, they will broadcast the message over and over again, even after the command post that sent it has been destroyed and the man who dictated it killed.

In the Minuteman launch control centers, crew members will copy the Emergency Action Message, however it is received, onto a prepared form and check it for authenticity. If it validates, the two launch officers will prepare for firing by following the steps on a checklist. (There are checklists for everything—diagnosing power failures, dealing with intruders, launching a nuclear attack—at every step of the nuclear command ladder.) Then they will insert separately two keys into two switches. One key in one switch will not be sufficient, and the switches have been separated so that one man cannot reach both. Turning the keys will set off ringing bells and flashing lights in the other four launch control centers in the squadron; to set the missiles off, one other crew must turn its keys as well.

If a missile launch center has been destroyed but its missiles have not, the two-key procedure will be followed by officers flying overhead in an Airborne Launch Control Center plane that took off at the first sign of attack. If the ALCC did not make it up, the general flying aboard the Looking Glass will remove a key he wears around his neck and insert it in one of two locks in the red safe next to his desk. Another Looking Glass officer will open a second lock and open the box. (So that no one can sneak into the box unnoticed, a clattering sound, like jokeshop chattering false teeth, only louder, issues from the box whenever it is open.) The general and the second officer will remove two more keys from inside the safe, insert them into Airborne Launch Control System consoles overhead, and turn them. In each silo below, rubber braces holding the missile will fall back, the umbilical cord that brought the launch signal to the missile's nose will blow away, the silo door will snap open, and, covered with flame from its own exhaust, the missile will lift heavily out of its hole. Thirty minutes later its warheads will explode over one, two, or three targets in the Soviet Union.

Over the Atlantic and Pacific oceans, the Emergency Action

Message will be relayed to cruising submarines by Navy TACAMO (Take Charge and Move Out) aircraft, which, like the Looking Glass, are always in the air. The launch procedures on a submarine are more elaborate than in a Minuteman launch control center, because, while land-based missiles (and aircraft-carried bombs) cannot be fired unless the proper eight-digit enabling code, embedded in the EAM, is dialed into the launch system, submarine-based missiles are subject to no outside control. It is feared that the technical difficulties of communicating the proper code to submerged submarines might prevent their missiles from being fired when they are wanted. One consequence of this is that a submarine full of crazy sailors could launch nuclear war on its own, but that would require a substantial number of crazy sailors. Submarine launch procedures involve the cooperation of a (secret) number of officers in widely separated sections of the boat. Once launched, the missiles will start exploding over their targets in less than fifteen minutes.

SAC's nuclear-armed bombers that were not caught on the ground by incoming missiles will receive their orders to attack as they fly toward or at their "positive control" points a few hundred miles outside Soviet airspace. The crews will authenticate the message and then set course for their targets, entering Russia at points where intelligence indicates air defenses are weakest or where preceding American missiles have already atomized defenses. The first bombers in, from those American bases that are the closest to Russia, will attack remaining air defense targets under a "rollback" strategy, softening things up for the bombers that will follow. All the bombers will be broadcasting signals and dispensing chaff to confuse Russian radar and dropping decoy flares to attract heat-seeking surface-to-air missiles.

The sight of the incoming B-52s will be awesome. Massive eight-engined airplanes, with wingspans so wide that little "training wheels" are attached under their wingtips to keep them from bouncing onto the runway during takeoff, the bombers will come screeching into Russia just over the treetops. To complicate the task of antiaircraft gunners and radar operators, they will fly hundreds of miles over Soviet territory at altitudes of three hundred feet or below. (An automatic terrain-following system on the FB-111s can be set to give the crew a hard, medium, or soft ride as it hugs the ground. Crews attacking Russia will select hard.) To protect the pilots' eyes from the flash of exploding bombs, the cockpit windows will be covered with reflector shields. Crewmen will watch where they are going on cockpit television monitors linked to cameras and infrared sensors on the noses of their planes. As they approach their targets, they will fire nuclear Short Range Attack Missiles, capable of traveling the last eighty-five miles on their own with 170-kiloton warheads, to attack enemy defenses. Then the bombers will fly in, staying low, dropping their bombs on slow-descending parachutes to allow themselves a few more seconds to escape being blown up by their own weapons as they fly away beneath the spreading mushroom clouds.

All of this will be easier on bomber crews in the future, as air-launched cruise missiles, which can be dropped 1,500 miles from their targets at the edge of Soviet airspace and then continue on their own, are now being fitted on some B-52s. In the meantime, every SAC bomber is equipped, for the benefit of those who do not make it out of Russia, with down sleeping bags, a saw, rations, a life raft, and .38-calibre pistols. Every parachute pack contains a water carrier and three fishhooks. And every crewman is given, and carries in his wallet, a little card (SAC Form 673) headed "Radiation Data." The card lists thirty-one tips for surviving if forced down in territory that may be radioactive. "Make [a] shelter large enough to rest," it says. "Lie down, keep warm and rest/sleep as much as possible. . . . Potatoes, turnips, carrots and other plants whose edible portions were growing underground during the fallout period are edible. . . . Avoid traveling within ten miles of any known ground zero. . . . Be alert for enemy warning signs marking any contaminated areas. . . . STAY COOL, USE YOUR HEAD, YOU WILL SURVIVE."

While bombers are screaming in over the Russian treetops, past radioactive wastelands created a few hours before by American missiles, many other American bombers and missiles will still be waiting. The first American nuclear strike against the Soviet Union will be a limited one. The National Command Authority who orders it will be sending not only weapons against Russia; he will also be sending a message. The scope of the message will depend upon what the NCA is responding to—a massive Russian attack, a smaller Russian attack, an anticipated Russian attack, or no attack at all. In any case, the purpose of the first American strike will not be to bring about the end of Russia, but rather to bring about the end of the war.

The theory behind this is known as "escalation control" (because control is at the heart of it) or "intrawar deterrence" (because deterrence theory, even after failing to prevent an initial nuclear attack, will not be abandoned). It was spelled out at some length by Secretary of Defense Harold Brown in his annual report to Congress for fiscal year 1982: "Plans for the controlled use of nuclear weapons, along with other appropriate military and political actions, would enable us to provide leverage for a negotiated termination of the fighting. At an early stage in the conflict, we must convince the enemy that further escalation will not result in achievement of his objectives, that it will not mean 'success,' but rather additional costs. To do this, we must leave the enemy with sufficient highly valued military, economic, and political resources still surviving but still clearly at risk, so that he has a strong incentive to seek an end to the conflict." So we will not hit the Soviets with everything we have; we will hit them selectively and let them know that we retain the ability to hit them with everything we have. And this will "provide leverage for a negotiated termination of the fighting."

Brown himself doubted that this strategy could ever work. "I remain highly skeptical that escalation of a limited nuclear exchange can be controlled, or that it can be stopped short of an all-out massive exchange," he wrote in the paragraph preceding the one above. A few months later, a Senate committee asked the new secretary of defense, Caspar Weinberger, if he believed a limited nuclear exchange could remain limited. "Senator," he replied, "I cannot even win a wager on a presidential election, so I don't have any idea what the odds would be on that." Soon after, however, in his first annual report to Congress, he reaffirmed that one purpose of American nuclear weapons is "to impose termination of a major war—on terms favorable to the United States and our allies—even if nuclear weapons have been used—and in particular to deter escalation in the level of hostilities."

Critics of both the Carter and Reagan administrations have denounced such thinking as dangerous madness. "Once a nuclear war started," former defense secretary Robert McNamara wrote in 1983, "there would be no way to contain it." Soviet officials have said the same thing. Possible drawbacks of the policy were considered (at least in the Carter administration) even by the men who made it. But policy debates are beside the point. The operational plans for limited nuclear war fighting have been made, and in place, for years.

They are being maintained right now by the three hundred men and women of the Joint Strategic Target Planning Staff in their offices at SAC headquarters. The full-time job of the JSTPS is assembling two "products": the National Strategic Target List (NSTL), a list of more than forty thousand places and things in Russia, Eastern Europe, and elsewhere deemed worthy of being destroyed in a nuclear war, and the Single Integrated Operational Plan (SIOP), the plan for destroying the places and things on the NSTL. This curious task of selection and planning is carried on with the aid of powerful computers, based on intelligence gathered by reconnaissance satellites and aircraft, and worked out in meticulous detail. "The NSTL," says a former defense consultant who has seen part of it, "includes every damn bridge in the Soviet Union, and not just the big ones. The location of every target is spelled out precisely, and they're all ranked according to importance." The SIOP, which Air Force press releases describe as "one of the most comprehensive plans ever conceived," carefully matches Soviet targets with the American weapons most suitable for destroying them (e.g., fast-arriving, relatively accurate Minuteman warheads set to explode at ground level to attack "hard, time-urgent" targets like Soviet ICBM silos; late-arriving airplane-dropped bombs set to explode in the air to attack "soft," dispersed, non-urgent targets like oil refineries). The effectiveness of the SIOP is regularly tested in computerized war games, in which the SIOP faces off against the RISOP (the presumed Red Integrated Strategic Operational Plan), winners determined, and the SIOP revised accordingly.

In the early days of American nuclear planning, the forerunners of the SIOP were devoted mainly to wreaking the greatest possible destruction on the Soviet Union in the shortest possible time, only taking care to organize things so that, a SAC officer explains, "you don't have one bomber dropping a one-megaton bomb and blowing another American bomber four miles away out of the sky." Over two decades, however, the SIOP has evolved from concentrating on a single massive attack to an emphasis on options and selectivity. "Our planning must provide a continuum of options, ranging from use of small numbers of strategic and/or theater nuclear weapons aimed at narrowly defined targets, to employment of large portions of our nuclear forces against a broad spectrum of targets," explained Secretary Brown. Taken as a whole, the SIOP is still a blueprint for attacking every target for which the United States has a weapon, but the total attack set has been broken into dozens of subsets—limited attack options that can be exercised individually or combined for attacks of any type and size desired.

To begin, the targets on the NSTL have been sorted into categories. First are Soviet nuclear forces, including missile silos and launch control centers, bomber and submarine bases, and nuclear weapon storage depots. Next are the nonnuclear military forces of Russia and other Warsaw Pact nations, including airfields, ammunition dumps, and places where tanks and troops are expected to gather in wartime. Third are the command posts that will house Soviet political and military leaders and the communications systems that will serve them. All such "organs of Soviet political and military leadership and control" have been emphasized in recent targeting plans, Secretary Brown told a Senate committee in 1980, because "in a time of great crisis what [Soviet leaders] most need to be deterred by is the thought that their power structure will not survive. That is even more important to them than their personal survival or survival of ten, twenty, or thirty million, or even fifty million of their fellow countrymen.... What most motivates them ... is their own personal power in a way that is not easily understood by someone who has come up through the American system." ("You have never run for the Senate; I can see that," replied Senator Paul Tsongas.)

The final category of targets is the one that has been on the list the longest—the facilities that make up Russia's industrial and economic base. Included are those that will contribute to the Russian war effort, such as oil refineries and truck factories, as well as those that will contribute to postwar recovery, such as fertilizer plants.

Russian *people* are not on the target list; cities will only be attacked because they happen to be where factories, airfields, warehouses, command posts, and other targets are found.

Working from the NSTL, SIOP planners have come up with a varied and flexible menu of attack options. "We plan to put together targeting packages that are building blocks that can be tailored to a situation," Harold Brown said in 1980. The result is new possibilities for a limited—and long—nuclear war. The United States must have the ability, according to a secret Reagan administration document leaked to *The New York Times,* to mount "controlled nuclear counterattacks over a protracted period."

In the field, America's nuclear forces are preparing to fight that war. "Back in the early sixties, it was common to say, 'We'll fight our war in ten minutes,' " says Lieutenant Colonel Paul Murphy, who was a missile crewman then and now is assistant deputy commander for operations of the 90th Strategic Missile Wing at F. E. Warren Air Force Base in Cheyenne, Wyoming. "Those were the days of massive retaliation. Now execution planning has become a lot more sophisticated, and the president has a lot more options than he used to."

One limitation on the president in the old days was technical. Each missile had only a single warhead with two preset targets. "It was simple," says Murphy's boss, Colonel Robert Gifford. "We'd hit a switch for target one or target two." And the missile would head off for one or the other. "We were considered to be a one-shot artillery piece buried in the ground," says another former missile crewman. "We were not responsive."

Today each of the two hundred Minuteman III missiles at the Warren base—a one-time cavalry post where the base liquor store is now called "Ground Zero"—has three independently targeted warheads. (Minutemen II missiles still have one; the MX missile is designed to have ten.) Each warhead can be sent to any one of four preset targets.* If those four are not enough, the Command Data Buffer system installed in launch control centers in the 1970s can re-

---

* "The average crew member doesn't care what the targets are," says Lieutenant Colonel Murphy. "It just doesn't seem that important." "The crews don't want to know the targets," says another former missile crewman. "They've said to me, 'That way I won't dream about the impact area.' "

166

target any missile remotely in thirty-six minutes. (To retarget a missile in the old days, the missile had to be taken off alert while a crew entered its silo and physically made the changes; the process took up to twenty-four hours.) This enables missile targets to be changed even after nuclear war has begun. "Political scientists can debate forever about what kind of targets you should pick," says Gifford, "but you never can tell what the target base is going to look like if it should ever come time to use the missiles. We want the flexibility to go after targets that are important to the war effort we might be involved in."

In pursuit of that flexibility, two hundred different SIOP attack options have been prepared and prestored in missile launch control center computers. "A plan will target the missiles, and time them [so you don't have American missiles flying into other American missiles over the targets], and hold some that are not being used in that war plan," says Gifford.

Exercising the plan will be easy. "If you get the message, say, to fight war number thirty-seven," says Murphy, "you'll dial it up, and those missiles that are supposed to go, go, and those that aren't, don't."

American bombers meanwhile will be heading toward their own carefully defined target sets. "The range of options for a particular sortie is pretty limited," says Lieutenant Colonel James Davis, chief of operations plans for the 42d Bombardment Wing at Loring Air Force Base in Limestone, Maine. "The ECM [electronic countermeasures] and navigation systems for each aircraft are set up for a specific corridor and a series of targets in that corridor. The EAM will tell the crew what to hit and what to bypass. But there's no way to tell a sortie to Leningrad to go to Moscow instead. . . . The map in the crew mission folder is of a corridor less than eighty miles wide, so if it's captured it will give away no information relating to other sorties.

"Each sortie is built for a purpose and may involve only six or eight airplanes. Every sortie must be target-pure; the planners spend a lot of time keeping them that way. One series might be Soviet weapon storage areas; another might be areas where you expect conventional forces to be massed. Say the Russians just wiped out four of our satellites and we've worked to put more up, and to show our intent [not to be intimidated] we want to go in and hit a limited objective, maybe their laser research facilities. We want to make that a surgical strike, so you don't get collateral damage of another type of target."

This will be one of the trickiest parts of fighting a limited nuclear war. It is one thing to plan an attack that is limited to laser research facilities. It is another to hit those facilities without a stray missile going haywire and landing in downtown Leningrad, especially if one of the facilities happens to be *near* downtown Leningrad. (And many important military and political targets in Russia are near population centers.)

Trickier still will be making sure Russian authorities understand that our limited attack is limited. When they see a flock of American missiles and bombers on their radar screens, and then begin to receive what will almost inevitably be vague and confusing reports of nuclear weapons exploding on Russian soil, they may not have the information to make fine distinctions about what kind of attack it is (or be in any mood to do so). In accordance with the limited-war theory articulated by Harold Brown, an initial American nuclear attack will spare "highly valued military, economic, and political resources," leaving them "still clearly at risk, so that [Russia] has a strong incentive to seek an end to the conflict." But it will all be for nought if the Russians cannot get a clear picture of what has happened, or do not believe the one they do get.

"The doctrine [of limited nuclear war] requires knowledge on the part of the other side of what our intent is when we initiate a certain option," SAC Commander in Chief General Richard Ellis told a Senate committee in 1981. So every effort will be made to see that the enemy gets that knowledge. "If he is unable to understand the intent," Ellis continued, "then in my opinion. . . ." At this point in the hearing transcript a censor deleted the rest of the sentence. But it is clear that what must follow will not be a happy turn of events either for limited-war theory or the American people.

"We'll be extremely careful to make sure all their command and control facilities are left intact, so they'll be able to perceive that our attack is limited to one particular target set, so we don't get into a war we don't want to fight," says Lieutenant Colonel Davis. To make the message explicit, the American president may simply call the Russians (or try to) and *tell* them what we have done, why we have done it, and what we might do next if the war continues.

Whether the Russians get the message will depend primarily on the capabilities of Russian "C^3" (Command, Control, and Communications), the name given to the systems by which military and political leaders will be sending out orders and receiving information. These will not be easy tasks in the middle of a nuclear war. Radar networks, satellite ground stations, and satellites themselves—all vital for spotting and assessing an incoming attack—may be among the first targets. Command posts and communications lines, even if not targeted deliberately, will be destroyed when they are located near other targets, and may be destroyed by errant missiles when they are not. Even if the American attack succeeds in leaving every Soviet C^3 facility intact, the facilities may still be degraded by nuclear weapons exploding dozens—or even hundreds—of miles away. Nuclear explosions disrupt the electrical properties of the atmosphere, interfering with long-distance radio and radar. High-altitude nuclear explosions also produce a lightninglike phenomenon called electromagnetic pulse (EMP) that can destroy unprotected electrical equipment—computers and other modern solid-state electronic devices are particularly vulnerable—over great distances; a 1962 nuclear test 248 miles over the Pacific caused street lights to fail and burglar alarms to ring in Hawaii, eight hundred miles away.

Even if every bit of Russian C^3 equipment is shielded against EMP, and is not targeted directly by American forces, and is not hit by accident, it still may not furnish Russian commanders with complete and accurate information. In *ordinary* wars messages are mislaid and misunderstood. (During the 1975 *Mayaguez* affair, American forces bombed Cambodian territory thirty minutes after President Gerald Ford ordered a halt to all attacks.) A nuclear war will have unpredictable effects on the people operating the equipment (and on national leaders). People will make mistakes; people will be confused; people will be vengeful; people will run outside and try to find their families.

All of these problems will also complicate American efforts to understand what is happening. It will be important for the president, in selecting among his SIOP options, to know if a Russian attack has destroyed half a dozen missile silos, or if it has destroyed

Detroit. If Detroit *has* been destroyed, he can't call somebody there to find out. To provide this kind of information, the Air Force maintains a classified program called Continental Airborne Reconnaissance and Damage Assessment; Air Force planes will fly over the spot where Detroit used to be and look for it. The United States is also installing Integrated Operational Nuclear Detonation Detection System (IONDS) sensors on navigation satellites; IONDS will detect nuclear blasts anywhere in the world and relay the information to earth, if the satellite earth stations have not been destroyed. This will, says the Pentagon, "provide nuclear trans- and post-attack damage assessment information to the NCA in a nuclear war, including protracted global conflict, to support force management decisions." Aboard the Looking Glass plane, meanwhile, Major Stalcup will be conducting his launch poll: "We'll get NUDET [nuclear detonation] information a number of ways. We'll contact all the launch centers we can and see if they might have heard from other launch centers. It's very possible that people might be there but you can't contact them. We could call someone and have them drive out and see if something is there. And we'll get information from *lack* of information. If we can't talk to the underground [SAC headquarters], we'll assume it's been blown up."

Once the NCA has figured out what is going on and decided on a response, the American attack order will go out over more than forty different channels, including SAC's Primary Alerting System and the Emergency Rocket Communications System. Unfortunately, SAC Commander Ellis warned in 1981, existing American C^3 systems "are essentially soft, fragile peacetime systems, conceived in the late 1950s and put into operation in the 1960s. Most are located at fixed sites or depend on ground communications networks and, like all terrestrial sites, are highly vulnerable to attack and destruction."

The systems were designed that way, Ellis explained, because they were conceived before the United States started preparing to fight a limited, protracted nuclear war. "We designed our command and control system to launch the force in a massive strike.... We were only worried about getting the message out. We were not worried about survival of that system. Today, our nuclear strategy has changed under national directive to the point where we are required

170

to have a flexible plan, to have options available to the president, to have an enduring capability that can last for an indefinite period, and to be able to exercise control over a reconstituted force after perhaps several exchanges."

Survivable C^3 is essential for all of this. "If deterrence fails," the Pentagon stated in 1981, "C^3 must provide the information, command facilities, and communications necessary to fight a nuclear war." Without C^3, the war will not be *fought* so much as just *happen*, in a chaos of uncontrolled, unlimited nuclear destruction.

And so lots of time and money have gone into developing C^3 systems that will survive the first round (and second, and third) of a long nuclear war. Looking Glass and NEACP planes are being shielded against EMP. (To study EMP effects on airplanes in flight, they are wheeled out onto a huge wooden structure in the New Mexico desert and zapped by two five-million-volt EMP simulators.) The Looking Glass and NEACP planes have been equipped with satellite communications terminals and five-mile-long Trailing Wire Antennas to unreel behind them as they fly to broadcast Emergency Action Messages on the very-low-frequency band. Communications satellites have been tested for EMP resistance by hanging them in caverns beneath the surface of the Nevada desert during underground nuclear tests. To talk to submerged submarines during a nuclear war, the Navy is building a huge antenna farm in the Midwest for extremely-low-frequency radio transmission and is experimenting with a system to shine laser beams up to space and reflect them off mirrors on satellites back down to the oceans. The Pentagon is experimenting with a radio system that will bounce its signals off ionized trails created by meteors while normal radio channels are disrupted by exploding nuclear weapons.

These programs and others are part of an $18 billion effort announced by the Reagan administration in 1981 to "upgrade the survivability and capability of command centers that would direct U.S. strategic forces during a nuclear war" and develop "a communications and control system that would endure for an extended period beyond the first nuclear attack." Part of that system will be a new generation of relatively invulnerable communications satellites, Secretary of Defense Caspar Weinberger promised in 1982, "so the President's orders can be passed from the national command center to the commanders of our forces and the forces themselves, and so we can better manage our forces in a protracted war."

After the first American salvo of the protracted nuclear war, there will be—if all goes well—an eerie pause. Aboard the president's or NCA's National Emergency Airborne Command Post, aboard the Looking Glass plane, in the National Military Command Center in the Pentagon, in the underground Alternate National Military Command Center at Fort Ritchie, Maryland, in every surviving missile launch control center and submarine and SAC command post, people will be waiting and watching for the Russians' next step. And wondering: Did the Russians understand that our attack was limited? Do they understand that we retain (at least for the moment) the ability to hit surviving highly valued targets if the war does not stop? Do they *care*?

There will also be questions about conditions more concrete than Russian generals' states of mind. Did our forces hit the targets at which they were aimed? Where are they now? What is destroyed? Who is dead?

Aboard the Looking Glass plane, the battle staff will be searching for this information to plan the next round of the war, if one is necessary. "Initially we'll only know what they have left because we'll know which of our forces didn't get off the ground," says Major Jennings. "Later bomber crews will come back and we'll get reconnaissance information. . . . The whole idea of our force is deterrence. But, should that fail, we'll want to maximize our situation relative to the Soviets postwar, post-SIOP."

"Our computer can come up with a listing of targets that have not been covered," says Major Stalcup. "The intelligence officer will suggest priorities and whether we have anything worth going back for and taking out. Then we come up with a plan and brief the general. If the general says yes, he asks the JCS for authority. They may have more data. Meanwhile we'll have sent messages to bomber units. We'll already have calculated with the TI-59 that they can make it to new targets. But now the unit will look at the plan and decide, yes, we can do it, or no, we can't."

The first bomber units the Looking Glass will contact will be those that did not take part in the previous attack, that took off from their bases and went into holding "buggy ride" orbits instead of flying to Russia. The Looking Glass will also be calling, for attack coordination, the Navy TACAMO planes flying over the oceans to relay messages to submarines still waiting underwater for their turns to fire. It may not be easy to communicate with the submarines, however. Present systems require them to send an antenna buoy up near the surface to receive messages, and such a buoy might advertise their presence to Soviet forces hunting them. The Navy says it is confident it can keep in touch with submarines throughout a nuclear war. (It will not say what a submarine captain is supposed to do with his missiles if suddenly all radio traffic stops and he suspects war has begun.) And the submarines are considered especially valuable for the latter rounds of a nuclear war. "The SLBM [submarine-launched ballistic missile] force ... is highly survivable at sea and able to endure without support for relatively long periods should a conflict erupt," the Joint Chiefs of Staff have reported. "These characteristics allow submarines to continue operations and to retarget their ballistic missiles as necessary to meet new objectives even after land-based systems have been neutralized or expended."

Stationary land-based missiles like the Minuteman will be the easiest for an enemy to "neutralize" because they will be the easiest for an enemy to find. To make things a little bit tougher for an attacker, the Minuteman force was given some extra protection against blast, shock, radiation, and EMP by a Silo Upgrade Program completed in 1980. Instead of sitting rigidly in their silos, the missiles are now slung on massive cables and braced with rubber and crushable foam. The 110-ton steel-and-concrete doors that cover the silos have been made harder. ("They protect the missiles from snow and rain and everything, and also from thermonuclear blast," a missile technician explained to a visitor at F. E. Warren Air Force Base.) When the signal to launch arrives, they will be yanked forward by an exploding pulley mechanism with enough force to push through a pile of postattack rubble. A sort of cowcatcher scoop will jut out of the door to catch debris that might otherwise fall into the silo and mess up the launch.

While unused missiles are swaying gently in their slings to the rhythm of Russian hydrogen bombs exploding nearby, surviving missile launch crews will be sitting tight in their aircraft-style seats, lap and shoulder belts fastened to keep them from being thrown to the floor by the shock waves. Their launch control capsules are mounted on giant shock absorbers. The above-ground antennas over which crews will receive high-frequency radio transmissions are built to break away. If one is blasted off, the crewmen can push a button and another will pop up. If that one is destroyed by the next incoming missile, another push will pop up another antenna. There are five in all. And the crewmen will ride it all out. "They will stay at the switch," says Colonel Gifford. "There are provisions for them to survive for an extended period of time. If there are any remaining missiles unexecuted, or missiles that were supposed to be executed but were unable to go and work is needed to make them operational, the crews will stay in their capsules until they are relieved." Or "neutralized."

And what are they supposed to do after their missiles are fired?

"Frankly," says Colonel Gifford, "not a great deal. But these gentlemen do not become civilians. Like anyone else in the military, they'd report to the nearest command center, which in their case is F. E. Warren Air Force Base, if we still have a viable command center here. If their commanding officer is not around, they'd report to the next in command and on down the line, even if those in the capsules were themselves the highest ranking."

In fact, says a former missile crewman, "We were only trained to the point of execution. There is an escape hatch to the surface, filled with sand to prevent blast damage, but we never trained with it. The crew has big poles to poke the sand out. But I think in a NUDET [nuclear detonation] sand will turn to glass. The launch control center also has emergency rations, and a .22 rifle. The idea is you can shoot rabbits with it."

While the missilemen are searching for a senior officer—or a rabbit—American submarines that have fired all their missiles will turn into attack submarines and start searching for Russian ships to sink. (The American subs are equipped with torpedoes as well as long-range missiles.)

Any American bombers that survive after hitting their targets will be flying out of Russia toward preselected recovery bases in Europe, Africa, and the Middle East. "It *may* be in an allied country

174

where we expect to have poststrike support," says Colonel Davis at Loring Air Force Base. "But there is fuel available all over the world." Wherever they land, the planes will be met—if all goes according to plan—by bomber recovery teams dispatched from their home air bases. They will be refueled and repaired, and reconnaissance photos they took during their missions will be removed for analysis. Then they will fly back to the United States to land at surviving airstrips, where they will be met by the Alternate Reconstitution Base teams that left their home bases to hide in the woods during the prewar crisis. Among the supplies the ARB teams will bring will be new nuclear weapons. The planes will be rearmed and made ready to attack once again.

"Everybody jokes that Tahiti will be the world's leading nuclear power after the war," says Colonel Davis, "because all the planes will go there. But I think they'll come home. Despite what's said, the American family is still important. [Air Force dependents will, like other civilians, participate in Crisis Relocation during the prewar crisis.] Also, I think there'll be a lot of curiosity to see if Chicago is still there."

And everybody will be waiting and getting ready for the next round of the war, and the round after that.

"Once initial execution is complete," SAC Commander Ellis said in 1981, "we must have sufficient feedback data and intelligence information to evaluate not only the effects of our retaliatory attack on the enemy but also our own resources remaining to continue the war. . . . Finally, we need communications in the trans- and postattack period to reconstitute our surviving forces, generate follow-on sorties and retarget our forces, as required. This complicated cycle is then repeated until hostilities are terminated."

How long might this go on?

A congressional General Accounting Office study of American nuclear strategy confirmed that the strategy "presumes that a protracted period of nuclear exchanges could occur." In the course of their research, GAO investigators spoke to officials of the Pentagon, the Joint Chiefs of Staff, the Joint Strategic Target Planning Staff, SAC, the Navy, and others. "We found no consensus on how long a protracted period might be," they reported. "Estimates ranged up to 180 days."

EIGHT

"We Sound a Little Crazy"

Dr. Edward Teller, the man popularly known as "the father of the hydrogen bomb," was carrying an old patched suitcase through Washington's National Airport on an autumn afternoon in 1981. He had come to Washington for a meeting of the FEMA Advisory Board, and now he was hurrying to catch the shuttle flight to New York. Although he had a small wheeled luggage cart with him, he was not using it to carry his bag. "It is not good on stairs," he explained to a reporter who was accompanying him (the departure gate was one flight down), "and they don't like it at check-in. So I separate it from the suitcase here and rejoin them at LaGuardia."

The reporter, anxious to keep up his end of the conversation, smiled brightly and groped for something to say to the world-famous physicist about his luggage cart.

"I've seen many stewardesses with them," he finally blurted out, "so I gather they must be very useful."

"Yes," Teller nodded, "a more useful invention than the hydrogen bomb."

Teller was correct, of course. You can carry a suitcase with a ten-dollar luggage cart, but what can you do with a hydrogen bomb? You can build the bombs and attach them to missiles and load them into airplanes, and you can *threaten* to use them against an enemy, but when your enemy has a few thousand hydrogen bombs of his own and will fire his at you if you fire yours at him, how can you ever actually *use* the damn things?

To some people, this problem has seemed to be no problem at

all but a solution. If hydrogen bombs are too horrible to use, and the world's major powers are armed with them, then it follows that the world's major powers cannot go to war. The horrible weapons have made war impossible, and good riddance.

This line of reasoning was adopted, even before the existence of the hydrogen bomb, by many Manhattan Project scientists in 1945. They argued that the atomic bomb should be dropped on Japan so the world would see how awful it was and thus learn that another world war was out of the question. Among those making this argument was Edward Teller. "If we have a slim chance of survival, it lies in the possibility to get rid of wars . . . ," Teller wrote to Leo Szilard a few weeks before the bombing of Hiroshima. "Our only hope is in getting the facts of our results before the people. This might help to convince everybody that the next war would be fatal. For this purpose actual combat-use might even be the best thing."

This view was repeated, not as a hope but as a prediction, by no less a military authority than General Henry Arnold, commander of the U.S. Army Air Forces, at a press conference a few days after the bombing of Nagasaki. Weapons of the future, Arnold said, would include "improved atomic bombs . . . destructive beyond the wildest nightmares of the imagination" and guided missiles able to carry them to almost any spot on earth. "What I am trying to tell you," he concluded, "is that this thing is so terrible in its aspects that there may not be any more wars."

A few years later, when it appeared that the world had not yet gotten the message, at least one young scientist working on those improved atomic bombs still clung to the end-of-war rationale. "A full-scale war between Russia and the U.S., in which A-bombs in their present form were used, would make this world unliveable, as far as I am concerned," physicist Theodore Taylor wrote to his parents in 1949. "And yet people in Congress (and, I suppose, in the Kremlin) talk about a future war as something indeed horrible—*but* they talk in terms of preparing to win it. . . . I think that there is only one realistic way to avoid war, and that is to make the world really afraid of it. . . . [T]here is only one thing to do: develop a bomb which will leave no doubt in *anyone's* mind."

By the end of the 1950s, this seemed finally to have been achieved. Hydrogen bombs were perfected and deployed. The threat of fallout had entered public consciousness. Popular movies and books depicted nuclear war as an end-of-the-world event. And political leaders—the men who could start a nuclear war, or not start one—routinely spoke of such a war as being too terrible to contemplate. The superpowers found themselves suspended in the uneasy stability of mutual deterrence—"where safety will be the sturdy child of terror," Churchill said, "and survival the twin brother of annihilation"—an uneasy stability that persists to this day.

But some people were not happy with the idea that nuclear weapons had made war unthinkable. They *missed* war. They didn't miss the death and destruction, and they didn't actually want to have a war. They wanted to avoid war as much as anybody else, they said. But they missed the diplomatic and political utility of the threat of war. If war had truly been made impossible, then much of international power politics was out the window. If war had become so awful that no national leader would ever start one, then all threats of war, explicit or implicit, were hollow and everyone would know it. "The more powerful the weapons . . . ," Henry Kissinger wrote in 1957, "the greater becomes the reluctance to use them. At a period of unparalleled military strength, President Dwight D. Eisenhower summed up the dilemma posed by the new weapons technology in the phrase 'there is no alternative to peace.' "

Kissinger sought a way out of this dilemma. His 1957 book, *Nuclear Weapons and Foreign Policy*, which grew out of a study group at the Council on Foreign Relations, was representative of the views of those who found the dilemma crippling. "The enormity of modern weapons makes the thought of all-out war repugnant," Kissinger wrote, "but the refusal to run any risks would amount to handing the Soviet leaders a blank check. . . . As the power of modern weapons grows, the threat of all-out war loses its credibility and therefore its political effectiveness." Credibility was the central problem here. The United States could threaten to go to war if the Soviet Union seized Berlin, say, or encouraged Communist rebels in some third-world country. But who would believe the threat? "Who can be certain," Kissinger asked, "that, faced with the catastrophe of all-out war, even Europe, long the keystone of our security, will seem worth the price?" The United States will be excessively cautious in confronting the Soviets, he warned, "if we must weigh each objective against the destruction of New York or Detroit, of Los Angeles or Chicago." This might encourage the Russians "to absorb the peripheral areas of Eurasia by means short of all-out war and to confront us with the choice of yielding or facing the destruction of American cities."

The solution to this problem, Kissinger concluded, was for the United States to develop strategies for using its military power, including its nuclear weapons, in less than full force. "Strategy can assist policy," he wrote, "only by developing a maximum number of stages between total peace (which may mean total surrender) and total war. It can increase the willingness of policy-makers to run risks only if it can demonstrate other means of preventing amputations [of the Free World by Russia] than the threat of suicide."

Kissinger and other nuclear strategists of the late 1950s thus began a quest that continues to this day. While the popular image of a nuclear stalemate has persisted—encouraged by the statements, if not always the actions, of political leaders—planners have spent twenty-five years looking for ways in which nuclear weapons can actually be used. Because a threat to launch total nuclear war may not be believed (because it is a threat to commit suicide), the United States has fashioned a range of threats for limited nuclear war. To make *those* threats credible, nuclear strategists have had to try to figure out just what kind of thing a limited nuclear war might be, and how such a thing could be fought, and how and why it would not automatically escalate into an all-out nuclear war. Over the years, the planners have devised scenarios for nuclear wars limited to specific geographic areas (like Europe and Iran), and they have concentrated lately on scenarios for nuclear wars that would reach the heartlands of the United States and Russia yet still remain limited. The threats to use nuclear weapons in limited geographic areas have been designed to deter Russian attacks in those areas. The threat to launch limited nuclear attacks against the Soviet Union itself has been designed to deter a limited nuclear attack by Russia against the United States (although exactly why the Russians might do such a thing has never been made clear).

"I don't see why we need to give more credibility to the fact that we might be willing to consider a limited exchange," protested Senator John Glenn during a 1980 Senate hearing at which Secretary of Defense Harold Brown explained the then-latest wrinkle in American planning for limited nuclear war. "It seems to me," Glenn said, "that the greatest deterrent we have is saying, 'If you ever drop a bomb on Atlanta; Columbus, Ohio; or in the desert someplace, you can expect that we may take out all your cities, we may take out all your missiles. . . .'"

"If you were in the Soviet Union," Brown replied, "and you heard that the Americans swore up and down that if one Minuteman site was taken out, then the Soviet Union would be visited with 100 million casualties, would that deter you from that one attack, or would you say that is not credible and the Americans are bluffing?"

Glenn: "It surely would give me more pause if I were a Soviet planner putting out a new directive than one which indicates, 'If you take out one site, we will respond by taking out a railhead or something like that.'"

Brown: "No. Let us have an example, that the Soviets take out one hundred Minutemen and our alternatives are only to do nothing or to go to an all-out urban-industrial attack. I think we might very well be deterred from [making the all-out attack], and I think they are smart enough to know that. I think it is important that they know that there are lots of other things we can do. . . . I think that is more credible than saying, 'No matter what you do, it is immediately going to lead to an all-out attack.' . . . In other words, 'Don't think that an attack on us will leave us with no options other than an immediate, mutual suicide option.'"

Glenn: "I get lost in what is credible and not credible. This whole thing gets so incredible when you consider wiping out whole nations, it is difficult to establish credibility."

Brown: "That is why we sound a little crazy when we talk about it."

Three months after the bombings of Hiroshima and Nagasaki, *Life* magazine offered its readers a profusely illustrated rendering of the war of the future, a war that would be fought with atomic bombs and missiles "so swift and terrible that the war might well be decided in 36 hours." One illustration showed "the U.S. as it might appear a very few years from now, with a great shower of enemy rockets falling on 13 key U.S. centers." Another showed a grotesquely costumed enemy soldier standing over the body of a blond American switchboard operator (in a tight sweater) killed at her post by one of those atomic rockets. "By the time enemy troops have landed ... some 40,000,000 people have been killed and all cities of more than 50,000 population have been leveled," said the text. (Nevertheless, a seemingly tacked-on conclusion assured that the United States was doing the same to the enemy and would emerge from the war victorious.)

The best defense against such a catastrophic attack, the magazine quoted General Henry Arnold as saying, "will rest on our ability to take immediate offensive action with overwhelming force. It must be apparent to a potential aggressor that an attack on the United States would be immediately followed by an immensely devastating air-atomic attack on him."

This is the logic of nuclear deterrence in its most basic form: that no nation will dare launch a nuclear attack against another if it can expect nuclear retaliation. The possession of nuclear weapons by one nation thus deters the use of nuclear weapons by others. And this, political scientist Bernard Brodie wrote in a widely quoted 1946 essay, is the only thing nuclear weapons are good for: "Thus far the chief purpose of a military establishment has been to win wars. From now on its chief purpose must be to avert them. It can have no other useful purpose."

Deterrence has been the cornerstone of American nuclear policy ever since. Liberals have accepted it as the best deal one can get in a nuclear-armed world, and even the most bellicose military hard-liners have felt obligated at least to pay lip service to the concept. (The two camps disagree, however, as to what constitutes an adequate deterrent.) But in the immediate aftermath of World War II the concept was a little premature. The United States was the only nation that had nuclear weapons; it could have used them freely without fear of retaliation. There was, of course, no war in which to use them, but planning proceeded nonetheless. A few weeks after the bombing of Hiroshima, the U.S. Army Air Forces prepared a draft study of American atom bomb stockpile needs for "the interim post-war era." "It is assumed," said the study, which was declassified in 1975, "that the United States may be required to conduct military operations against any other nation or combination of nations in the world [and that] the initial mission of the air force units allocated for preparation, transportation, and delivery of these atomic bombs should be the immediate destruction of the enemy centers of industry, transportation and population. An exhaustive analysis of the strategic vulnerability of all the nations of the world would require extensive research." To save time, the study said, it had analyzed the vulnerabilities of only one nation—Russia.

The study proceeded to list 66 Russian cities that produced most or all of the Soviet Union's aircraft, tanks, guns, trucks, steel, oil, aluminum, and so on. From the 66, it selected the 15 most important. "Based on our experience with the bombs dropped to date [in Japan]," it said, "three well-placed bombs would throw a modern city of any size into chaos and definitely incapacitate it for an appreciable period of time. Four of these cities would require only two bombs and one city only one bomb to completely destroy them." Adding up, the study found that 39 bombs would be needed to destroy those 15 cities. Ten bombs were allotted for the destruction of overseas air bases the Russians might establish for counterattacks on the United States. Another 10 bombs were allotted to hinder Russian troops on the move outside Russia (possible targets included the Dardanelles and the Suez Canal). Figuring that 48 percent of the American bombs would hit their targets (the rest would fall wide or would be on bombers that were shot down), the planners concluded that the American nuclear stockpile at the outbreak of the war should consist of at least 123 bombs. The ideal stockpile, with enough weapons to destroy the 66 most important Russian cities, would have 466 bombs.

The study was sent to General Leslie Groves, commander of the Manhattan Project, for comment. He replied that he found its requirements too high. The planners, he said, had underestimated the power of the atomic bomb. ("While at Hiroshima the frames of a number of reinforced concrete buildings remained intact the windows were blown out and the interiors were gutted," he noted.) Groves did not point out another flaw in the report—that the United States was not prepared at that time to manufacture 466 atomic bombs, 123, or even 23. The bombs dropped on Japan had been painstakingly assembled by scientists in laboratories, not manufactured on assembly lines, and it was a long time before the production process was speeded up. According to documents obtained by historian David Alan Rosenberg, in the fall of 1945 the United States possessed no more than two atomic bombs, if it had that many. As late as June 1947, it had only thirteen. This scarcity was probably the most closely guarded secret in the United States at the time. When President Truman was told of the actual size of the American atomic stockpile in early 1947, he was visibly shocked.

Meanwhile, Pentagon planners (who were denied access to the stockpile figures) were writing a series of plans for the next war. The role ascribed by the plans to the atomic bomb depended in part on which service was doing the planning. (The Army Air Force, later the U.S. Air Force, was the most enthusiastic about the new weapon because it had the most to do with delivering it.) Some military men downplayed the role of the bomb because they were reluctant to give up traditional ideas about war fighting or were afraid that the public might decide that the fantastic new weapon made large conventional forces unnecessary. In January 1946, Army Chief of Staff Dwight Eisenhower felt compelled to protest to the Joint Chiefs of Staff about their tendency "to depreciate the importance of the development of atomic weapons and to insist unnecessarily strongly that the conventional armed services will not be eliminated."

A few months later, the tests at Bikini demonstrated the power of the new weapon in a way the Pentagon could not ignore; General Curtis LeMay (who would become commander of the new Strategic Air Command in 1948) reported afterward that atomic bombs could "nullify any nation's military effort and demolish its social and economic structures" and made it possible to "depopulate vast areas of the earth's surface, leaving only vestigial remnants of man's material works." Plans for atomic bombing became part of every American war plan (although it would be several years before SAC had the planes, crews, bases, or bombs needed to carry out the planned attacks).

Ambivalence about the new weapon persisted, however, and was still apparent in 1949 when the Joint Chiefs of Staff prepared Plan Dropshot, a blueprint for a war against the Soviet Union assumed to begin on January 1, 1957. The war envisioned by Dropshot looked a lot like World War II. It was assumed that World War

III would begin with a successful Russian invasion of Western Europe, the Middle East, and Korea, and that it might last for several years.

Dropshot also assumed that the war would be atomic. Russian "air attacks, with the probable employment of atomic bombs and biological and chemical agents," were to be expected against the United States and Canada, it said. Complete protection against such attacks (via fighter planes and antiaircraft artillery) would not be "practicable" because it would tie up so many resources for defense that it would "weaken dangerously our offensive capabilities." Less important areas and installations would therefore have to be left undefended, the plan said, although they ought to be dispersed or duplicated ahead of time.

To minimize the impact of Russian attacks, Dropshot called for a massive American atomic attack against Russia "immediately after the outbreak of hostilities." It urged "that attacks against atomic-bomb production and storage facilities and important air bases from which atomic-bomb attacks are most likely to be launched should be given high priority." The plan also called for attacks against targets supporting conventional Russian forces (including supply depots and massed troops), against "the political, governmental, administrative, and technical and scientific elements of the Soviet nation," against urban areas, and against industry. In all, some 300 atomic bombs (and some conventional bombs) were to be dropped on some 200 targets in the first 30 days of the war. It was *hoped* that this would bring about a Soviet collapse, but it was not counted on to do so. "It is imprudent to assume that complete victory can be won by air offensive alone," the plan said. "Achievement of our war objectives will undoubtedly require occupation of certain strategic areas by major Allied land forces and may require a major land campaign."

Exactly why an atomic offensive might not win a war was spelled out by the report of a high-level Pentagon study group known as the Harmon Committee in the spring of 1949. The then-current SAC war plan Trojan called for dropping 133 atomic bombs on 70 Russian cities in 30 days. Such an attack, the Harmon Committee said, would eliminate less than 40 percent of Soviet industrial capacity, and "this loss would not be permanent." The attack would not seriously impair "the capability of Soviet armed forces to advance rapidly into selected areas of Western Europe, the Middle East, and the Far East," nor would it, "per se, bring about capitulation, destroy the roots of Communism, or critically weaken the power of Soviet leadership to dominate the people." On the other hand, it *would* "stimulate resentment against the United States, unify the people, and increase their will to fight," and the bitterness aroused would "complicate post-hostilities problems." Nevertheless, the committee recommended that a prompt and massive atomic attack be part of American war planning, because it "would constitute the only means of rapidly inflicting shock and serious damage to vital elements of the Soviet war-making capacity."

The points made by the Harmon Committee partially recapitulated an old debate about strategic bombing, one that had arisen earlier in the century when the invention of the airplane made it possible for the first time for a warring nation to attack an enemy's cities without first defeating its troops. There were objections then that it was not civilized to kill civilians instead of soldiers. Defenders of strategic bombardment (who were principally airmen) replied that the destruction of industry in cities was a shortcut to ending wars. "This will result in a diminished loss of life and treasure and will thus be a distinct benefit to civilization," General Billy Mitchell said in 1925.

Strategic bombing came of age in World War II, with massive applications by Germany, Britain, and the United States. After the war, the U.S. Strategic Bombing Survey examined the results of all the bombing and reported that it had not significantly reduced industrial production and had raised rather than broken civilian morale. Even the atomic bombing of Japan had not been decisive, the survey concluded: "Based on a detailed investigation of all the facts, and supported by the testimony of the surviving Japanese leaders involved, it is the Survey's opinion that certainly prior to 31 December 1945, and in all probability prior to 1 November 1945, Japan would have surrendered even if the atomic bombs had not been dropped, even if Russia had not entered the war and even if no invasion had been planned or contemplated."

Arguments against strategic bombing were carried on most vigorously after the war by the U.S. Navy, which was not happy to see

185

its role diminished by the growth of the new Air Force. (This was before the Navy was selected to operate ballistic missile submarines.) Naval officers raised practical objections to atomic warfare. "This kind of war is not as simple as the prophets of the ten day atomic blitz seem to think," Admiral Daniel Gallery wrote in a 1949 memorandum. "Some authorities estimate that the damage done by strategic bombing of Germany was equivalent to 500 Atomic Bombs. But Germany did not surrender until her armies were defeated. . . . In addition, levelling large cities has a tendency to alienate the affections of the inhabitants and does not create an atmosphere of international good will after the war." Moral objections were raised as well. "For a 'civilized society' like the United States, the broad purpose of a war cannot be simply destruction and annihilation of the enemy," wrote Gallery. The Navy went public with its criticisms in a series of congressional hearings in October 1949 that became known as the "admirals' revolt." But the admirals were rejected on every point.*

The explosion of the first Russian atomic bomb a few weeks before the admirals' testimony, the subsequent decision to build the American hydrogen bomb, and the ensuing rapid growth in the power and numbers of nuclear weapons soon overwhelmed all practical (if not moral) objections to nuclear warfare. After all, it didn't much matter whether strategic bombing would lower or raise civilian morale if the new bombs weren't going to leave many civilians alive to *have* morale.†

And 1952 saw the election of a new American president—Dwight Eisenhower—who firmly believed, he wrote later, "that it

---

* Two years later, participants in a Pentagon-funded study called Project Vista, who included J. Robert Oppenheimer, recommended the development of tactical nuclear weapons so that "the battle could be brought back to the battlefield." This was seen, like the admirals' revolt, as an attack on SAC and strategic bombing, and SAC's supporters counterattacked by questioning Oppenheimer's loyalty and patriotism.

† In 1955, when the American war plan called for an attack on Russia and its allies that would kill 60 million people and injure 17 million more, the Pentagon engaged a group of psychologists to evaluate "the will of the Soviets to continue to wage war." The psychologists reported that "there presently exists no basis on which to assess quantitatively the effect on the Soviet will to continue to fight. Nevertheless, casualties of such magnitude and the total loss of 118 out of the 134 major Soviet cities would have a calamitous effect. . . . Whether such losses would cause the Soviets to lose the will to continue to fight remains for the present a matter of judgment rather than of deduction or evaluation."

would be impossible for the United States to maintain the military commitments which it now sustains around the world (without turning into a garrison state) did we not possess atomic weapons and the will to use them when necessary." Eisenhower began his presidency by threatening that use. The Korean War had stalemated, and so had the negotiations seeking its resolution, a situation Eisenhower found intolerable. He decided "to let the Communist authorities understand that, in the absence of satisfactory progress, we intended to move decisively without inhibition in our use of weapons, and would no longer be responsible for confining hostilities to the Korean Peninsula. . . . In India and in the Formosa Straits area, and at the truce negotiations at Panmunjom, we dropped the word, discreetly, of our intention. We felt quite sure it would reach Soviet and Chinese Communist ears. Soon the prospects for armistice negotiations seemed to improve." A truce was signed in July 1953.

Early the next year, in a now-famous speech to the Council on Foreign Relations, Secretary of State John Foster Dulles gave credit for the truce to Eisenhower's nuclear threat. "The fighting was stopped on honorable terms," Dulles said, "because the aggressor . . . was faced with the possibility that the fighting might, to his own great peril, soon spread beyond the limits and methods which he had selected." In the future, Dulles said, this possibility would be the rule. "There is no local defense which alone will contain the mighty landpower of the Communist world," he said. Therefore the United States would "depend primarily upon a great capacity to retaliate, instantly, by means and at places of our own choosing."

This doctrine, which became known as "massive retaliation," sounded like a promise to destroy Russia if it were ever again involved in a local war against American interests. "Rather than let the Communists nibble us to death all over the world in little wars we would rely in the future primarily on our massive mobile retaliatory power which we could use in our discretion against the major source of aggression at times and places that we choose," Vice President Richard Nixon explained. Dulles himself soon sought to modify that explanation—Russian and Chinese cities would not necessarily be bombed, he wrote, "if there is a Communist attack somewhere in Asia." But Dulles's speech had accurately reflected the Eisenhower administration's emphasis on nuclear weapons at every level of warfare. The administration called this emphasis the New Look.* It was appealing at a time when the United States had overwhelming nuclear superiority over the Soviet Union, and it looked good for financial reasons as well. Eisenhower had campaigned on a pledge to reduce defense spending, and nuclear weapons were a relative bargain. Dollar for dollar, they produced more death and destruction than conventional explosives or expensive masses of salaried soldiers. "With the shift in emphasis to the full exploitation of air power and modern weapons," Eisenhower explained, "we are in a position to support strong national security programs over an indefinite period with less of a drain on our manpower, material, and financial resources."

The first battlefield nuclear weapons were deployed in Europe in 1953, and administration spokesmen stated repeatedly that they were to be used as freely as conventional weapons should war break out. "Where these things are used on strictly military targets and for strictly military purposes, I see no reason why they shouldn't be used just exactly as you would use a bullet or anything else," Eisenhower himself said in 1955. Should a general war begin, the Strategic Air Command, growing more powerful every year, had plans for a massive nuclear strike against the Soviet Union. Ideally, a SAC general told other officers at a classified briefing in 1954, SAC would have time to deploy its bombers and tankers to overseas bases before the attack. SAC would then be prepared to drop more than six hundred atomic and hydrogen bombs on Russia in a single blow. "The final impression," reported a naval officer present at the briefing, "was that virtually all of Russia would be nothing but a smoking, radiating ruin at the end of two hours."

The SAC target list of that era included three categories of targets: Bravo (for "blunting") missions were aimed at Soviet nuclear forces that, if not destroyed promptly, could be used to attack the United States. Romeo (for "retardation") missions were aimed at industrial facilities like oil refineries that would provide crucial support to conventional Soviet forces on the attack. Delta (for "disruption") missions were aimed at the general Soviet industrial

---

* Its name was borrowed, Eisenhower explained, from a then-current fashion phrase "coined to describe noticeable changes in the style of women's dresses (not entirely an improvement, some men felt)."

base. While the target types were separate, the planned attacks on them were not. The first Single Integrated Operational Plan, written in 1960 (prior to which every service command made its own nuclear war plans), called for dropping all available American nuclear weapons on military and urban targets in the Soviet Union, Eastern Europe, and China at the first sign of even a nonnuclear Russian attack.

The Eisenhower administration was not oblivious to the fact that the threat of massive nuclear attack might have only limited utility against a nuclear-armed adversary. "As general war becomes more devastating for both sides the threat to resort to it becomes less available as a sanction against local aggression," acknowledged a 1953 National Security Council paper that laid out the principles of the New Look. And Eisenhower stressed the development of tactical as well as strategic nuclear weapons; tens of thousands of American soldiers took part in tactical nuclear war-fighting exercises at the Nevada test site (exercises which resulted in delayed radiation effects and lawsuits decades later).

Theorists like Henry Kissinger, however, worried that the administration's nuclear strategy emphasized options too massive to meet likely Cold War threats. "Limited war," Kissinger wrote, "represents the only means for preventing the Soviet bloc, at an acceptable cost, from overrunning the peripheral areas of Eurasia." And so, he wrote, the United States should prepare for limited war— including limited nuclear war. We should not "be defeatist about the possibility of limiting nuclear war," Kissinger admonished, "or about the casualties it might involve. It is far from certain that a conventional war involving fixed positions would produce less devastation than a nuclear war, and in certain circumstances it may produce more."

There was, in fact, some evidence that Kissinger was wrong about this. In Operation Sagebrush, a war game played by American forces in Louisiana, seventy mock nuclear weapons were dropped on military targets and the game's umpire then ruled that all life in the state had "ceased to exist." In Operation Carte Blanche, two days of mock tactical nuclear warfare in West Germany left 10 percent of the civilian population "killed" or "wounded."

Undeterred, Kissinger (who later did modify his views on the subject) presented his own detailed plan for limited nuclear warfare in 1957: "We might propose that neither bases of the opposing strategic air forces nor towns above a certain size would be attacked, provided these bases would not be used to support tactical operations and that the towns would not contain military installations useful against armed forces. . . . [A]ll cities within five hundred miles of the battle zone would be immune from nuclear attack if they were declared 'open' and if their status were certified by inspectors. . . . The inspectors might consist of a commission of neutrals; it would be preferable if they were experts of the other side because this would give their reports a much higher credibility. The inspectors would have their own communications system and would operate even during hostilities."

Standing behind these rules (and there were others), Kissinger warned, had to be the threat of all-out nuclear war. "We can make a strategy of limited war stick only if we leave no doubt about our readiness and our ability to face a final showdown. Its effectiveness will depend on our willingness to face up to the risks of Armageddon." If we were willing to take that chance, he wrote, and then started to fight a limited nuclear war, the Soviet Union would have the choice of fighting by the rules or finding itself in an all-out nuclear war; with those choices, it might well choose to follow the rules.

An extension of the rules even into strategic nuclear warfare was proposed by Herman Kahn. "It would be irresponsible to be so unprepared to cope with crisis options as to have no choices other than holocaust or surrender," Kahn wrote. And he offered choices, forty-four in all, on an "escalation ladder" that began with Rung 1, "Ostensible Crisis," in which "vague or explicit threats" are made regarding some dispute, and ended with Rung 44, "Spasm or Insensate War," in which "all the buttons are pressed, and the decisionmakers and their staffs go home—if they still have homes." (Kahn also described this as a "war-gasm.")

Intermediate rungs on the escalation ladder included Show of Force (Rung 5), Large Conventional War (Rung 12), Local Nuclear

War—Exemplary (Rung 21), Slow-Motion Countercity War (Rung 39), and Civilian Devastation Attack (Rung 42). Midway on the ladder was Declaration of Limited Nuclear War (Rung 22), at which point "it might be judged desirable to make a formal declaration of limited nuclear war—perhaps in hope of setting out relatively exact limits and establishing expectations about the types of nuclear action that the declarer intends to initiate and that he is prepared to countenance from the enemy without escalating further himself."*

Like Kissinger, and most others who advocated preparations for limited nuclear war fighting (and who advocate such preparations today), Kahn was a strong proponent of civil defense. A limited nuclear war, after all, would not be limited if everybody were killed right away. And, Kissinger pointed out, "a power whose population is protected to some degree by a deep shelter program can run greater risks than an enemy whose people are totally exposed to attack."

Also like Kissinger, Kahn was concerned by the fact that "probably never in the history of the world has there been so widespread a conviction that 'war is unthinkable' or 'impossible,' and so extensive a belief that a serious concern with the problems in fighting and surviving a war—as opposed to deterring it—is misguided and perhaps even immoral." Kahn complained that this "psychological obstacle" had resulted in a lack of "serious, sophisticated

---

* Mutual threats to escalate from rung to rung during a crisis or war, Kahn wrote, could be compared to the game of "chicken," in which two teenage drivers speed toward one another and the first to turn away loses. "Some teenagers utilize interesting tactics in playing 'chicken,' " Kahn observed. "The 'skillful' player may get into the car quite drunk, throwing whiskey bottles out the window to make it clear to everybody just how drunk he is. He wears very dark glasses so that it is obvious he cannot see much, if anything. As soon as the car reaches high speed, he takes the steering wheel and throws it out the window." And by appearing to be so reckless, he scares his opponent into giving way. Kahn noted that some people believed it useful for American leaders to behave this way during crises, "that if our decision-makers can only give the appearance of being drunk, blind, and without a steering wheel, they will 'win' in negotiations with the Soviets on crucial issues." Among those who believed this, it turned out a few years later, was President Richard Nixon, who came into office intending to use the strategy against the North Vietnamese. "I call it the Madman Theory, Bob," he explained to H. R. Haldeman. "I want the North Vietnamese to believe I've reached the point where I might do *anything* to stop the war. We'll just slip the word to them that, 'for God's sake, you know Nixon is obsessed about Communists. We can't restrain him when he's angry—and he has his hand on the nuclear button'— and Ho Chi Minh himself will be in Paris in two days begging for peace." Ho Chi Minh called Nixon's bluff and won.

consideration of the military requirements, advantages, and weaknesses of various strategies and tactics for the middle and upper rungs of the escalation ladder." The growth of the Soviet nuclear arsenal had reinforced the popular feeling that "war really is obsolete," he wrote. But, he asserted, "even if the balance of terror becomes relatively stable, war can still occur. And particularly in a balance-of-terror situation, the difference between intelligent, sophisticated, and rational use of weapons, and stupid, thoughtless, or emotional use, would loom very large."

President John F. Kennedy often spoke of the horrors of nuclear war, and he accepted the traditional view that the first order of business for American nuclear policy was to maintain a force capable of retaliating so devastatingly after any Russian attack that the Russians would be deterred from ever launching an attack. But he agreed with the limited war advocates that less drastic nuclear capabilities were required as well. "We intend to have a wider choice than humiliation or all-out nuclear action," he announced during the 1961 Berlin crisis.

Kennedy's secretary of defense, Robert McNamara, acted on that intention. Heavily influenced in his thinking by strategists affiliated with the RAND Corporation, the Air Force–funded "think tank" where many of the concepts of limited nuclear warfare were developed, he hired several RAND staff members, including Daniel Ellsberg, to work in the Pentagon. McNamara soon adopted and enunciated in public statements—aimed as much at Soviet leaders as at his American audiences—new principles of nuclear war fighting and planning that to this day form the basis of American nuclear policy.

"The U.S. has come to the conclusion," McNamara said in a 1962 address at the University of Michigan, "that, to the extent feasible, basic military strategy in a possible general war should be approached in much the same way that the more conventional military operations have been regarded in the past. That is to say, principal military objectives, in the event of a nuclear war stemming from a major attack on the [NATO] Alliance, should be the destruction of the enemy's military forces, not of his civilian population."

Eisenhower-era plans for nuclear war had included plans for such "counterforce" attacks against Soviet nuclear weapons and other military targets, but the counterforce targets were to be attacked along with Soviet urban-industrial targets (known as "countervalue" targets) in a single massive strike at the outbreak of war. McNamara rejected that strategy. Evoking a hypothetical scenario that has preoccupied American nuclear strategists ever since, he wrote that a Soviet first "strike might be directed solely at our military installations, leaving our cities as hostages for later negotiations. In that event, we might find it to our advantage to direct our immediate retaliatory blow against their military installations, and to withhold our attack on their cities, keeping the forces required to destroy their urban-industrial complex in a protected reserve for some kind of period of time." (Such a capability would not only give us a means for appropriately limited retaliation against a Soviet counterforce attack, McNamara added, but it might also encourage the Russians, if they were resolved to attack us, to spare our cities in the first round. "In talking about global nuclear war, the Soviet leaders always say that they would strike at the entire complex of our military power including government and production centers, meaning our cities . . . ," McNamara wrote. "By building into our forces a flexible capability, we at least eliminate the prospect that we could strike back in only one way, namely, against the entire Soviet target system including their cities. Such a prospect would give the Soviet Union no incentive to withhold attack against our cities in a first strike. We want to give them a better alternative.")

McNamara ordered the Joint Chiefs of Staff to prepare a doctrine that "would permit controlled response and negotiating pauses in the event of thermo-nuclear war." The result was a new Single Integrated Operational Plan, with options to attack Soviet counterforce targets only, while holding more weapons in reserve to threaten Soviet cities during intrawar negotiations. (To facilitate such negotiations, Moscow was removed from the list of targets to be struck immediately.) The prospect of launching American nuclear forces not in a single spasm but "in waves, if you will," McNamara pointed out, required that American weapons and command, control, and communications facilities be protected from enemy nuclear strikes during what could be a protracted war. The new Minuteman missile force was given additional targeting options, and nonstop Looking Glass flights began during the second month of the Kennedy administration. "We are providing alternate command posts at sea and in the air, with communications links to all elements of our strategic force," McNamara said. "With this protected command and control system, our forces can be used in several different ways. We may have to retaliate with a single massive attack. Or, we may be able to use our retaliatory forces to limit damage done to ourselves, and our allies, by knocking out the enemy's bases before he has had time to launch his second salvos. We may seek to terminate a war on favorable terms by using our forces as a bargaining weapon—by threatening further attack."

McNamara thus laid the groundwork—rhetorically and operationally—for the present American plans for protracted, limited nuclear war. There were objections, then as now, that such planning made nuclear war more thinkable, and thus more likely. The Russians protested that war was war, and that they wouldn't play according to McNamara's rules should it come. Both the Russians and American liberals pointed out that planning for counterforce strikes against remaining Russian weapons after a Russian first strike was indistinguishable from planning for an American first strike against Russian weapons. (The Russians "undoubtedly reasoned that if our buildup were to continue at its accelerated pace, we might conceivably reach, in time, a credible first-strike capability against the Soviet Union," McNamara later acknowledged.)* Worst of all, from McNamara's point of view, the American armed services saw the counterforce strategy as a green light for huge new expenditures on more accurate, more powerful, and more numerous nuclear weapons.

So McNamara retreated. His public statements began to downplay "damage limitation" programs—which included counterforce targeting (which would destroy Soviet weapons before they could damage American targets), Kennedy's short-lived civil-defense buildup, and proposed anti-ballistic-missile (ABM) systems. Instead, McNamara began to emphasize something he called "assured

---

* In fact, the Russians *were* worried about the Americans. Russian agents controlling an American soldier spying for them in France in 1963 instructed him to contact an address in Switzerland if he got word of an impending American attack. He was to send an order for railroad ties to the address. The number of ties ordered (930, for example) would correspond to the time of the planned attack.

destruction." "Damage limiting programs, no matter how much we spend on them, can never substitute for an Assured Destruction capability in the deterrent role," McNamara wrote in 1967. "It is our ability to destroy an attacker as a viable 20th Century nation that provides the deterrent, not our ability to partially limit damage to ourselves." In characteristic fashion, McNamara quantified America's assured destruction goals. He set them originally at the ability to destroy two-thirds of Soviet industry and kill one-quarter to one-third of the Soviet population; later he reduced the goals to one-half of Soviet industry and one-fifth to one-fourth of the population (as well as half of *Chinese* industry destroyed and fifty million Chinese people killed). Assured destruction provided McNamara with a means to resist the Pentagon's spending demands. Once the United States had enough weapons to meet assured destruction goals—and McNamara could produce charts and graphs to show that this was the case—any additional nuclear weapons were obviously superfluous.

Ultimately, McNamara would carry his assured destruction argument even further. Just as the American ability to wreak assured destruction on the Soviet Union prevented any Soviet attack on the United States, he said, so the developing Soviet ability to do the same to the United States—despite any American damage-limiting efforts—would prevent an American attack. "No nation can possibly win a full-scale thermonuclear exchange," he wrote. "The two world powers that have now achieved mutual assured-destruction capability fully realize that." And mutual assured destruction (which became known as MAD) might not be such a bad thing, he said; if both sides had nuclear retaliatory forces that could survive a first strike, then preemptive first strikes would lose their appeal, and the result would be "a more stable balance of terror."*

Despite all his talk about assured destruction of Soviet industries and people, however, McNamara did not dismantle the counterforce options in the new SIOP, nor did he undo improvements in

---

[6] Statements like this got McNamara in trouble with right-wingers like Phyllis Schlafly, later renowned for her crusade against the Equal Rights Amendment. Favorable statements about a "stable balance of terror," Schlafly wrote in a 1964 pro-Goldwater booklet, were based on the false assumption that "all the Soviets want is to feel secure against possible aggression. . . . On this absurd theory, we should erect a national monument to Klaus Fuchs for supplying our atomic secrets to the Soviets!"

American nuclear weapons and C³ facilities that made a limited counterforce nuclear war theoretically possible. Not for the first time, nor the last, a gap opened between the strategic doctrine enunciated by political leaders and the actual operational plans for fighting a nuclear war. "All public officials have learned to talk only about deterrence and city attacks," strategic historian Desmond Ball has quoted an unnamed assistant secretary of defense in the Johnson administration as saying. "No war-fighting; no city-sparing. Too many critics can make too much trouble (no-cities talk weakens deterrence, the argument goes), so public officials have run for cover. That included me when I was one of them. But the targeting philosophy, the options and the order of choice remain unchanged."

So did all the routine planning for war that professional soldiers carry out as part of their jobs no matter how many presidents say war is unthinkable. No detail was overlooked. An annual "Military Chaplains' Nuclear Training Course" was conducted in Albuquerque, where the chaplains were told, "Since nuclear science is a gift from God, it is inherently good. . . . It is in the area of the limits to the fighting that the specter of the nuclear weapon really raises its moral or immoral head." Information of a more practical nature was supplied in an Army study of "The Impact of the Radioactive Environment Upon Traditional Chaplain Ministry." "In ministering to radioactive casualties," it advised, chaplains should "wear gloves if possible, preferably rubber."

Meanwhile, the Pentagon was preparing and publishing a pocket Russian language guide for American soldiers. "Knowing a little Russian will help you get along with the people," it said, "for they will naturally be pleased to see a stranger showing enough interest in them to try to learn their language." Among the phrases translated in the book were "I want cigarettes," "I am an American," "I am your friend," "We are wounded," "Where are the soldiers?," "Which is the road to Moscow?," "Draw me a map," "Stop!" and "Take cover!"

The public rhetoric of American leaders shifted once again toward limited nuclear warfare during the administration of Richard Nixon. "Should a President," Nixon asked, "in the event of a nuclear attack, be left with the single option of ordering the mass destruction of enemy civilians, in the face of certainty that it would be followed by the mass slaughter of Americans?" He thought not. In January 1974, following the appointment of former RAND Corporation official James Schlesinger as secretary of defense, Nixon signed a secret National Security Decision Memorandum instructing that plans be developed "for limited employment options which enable the United States to conduct selected nuclear operations." If total war broke out, Nixon ordered, the United States should destroy "the political, economic and military resources critical to the enemy's postwar power, influence and ability to recover ... as a major power." But the United States should seek to avoid total war, he said, by developing the ability to launch selected nuclear operations while holding "some vital enemy targets hostage to subsequent destruction by survivable nuclear forces."

Schlesinger took the lead in informing the American public (and thus the Soviets, who read the papers) about the new American policy. He acknowledged that the nuclear war plans Nixon had inherited from previous administrations included counterforce options short of total war. "The overt public doctrine stressed only going against cities," Schlesinger said, but "in fact, this is not the way the forces were targeted." Nevertheless, he complained, all of the old options were too large. "In the past we have had massive preplanned strikes in which one would be dumping literally thousands of weapons on the Soviet Union. Some of those strikes could to some extent be withheld from going directly against cities, but that was limited even then."

The reason those strikes were so large was that the Soviet nuclear arsenal had grown. In the McNamara era, the smallest SIOP option—the one for an attack against Soviet nuclear weapons only—had in fact been relatively small, because the Soviets didn't have very many nuclear weapons. By the early 1970s, the Soviet nuclear arsenal had increased to the point where the SIOP's limited counterforce option required firing 2,500 nuclear weapons against the Soviet Union—hardly a limited option. Schlesinger sought to rectify the situation. He ordered the development of new options giving "the President of the United States, whoever he may be, the option of limiting strikes down to a few weapons."

The reason for adding these limited options, naturally, was "credibility." "Once the Soviet Union built up a counter-deterrent," Schlesinger said, "assured destruction became a logically incredible kind of threat. It is not psychologically incredible, but it is logically incredible." This was a particular problem for America's relationship with its NATO allies, he said. The Western Europeans had always had cause to doubt that the United States would willingly risk total nuclear war—and thus New York and Chicago—to defend Paris and Bonn. American soldiers with tactical nuclear weapons had originally been stationed in Europe not so much to defeat a Russian invasion as to guarantee that such an invasion would involve American casualties and the firing of nuclear weapons, and so bring the United States into the war. (In a triumph of mixed metaphors, Schlesinger described this as "the trip-wire strategy, sometimes called the plate glass window, [which] was designed to have a small force sometimes referred to as a corporal's guard up front so that the nuclear bell could ring.") American planning for limited nuclear attacks, Schlesinger said, "means U.S. strategic forces are still credibly part of the overall deterrent for Europe." That is, the Europeans (and Russians) would be more likely to believe that the United States would fire nuclear weapons in defense of Europe if they knew that the United States had plans for doing so that minimized the risk to New York and Chicago. European reaction, Schlesinger said, was "joyous."

Testifying before a Senate committee, Schlesinger explained how limited nuclear options might work in practice: "One circumstance I can think of is the possibility of the overrunning of Western Europe [by the Russians]. . . . If, for example, under those circumstances, one were to go after their oil production capacity—just take that as an illustration of a target set—the removal of that capacity would have a crippling effect on the Soviet ability to wage war against Western Europe."

Senator William Fulbright: "Do you mean that if we did that you don't think they would respond with nuclear weapons against us?"

Schlesinger: "They might well. I think that they would. . . . But I believe, Senator, if we were to maintain continued communications with the Soviet leaders during the war, and if we were to describe precisely and meticulously the limited nature of our actions, including the desire to avoid attacking their urban industrial base, that in spite of whatever one says historically in advance that everything must go all out, when the existential circumstances arise, political leaders on both sides will be under powerful pressure to continue to be sensible. Both sides under those circumstances will continue to have the capacity at any time to destroy the urban industrial base of the others. The leaders on both sides will know that. Those are circumstances in which I believe that leaders will be rational and prudent. I hope I am not being too optimistic."

Senator Clifford Case: "And you argue further that, because this is a possibility, therefore the Russians won't go into Western Europe with massive conventional force?"

Schlesinger: "That is our hope."

The senators were skeptical, especially when Schlesinger said that a limited Russian nuclear attack on the United States —the deterrence of which, he said, required an American ability to launch a limited nuclear attack on Russia—would cause relatively few casualties. "I am talking here about casualties of 15,000, 20,000, 25,000—a horrendous event, as we all recognize, but one far better than the alternative [of total nuclear war]."

The senators asked Schlesinger to double-check those figures, and he returned a few months later with new ones. A Russian attack on American missile fields and nothing else, Schlesinger now said, would kill 800,000 Americans.

The senators were still skeptical. They recruited the Congressional Office of Technology Assessment to review the calculations with the Defense Department. The report came back that the estimate of 800,000 dead, not to mention the estimate of 15,000 dead, had been based on a number of very optimistic assumptions. (Senator Stuart Symington called the earlier numbers a "hoax.") The new study found that an attack against missile silos alone could kill more than 18 million Americans.

This seemed to undercut the entire rationale for limited nuclear options. It might not be credible to threaten all-out nuclear war to deter an attack that would kill 15,000 Americans, but it might well be credible to threaten massive retaliation against an attack that would kill 18 million. "I myself," noted Harold Brown, who became secretary of defense upon the election of Jimmy Carter, "continue to doubt that a Soviet attack on our strategic forces whose collateral damage involved 'only' a few million American deaths could appropriately be responded to without including some urban-industrial targets in the response."

Nevertheless, Brown proceeded to preside over a further refinement in American planning for limited nuclear attacks. "A strategy based on assured destruction alone is no longer credible," Brown wrote in his fiscal year 1980 report to Congress. He did not hide his doubts about the new strategy. "I am not at all persuaded that what started as a demonstration, or even a tightly controlled use of the strategic forces for larger purposes, could be kept from escalating to a full-scale thermonuclear exchange," he reported a year later. But, he insisted, "to deter Soviet attacks of less than all-out scale," the United States had to be able to attack, "in a selective and measured way, a range of military, industrial, and political control targets, while retaining our assured destruction capacity in reserve."

The new Carter policy was formalized in the summer of 1980 in Presidential Directive 59. PD-59 is still classified, but its contents were almost immediately leaked to the press and were discussed extensively by Harold Brown. "Deterrence remains, as it has been historically, our fundamental strategic objective," he said. But deterrence must be flexible and credible, and so, "in our analysis and planning, we are necessarily giving greater attention to how a nuclear war would actually be fought by both sides if deterrence fails." That meant reinforcing the emphasis of previous targeting policies on striking Soviet nuclear forces and on organizing American attacks around small "targeting packages" that could be mixed and matched to destroy selected isolated targets or to send very particular messages to the Russian leaders during a war.

Brown insisted that PD-59 marked only "a modest change" in the "conceptual foundation built over a generation by men like Robert McNamara and James Schlesinger." But it included some significant developments. Past targeting strategies, including Schlesinger's, had emphasized as the ultimate deterrent the destruction of factories and other facilities that the Soviet Union would need to recover from a nuclear war. Carter's nuclear policy reduced the emphasis on recovery targets and paid special attention to "political control targets." These include regional offices of the Communist Party and the KGB (the destruction of which, especially in non-Russian Soviet republics, might weaken central Soviet control), and Soviet troop concentrations in Eastern Europe and along the Chinese border (the destruction of which might encourage uprisings in Poland or a Chinese invasion). Explained Brown: "We have to target or have options to target . . . all the elements of Soviet power that are most important to the Soviet leadership."

PD-59 was issued at a time when the kind of precision nuclear attacks necessary to fight a limited nuclear war were more feasible than they had ever been before. American nuclear strategists of earlier eras may have planned for attacks against Russian missile silos and hardened C^3 centers, but to destroy such targets you must, first, know exactly where they are and, second, have weapons accurate enough to land practically on top of them. In the 1950s and 1960s, this was far from being the case. The first American missiles were barely accurate enough to hit large cities, let alone hardened holes in the ground. By the mid-1970s, however, technological improvements encouraged planning for limited nuclear warfare. Incredibly sensitive spy satellites revealed the precise locations of enemy weapons; improved missile and bomber guidance systems promised to land attacking weapons on their targets; and computerized remote targeting systems made it possible to change the target sets in unfired missiles rapidly as a nuclear war unfolded.

To further enhance the nation's capability for limited nuclear war fighting, the Carter administration increased spending on C^3 systems supporting nuclear weapons. Carter signed Presidential Directive 53, a companion to PD-59, proclaiming the need for "a survivable communications system" to provide "connectivity between the National Command Authority and strategic and other appropriate forces to support flexible execution of retaliatory strikes during and after an enemy attack." American communications, it said, must provide "responsive support for operational control of the armed forces, even during a protracted nuclear conflict."

PD-59 soon led to calls for other nuclear spending. Years before, Robert McNamara had stopped talking about counterforce and started talking about assured destruction largely to keep the lid on the military budget. Even James Schlesinger had told Congress that, to implement his new targeting doctrine, "we do not have to acquire a single additional weapon." (All that was needed, he said, was improved planning and C^3.) With PD-59, however, Carter let the Pentagon loose.

PD-59 "codifies the evolution of our national nuclear strategy from one of massive assured destruction toward a strategy that combines both countervalue and counterforce targeting . . . ," Admiral Powell Carter, the Navy's director of nuclear warfare, testified during fiscal year 1982 budget hearings. "The current Navy nuclear forces were designed in the fifties and the early sixties when the national policy was one of massive assured destruction. They were designed to be survivable and enduring and have the capability to do unacceptable damage to soft Soviet urban and industrial targets. . . . As the national strategy has evolved our forces have aged, and they now require modernization." What was needed, Admiral Carter said, were new weapons with "the ability to attack time urgent hard targets such as enemy missile silos and command and control centers." It just so happened that technological development had recently made such weapons possible. (And the very fact that they existed, of course, hastened the development of doctrine that required their deployment.) By 1980, a new generation of super-accurate "silo-busting" missiles was on the way: the MX (to be based on land), the Pershing II (to be based in Europe), the Trident II (to be based on the new Trident submarine), and cruise missiles (to be based almost everywhere).

One conceptual problem with such missiles is that they look like first-strike weapons. The Pentagon insists that American counterforce weapons are intended to be used, *after* a Soviet first strike, against unfired Soviet nuclear weapons threatening surviving American targets. But there is no difference between a missile that can destroy a Soviet weapon after a Soviet first strike and a missile that can destroy a Soviet weapon *before* any Soviet strike. Building such missiles not only amounts to bad public relations; it could in itself be the cause of a nuclear war. "A U.S. second-strike counterforce capability might be indistinguishable to the Soviet Union from a first-strike force . . . ," notes a Congressional Budget Office briefing paper. "As a result, a Soviet leadership facing a serious international crisis might feel strong incentives to launch a preemptive strike against U.S. strategic forces before their own land-based missiles could be destroyed."

This dangerous situation—known in arms control jargon as "crisis instability"—is one that the United States had pledged for years to avoid. "In the interests of stability," Harold Brown wrote in 1979, "we avoid the capability of eliminating the other side's deterrent, insofar as we might be able to do so. In short, we must be quite willing—as we have been for some time—to accept the principle of mutual deterrence, and design our defense posture in light of that principle." The new counterforce weapons would not undercut that principle, Brown insisted, because some Soviet land-based missiles and many Soviet sea-based missiles could survive any American attack. Besides, he said, "if the Soviets find unacceptable the prospect of a U.S. capability to threaten a large part of their silo-based ICBMs in a pre-emptive U.S. strike, they could respond by increased reliance on launch-under-attack (LUA) or by reducing the vulnerability of their ICBMs." If this statement sounded a little cavalier, especially in its untroubled suggestion that the Soviets adopt a hair-trigger LUA posture, at least it demonstrated an effort to preserve some semblance of the principle of mutual deterrence.

In the Reagan era, the principle of mutual deterrence has had a harder time of it. Mutual assured destruction has long been an easy mark because of its unfortunate acronym, and in recent years its critics have flourished. The 1980 Republican Party platform denounced MAD and endorsed as an alternative "a credible strategy which will deter a Soviet attack by the sheer capability of our forces to survive and ultimately to destroy Soviet military targets." The Republicans have been joined in deriding MAD by others who yearn for clear-cut American nuclear superiority, who believe it is important to plan to fight a nuclear war, and who advocate civil defense and other measures to protect the American people during a nuclear war (and who believe that such measures really *can* protect the American people during a nuclear war). They often attack MAD as if it were a theory foisted upon America by lily-livered liberals and Communist dupes instead of a simple fact of international politics and the laws of physics. "MAD ... is a SALT I 'Whiz-Kid' delusion that exposes our American population to adversary slaughter ...," stated the *Journal of Civil Defense* in 1980. "It means simply that you and yours are today blood and flesh sacrifices in the hands of potential enemies and may be summarily executed at their pleasure."

It is an irony of the strategic debate that those who would risk upsetting the balance that upholds deterrence by preparing to fight and even win a nuclear war have been able to seize the rhetoric of the moral high ground. "This author has difficulty seeing merit (let alone moral justification) in executing the posthumous punishment of an adversary's society, possibly to a genocidal level of catastrophic damage," one critic of MAD has written. And what kind of monster, implies the *Journal of Civil Defense*, would force you and yours to be "blood and flesh sacrifices"?

The answer, of course, is no kind of monster at all, just men and women who can accept facts when they see them. "We live in an inherently MAD world," wrote physicist Wolfgang Panofsky and former Arms Control and Disarmament Agency official Spurgeon Keeny, Jr., in 1981, simply because "effective protection of the population against large-scale nuclear attack is not possible. This pessimistic technical assessment ... follows inexorably from the devastating power of nuclear weapons." Panofsky and Keeny called their article "MAD Versus NUTS" in an effort to rectify the rhetorical balance. "For convenience, and not in any spirit of trading epithets, we have chosen the acronym of NUTS [Nuclear Utilization Target Selection] to characterize the various doctrines that seek to utilize nuclear weapons against specific targets in a complex of nuclear war-fighting situations intended to be limited ...," they wrote. "Readers not familiar with the colloquial American usage may need to be told that 'nuts' is an adjective meaning 'crazy or demented.' For everyday purposes it is a synonym for 'mad.'" Panofsky and Keeny granted that some NUTS theories might extend "the credibility of our nuclear deterrent," but they warned that "the profusion of proposed NUTS approaches has not offered an escape from the MAD world, but rather constitutes a major danger in encouraging the illusion that limited or controlled nuclear war can be waged free from the grim realities of a MAD world."*

In a nationally televised speech in the spring of 1983, Ronald Reagan offered a fanciful escape from those grim realities as he renewed the attack on MAD from the office of the president. "Deterrence of aggression through the promise of retaliation" *has* "succeeded in preventing nuclear war for more than three decades," Reagan acknowledged. But, he said, "to rely on the specter of retaliation—on mutual threat . . . is a sad commentary on the human condition." (And it is dangerous, too, he added a few days later: "The great nations of the world . . . sit here like people facing [one another] across a table, each with a cocked gun, and no one knowing whether someone might tighten the finger on the trigger.") "The human spirit," Reagan said, "must be capable of rising above dealing with other nations and human beings by threatening their existence."

Reagan proposed that the human spirit rise above mutual deterrence by developing space-based beam weapons that could destroy Soviet missiles in flight and thus eliminate at least American fear of retaliation in a nuclear war. (And perhaps Russian fear, too. If such weapons are developed, Reagan said a few days after his speech, the American president "could offer to give that same defensive weapon to [the Russians] to prove to them that there was no longer any need for keeping these missiles.")

For the foreseeable future, however, the success of such weapons is unlikely. Even if they could perform the amazing technological feat of spotting and destroying every enemy missile in a massive attack—destroying *most* would not be good enough— they would still be vulnerable to being attacked themselves *before* a missile attack was launched. (And an enemy could still blow big holes in the United States with the smuggled-in "suitcase bombs" the FBI was worried about in 1954.) Reagan himself cautioned that the develop-

---

* Even James Schlesinger seemed to accept those realities when he said, in 1974, that the Russians "now have a deterrent posture that is beyond the capacity of the United States to take away. Some welcome that. Some do not welcome that. But I think it is a fact of life."

ment of such weapons "may not be accomplished before the end of this century."*

Even before what critics called Reagan's Buck Rogers speech (and a subsequent surge in spending on beam-weapon research), the Reagan administration had undertaken other damage-limitation strategies more enthusiastically than its predecessors. A multi-billion-dollar program to build up American defenses against Soviet bombers is under way, as is a large research and development program for an (earthbound) anti-ballistic-missile system to defend American missile silos. Reagan has also proposed increases in the budget for civil defense, but he has had trouble getting those through Congress.

As for the limited nuclear war-fighting strategies of its predecessors, the Reagan administration has stayed the course. "Our top priority," Secretary of Defense Caspar Weinberger told Congress in 1981, "is on doing whatever is necessary to ensure nuclear force parity, *across the full range of plausible nuclear warfighting scenarios*, with the Soviet Union." (The italics were in the printed text of Weinberger's testimony distributed by the Pentagon.) The White House announcement of Reagan's $180 billion nuclear weapons program a few weeks later stressed the need for C^3 systems that would "direct U.S. strategic forces during a nuclear war" and would "endure for an extended period beyond the first nuclear attack."

The Reagan program also continued the push for the development of counterforce weapons, the new accurate missiles at least theoretically capable of destroying Russian missiles in their silos. "Today we have principally a bag of nuclear weapons that were procured for a different strategy, the strategy of mutual assured destruction—large weapons with not very good accuracies," SAC commander General Bennie Davis told a Senate budget hearing in

---

* Reagan's proposal revived the debate that preceded the signing of the 1972 U.S.-Soviet treaty banning the deployment of nationwide anti-ballistic-missile (ABM) systems. Adherents to mutual deterrence had argued that ABM systems would upset the balance that maintained the peace, and the Joint Chiefs of Staff said afterward that the treaty was indeed based "primarily on a philosophy of mutual vulnerability to retaliatory attack." But the treaty was based also on the facts that proposed ABM systems were very expensive, that it was doubtful they would work, that they would defend against incoming nuclear weapons by exploding intercepting nuclear weapons over the defender's own homeland, and that their development would encourage an arms race to build offensive weapons to overwhelm the ABMs.

1982. "With our current strategy we need to buy weapons that are smaller and more accurate, that is, more surgical-type weapons."

Asked a senator: "Our national strategic policy is no longer mutually assured destruction, do I gather that?"

Davis said he was correct.

"And what is it referred to as now?" asked the senator.

"Counterforce . . . ," said Davis, "or 'war fighting.' The two are synonymous."

(The new "surgical-type" weapons, Davis went on to explain, will be able to destroy military targets while minimizing collateral civilian deaths, a requirement of limited nuclear war fighting.)

Reagan's nuclear war-fighting weapons and strategies have been justified, as always, in the name of deterrence. "Our entire strategic program, including the development of a protracted response capability that has been so maligned in the press recently, has been developed with the express intention of assuring that nuclear war will never be fought," Caspar Weinberger said in 1982. But weapons and strategies designed to fight a nuclear war can obviously be used not only to deter but to fight a nuclear war, and the Reagan years have seen an upsurge of discussions of nuclear war-fighting preparations for the sake of nuclear war fighting—and even nuclear war winning.

Of course, nuclear war-fighting strategies were always designed to be used to fight and win a nuclear war, if push came to shove. PD-59 "does *not* assume, or assert, that we can 'win' a limited nuclear war, nor does it pretend or intend to enable us to do so," Harold Brown insisted. But Brown also said (a few years earlier) that "the U.S. objective of maximizing the resultant political, economic and military power of the United States relative to the enemy in a postwar period in order to preclude enemy domination continues to remain valid and achievable."

In recent years, the rhetoric has been less euphemistic. Much of it has come from, or been inspired by, academic or academic-style nuclear theorists. For decades, deskbound nuclear warriors at the RAND Corporation, the Hudson Institute (founded by Herman Kahn), and dozens of other think tanks have made comfortable livings spinning out nuclear war scenarios on contracts from the Pentagon and the Federal Emergency Management Agency and its predecessors. Full-fledged professors of political science and history at American universities have done the same kind of thing for free, publishing their papers in academic/military journals. (Not to be left out, many career military officers have taken graduate degrees and joined in the scholarly roundtable.) The military academicians, comfortable in the realm of pure, untested (and untestable) theory, have tended to specialize in nuclear topics exclusively, leaving conventional military strategizing to professional soldiers. "Most of [the civilian strategists] have been attracted to nuclear issues because the issues offer a first order conundrum of great political significance complicated by a mass of second order technical diversions that appeal to a certain cast of mind," observed Lawrence Freedman, a historian of strategic doctrine. "Conversely, in the areas of conventional warfare, civilian strategists often have no military training, do not properly understand things like logistics and lines of command, and tend to get discouraged by the large numbers of bits and pieces of hardware with which they ought to be familiar. Moreover, a civilian is derided when he suggests radical ways of organizing conventional warfare, whereas one can suggest quite absurd and terrible things in the nuclear area, and nobody seems to mind at all." Some people do mind—Harold Brown once complained of civilian strategists "who consider forty-kiloton weapons to be nuclear confetti"—but civilian strategists have been influential in every American administration since that of John Kennedy.

Prominent in the academic/military journals in recent years has been Colin Gray, formerly of the Hudson Institute and now of his own National Institute for Public Policy, a consultant to the Departments of State and Defense and a Reagan appointee to the advisory board of the Arms Control and Disarmament Agency. Gray's best-known articles are "Nuclear Strategy: the Case for a Theory of Victory" (published in *International Security* in 1979) and the more directly titled "Victory Is Possible" (co-written with Keith Payne and published in *Foreign Policy* in 1980). In them, Gray complains that "because the U.S. defense community has refused to recognize the importance of the possibility that a nuclear war could be won or lost, it has neglected to think beyond a punitive sequence of targeting options." He criticizes as ineffective the strategy of threatening to wreak progressively greater destruction against the urban-indus-

208

trial base of the Soviet Union during a nuclear war: "The Soviet Union, like Czarist Russia, knows that it can absorb an enormous amount of punishment (loss of life, industry, productive agricultural land, and even territory), recover, and endure until final victory— provided the *essential assets of the state* remain intact." He therefore recommends as a more effective threat the "counter-control" targeting that appeared in PD-59 (which Gray called "a useful step forward"):

> Soviet leaders would be less impressed by American willingness to launch [a limited nuclear attack] than they would be by a plausible American victory strategy. Such a theory would have to envisage the demise of the Soviet state. The United States should plan to defeat the Soviet Union and to do so at a cost that would not prohibit U.S. recovery. ["A combination of counterforce offensive targeting, civil defense, and ballistic missile and air defense should hold U.S. casualties down to a level compatible with national survival and recovery," Gray adds later.] Washington should identify war aims that in the last resort would contemplate the destruction of Soviet political authority and the emergence of a postwar world order compatible with Western values. . . . [T]he United States should be able to destroy key leadership cadres, their means of communication, and some of the instruments of domestic control. . . . The Soviet Union might cease to function if its security agency, the KGB, were severely crippled. If the Moscow bureaucracy could be eliminated, damaged, or isolated, the USSR might disintegrate into anarchy. . . . Soviet political control of its territory in Central Asia and in the Far East could be weakened by discriminate nuclear targeting. The same applies to Transcaucasia and Eastern Europe.

All of this, of course, is justified in the name of more credible, more effective deterrence.*

In a 1981 letter replying to a critical article, Gray took exception to a description of his work as "isolated." "It does so happen,"

---

* Along the same lines, a 1978 report prepared for the Pentagon by SRI International, a Virginia think tank, urged that American nuclear weapons be targeted at Soviet military forces in Eastern Europe and the non-Russian Soviet republics. "Thus, the U.S. strategic nuclear forces become a 'liberation force' for these subject peoples rather than a threat to their survival. . . . This goal is in full consonance with the American foreign policy traditions: Wilson's Fourteen Points; Roosevelt's Four Freedoms; and . . . the current human rights campaign of President Carter."

he protested, "that the argument in my recent articles in *International Security* and *Foreign Policy* are about as close to current U.S. official (if still substantially private) thinking as one is likely to find in the public domain."

About this, if nothing else, Gray appears to be correct.

"Fiscal Year 1984–1988 Defense Guidance," a classified Pentagon document obtained by *The New York Times* in 1982, called for American nuclear forces to be able to "render ineffective the total Soviet (and Soviet-allied) military and political power structure through attacks on the political and military leadership." It called for C^3 systems "capable of supporting controlled nuclear counterattacks over a protracted period." And, it said, "should deterrence fail and strategic nuclear war with the USSR occur, the United States must prevail and be able to force the Soviet Union to seek earliest termination of hostilities on terms favorable to the United States."

The Reagan administration was widely criticized for believing the United States could "prevail" in a nuclear war. "I've been to several meetings at which the word 'prevail' has been hurled at me with great venom by some fellow, usually in the back of the room," Caspar Weinberger complained.

"We've said many times we don't think nuclear war is winnable," Weinberger insisted. There followed considerable public debate as to whether or not "prevail" and "win" are synonyms.

In any case, Weinberger did acknowledge, "we certainly are not planning to be defeated." Only "effective contingency plans," he said, could establish "successful deterrence."

And, as for that venomous fellow in the back of the room, Weinberger asked, "What does he want? Does he want us not to prevail? You show me a secretary of defense who's planning not to prevail and I'll show you a secretary of defense who ought to be impeached."

NINE

Continuity
of Government

Twice each day, the National Weather Service prepares and feeds wind forecasts into computers maintained by the Federal Emergency Management Agency to assess the effects of a nuclear war. The forecasts are based on measurements made by meteorologists at 134 weather stations across the United States, Canada, and the Caribbean, who release balloons at noon and midnight Greenwich Mean Time. Their data are organized to predict wind patterns 12, 18, and 24 hours into the future. If nuclear war breaks out before the next balloons go up, the FEMA computers will use the data on hand to predict the spread of radioactive fallout over the United States. (The only weak point in the system, says a FEMA damage-assessment expert, is this: "How often is the weatherman right?")

Weather forecasts are only one speck in the giant maw of FEMA's damage-assessment computers. For decades, they have been gearing up to provide surviving government officials with prompt estimates of what has been destroyed and what has not following a nuclear attack. To determine what is gone, of course, will require knowing what once was, and so the computers have been stuffed full of information on almost two million places, things, and groups of people deemed worth keeping track of in a nuclear war. The data base includes 10,873 grain silos, 4,746 savings and loan associations, 8,184 hospitals, and 1,039 television stations. There are population data for 65,000 geographical subdivisions and agricultural data on 3,050 counties. There are listings for 326,525 retail stores and for 316 mines and caves "suitable for post-attack industrial occupation." And more. "It is one of the most comprehensive data banks on U.S. resources ever assembled," boasts FEMA's *Resource Data Catalog*. Every facility in the data base has been assigned a "vulnerability number" based on its type of construction, and every facility is listed by its precise location. "We prefer to get data by latitude and longitude," says William Fehlberg, a FEMA computer division executive, "but sometimes we don't. We know the coordinates for every ZIP code, so we use that instead."

Fehlberg works underground, at FEMA's Federal Regional Center in Olney, Maryland. Surrounded by farms—cows graze around the installation's above-ground radio towers—the Olney FRC is entered through a small concrete building adorned by an American flag and a sign: "Welcome to your Federal Regional Center. Warning, the following are prohibited: cameras, firearms, voice and video recorders, explosive devices." Visitors descend a curving concrete staircase and pass through a vaultlike blast door to enter the FRC proper. FEMA maintains six underground FRCs around the country, but Olney is special. Not only will it house regional federal officials after a nuclear attack; it is also the permanent prewar site of the Alternate National Warning Center (backing up the main center inside Cheyenne Mountain, Colorado) and of one of FEMA's three main computers.

The computers keep track of data for FEMA's own operations, including a list of two million American buildings that have been surveyed for their fallout-protection characteristics. "We print it out twice a year to distribute to local civil-defense organizations," says Fehlberg. "We say that if you collected all the print-out paper, you could *build* a pretty good fallout shelter." The computers also maintain a list of every radiation-measuring instrument distributed around the country—and the dates their batteries were last checked—in addition to the data base for postattack damage assessment.

"Our damage-estimation programs work on the principle that you calculate the distance between the weapon detonation and the resource, calculate the overpressure, and compare it to the vulnerability factor," Fehlberg explains. This will yield a probability that a particular resource has been flattened and/or incinerated. The main damage-estimation program—READY—will then be able to produce neatly printed tables detailing, for example, what percentage of the American bus-manufacturing industry has been destroyed, what percentage has been damaged, and how this will affect bus production during the first postattack year. READY will also produce, among many other things, casualty estimates for people, hogs, milk cows, sheep, chickens, and turkeys.

READY has already been used in many simulated nuclear wars. Following a 1973 exercise that assumed a Russian attack on the United States with twelve hundred nuclear weapons totaling six thousand megatons, READY spewed out hundreds of pages of tables containing mixed conclusions about the postattack situation. It found, for example, that the survival rate of the general population would be higher than that of food-processing plants. "The increased use of unprocessed . . . foods, however, could be counted on to maintain an adequate diet for the survivors," the exercise analysis reported. Tobacco and alcoholic beverage production capacity would survive at, respectively, one-half and one-third the population survival rate, producing "the necessity for drastic rationing of those products among the surviving population. . . . The cut in printing and publishing to almost one-third of the population survival level practically eliminates all but the essential printed material. Very little newspaper, magazine, or direct mail advertising could be accommodated."

When a real nuclear war begins, FEMA will rely on NORAD (the North American Aerospace Defense Command) for early estimates of where nuclear detonations—known in the trade as NUDETS—have occurred. NORAD's warning radars, spotting incoming enemy missiles, will not be able to determine *exactly* where each missile is headed, or how large a warhead it carries, or whether it is set to explode on the ground or in the air—all crucial data for damage estimation. But the radars will be able to determine *approximately* where each missile is headed. A classified *Attack Gazetteer* divides the country into ten-mile-radius circles and lists every likely enemy target in every circle. NORAD will report which circle each incoming weapon is headed for, and the FEMA computers will assume that the first weapon heading for each circle is aimed at the most important target in that circle, and so on down the line. The computers will assume that every missile carries a warhead of a size appropriate to destroy the target it is assumed to be aimed at, and that every missile is set to explode at a height appropriate for destroying that target (e.g., ground level for hardened missile silos, airburst for spread-out steel mills).

All these assumptions will be rapidly combined with the preattack wind forecasts and the computers' knowledge of which nontarget resources (TV stations, cows, Sears stores) are in which circles. Within minutes of the attack, surviving government officials with access to computer terminals and working telephone lines will be able to call up the computers (if *they* have survived) and begin to get estimates of what has been destroyed, what has been damaged, who has been killed, and what areas will be covered by dangerous fallout for how long.

For the speediest estimates, a simplified program called REACT will work with an abbreviated version of the resource data base. REACT was designed "to meet the need for quick response to queries from top level decision makers concerning the probable trans-attack status of high interest resources," explains the *REACT User's Guide*. "Structural damage, casualty, and fire effects are re-estimated each time a weapon report is received, thus providing current resource status predictions."

REACT assumes no special knowledge of computers; it will respond to simple, English-language queries. The *REACT User's Guide* provides examples of the questions REACT will be prepared to answer even as the bombs are falling:

WHICH OCEAN PORTS REGION 1 OPERABLE WITH NO FIRE?

HOW MANY KEY POSTAL FACILITIES IN NEW JERSEY DESTROYED WITH FIRE?

The decision makers will also be able to call up, if they can bear to look, casualty estimates for their own home towns, but they'll have no way of knowing for sure if the answers they get are accurate. "We've never had a war to calibrate our programs," Fehlberg notes. But the probabilities of accuracy will be indicated, and the system is ready to go on no notice at all, ready to provide surviving government officials in their postattack bunkers with the information they will need to begin reorganizing the United States of America.

•   •   •

"It's hard not to be cynical," said William Baird shortly before his recent retirement as FEMA's assistant associate director for national security plans and preparedness, a job that included responsibility for postattack "continuity of government." "This is a damned hard program to manage. We're dealing with preparedness for a circumstance none of us wants to recognize ever happening. People don't want to give time to it—the average guy has enough on his desk—and I've heard it said, 'There's nothing we can do.'

"But," Baird continued, "there's been enough study to know there's a *lot* we can do. If we lose fifty million people, there'll still be a substantial population remaining that needs national leadership and direction. The surviving will try to continue to survive. And what happens to them? Do we break up into tribes? Or try to continue to operate as a nation? Someone has to try to direct things for the common good. Otherwise it will be dog eat dog, which we don't want to see. There's got to be law and order, and everything else."

The government has been working on post-nuclear-war law and order for more than thirty years. Its concern began a few months after the explosion of the first Russian atom bomb in 1949, when a prominent congressman proposed that immediate steps be taken to designate an alternate national capital, perhaps underground. "The continuity of government functions in a period of national emergency created by atomic or hydrogen bomb disaster must be guaranteed," he said. "Such guarantee does not exist at the present time."

The Eisenhower administration sought to create one. It began the construction of underground government installations and launched an annual series of nationwide nuclear war drills called Operation Alert. During Operation Alert 1955, President Eisenhower, en route to the tent serving as temporary White House (more elaborate underground facilities had not yet been completed), signed a mock order of "Civil Defense emergency." (An ensuing mock emergency order from the Department of Agriculture removing marketing quotas on major crops was mistakenly reported as an actual order, prompting irate protests from farmers all over the country.) "We are here," Eisenhower said in a live radio and television address from his tent, "to determine whether or not the government is prepared in time of emergency to continue the function of government so that there will be no interruption in the business that must be carried out." On the second day of the exercise, Eisenhower said that it had revealed "more complications than I ever believed possible," and he issued a mock declaration of martial law, arousing protests from civil libertarians.

President Kennedy, as concerned about postattack continuity of government as he was about civil defense, ordered a secret study of the problem in 1962. The study panel was instructed that "nationwide martial law is not an acceptable planning assumption," and that "some segment of representative civil government must remain in control of government operations." The committee reported that current planning for continuity of government was inadequate. It recommended that every important government agency *permanently* station at least one top official and a supporting staff at "fallout-protected sites" outside Washington, and that consideration be given to ordering that at least one designated presidential successor, "on a rotational basis, shall at all times be outside the Washington target area at one of the prelocation sites or a mobile command post."

Those recommendations were not implemented, but improvements were made in the Eisenhower-era relocation plans. In 1964, the Office of Emergency Preparedness published the *National Plan for Emergency Preparedness*, which is still theoretically in effect (a revised edition has been in the works for years). The *Plan* spells out the postattack responsibilities of numerous federal agencies and declares: "To continue to exist as a sovereign power, the Nation must be able not only to withstand an initial nuclear assault but also to restore its social, political, and economic systems. This entire survival and recovery period would probably last for several years. . . . Although the Government must and would take whatever action is required to insure national survival in times of great peril, this does not mean the end of personal and political freedoms. On the contrary, one of the fundamental policies of the emergency preparedness program is [to proceed] without undue infringement of individual rights and with minimum disruption of the political, economic, and social structure of the Nation."

To those ends, continuity-of-government planning proceeded. Then as now, it was done quietly and secretly, and it was not often a matter of public discussion.* Gradually, planning for the protection of the president led to the development of the National Emergency Airborne Command Post, designed to fly above nuclear explosions; more than seventy-five secret "Presidential Emergency Facilities" scattered around the country; detailed secret procedures for delegating presidential authority and passing it on to successors; and the Central Locator System, which keeps track of every official in the presidential line of succession and sends out a warning if all of them are scheduled to gather in the same place so that one can be told to stay away. "And we did one thing we hadn't done before at Reagan's inauguration in 1981," says William Baird. "Ordinarily, Cabinet members go out of office when the president does. We brought the matter up, and both sides agreed that something should be done. So Secretary [of Defense Harold] Brown stayed on in office until later that day, so we had a potential leader if all the others were gone."

Plans have been developed as well for the protection of the justices of the Supreme Court and the leaders of Congress (two of whom—the Speaker of the House and the president pro tempore of the Senate—are second and third in the presidential line of succession). "They have a plan for the leadership . . . ," Speaker Thomas "Tip" O'Neill told a reporter in 1982. "It's something that's highly privileged and confidential, and I wouldn't be able to discuss."

And, as for the bureaucrats, the rank and file in the Executive departments who make up the bulk of the working government . . . Richard L. (who wishes not to be further identified) received his instructions one day in 1979. Then employed as a principal assistant to a Cabinet officer, Richard was sitting in his office when the memo, marked PERSONAL ATTENTION, arrived. It began: "This is your official notification that you have an emergency duty assignment . . ."

---

* A rare exception was the introduction by Walter Cronkite to a 1968 book called *Who Speaks for Civil Defense?* "We must not merely prepare for the survival of individuals but also for the survival of our democratic system," Cronkite wrote. "To insure that, the pre-war government has an obligation of highest priority to be certain that everything is done to preserve the post-war population's confidence in government." Otherwise, Cronkite warned, nuclear war could result in "anarchy."

"It was a one-page piece of paper," Richard recalls, "instructing me that I had been assigned to go such and so in case of nuclear attack. I got the impression I was in the most select group."

How did he feel about that?

"I was somewhat honored to be included."

If a nuclear war is ever considered imminent, Richard L. and several thousand other federal bureaucrats will receive telephone calls. "This is————. I have an emergency message for [your name]," each bureaucrat will be told, according to the emergency message format spelled out in the *Emergency Management Team Member's Handbook* of the Department of Health and Human Services.

"Readiness level————has been declared," each caller will continue. There are four readiness levels—communications watch, initial alert, advanced alert, and attack warning—and the appropriate one will be named. "Repeat. Readiness level————has been declared. Please acknowledge by repeating the message I have given you."

Then, instructs the HHS *Handbook*, "You will repeat the message verbatim, and—upon confirmation of correctness—write it verbatim, note the date and time, and—if any persons are named below you on the diagram [the HHS *Handbook*, like other agencies' emergency guides, organizes emergency team members into a telephone tree]:

"a. Relay the message verbatim to all persons in the block(s) immediately below yours on the diagram. . . .

"b. If you can not immediately contact one of the people at office, home, or alternate number, you *must* make his or her calls, if any, as indicated on the diagram. *The chain must not be broken.*"*

---

* The telephone chains are tested regularly by several agencies, including the Department of Health and Human Services, with less than perfect results. In an HHS drill during a 1980 government-wide continuity-of-government exercise, 22 percent of those on the phone tree were reached within half an hour, 56 percent were reached within an hour, and 80 percent were reached within five hours, when the test ended. The test was conducted during regular office hours and with some advance notification.

Telephoning completed, each bureaucrat will then act according to which readiness level has been declared.

A *communications watch*, the lowest level, will require no individual action. At agency offices, communications equipment will be manned around the clock.

An *initial alert* will require each emergency team member to "be sure your automobile is available with gasoline tank filled. Make stand-by carpool arrangements in case you need transportation during relocation. . . . If you must be away from home or office for any extended time, give an alternate telephone number to the person who (according to the alerting chart) would call you."

An *advanced alert* will mean that things are getting very threatening: "Make arrangements for your family's protection and safety. Keep the person above you on the alerting diagram informed of your whereabouts at all times. . . . Cancel your travel or leave plans; obtain a travel order if you have a relocation assignment. Assemble a personal kit of subsistence and survival items. . . . Stand by for individual instructions or an attack warning."

An *attack warning*, if it comes next, will render the entire system almost useless. It will mean that missiles are on their way, and it is too late to relocate, too late to do much of anything except "take immediate protective action and follow local and building civil defense instructions."

Before an attack warning, however, plans call for the president to order emergency team members to relocate. Relocation plans have been devised for some four dozen "Category A" and "Category B" federal agencies. Category A agencies, which include every Cabinet department as well as independent agencies ranging from the CIA to the TVA, are those deemed to require "a capability for uninterrupted emergency operations" during "the immediate preattack, transattack and immediate postattack periods." Category B agencies, which include the National Science Foundation and the Federal Home Loan Bank Board, are deemed to have "a requirement for postattack reconstitution as soon as conditions permit." (Category C agencies do not rate relocation teams. They are supposed "to defer reconstitution until directed by appropriate authority." In the meantime, their surviving postattack employees are instructed "to make themselves available for other emergency duty.")

Overall authority for this planning is given by Executive Order 11490, which was issued by Richard Nixon in 1969 and has been updated periodically. It charges every federal agency with "the duty of assuring the continuity of the Federal Government in any national emergency . . . including a massive nuclear attack." The order also assigns specific postattack duties to the agencies. It commands the Department of Justice, for example, to make plans for establishing "the location, restraint, or custody of alien enemies" following a nuclear attack. The Securities and Exchange Commission is instructed to develop plans "to reestablish and maintain an orderly market for securities when the situation permits." The Railroad Retirement Board is to plan for administering the Railroad Retirement Act "consistent with overall Federal plans for continuation of benefit payments after an enemy attack."

Additional guidance for planning during the "preattack period," i.e., now, is contained in Federal Preparedness Circulars, which were issued originally by the Office of Emergency Planning, then by its successor, the Federal Preparedness Agency, and now by *its* successor, the Federal Emergency Management Agency. FPC #14, for example, orders Category A and Category B agencies to establish emergency succession lists for the replacement of suddenly deceased key officials. "Succession should be established to a minimum depth of six where designation of successors located outside of the Washington capital area is not feasible," it says. "In this instance, it is desirable to designate several executives who are frequent travellers and thus increase the likelihood that all successors will not be concentrated in the Washington capital area at any given time." In compliance with this directive, the Department of Labor, for one, has published its list of who will succeed whom following a nuclear attack. If the assistant secretary of labor for occupational safety and health is killed, he or she will be replaced by the deputy assistant secretary for operating programs, or, if *he* is dead too, one of five other designated successors ranging in rank down to the associate assistant secretary for training, education and consultation programs.

All agencies have also been required to determine which of their functions are "essential and uninterruptible" during and immediately following a nuclear war. The Treasury Department, for one, has decided that its uninterruptible functions include advising the president, guarding federal bullion, and providing "central payment service for most agencies," while printing currency and managing the public debt are interruptible. The Postal Service decided at first that mail delivery—not just postattack survivor registration and mail forwarding but ordinary, everyday mail delivery—was an essential, uninterruptible function during a nuclear war. "We convinced them to change it," says William Baird. The only mail delivery now considered uninterruptible is that to the secret federal relocation sites.

Keeping their essential uninterruptible functions in mind, the agencies have recruited their emergency relocation teams. The Department of Agriculture has allotted some of the spaces on its 62-member team as follows:

- 11 places to the Office of the Secretary, whose members have the essential, uninterruptible function of providing "executive policy and direction" in the immediate preattack, transattack, and immediate postattack periods.
- 24 places to the Agricultural Stabilization and Conservation Service, to direct "use of food resources . . . and agricultural production." ("If the crisis involves nuclear radiation of fresh foods and this food receives less than 5 mr[millirem]/hr radiation within a 24-hour period, that food if otherwise wholesome will be deemed safe for human consumption.")
- 2 places to the Soil Conservation Service, to estimate "effects of radiation on agricultural soils and water."
- 3 places to the Forest Service, to estimate "the extent and effects of fire in rural areas."
- 3 places to the Food and Nutrition Service, to authorize "the distribution of USDA donated foods and emergency use of food stamps."
- 2 places to the Office of the General Counsel, to provide "legal advice on emergency actions."

Each Category A agency has assembled not one but *three* emergency management teams—an A Team, a B Team, and a C Team. (The Agriculture team described above is its A Team.) When the order to relocate goes out during the pre-nuclear-war crisis, the three teams will disperse.

The A teams, which are headed by Cabinet secretaries and other agency chiefs, will remain at normal agency headquarters—although, in most cases, they will move to the basement. "The 'A' team is designated to remain at headquarters to carry out departmental functions as long as is feasible," explains the *Emergency Management Team Member's Handbook* of the Department of Health and Human Services. In the case of HHS, that will be relatively comfortable service—unless and until Washington is bombed. The HHS headquarters building is new, and its A Team site is well designed and well maintained. (It is also easy to find. A sign by the elevator in the building's main lobby says "Secretary's Emergency Operating Center, Room 3B-10" and bears a downward-pointing arrow.)*

The HHS emergency center shares a basement floor with an underground garage and can be reached by regular elevator or a special private elevator from the Secretary's office (which some Secretaries have used to get to their cars). A Team members will enter the center through a vestibule that doubles as an air lock. If necessary, they will detour through a shower room, where they will discard their fallout-contaminated clothing, wash themselves, and don fresh clothes that are already stockpiled in the center. Uninvited guests will be turned away by the Secretary's bodyguards.

The main room in the center is a large and well-lighted conference room, furnished with long tables, orange padded chairs, telephones, a Xerox machine, a color TV, a blackboard, a movie screen, a machine for making slide graphs and charts, and a lectern with a

---

* The HHS center is also the A Team site for the Public Health Service, which was originally supposed to use the basement of its own building in suburban Rockville, Maryland. Owing to the slope of the land on the Rockville site, however, half the basement became the ground floor. "This was an A Team site, but you'd have to be morons to come here," explains Harold Gracey, emergency coordinator of the Public Health Service, whose office is in the Rockville half-basement. "This wall is underground, but across the hall there are windows facing D.C. In an attack, we'd be blown out into the parking lot—after we were compressed up against the wall."

microphone. Behind it is a smaller meeting room, soundproofed for classified postattack briefings. The complex also includes an infirmary, a computer terminal for communicating with FEMA's damage-assessment computers, a well, an emergency generator, a radio room, file rooms, and a kitchen stocked with enough Mountain House freeze-dried food—including shrimp Creole and chocolate pudding—to feed three dozen people for a month. There is a private office off the main conference room for the Secretary and, behind that, a small private bedroom and bath. The walls of the Secretary's office are decorated with photographs of Hiroshima and Nagasaki.

Finally, there are two bunk-bedded dormitories for the rest of the A Team members. The HHS A Team consists of thirty executives and four secretaries, so—and this is somewhat embarrassing in a department currently headed by a woman—there are thirty beds in the men's dormitory and four in the women's. Current plans are to partition the "men's" dormitory as needed during a nuclear war.

While A Team members throughout the government are heading into basements (few of which are as well equipped as the one at HHS), all B Team members will be embarking on a fifty-mile trip west into the Blue Ridge Mountains of Virginia. There they will gather inside Mount Weather, a hollowed-out mountain fortress constructed during the 1950s to be the alternate national capital. Almost everything about the Mount Weather installation, known officially only as the "Special Facility," is classified, but reports over the years have described it as including offices, residences, streets where electric cars travel, and a lake-sized reservoir, all *inside* the mountain. "It's kind of mind-boggling," says Buford Macklin, emergency coordinator of the Department of Housing and Urban Development, who has been there. "*Dr. Strangelove* is one of my favorite movies, and you can fantasize about that site in similar ways. It's otherworldly—just the size and weight and massiveness of the doors. It's a mini-city—like a space station." It is apparently not, however, luxurious. "It's austere," says Richard Pidgeon, emergency coordinator of the Department of Commerce. "Believe me. I've been there. The secretary of commerce has a small cubicle. He wouldn't have to share a bed. Everybody else would." (Bed-sharers would presumably sleep in shifts, not together.)

A rare official statement on Mount Weather was submitted by

FEMA to Congress in 1981 when, because of a legal technicality, FEMA had to ask for a bill authorizing the operation of buses to carry Mount Weather's permanent employees to work. "There are presently more than three hundred FEMA employees permanently assigned to the Special Facility," the report explained.

> The installation is kept in a constant state of readiness to perform its mission in the event of an emergency that requires the relocation of key Government officials. These employees are required to have top secret clearance, to reside within an hour's ride of the Special Facility, and to be available 24 hours a day to report for duty at the Special Facility in the event of an emergency.
>
> Because of the remote location of the Special Facility, as well as its top secret classification, the employees assigned there are not able to use public transportation to travel between their homes and their jobs. Therefore, for many years a bus transportation service, at reasonable rates of fare to the employees, has been operated by the Government between the Special Facility and the nearby communities where the employees reside. The buses remain nightly at predesignated community rendezvous points to ensure transportation for employees to the Special Facility in the event of after-duty-hour recall.

Among those permanently employed at Mount Weather is the staff, including a doctor, of the facility hospital, designated Health Unit #1 of the Public Health Service. All B Team members are entitled to free checkups there at any time, so that any medications they may need can be identified and added to Mount Weather's emergency supplies.

While B Team members are settling into the mountain during the preattack crisis, C Team members will be dispersing to individual agency relocation sites scattered within a few hours drive north, west, and south of Washington in what is referred to as the Federal Relocation Arc. To back up Mount Weather, every Category A agency is charged with maintaining a site in the Arc, making sure it is protected, and equipping it with communications gear. Some of the sites are self-sufficient and fallout-protected and some are not.

"We make agreements with local motels for housing," says David Madden, a security manager for the U. S. Postal Service. "In the long run, though, it won't matter. There'll be martial law, and we'll just take it." (This attitude seems to conflict with the Postal Service's *Emergency Planning Manual*, which admonishes all postal relocatees "to respect all local laws and the rights of others. . . . They should not engage in any activities which might lessen the confidence of local citizens in the government mission should it become known.")

Each agency is also responsible for stocking its Arc site with copies of records that will be needed to resume the agency's operations after a nuclear war. A Labor Department emergency manual recommends that such records be carefully wrapped in "protective paper," as "experience has revealed that unprotected records not wrapped and sealed are often damaged by dust and moisture."

To speed them in their crisis commutes to Mount Weather and the Arc facilities, all emergency team members have been issued Federal Employee Emergency Identification Cards, each of which bears its owner's name, photo, blood type, and the message: THE PERSON DESCRIBED ON THIS CARD HAS ESSENTIAL EMERGENCY DUTIES WITH THE FEDERAL GOVERNMENT. REQUEST FULL ASSISTANCE AND UNRESTRICTED MOVEMENT BE AFFORDED THE PERSON TO WHOM THIS CARD IS ISSUED. With considerable expense and bureaucratic effort, the cards were distributed throughout the government in 1980, only to be recalled in 1981 because the new director of FEMA, Louis Giuffrida, did not like the old FEMA seal—a white triangle within a square with rounded corners. Giuffrida presided over the design of a new agency emblem featuring a bald eagle clutching arrows and an olive branch beneath a Latin motto meaning "Service in Peace and War." The Emergency Identification Cards were redesigned, and a new set was issued.

Despite the cards, the telephone trees, and annual exercises in which emergency team members gather at Mount Weather and practice running the country after a nuclear war, problems with planning for continuity of government persist. While many agencies are diligent and enthusiastic about the program and have large full-time emergency-planning staffs, others are less enthusiastic. One agency's emergency coordinator, who is responsible for all his department's postattack planning, when asked which relocation team he himself is on, replied, "I'm on the team that goes home and drinks gin and tonic until the bomb drops."

Continuity-of-government planners, a 1978 General Accounting Office report noted, have "an unenviable task, considering that many people, both in and out of government, believe that (1) a nuclear war will probably not occur and (2) if it does, they most likely will not survive."

The GAO surveyed 534 emergency team members in six federal departments and found that only 56 percent of them had been informed of their emergency duties. (The Department of Defense ranked highest on this question, 79 percent of its emergency team members having been told what they are supposed to do in a war.) Less than half those surveyed said they felt prepared to travel to their relocation sites or perform their postattack duties, and 20 percent said they were not particularly likely to report for duty if the call came while they were at home.

Most of those surveyed said that the chances of their reporting as ordered would improve if better arrangements were made for their families. As things stand, almost no provisions have been made for them. (In fact, most departments instruct their team members that, when making an emergency alert call to a colleague, they are *not* to leave messages with family members.) "I consider it a weakness in the program," says Richard Pidgeon, the Commerce Department's emergency coordinator. "Team members are supposed to make their own arrangements: 'If I have to go, honey, take the kids and go up to Aunt Bessie's.' I think that's asking a hell of a lot."

A notable exception to this is the Federal Reserve System, where team members will be able to take their families with them to relocation sites. "The Board discussed this and it was generally felt that the chance of getting our essential staff to go without their families was pretty slim," explains Federal Reserve Board Emergency Coordinator Harry Guinter. The Treasury Department has not gone that far, but it, too, has made some plans for families. "When someone's assigned to an emergency executive team, we ask him how many family members need to be provided for," says Emergency Coordinator Robert Merchant. "We have written agreements that are renewed periodically with establishments that have the capability to house and feed people. They're not picked for their nearness to relocation sites; they're picked for being in low-risk areas. When the emergency teams relocate, their dependents will relocate to these establishments. The team member agrees to bear the expense, and the families have to get to the low-risk areas themselves, but we have assigned a Treasury coordinator to try to be there when they arrive and act as liaison between the dependents and the installation's management."

More typically, the HHS *Team Member's Handbook* only advises: "Establish an emergency survival plan for your family. Remember that your emergency duties may prevent you from being with your family during an attack, and make sure that they know the steps to be taken when you are away." To help out, HHS gives each team member a copy of FEMA's standard civil-defense booklet.

At least one emergency coordinator, however, has his own ideas about this. "There's a fifty-fifty chance I'd go," says the coordinator, who has been assigned to Mount Weather. "And if I do go I'll probably take my family with me. What are the guards going to do? I don't think they'll capture me and take me inside. They could turn us all away, but that would miss the whole point of the thing."

While A, B, and C team members from federal agencies in Washington are heading into basements or for the hills, regional officials of Category A agencies will be dividing into two teams, one to stay at regional headquarters and one to go to a Federal Regional Center like the one in Maynard, Massachusetts. Built in 1968, the Maynard FRC is a two-story office building underground; FEMA employees who work there call it "the mushroom factory." It has a fallout protection factor of one thousand (meaning that only one-thousandth of the radiation on the outside will get inside), its communication and electronic equipment is shielded against the destructive electromagnetic pulse of distant nuclear explosions, and it is designed to withstand the blast of a one-megaton bomb less than two and a half miles away. It has massive vault doors, valves in its ventilation shafts that will snap shut automatically upon sensing the flash of a nuclear explosion, its own wells and generators, some nice wooden furniture obtained from the Boston office of the Community Services Administration when the CSA was shut down by the Reagan administration, and enough freeze-dried food to feed 317 people for a month. "We ate it for a week during the blizzard of seventy-eight," says a Maynard employee. "Some of it's not bad, but we *did* learn to stay away from the pork chops."

Continuity of *state* government during a nuclear war has not been overlooked. During the early 1960s, more than two dozen states passed "survival amendments" to their constitutions, granting emergency war powers to governors and legislatures. And most states have constructed their own protected underground facilities. One of the more elaborate of these is the New York State Emergency Operating Center and Alternate Seat of Government, an underground complex for seven hundred state officials in Albany. Constructed during the administration of Governor Nelson Rockefeller, the shelter houses files containing, among other things, microfilmed duplicates of New York State birth and death records for postattack reference. To avoid blast damage, the mirrors in the facility's bathrooms are of polished metal—glass has been banished—and the toilet pipes are of shatterproof flexible plastic. (The facility does lack, however, something included in the newer and smaller state bunker in Framingham, Massachusetts—a piece of equipment that looks like an oversized file cabinet but is labeled "Refrigerated Morgue for Two Bodies.")

Continuity of *local* government will be maintained at more than 2,100 city and county Emergency Operating Centers, many of which are in the basements of city halls and police headquarters. Federal civil-defense funds pay half the cost of the EOCs, which are required to be blast- and fallout-resistant and to have several redundant types of communications equipment. "Our current program also requires that the EOC be manned twenty-four hours a day, that it must be occupied by the local civil-defense director, and that he has to have a legal charter to run it in a major emergency," says Joseph Mealy, FEMA's chief of emergency management systems support. "So applicants know that they must have real interest in civil defense and not just want help building a new basement for the sheriff's department." Some local EOCs are in excellent shape, like the one beneath the modern police headquarters in Plattsburgh, New York, which has a standing order with a wholesale grocer to deliver food during a national emergency, has offices for the mayor and the common council, and is supplied with sixty-four pairs of Montgomery Ward overalls in case the mayor and councillors have to discard fallout-contaminated clothing when they enter. (The EOC is, however, just one mile from a Strategic Air Command bomber base, so its survival in a nuclear war is not likely.) Other EOCs are not so well equipped, like the one in the half-basement beneath the old fire station in Greenfield, Massachusetts, where supplies include thirty-year-old survival biscuits, twenty-eight-year-old radios, and several fallout shelter toilet kits (each consisting of ten rolls of toilet paper, a plastic bag, and a makeshift seat inside a metal drum) of uncertain vintage.

During the prewar crisis, local EOCs will coordinate all local civil-defense activities—piling up dirt around buildings, testing sirens, alerting and training police and hospital workers, and so on. They will also participate in FEMA's Civil Defense Emergency Operations Reporting System, because, according to the CDEORS manual, it will "be vitally important for key national officials to know what IR [Increased Readiness] actions had been taken by localities throughout the country." Once a day, local EOCs will fill in DCPA Form 902 (which will be supplied to them in pads of fifty), filling in the blanks to indicate whether or not they have stepped up their distribution of civil-defense literature, whether the EOC itself is fully manned and ready, how many fallout shelter managers have been trained, how much above normal retail sales of food and gasoline are running, and how many evacuees have arrived in or departed from the area. ("This number can be determined through coordination with local utility companies," advises the manual. "There is a correlation between the amount of electricity and water used and the population.")

The answers to these questions and others will be sent, by radio or telephone, to state-level EOCs every day before 6:00 p.m., and the reports will then be collated and forwarded to the nearest Federal Regional Center before midnight. Each state EOC will also report on its own activities, filling in Form 901 to let the FRC know if the governor has been briefed, if he has urged local officials to increase local readiness, if he has urged the public to make limited civil-defense preparations, or if, as the international situation deteriorates, he has urged the public "to make final crisis preparations short of taking shelter."

When the incoming enemy attack is spotted, Air Force helicopters that have been standing by will swoop down to pick up Cabinet officers from the A Team bunkers beneath their headquarters in Washington. Along with the Speaker of the House and the president pro tem of the Senate, they will be flown to presumed nontarget areas to wait out the attack and see which of them, if any, is the new president. If all the successors are killed, surviving House or Senate members could, in theory, gather to elect a new Speaker or president pro tem, who would then become president. If there are no surviving House or Senate members, surviving governors or state legislators could select new senators who could elect a new president pro tem, who would then become president.

The rest of the A Team members will be left behind, wondering not if they are about to become president but if they are about to die. "Emergency Team Alpha [A] will continue in charge of Departmental emergency operations until it is unable to function," explains the Labor Department's *National Office Alerting Plan*, "at which time Emergency Team Bravo [the B Team at Mount Weather] will assume command responsibility. Notification will normally take the form of data output from the damage assessment program indicating the destruction of the headquarters emergency operations center. . . . Emergency Team Charlie [the C Team at the Arc site] will not assume operational command until a clear indication is received that communications are no longer possible with the Special Facility [Mount Weather] or damage-assessment reports indicate it has been destroyed."

On the local government level, city and county Emergency Operating Centers will be supervising fire-fighting and rescue operations. Such operations will be restricted, warns the *FEMA Attack Environment Manual*, if the local fallout dose rate exceeds 50 roentgens an hour, which will be the approximate rate 60 miles downwind six hours after a single two-megaton blast. (A cumulative dose of 200 roentgens will kill some people; a dose of 600 roentgens will kill almost anyone.) "Below 50 R/hr, outside operations are generally feasible," FEMA instructs local governments. "Operations should be confined to essential tasks, such as search and rescue, resupply of shelters, and reconstitution of urgent utility services. Exposure of persons conducting such operations can be controlled by rotation of work crews ... Above 50 R/hr, few outside operations are feasible without risking incapacitating exposure. Only desperate needs, such as protecting the population against fire, would justify emergency operations." To facilitate planning, FEMA has developed a ladder of nine "Basic Operating Situations," ranging from #1, NEGRAD NEGFIRE (negligible radiation and negligible fire), to #9, HIRAD HIFIRE. It estimates that 17 percent of those Americans surviving the immediate effects of a massive nuclear attack would find themselves in BOS #9.

Local EOCs will also be responsible for keeping in touch, via radio or telephone, with local fallout shelters, telling shelter managers about conditions in the outside world and, eventually, notifying them that it is safe to emerge. "It is essential that you maintain communication with the Emergency Operating Center ... ," advises FEMA's manual for fallout shelter management, "so that your population will know at all times that they are part of a nation that is preparing for survival and recovery."

Local EOCs will be communicating back up the command chain as well, filing reports with state EOCs about local conditions. Sample local status reports are given in FEMA's Civil Defense Emergency Operations Reporting System manual:

MAJOR FIRE SW OF LA GRAND ADVANCING NE AT 10 MILES PER HOUR. . . .

NO CONTACT WITH JURISDICTIONS SOUTH OF COUNTY SEAT. CHIEF ELECTED OFFICIAL AT POLK COUNTY EOC IS THE COUNTY ASSESSOR. . . .

LOCAL HOSPITALS AND HEALTH DEPT REPORT 3,000 PLUS CASES OF CARBUNCLE-LIKE LESIONS ON THE SKIN CHIEFLY AMONG FARMERS. . . .

CRITICAL SHORTAGE . . . FOOD — 20 DAYS [SUPPLY ON HAND],

MED SUPPLIES — 10 DAYS. . . . COUNTY-IMPOSED RATIONING NOW IN
EFFECT FOR ABOVE ITEMS. . . .

REQUEST FOR AID . . . MEDICAL EQUIPMENT AND PERSONNEL FOR
13,000 PEOPLE FROM THE PORTLAND AREA SUFFERING FROM INJURIES
AND RADIATION SICKNESS.

During the attack itself, local EOCs will be forwarding reports
from Weapons Effects Reporting Stations, one of which should be
established, FEMA says, for every hundred square miles in rural
areas and every nine square miles in cities. ("I think you could go
from coast to coast today and not find anyone who'll admit to being
a weapons effects reporter," says FEMA's Joseph Mealy, but he
suggests that, during a crisis, reporters could be recruited among
public safety employees, shelter managers, and volunteer tornado-
watchers.) It will be the job of WER stations to file reports of
NUDET (nuclear detonation) sightings with the nearest EOC.
"Sightings are reported based on the light flash or resulting stem or
cloud of a weapon, in terms of the 16 points of the compass," instructs the WER station procedures manual. "A sample message
format for this report follows: 'POLK COUNTY EOC. THIS IS REPORT-
ING STATION 9. . . . NUDET NORTH-NORTHEAST AT 10:30 A.M.' " WER
stations will also file reports on blast damage, glass breakage, and
fallout intensity. Local EOCs will forward the reports to state EOCs,
which will pass them on to Federal Regional Centers and the EOCs
of interested neighboring states. A sample interstate message is supplied in the CDEORS manual:

WASHINGTON, THIS IS IDAHO. NUDET SIGHTING REPORT. RE-
PORTING AREA IDAHO 6 REPORTED NUDET TO WEST-NORTHWEST AT
0400Z, POSSIBLY SPOKANE.

It is all too possible, postattack planners realize, that Weapons
Effects Reporting Stations in the mid-Atlantic region will be sighting NUDET after NUDET in the vicinity of Mount Weather and
other federal relocation sites. The location of Mount Weather,
theoretically a secret, was fatally compromised when a TWA flight
from Columbus crashed into the mountain in 1974. Now a road map
to Mount Weather is included in the Department of Health and
Human Services' *Emergency Management Team Member's Hand-*

book, an unclassified document. The Russians certainly know where to find the place, if they want it.

"Our program started in 1954," says John Policastro, director of FEMA's division of continuity-of-government planning. "Wouldn't it be prudent to assume that the Russians have found out where these facilities are and have targeted them? With modern weapons, they can dig out anything they want. . . . Mount Weather still has lots of utility for a situation less than nuclear war. Its capital costs are amortized, and the operating costs of a place like that are pretty cheap. And it *might* survive an attack. Do you scrap something like that? Maybe at some point, when you have sufficient alternatives, you close it."

Alternatives to Mount Weather and the Federal Relocation Arc are being developed now. The National Security Council ordered a classified study of continuity of government during the administration of Jimmy Carter; it resulted in Carter's issuance of Presidential Directive 58, a secret document outlining a new plan for dispersing and protecting government officials in a crisis.*

Details of PD-58 are still closely held, but it apparently called for a decentralized "shell game" concept (like Carter's MX missile proposal) in which more relocation sites would be established than would be used. (Schools would serve well as such sites, one FEMA planner points out, with their swimming pools—to drink from, not swim in—and their kitchens.) "We probably would not reconstitute in Washington," General William Hilsman, manager of the National Communications System, said in 1982. "Surviving government would be in Augusta, or in Hartford, or some other place; and decision makers are likely to be moving around." There have also been suggestions that the new system builds on federal employees who already work outside of Washington and on the "Federal Re-

---

* Published accounts of PD-58 and other continuity-of-government planning have provoked an unusual assortment of critics. *Tass* denounced "Carter, Brzezinski and Co." for making plans for their own survival while risking the lives of tens of millions of other Americans with a nuclear strategy (PD-59) "fraught with a nuclear holocaust for the whole world." Agreeing with *Tass*, up to a point, was a contributor to the hawkish *Journal of Civil Defense*, who demanded to know why "key military and government crews will fan out to buried bunkers" while "the children, the women, the people . . . will be left to fry, sizzle and pop under the attack." Columnist Russell Baker only wondered if the fact that he had once been admitted to Studio 54 would qualify him for admission to a government hide-out in a nuclear war.

gional Reconstitution Area" concept, under which regional federal officials have picked out small towns and cities with no obvious military or industrial targets as potential government centers for post-attack America.

"Weapons are getting smaller and more accurate," says one FEMA planner. "There are more places to hide now than there were ten years ago. You can go and pick little towns all over the country. ... If you can disperse your people so that if the Russians want to target them it would soak up a large number of weapons, they'd have to judge, 'Is it worth expending so many weapons to get to the governors, to the regions, to the president?' If you build that kind of a system, what have you done? You've assured the survival of Washington."

The Reagan administration has, if anything, expanded on Carter's continuity-of-government program. "In the past, in too many instances, continuity of government was limited to succession to the presidency," FEMA Director Louis Giuffrida said in 1981. "Now that didn't make sense to me. It doesn't make a great deal of sense to have a president if you don't have the rest of the structure, so we have expanded the continuity-of-government [program] to include the rest of the federal government, and also state and local."

And so, if all goes well, somewhere—in a Washington basement, inside Mount Weather, or in a high school gym in Arkansas—the postattack government of the United States of America will get to work, freezing wages and prices, rounding up enemy aliens, managing housing for refugees. "A long-term recovery phase would follow the immediate post-attack period," says a Labor Department emergency manual. "The relatively small emergency cadre group would be joined by regular employees who had survived." Allowances will be made for those who are late. "Employees instructed to report to the agency relocation site immediately after an attack who are delayed in reporting for work due to disaster conditions ... (road conditions, radioactive fallout, and so on) should be granted administrative leave for the full period of time it took to reach the relocation site," notes a government personnel regulation.

Until 1979, the Office of Personnel Management (formerly the Civil Service Commission) supplied post offices with cards to be filled out by federal employees who could not reach their normal places of employment after a nuclear attack or whose places of employment no longer existed. The cards were to be sent to their own employers or the nearest functioning OPM office. "In a lot of people's minds," acknowledges an OPM planner, "this presented an image of Joe Bureaucrat going to an incinerated post office to fill out an incinerated form." OPM has discontinued the old cards and is now developing a new postattack registration system. "It will be some way of getting employees in touch with their own agencies or, if that's not possible, with us," says the planner. "It will take a lot of people to run the system, but after a nuclear attack a lot of things we do day-to-day we're not going to do for a while, and this is one of the programs we'll focus on." The planner adds that the new system will adhere to the basic principles of the old one: "The preferred option will be for people to go to work at their old job. If that's not available, they'll take another necessary federal job. If that's not available, they'll volunteer for civil-defense work. Whatever they do, they'll stay in the same pay status."

To meet postattack payrolls, the Treasury Department has prepared an *Emergency Disbursing Plan*. Relocation sites have been selected for every federal payroll office—the Chicago office, for example, will move to the post office in Oconomowoc, Wisconsin—and "emergency disbursing kits" have been stored at each site. The kits include stockpiles of blank checks marked with "emergency disbursing symbols." The Treasury also maintains a list of "printing establishments in non-critical target areas having plants capable of printing continuous-form paper checks with whom prior arrangements have been made." (If payroll checks still do not arrive, the Postal Service manual authorizes postmasters to pay local employees with cash or postal money orders.)

Postattack federal employees, meanwhile, will be dusting off Federal Emergency Plan D, the compendium of post-nuclear-war actions and policies that has already been prepared and distributed to relocation sites, and the "Other Than D" documents, which will be used instead if Congress is still functioning. Both Plan D and the Other Than D documents are classified, but one old Plan D proclamation was recently declassified by the Treasury Department and provides a sample of the form:

PROCLAMATION NO. _____

AUTHORIZING THE SECRETARY OF THE TREASURY TO EXTEND THE TIME PRESCRIBED FOR THE PERFORMANCE OF ANY ACT REQUIRED BY THE TARIFF ACT OF 1930 AND TO PERMIT THE ENTRY FREE OF DUTY OF CERTAIN EMERGENCY SUPPLIES.

A PROCLAMATION

WHEREAS an unprovoked armed attack has been launched against the United States by foreign military forces; and

WHEREAS I have this day proclaimed the existence of an unlimited national emergency and a state of civil defense emergency; and

WHEREAS the exigencies of the international situation and of the national defense require the suspension of import restrictions, as necessary, to facilitate the receiving of necessary supplies . . .

NOW THEREFORE, I, _____, President of the United States, under, and by virtue of, the authority vested in me by the Constitution and laws of the United States . . . do hereby authorize the Secretary of the Treasury [to waive certain import requirements, etc.]

More federal postattack plans and policies are spelled out in detail in the *Code of Emergency Federal Regulations*, which has been distributed to federal relocation sites and will go into effect following a nuclear attack. The *CEFR*, several hundred pages long, includes the Agriculture Department's postattack rationing scheme and a plan for emergency loans to farmers. Farmers will be allowed to use the loans to pay for feed and seed, to replace "livestock lost, destroyed, or disposed of as the result of a military attack or a natural disaster occurring after the attack," and to pay premiums "on reasonable amounts of health and life insurance, and reasonable expenses for medical care." The *CEFR* also includes a suspension of the ban on nepotism in federal employment, Interstate Commerce Commission orders allowing regulated bus companies to modify and expand their routes to and from cities "within any area of attack," and regulations authorizing federal agencies to requisition private property "without regard to the willingness of owners or suppliers to provide such property or services." A blank requisitioning form is included, with instructions on filling it out: "The original and one copy of the Order of Taking are to be given to the owner or other person in possession. If no such person is available, the original and the copy should be posted in a conspicuous place on or near the property . . . and a true copy should be filed, if feasible, at the appropriate location where real property records of the jurisdiction in question are maintained. If personal property, the original and the copy should be posted in a conspicuous place or delivered to a responsible local inhabitant who will endeavor to deliver them to the owner."

The Office of the Federal Register, which publishes the *Code of Emergency Federal Regulations*, urges all federal agencies to take advantage of it. "By making use of this valuable tool now," says the OFR, "they will be taking the soundest approach to the problem of emergency promulgation." For those federal agencies caught short by a nuclear attack, however, there will still be ways to promulgate emergency regulations. The *Emergency Federal Register*, a postattack version of the peacetime *Federal Register*, in which all federal regulations are published, will commence publication as soon as possible after a nuclear war. "Initially, at least, only a few hundred copies would be printed and distribution would be limited," cautions the OFR. As for the immediate postattack period, when even the *Emergency Federal Register* will not be available, the OFR advises agencies to "promulgate their own documents by any means at their disposal including radio or other means of electronic transmission. They would, however, retain the signed, original document and two certified copies for eventual filing with the Office of the Emergency Federal Register."

And if the whole system falls apart—the A, B, and C teams are killed in their hideouts or fatally demoralized, surviving Americans pay no heed to federal regulations, no one is quite sure who is president, survivors *do* band together in tribes, anarchy reigns—and the United States of America ceases to exist as a nation . . . there will still be one final backup, one more preattack preparation that may yet bear fruit, that may, someday, point the way for descendants of the survivors to reestablish our republican system of government.

The special protective ceremony is rehearsed once a day at the National Archives in Washington. Under the building's great rotunda, a uniformed guard approaches the display case that holds the Declaration of Independence and the Constitution of the United States, unlocks a switch, and starts the documents on a long slow descent into a fifty-ton vault that was designed to protect them from fire, shock, heat, water—and nuclear explosion. The vault, President Harry Truman said as he dedicated it in 1952, "is as safe from destruction as anything that the wit of modern man can devise. . . . So I confidently predict that what we are doing today is placing before the eyes of many generations to come the symbols of a living faith."

The documents are lowered into their vault every night at closing time and brought up again every morning. During a nuclear attack, they will be lowered for what may be a longer rest.

"We have a hot line to the Pentagon down in the guard's office," says Larry Oberg, a National Archives security manager. "They'd call and say the attack is under way. The guard is supposed to come up here and activate this. I hope they get the right guard— one who's not going to run out and go home."

TEN

"Comrade, What Is This?"

A few years ago Leon Gouré went to Moscow on a tourist visa to look for blast and fallout shelters. "I wandered around courtyards and around buildings," Gouré explained later to a congressional committee, "and I assumed that the most evident sign of a shelter would be the emergency exits." He spotted a number of large concrete blocks with louvered grates. "It could be a ventilation shaft, could be anything . . . ," Gouré recounted. "What I usually did was to palm some Soviet citizen coming down the path, digging him in the ribs and saying, 'Comrade, what is this?' And it never failed. They always said it was a shelter exit."

This was the confirmation Gouré was looking for. For more than two decades his career has been largely devoted to studying and describing Soviet civil defense and issuing warnings about its size, its effectiveness, and its dangerous influence on the international balance of power. "The Soviet Union has the largest and most comprehensive war-survival program in the world today," Gouré wrote in his book, *War Survival in Soviet Strategy: USSR Civil Defense* (which followed his books *Civil Defense in the Soviet Union* and *Soviet Civil Defense Revisited 1966–1969* and preceded *The Soviet Civil Defense Shelter Program* and *Shelters in Soviet War Survival Strategy*). "[T]he Soviet leadership has come to view civil defense as a critical 'strategic factor' which, in a large measure, can determine the course and outcome of a nuclear war," Gouré concluded in *War Survival in Soviet Strategy*. That book was based, according to its preface, on Soviet literature and interviews with emigrés and was "verif[ied] . . . by direct observations made during a visit to the Soviet Union."

The Soviet civil-defense effort, Gouré warns (as do others who have followed his lead), has produced a civil-defense gap between a fine Russian program and a weak American one. More important, they claim, it is indicative of an attitude-toward-nuclear-war gap that puts the United States at a significant disadvantage. "There is something innately destabilizing in the very fact that we consider nuclear war unfeasible and suicidal for both, and our chief adversary views it as feasible and winnable for himself," wrote Richard Pipes, a Harvard historian who later joined the staff of Ronald Reagan's National Security Council, in an influential 1977 *Commentary* article called "Why the Soviet Union Thinks It Could Fight and Win a Nuclear War."

"I have my doubts as to whether the present Soviet leadership believe that," Harold Brown said in 1980, yet he justified Jimmy Carter's Presidential Directive 59, with its emphasis on nuclear war fighting, as a corrective to the alleged attitude gap. "[PD-59] does seek both to prevent the Soviets from being able to win such a war and to convince them that they could not win such a war," Brown told a Senate committee. "I do not believe that either side could win a limited nuclear war; and I want to insure as best we can that the Soviets do not believe so either."

The Reagan administration came into office with no doubts about what the Soviets believe, or what the United States should do about it. "It's difficult for me to think that there's a winnable nuclear war," Ronald Reagan told reporters in 1981, "but where our great risk falls is that the Soviet Union has made it very plain that among themselves they believe it is winnable. And believing that, that makes them constitute a threat."

A few weeks later, defending the president's $180 billion nuclear weapons program, Caspar Weinberger told a Senate committee, "I do feel confident that the Soviets must believe they can [win a nuclear war], and that they are planning, deploying and developing techniques . . . which clearly indicates that they have that belief. Therefore, I think, if we are going to maintain the strategic balance, we have to acquire similar capabilities."

• • •

For the first few years after the atomic bombing of Hiroshima, the official public attitude of the Kremlin toward the fantastic new weapon was to ignore it. As long as the United States had the atomic bomb and the Soviet Union did not, it seemed it would little profit Communist morale to make a fuss about the thing. When Soviet spokesmen mentioned it at all, they denounced it. The West was sadly mistaken, said a Soviet air marshal in 1949, in thinking "that the peoples of the USSR and the People's Democracies will be intimidated by the so-called 'atomic' or 'push-button' war."

The Soviets denounced as well the doctrine of strategic bombing, of which atomic bombing was the ultimate manifestation. While the United States and Britain had pummeled German and Japanese cities during World War II, the Soviet Union had concentrated its firepower on the battlefield. "At first, the Soviets did not seem to recognize the potential of strategic bombing," wrote the staunchly anti-Communist authors of a 1954 book about the hydrogen bomb. "During the war, U.S. Air General Hoyt Vandenberg went to Moscow to explain strategic bombing to the Russians and convince them that it was worth while." After the war, Russian doctrine continued (and continues still) to minimize the bombing of enemy cities. "This negative attitude to bombing of civilians is conditioned not by humanitarian considerations," Richard Pipes took care to point out in his *Commentary* article, "but by cold, professional assessments of the [minimal] effects of that kind of strategic bombing as revealed by the [post-World War II] Allied Strategic Bombing Surveys."

None of this, of course, prevented the Soviets from working to develop their own atomic bomb as quickly as they could. But even after Russia became a substantial nuclear power a significant line of Soviet thought continued to insist that nuclear weapons were not as all-powerful as they were widely considered to be in the West. "In the opinion of [Western] bourgeois ideologues, a nuclear war, if such a war arises, will deprive the masses of any possibility of influencing its outcome and may have only one result—the physical annihilation of mankind . . . ," wrote the authors of *The Philosophical Heritage of V.I. Lenin and Problems of Contemporary War*, a

1972 Soviet publication. "While weapons of mass destruction should not be underrated, neither should they be overrated, viewed as some kind of mystical force detached from society."*

Problems of Contemporary War manages to quote Lenin himself, who died in 1924, on the error of overestimating the effects of nuclear war: " 'Regardless of the degree of destruction of civilization,' wrote Lenin, 'it cannot be erased from history.' " The book makes clear the ideological underpinnings of its stance: "If the imperialists unleash a new world war, the toilers will ... mercilessly and irrevocably sweep capitalism from the face of the earth. Of course losses may be extremely high in the decisive clash between two opposing forces. Much, however, depends on the activeness of the masses. The more vigorously and resolutely they oppose the actions of the aggressor, the less damage will be inflicted on world civilization."

It is here, in underestimating the role of the masses, that Western "fatalists" are said to overestimate the role of nuclear weapons: "There is profound error and harm in the disorienting claims of bourgeois ideologues that there will be no victor in a thermonuclear world war. The peoples of the world will put an end to imperialism, which is causing mankind incalculable suffering."

To the Marxist-Leninist theoretician, the working class is at least as powerful as a hydrogen bomb.

Still, the power of the bomb is not unacknowledged. "It would hardly be possible for anyone to visualize and accurately reproduce the picture of a possible nuclear missile war ...," writes the author of *The People, the Army, the Commander*, published in Moscow in 1970. "The belligerent parties will sustain losses without precedent in the history of warfare." Quoting Leonid Brezhnev, *Problems of Contemporary War* declares that "a nuclear world war could result in hundreds of millions of deaths, in the destruction of entire coun-

---

* Quotations from this book, which will henceforth be referred to as *Problems of Contemporary War*, and from *The People, the Army, the Commander* and *Civil Defense*, which will be quoted below, are from translations of these works prepared and published under the auspices of the U.S. Air Force in a series called "Soviet Military Thought." Each of the books, which are filled with declarations about the triumphs of Communism, past and future, is prefaced with the disclaimer that "the translation and publication of [this book] does not constitute approval by any U.S. Government organization of the inferences, findings and conclusions contained therein."

tries, in contamination of the earth's surface and atmosphere."

The prospective damage of a nuclear war is in fact maximized in Soviet literature by the absence of any consideration of the limited nuclear war scenarios so often discussed in the United States. "Could anyone in his right mind speak seriously of any limited nuclear war?" demanded Soviet Defense Minister Dmitri Ustinov in 1981. "It should be quite clear that the aggressor's actions will instantly and inevitably trigger a devastating counterstrike by the other side. None but completely irresponsible people could maintain that a nuclear war may be made to follow rules adopted beforehand, with nuclear missiles exploding in 'gentlemanly manner' over strictly designated targets and sparing the population."

This Soviet promise of a devastating counterstrike followed the issuance of PD-59 and ensuing discussion of American plans to attempt to control a nuclear war by limiting an initial attack to selected targets while leaving important Soviet targets unhit but still at risk. (This will "provide leverage for a negotiated termination of the fighting," explained Harold Brown.) Despite Ustinov's disparaging remark about "gentlemanly" rules, the American strategy does not in fact depend on prewar agreements. It is based on coercion, not etiquette. But if it is to work the Soviets must understand how and why they are being coerced. American critics of the American strategy have pointed out that such understanding may be difficult to come by in the middle of a nuclear war. And the Soviets have rejected it out of hand. "This cannot be done in practice," General A. Slobodenko wrote in a Soviet military journal in 1981. "Even the [Western] press emphasizes that when one side launches its missiles (even in a limited number), the opposing side will not know what targets they are aimed at (military or civilian), what objective is being pursued (limited or unlimited), what warheads and of what yields they are carrying, etc. Naturally, in such circumstances, the only justified decision by the opposing side must be the launching of a powerful retaliatory strike."

Soviet declarations that Russia will respond massively to any attack might or might not turn out to be true; it is certainly in Russia's interest to take that position now, for the sake of deterring an American attack. But the Soviet promise that any nuclear war will be massive does create problems for the consistency of Soviet literature, which asserts on one hand that nuclear war will be such a terrible thing that the capitalists had better not start one, and asserts on the other that the Soviet masses will not be intimidated by the threat of nuclear war because they know that through concerted action they can overcome its effects and emerge victorious, sweeping capitalism into the garbage bin of history.

The Soviet dilemma is evident in the attempts of *Problems of Contemporary War* to uphold the dictum of Karl von Clausewitz, embraced by Lenin, that war is a continuation of policy by other means. The book denounces the efforts of "bourgeois ideologues" to put nuclear war, because of its unprecedented destructiveness, in a category beyond politics as usual. "The concept of nuclear fatalism breaks with the Leninist concept of the essence of war and metaphysically detaches armed struggle from politics. This concept diminishes the role of the masses, viewing them as a passive object of weapons of mass destruction. It is harmful in that it promotes an attitude of defeatism and doom and hinders the development of mass activeness." Yet the book also states, "There is certainly no question about the fact that nuclear missile weapons have introduced substantial changes in the relationship between politics and war. This new and ominous weapon has transformed war into an exceptionally dangerous and destructive means of implementing policy. It is precisely for this reason that thermonuclear war cannot serve as an implement to achieve political goals." The book resolves its conflicts as best it can: "The conclusion that imperialism will suffer defeat if it forces a new world war on mankind does not in any way signify that we should strive toward a military confrontation." And later, "This lies behind the important conclusion stated in the CPSU [Communist Party of the Soviet Union] program that nuclear war *'cannot and shall not serve as a means of settling international disputes.'* "

To complicate the record further, Soviet leaders have in recent years scored political points by speaking of nuclear war in terms very like those of the previously despised "bourgeois ideologues." After Ronald Reagan remarked in 1981 that he thought the exchange of tactical nuclear weapons on a battlefield would not necessarily lead to all-out nuclear war, Leonid Brezhnev replied, "Only he who has decided to commit suicide can start a nuclear war in the hope of emerging a victor from it." In response to a 1982 appeal to Reagan and Brezhnev by a group called International Physicians for the Prevention of Nuclear War, Brezhnev said he agreed with the physicians that "nuclear war would be fatal for any country or any people subjected to the use of this weapon." In 1983, Soviet Foreign Minister Andrei Gromyko proclaimed that "there will be no winners in a nuclear war," and charged that it was in the United States, not the Soviet Union, that "nuclear war is pronounced to be permissible and even feasible."

All of this has provided a rich lode of material for those participating in the great debate about what the Russians really think. Those who assert that the Russians really have a respectful and realistic (i.e., pessimistic) attitude about the effects of nuclear war can point to Brezhnev's comments about nuclear suicide. Those who assert that the Russians really believe nuclear war is winnable (while we, presumably, do not) argue that comments like Brezhnev's are propaganda for export only and that true expressions of Soviet beliefs must be sought elsewhere.* "Soviet military literature . . . is written in an elaborate code language . . . ," Richard Pipes claimed in his*Commentary* article. "Buried in the flood of seemingly meaningless verbiage, nuggets of precious information on Soviet perceptions and intentions can . . . be unearthed by a trained reader." Pipes cites one such "code phrase" from *Military Strategy*, a 1962 Soviet volume edited by Marshal V. D. Sokolovskii. The phrase in question elaborates on the dictum of Clausewitz of which Lenin was so fond: "It is well known that the essential nature of war as a continuation of politics does not change with changing technology and ar-

---

* When dramatic statements about the effects of nuclear war were made by the International Physicians for the Prevention of Nuclear War in 1981, some American publications protested that the physicians' campaign was one-sided. "No such accounts of horror of nuclear war ever reach the Soviet public," the*Omaha World-Herald* quoted a critic of the Russians as saying. In fact, IPPNW meetings and statements by prominent Soviet doctors who joined the organization received wide coverage in the Soviet press. *Pravda*, for example, quoted Dr. Yevgeny Chazov, Brezhnev's cardiologist, on "the danger to life on earth inherent in the use of nuclear arms." In 1982, Soviet television carried a one-hour panel discussion on the effects of nuclear war by three Soviet and three American doctors, one of whom used the occasion to denounce civil defense as "insane." The program was offered to, and rejected by, the three American commercial networks and finally appeared in this country on public television.

mament." According to Pipes, this single sentence, with its oblique reference to nuclear weapons, "spells the rejection of the whole basis on which U.S. strategy has come to rest: thermonuclear war is not suicidal, it can be fought and won, and thus resort to war must not be ruled out."

(Pipes is scornful of the nuclear doctrine he attributes to the United States—the view that the superpowers' nuclear arsenals are so destructive that "neither country could rationally contemplate resort to war." This conclusion, he writes, "was reached without much reference to the analysis of the effects of atomic weapons carried out by the military. . . . It represented, rather, an act of faith on the part of an intellectual community which held strong pacifist convictions and felt deep guilt at having participated in the creation of a weapon of such destructive power." That the Soviets have adopted a different view (as, apparently, has Pipes) has unfortunately been difficult for Americans to accept, Pipes writes:

> In the United States, the consensus of the educated and affluent holds all recourse to force to be the result of an inability or an unwillingness to apply rational analysis and patient negotiation to disagreements. . . . [T]his entire middle-class, commercial, essentially Protestant ethos is absent from Soviet culture. . . . The Communist revolution of 1917 . . . installed in power the *muzhik*, the Russian peasant. And the *muzhik* had been taught by long historical experience that cunning and coercion alone ensured survival. . . . Middle-class American intellectuals simply cannot assimilate this mentality, so alien is it to their experience and view of human nature. . . . How ironic that the very people who have failed so dismally to persuade American television networks to eliminate violence from their programs, nevertheless feel confident that they can talk the Soviet leadership into eliminating violence from its political arsenal!

Quoting the Russians is a game anyone can play. Liberal critics of Pipes have pointed out that he neglected to mention passages from Sokolovskii's book that describe nuclear war as an unacceptable disaster that must be avoided. In 1980, Harold Brown provided a Senate committee with the following statement from Marshal Nikolai Ogarkov, the Soviet chief of staff, as an illustration of the Soviet attitude toward nuclear war:

246

The possibility cannot be excluded that the war could also be protracted. Soviet military strategy proceeds from the fact that if a nuclear war is foisted upon the Soviet Union, then the Soviet people and their armed forces must be ready for the most severe and prolonged trials. In this case, the Soviet Union and the fraternal Socialist states . . . [have] objective possibilities for achieving victory.

Brown's critics soon came up with the full text of the statement Brown had excerpted (in a slightly different translation), and it turned out to be rather less ominous:

> *It is considered that in light of modern means of destruction, world nuclear war would be comparatively brief. However, taking into account the enormous potential military and economic resources of the coalition of belligerent states,* one cannot exclude the fact that it might also be prolonged. Soviet military strategy is based on the fact that should the Soviet Union be thrust into a nuclear war, the Soviet people and their armed forces need to be prepared for most severe and protracted trials. In this case the Soviet Union and fraternal socialist states, *in comparison to the imperialist states, will have definite advantages stemming from the just goals of the war and the advanced nature of their social and state system. This creates* objective possibilities for them to achieve victory. [Words in italics were omitted by Brown.]

The quotemasters volley back and forth like Talmudic scholars, providing for every Soviet quotation an equal and opposite Soviet quotation. In 1982, Caspar Weinberger managed to avoid such complications by asserting that "we have a great deal of evidence that the Soviets believe nuclear war is winnable" and then declining to make any of that evidence public on the ground that it was too sensitive.

While those who ascribe the most dangerous views to the Soviets *have* assembled a sizable body of Soviet quotations asserting that nuclear war is winnable, they can only brandish them so accusingly because of the presumption that *we* would never think like that. And that is not necessarily so. Weinberger's statements about "prevailing" in a nuclear war come immediately to mind, but there is nothing new about such statements in the *American* military literature.

A 1977 memorandum from the Joint Chiefs of Staff to Senator William Proxmire rehearsed the assertions that the Soviet Union believes "success in war, even nuclear war, is attainable" and that the Soviets therefore were preparing "to fight, survive, and win a nuclear war." American nuclear strategy, on the other hand, "is more accurately described as maintaining military strength sufficient to deter attack," the memo said. But then it elaborated on the American position. "In the event deterrence fails," it said, it is American policy to have strength "sufficient to provide a warfighting capability to respond to a wide range of conflict in order to control escalation and terminate the war on terms acceptable to the United States. To the extent that escalation cannot be controlled, the U.S. objective is to maximize the resultant political, economic, and military power of the United States relative to the enemy in the post-war period."

This is certainly a fine distinction. The Soviet Union seeks to "win" a nuclear war. The United States seeks only to "terminate the war on terms acceptable to the United States" or to "maximize the resultant political, economic, and military power of the United States relative to the enemy in the post-war period." One could be excused for thinking that sounds like winning too.

A country that believes nuclear war can be fought, survived, and won will have—must have—an excellent program of civil defense, and here those who are alarmed about Soviet attitudes make a large part of their case. "Nothing illustrates better the fundamental differences between [Soviet and American] strategic doctrines than their attitudes to defense against a nuclear attack," wrote Richard Pipes. He cited, as have others, the Russians' small anti-ballistic-missile system around Moscow, their substantial antiaircraft defense system, and their "serious program of civil defense."

The Soviets do have an ambitious civil-defense program, headed by a deputy minister of defense, employing (according to a 1978 American intelligence estimate) more than 100,000 people, and providing compulsory civil-defense courses to all Soviet citizens. "Preserving the population—the basic productive force of the economy—ensuring economic stability, and preserving the material and technical resources are matters of paramount importance during a war. Thus, under modern conditions, *civil defense has become a factor of strategic importance*," declares *Civil Defense*, a 1970 Soviet college textbook that is typical of Soviet literature on the subject.

Civil Defense outlines a large and varied program that includes planning for the evacuation of cities, which may reduce urban casualties in a nuclear war, it says, "to several percent of the total population." Key workers, it says, will be evacuated to suburban areas, from which they can commute to their jobs. Others will be sent farther away.

> When the situation warrants it, the population will be given the sequence of evacuation, the times to assemble at the evacuation points . . . for loading on transport, the marching routes to be followed, the list of necessary documents to take along, the permissible baggage weight, and other information. . . . Citizens should take only what is absolutely necessary: clothes, underwear, bedding, toilet articles, and the necessary personal documents. It is recommended that a tag be sewn to the clothing of preschool-age children, indicating first and last name, patronymic, year of birth, permanent address, and final evacuation point. . . . The evacuees do not have a right to independently select a living place. . . . When an evacuee from a city has arrived and has been assigned to a rural locality, he must prepare cover [a fallout shelter] and continuously improve its protective qualities. . . . The Party committees of each enterprise must assign Party-Komsomol and trade-union activists among the evacuation collection points, trains, and convoys. These activists conduct agitation work, counteract panic, and inform those being evacuated of the rules of conduct. . . . Primary attention must be directed to . . . fostering faith in the righteousness of our cause and in the certainty of victory over the enemy.

Civil Defense also describes plans for the construction of blast and fallout shelters (it suggests that shelters be used for "patriotic displays" or "exhibits of craftsmanship" during peacetime), and it lays out the rules for shelter living: "It is forbidden to wander through the shelter, to make noise, to smoke, to burn kerosene lamps. . . ." It describes ways to protect industrial equipment from blast damage and how to bulldoze paths through postattack rubble. It even prescribes rules for urban planning to minimize nuclear war rubble: "It is very important to construct major thoroughfares in a city [wide enough so that they] would not be clogged [by rubble] if buildings were destroyed."

Other Soviet texts take up where *Civil Defense* leaves off. A 1980 manual for instructors at Young Pioneer summer camps includes directions for teaching campers how to don gas masks, how to dig trench shelters, and how to wash radioactive particles off their clothes. The manual suggests that competitive quizzes be given, with the winners awarded pies and excursions. Among the quiz questions: "Name four groups of poison gases." "Name the place in the individual medical kit where the nerve-gas antidote is kept." "What means of defense of the population from weapons of mass destruction do you know?" And this one:

> Several youngsters noticed the flash of a nuclear explosion. The first one lay down in a ditch, the second sheltered himself behind a tall stone wall, the third at the wall of a building, the fourth behind a tree stump. The fifth and sixth remained on the spot and stood looking at the flash. Who of the youngsters acted correctly, and who did not?
>
> Answer: The following youngsters acted correctly: the first, who lay in a ditch, and the fourth, who sheltered himself behind a stump. The others acted incorrectly.

The current Soviet civil-defense program was organized in 1961, but it was not until the mid-1970s that its significance became an issue in the United States. In 1975, Harriet Fast Scott, a writer and editor who had lived in Moscow for four years while her husband was air attaché at the American embassy, published an article in *Air Force Magazine* describing Soviet civil defense as an important and overlooked element in the strategic balance. "The Soviet leadership has physically and psychologically prepared its people for the possibility of nuclear war," she concluded. "Western leaders have not." A few months later, Leon Gouré testified at a congressional hearing that "the Soviet war-survival capability is intended, as Soviet spokesmen admit, to deprive the United States of its ability to threaten the Soviet Union with 'assured destruction.' " As a result, Gouré said, the United States would be "increasingly vulnerable to Soviet blackmail." At the same hearing, T. K. Jones, then a Boeing executive, testified that "the entire premise of the Soviet civil-defense preparation is contrary to the widely held American belief that nuclear war is 'unthinkable' and would be 'the end of all mankind.' " If Soviet cities were evacuated according to the directions in Soviet manuals and the evacuees then constructed "simple shelters," Jones said, the Soviet Union would lose only 2 percent of its population in a nuclear war. The Soviet Union could recover from such a war, Jones told another congressional committee, in two to four years.

These views were seconded by General George Keegan, who retired as chief of Air Force Intelligence in 1977 and proceeded to travel the country speaking before conservative audiences and being interviewed for publications ranging from *Human Events* to *Oui*. His repeated message was that, in the Soviet Union, "we are in fact observing the preparation for World War III." This fact was being ignored, Keegan complained, by "left-wing radicals" in the Carter administration, despite "explicit . . . documentary evidence" developed by Air Force Intelligence. (Keegan did acknowledge, however, that some of his evidence was contested not only by left-wing radicals like Harold Brown but also by "the balance of the intelligence community.") "The Soviets have undertaken to fulfill the judgment [that their country can survive a nuclear war] by hardening their cities, by placing their factories underground, by assuring that in every city in every apartment house there is a basement shelter that is capable of protecting the local civilian population," Keegan said. He concluded that those preparations, combined with the evacuation of Soviet cities, would reduce Russian casualties in a nuclear war to less than one thirty-second the level of American casualties; fewer than 5 million Russians would die, compared to 160 million Americans.

This presumed imbalance in nuclear war casualties was cited again and again by the harbingers of the civil-defense gap. It would, they said, substantially strengthen the hand of the Soviet Union in international crises. ("Let's say you [the Soviets] were into a crisis over South Africa and you decided to close the Persian Gulf for some reason," said Keegan. "Who's going to challenge you?") A nuclear war would be fatal for the United States, they said, while the same nuclear war would produce fewer Russian casualties than had World War II (and the Russians would be able to make up for material losses by seizing Western Europe relatively intact). Besides, the Russians were *used* to having their country devastated. "A country that since 1914 has lost, as a result of two world wars, a civil war, famine, and various 'purges,' perhaps up to 60 million citizens, must define 'unacceptable damage' differently from the United States," wrote Richard Pipes. "I firmly believe that the present Soviet leadership would have no qualms in risking the loss of 20 million or so of its population," said T. K. Jones.

This alarm over Soviet civil defense was seized upon by the Defense Civil Preparedness Agency (a predecessor of the Federal Emergency Management Agency) to lobby for an improved American program, and concern percolated to the highest levels of the Pentagon. "During the last six months we have become more aware of the magnitude of Soviet Civil Defense efforts . . . ," Secretary of Defense Donald Rumsfeld wrote in his January 1977 report to Congress. "This civil defense capability . . . could adversely affect our ability to implement the U.S. deterrent strategy. Thus, it could provide the Soviets with both a political and a military advantage in the event of a nuclear crisis."

But none of this went unchallenged. Critics of the civil-defense Cassandras questioned whether the Soviet Union, having lost 20 million lives in World War II, would gladly risk 20 million more. More fundamentally, they challenged the conclusion that Soviet civil defense could reduce casualties to anywhere near that level. The Soviet program might look good on paper, they said, but there was a mighty big leap between writing out guidelines for civil defense and using those guidelines to save 100 million people from nuclear weapons. "People read the Soviet manuals and assume that's what will happen," said an official of the U.S. Arms Control and Disarmament Agency. "That's the same thing as reading an AAA manual on avoiding auto accidents and assuming that there aren't any accidents."

In April 1977, the Joint Congressional Committee on Defense Production concluded a study of Soviet civil defense and reported "there appears to be little warrant for the belief that the Soviet Union could survive even a modest yet carefully configured nuclear attack in any but the most primitive economic circumstances." An Arms Control and Disarmament Agency study the following year concluded that the United States and the Soviet Union were "roughly equally vulnerable" to nuclear attack. It acknowledged that urban evacuation could significantly reduce short-term casualties—Russia might lose as few as 23 million lives with an effective program, it said—but it questioned how effective a program the Russians actually have:

> Who is better equipped for evacuation? The U.S. with one car for every two citizens and a vast highway system? Or the Soviet Union with a plan but limited transportation? ... Who is better equipped for sustaining the evacuees? The U.S. with large surpluses of goods and food and many non-urban housing facilities? Or the Soviet Union with chronic shortages, limited distribution capabilities, and limited non-urban housing? Finally, it should be kept in mind that, while no one has practiced evacuation, on every major holiday approximately 50 million Americans "evacuate" their homes and travel to resort areas. The Soviet Union has no comparable capability.

The shortcomings of the Soviet plan were enumerated in a detailed critique by Congressman Les Aspin. Within the Soviet Union, he said, civil-defense training is "the topic of numerous jokes; apathy is pervasive, the program riddled with bureaucratic indifference and incompetence; factory managers often deliberately schedule [civil-defense] exercises during the busiest work periods so they can be postponed, often cancelled." Soviet evacuation plans, Aspin pointed out, call for many urban residents to *walk* into the countryside, where they might or might not find the supplies they need to construct fallout shelters. Even if Soviet cities were evacuated, he said, the destruction of the empty cities would leave Soviet leaders with a large population and a decimated industrial base; the result would be "widespread internal revolt, to say nothing of disease, hunger and prolonged socioeconomic agony." Perceptions that the flawed Soviet civil-defense program would put the United States at a disadvantage in a crisis, Aspin asserted, "are largely the making of a mere handful of U.S. defense analysts who have shrewdly propagated their studies far and wide. . . . They have no connection with the findings of the intelligence community or with the widely accessible facts about the Soviet economic structure."

Skepticism about Soviet civil defense has been supported by some American observers in Moscow. A *New York Times* correspondent, asked to send Soviet civil-defense posters to New York to illustrate a 1979 article, cautioned his editors to be "careful to differentiate between what is in the posters and handbooks and what exists in reality." The posters, he warned, make "the civil defense program look more pervasive and efficient than it is. . . . They are no more truthful than the unity of the party and the people." In 1982, a young American who spent a year working at the Novosti news agency in Moscow reported that at the one compulsory civil-defense lecture he had attended he saw his co-workers catching up on their reading and taking naps.

Soviet civil-defense officials themselves, in the Soviet tradition of self-criticism, have described failings in their own program. "The shortcomings of our propagandists should . . . be pointed out . . . ," General A. Altunin, the Soviet civil-defense chief, wrote in a 1978 article. "Many of them are not achieving the goals and are not convincing the listeners of the effectiveness of CD measures." Altunin reported successes as well, but, sounding like Leon Gouré in reverse, he justified the Soviet program as a response to highly effective *American* civil defense:

> The U.S. "lag" in civil defense has . . . emerged in order to extort additional appropriations from Congress, to dupe the taxpayer, and to take new steps to strengthen civil defense, which as it is was long ago transformed in the United States into a state system which is assuming ever greater fundamental strategic importance. . . . Modern underground federal control centers which provide protection from nuclear weapons have been established. . . . Construction of communications and warning centers for all local government agencies is underway on a broad scale. . . . About 232,000 protective structures with a capacity for over 200 million people . . . were recorded back in 1975. . . . Civil defense is receiving more and more effective assistance from the U.S. Armed Forces . . . and the entire population is being trained in civil defense.

254

What can be said in regard to this? The imperialists will be waiting in vain for us to sit idle in the face of such facts.

Anyone reading this had to wonder whether those raising the alarm about Russian civil defense might be as deluded about the Soviet program as Altunin seemed to be about the American program—which does, after all, look good on paper.

Leon Gouré and the others insisted, of course, that it was not they who were deluded but their critics. The two camps traded charges and countercharges of dealing in incorrect facts and reaching fanciful conclusions. Gouré himself acknowledged shortcomings in the Soviet program but maintained that it did amount to more than paper plans. Sitting in his office beneath a wall map of Moscow marked with circles denoting the blast damage radii of nuclear weapons dropped at various points, Gouré told a reporter, "People argue that the Soviet population is apathetic toward civil defense. They've had this beaten over their ears for thirty years. Anybody would be bored. But in a crisis they know what to do."

In any case, those concerned about a civil-defense gap argued, it didn't really matter what Les Aspin—or any American—thought of the Soviet program. "It makes no difference whether *you* believe the Soviet program will work," an official of the Defense Civil Preparedness Agency told a reporter. "All that matters is whether *they* believe it." If *they* believe it, the argument went, *they* might feel secure in raising a little hell here and there around the world, even to the point of risking a nuclear war.

In 1978, the entire controversy was dumped into the lap of an interagency intelligence group chaired by the CIA. The group included representatives of the military intelligence agencies and the DCPA, which tended to be alarmed about Soviet civil defense, the CIA itself, which tended to be less concerned, and other federal intelligence organizations. Its conclusions were hammered out after long negotiations. ("It was fought bitterly," said one DCPA official.) The group's final report contained something for everyone, and all participants in the debate about Soviet civil defense promptly began quoting their favorite passages (and quote them to this day). These were among the report's findings:

- The Soviet civil-defense program includes blast-hardened command posts for 110,000 political leaders and shelters at key factories for 12 to 24 percent of the total work force. Many leaders and key workers would survive a nuclear attack. On the other hand, "all fixed leadership shelters which have been identified would be vulnerable to direct attack."
- "Nearly every Soviet citizen receives civil defense instruction either in school or through training courses, lectures, and exercises at places of work. Public attitudes about surviving a nuclear war remain skeptical, however, and there is evidence that many people do not take the program seriously. Nevertheless, the Soviet people would respond to directions from civil defense authorities."
- Following Soviet evacuation plans, "the major portion of the Soviet urban population" could be evacuated in two or three days. With a week or more to evacuate and build rural shelters for the evacuees, followed by a Soviet first strike, the Soviets could reduce short-term casualties from the American retaliatory attack "to the low tens of millions, about half of which would be fatalities." These figures were based on the unlikely assumption, however, that the Soviet evacuation would not cause American leaders to put U.S. nuclear forces on a higher than ordinary state of alert.
- Despite Soviet literature on the subject, "little evidence exists that would suggest a comprehensive program for hardening economic installations. . . . Soviet measures to protect the economy could not prevent massive industrial damage."

On the crucial question of what the Soviets themselves believe about Soviet civil defense and how their beliefs might influence their actions, the report wended its way past one "almost certainly" and one "however" to end up on the side of the skeptics:

> The Soviets almost certainly believe their present civil defenses would improve their ability to conduct military operations and would enhance the USSR's chances for survival following a nuclear exchange. They cannot have confidence, however, in the degree of protection their civil defenses would afford them, given the many

uncertainties attendant to a nuclear exchange. We do not believe that the Soviets' present civil defenses would embolden them deliberately to expose the USSR to a higher risk of nuclear attack.

Nevertheless, two months after the release of the intelligence report, President Jimmy Carter signed Presidential Directive 41. "Civil defense," it said, "as an element of the strategic balance, should assist in maintaining perceptions of that balance favorable to the U.S." And it endorsed American evacuation planning.

If the Soviet civil-defense program is as hollow as the skeptics claim, it would not be the first time the United States has overestimated a Soviet military capability. In the mid-1950s, concern about a "bomber gap" followed American intelligence estimates of a substantial Soviet buildup. The estimates were based in part on a display of "Bison" intercontinental bombers at the Soviet Air Force Day celebration in 1955. While Western air attachés stood on reviewing stands below and kept count, every Bison in the Soviet fleet flew by overhead. Once out of sight, the Bisons circled back and flew by—and were counted—once again.

Photos taken by a U-2 spy plane the following year established that the bomber gap did not exist. But it was soon replaced by the "missile gap." American intelligence agencies, led by Air Force Intelligence, predicted that by the early 1960s the Soviet Union would have a commanding lead in intercontinental ballistic missiles; John Kennedy made the alleged gap a major issue in his 1960 presidential campaign.

The missile gap was exposed as illusory when American spy satellites, new that year, were unable to find more than four operational ICBMs in Russia. The Air Force held out against this evidence—it pointed to grain silos and a Crimean War memorial where it said missiles might be hidden—but everyone else soon accepted that there was actually a *reverse* missile gap; the United States was ahead of the Soviet Union.

This situation, emphasized by Khrushchev's retreat in the 1962

Cuban missile crisis, was one the Soviets eventually set out to remedy. Today, although dubious alarms are still raised about various rumored and barely operational new Soviet weapons, there is no question about the basic capability of Russian nuclear forces. The Soviet Union has built itself into a formidable nuclear power, on the same level as the United States. Precise comparisons are complicated, but defense officials in recent American administrations—before Reagan—have spoken of "parity" between the two nations' forces, or "essential equivalence." It is clear that either superpower could deal the other a terrible blow.

In 1981, the Reagan administration came into office with a different view. "The truth of the matter," the president told a press conference, "is that on balance the Soviet Union does have a definite margin of superiority." This had been created, he explained on another occasion, by the fact that during the 1970s, while the Soviets were undergoing "the greatest buildup of military strength in world history," the United States had been "unilaterally disarming." A lot of people did not find it easy to survey the American nuclear arsenal and think of it as the product of any kind of disarmament, unilateral or otherwise, and some of them had a chance to call administration officials on this. During a 1982 Senate hearing, after General John Vessey, Jr., just nominated to be chairman of the Joint Chiefs of Staff, said the Soviets were "superior to us" in "intercontinental ballistic missiles and . . . nuclear explosive power," a senator asked Vessey if he would therefore be willing to trade American military forces for Soviet forces. "Not on your life," Vessey replied. The same question was put to President Reagan a few weeks after he told a national television audience (in November 1982) that "today, in virtually every measure of military power, the Soviet Union enjoys a decided advantage." Like Vessey, Reagan said he would not trade, but he added that that was only "because of my faith in America and in the young men and women of America who are in our armed forces."

There are many ways to compare military strength, and Reagan, to prove his point that America was inferior and thus justify his huge defense budget requests, naturally selected those measures that served his purpose. During his November 1982 address to the nation, Reagan produced a colored graph that showed Soviet military spending ("now follow the red line") soaring ahead of American military spending. Reagan did not mention that estimating the Soviet military budget is an exceptionally inexact business. The figure is not published by the Russians, so American analysts must try to count every soldier and weapon in the Soviet Union. The dollar/ruble exchange rate is an artificial one, so the analysts put the cost of Soviet forces at what it would cost to pay those soldiers and produce those weapons in the United States. That means every time American soldiers get a raise, or an American weapon has a cost overrun, the Soviet military budget goes up—even if, in Russia, nothing has changed.

Reagan's address was also illustrated with charts comparing the numbers of American and Soviet intercontinental missiles. Once again, the red line rose over the blue. "I could show you chart after chart," Reagan said, "where there is a great deal of red and a much lesser amount of U.S. blue." Reagan chose not to show, however, a chart comparing the total number of nuclear weapons—warheads and bombs—carried by American and Soviet intercontinental missiles and bombers. (It's not the missiles themselves that explode; it's the warheads they carry.) Such a chart would have shown more blue than red. The absence of such a chart did not proceed from some principled reason for counting missiles instead of warheads. Reagan did display a chart showing the number of warheads carried on intermediate-range missiles, which had the effect of emphasizing a Russian lead in that area. When counting warheads made his charts look better, Reagan used warheads.*

In 1981, the Department of Defense took the unusual step of publishing a lavishly illustrated booklet called *Soviet Military Power*

---

* Reagan's taste for graphics was also manifested, according to *Armed Forces Journal International*, during the preparation of his first military budget. Pentagon officers prepared bar charts and graphs comparing various budget options for the president's consideration, the magazine reported, but they were instructed to redo them in the form of cartoons. The relative sizes of three alternate budgets for nuclear weapons were finally illustrated with three mushroom clouds—a small mushroom cloud representing the lame-duck Carter budget, a medium-sized mushroom cloud representing the budget backed by budget director David Stockman, and a large mushroom cloud representing the budget proposed by Secretary of Defense Caspar Weinberger.

as part of its campaign to make clear "the threat to Western strategic interests posed by the growth and power projection of the Soviet Armed Forces." *Soviet Military Power* (which was revised and reissued in 1983) was packed full of information—some of which had previously been classified to protect American intelligence methods—about everything from the newest Soviet missiles to alleged improvements in Soviet welding techniques. The booklet generally avoided, however, making meaningful comparisons between Soviet and American forces. On one page, it superimposed an outline of a major Russian tank factory over a map of downtown Washington, D.C. (to emphasize the size of the factory). Another illustration depicted a Soviet "Typhoon" submarine standing on its tail next to the Washington Monument. The Russian submarine and the monument are indeed the same height, but so is the American Trident submarine, which was not pictured. (And would a missile-launching submarine as long as Long Island, say, necessarily be a better weapon?)

Fighting booklet with booklet, the Russians replied to *Soviet Military Power* with *Whence the Threat to Peace*, a similar-looking publication that denounced the American booklet as containing "tendentiously selected and deliberately distorted information ... designed to frighten the public." *Whence the Threat to Peace* asserted that it was not Soviet but American military doctrine that considered nuclear war winnable, and the booklet matched *Soviet Military Power*'s descriptions of Russian weapons with its own descriptions of American weapons. *Whence the Threat to Peace* even responded to the American map showing the Soviet tank factory dwarfing downtown Washington; it reprinted the map but added, beyond the outline of the Soviet factory, the even larger outline of an otherwise unidentified "tank complex in Detroit."

The Soviet booklet repeated earlier Soviet assertions that "an approximate military balance" existed between Russian and American forces and that it was the United States that was seeking to pull ahead. Reagan administration officials insisted that the Soviet Union was already ahead and that this had grave consequences not only for wartime but also for peace. "The nuclear balance inevitably affects the political and psychological environment within which deep international crises must be managed . . . ," Secretary of State Alexander Haig said in 1981. "Short of crisis, nuclear weapons perform an important function in the conduct of day-to-day diplomacy." In a crisis, Haig said, doubts about America's nuclear strength could lead to Russian "blackmail" and "intimidation." In day-to-day diplomacy, he said, "the strategic nuclear balance casts a shadow which affects every geopolitical decision of significance."

Why this should be so has never been made clear. If one nation has eight thousand nuclear weapons and another has nine thousand, and a mere few hundred can inflict unprecedented damage on an adversary, then what is the significance of that extra one thousand, in war or in peace? "What in the name of God is strategic superiority?" Henry Kissinger demanded in 1974. "What is the significance of it, politically, militarily, operationally, at these levels of numbers? What do you do with it?"

According to Haig, you benefit from it in "every geopolitical decision of significance." And Haig was only echoing previous statements by top-ranking members of the Carter administration. "Perceptions can be as important as realities in the international arena . . . ," Harold Brown wrote in 1981. "Indeed, in some sense, the political advantages of being seen as the superior strategic power are more real and more usable than the military advantages of in fact being superior." The 1981 report of the chairman of the Joint Chiefs of Staff identified the invasion of Afghanistan as just the kind of thing that the perception of superiority could lead the Soviets to undertake: "I anticipate [projected Soviet superiority] would be reflected in a more confident Soviet leadership, increasingly inclined toward more adventurous behavior. . . . The Soviet invasion of Afghanistan could well be a 'leading edge' event reflecting precisely such a heightened confidence."

The great irony of all this—if any of it is true—is that the perception of Soviet superiority that allegedly gives Soviet leaders the confidence to blackmail and intimidate the United States and its allies, and to invade Afghanistan, has been assiduously created by the American government. By publishing *Soviet Military Power*, the Arms Control Association pointed out, our Department of Defense "runs the risk of becoming the chief public relations firm for the

Red Army." Every time Ronald Reagan proclaimed American military inferiority, he strengthened the Russians' hand.

If perceptions are as important as American officials say they are, then the Soviets have surely been gratified in recent years by the many declarations from Washington that American ICBMs have become, or are about to become, vulnerable to Soviet missiles. Beginning in the late 1960s, American defense and intelligence officials began to warn that improvements in the accuracy of Soviet missiles would soon make it possible for a Soviet first strike to destroy American ICBMs in their hardened steel-and-concrete silos. The initial warnings were premature, but, by the late 1970s, the Soviets *were* making substantial improvements in the accuracy of their missiles.

Exactly how accurate the new Soviet missiles—or *any* missiles—could be was a matter of some debate. "I believe that there is some misunderstanding about the degree of reliability and accuracy of missiles . . . ," James Schlesinger had said in 1974. "It is impossible for either side to acquire the degree of accuracy that would give them a high confidence first strike because we will not know what the actual accuracy will be like in a real-world context. . . . I want the President of the United States to know that for all the future years, and I want the Soviet leadership to know that for all the future years." Schlesinger's statement was based on the fact that American and Soviet missiles have never been test-flown—for obvious reasons—over the routes they will take in a war. Some scientists have asserted that gravitational, magnetic, and atmospheric peculiarities of those routes are likely to produce an aiming "bias" that will cause missiles to fall a few hundred yards wide of their targets. A few hundred yards won't make any difference to a missile aimed at downtown Detroit, but it could make the difference between destroying a Minuteman missile in its underground silo and just giving it a bad shaking up. "Not only have ICBMs never been tested in flying operational trajectories against operational targets, they have not been tested flying north [the direction they would fly in a war]; and this may or may not introduce certain areas of bias in the estimation of accuracy," Schlesinger told a Senate committee in 1982, long after Minuteman vulnerability had been generally accepted as a fact of life.

The Pentagon, defending the accuracy of its own missiles, insists that bias is not a problem, and the debate cannot be conclusively resolved without having a nuclear war. But even if the Soviet missiles are as accurate as they are cracked up to be, even if a Soviet first strike could catch and destroy every single American land-based ICBM in its silo, so what? Slightly fewer than one-fourth of America's long-range nuclear weapons are on land-based ICBMs. Another one-fourth are on American bombers, some of which would get off the ground at first sign of a Soviet attack, and fully one-half of America's strategic warheads are carried on relatively invulnerable missile-launching submarines. Moreover, intermediate-range American nuclear weapons capable of hitting Soviet targets are based in Europe and Asia and on American ships around the world. So if the entire Minuteman force disappeared tomorrow—in a Soviet attack or a snowball fight—the United States would hardly be disarmed.

Harold Brown, who spent much of his term as secretary of defense working on a cure for Minuteman vulnerability, acknowledged as much in his 1981 report to Congress. "Even if the Soviets were able ... to eliminate most of our ICBMs, all our non-alert bombers, and all our ballistic missile submarines in port," he wrote, "we would still be able to launch several thousand warheads at targets in the Soviet Union in retaliation." So why make a fuss about Minuteman vulnerability? For one thing, Pentagon spokesmen said, if we tolerate a Soviet threat to American ICBMs today, the Russians might devise a way to threaten American submarines tomorrow, and then we'd really be in trouble. (The Navy, according to *The New York Times*, protested this lack of confidence in its submarines, and Brown acknowledged that some of his aides "may have exaggerated" potential submarine vulnerability.)

Another reason offered by Brown had to do with perceptions: "If we do not respond, it will create perceptual problems." In 1983, Secretary of State George Shultz made a dire prediction about the results of those problems: "If the Soviets can strike effectively at our land-based ICBMs while our land-based deterrent does not have comparable capability, the Soviets might believe that they have a significant advantage in a crucial dimension of the strategic balance: they could seek to gain political leverage by a threat of nuclear blackmail.... Such a crucial imbalance in strategic capabilities could well make them bolder in a regional conflict or in a major crisis."

Other members of the Carter and Reagan administrations and outside defense consultants explained how that nuclear blackmail might work. This is the nightmarish scenario they described:

The Soviet Union, seeking to have its way in a major crisis, launches a portion of its accurate missile force at American ICBMs. The American ICBMs are destroyed, and between five and twenty million Americans are killed. American cities have been spared. The Soviet premier calls the American president and tells him to accede to Soviet terms or face an attack on American cities. The president has the choice of surrendering or prosecuting the war. If he surrenders, fewer than 20 million Americans will have died. If he fights, more than 100 million Americans will die. He surrenders.

An additional wrinkle in this scenario has the president giving in to Soviet terms in a crisis even without a Soviet attack on American ICBMs, because the president *knows* that the Russians can launch such an attack, and he knows what a bind it will put him in. So the Soviets have their way without firing a shot. This is the ultimate perceptual problem.

Some purveyors of the nightmare scenario have linked it to the alleged civil-defense gap as well as to Minuteman vulnerability. "The absence of a U.S. capability to protect its own population gives the Soviet Union an asymmetrical possibility of holding the U.S. population as a hostage to deter retaliation following a Soviet attack on U.S. forces," Paul Nitze warned in 1976.

Every time it is raised, in whatever context, the nightmare scenario rests directly on the assumption that the Soviet Union would be willing to make the greatest gamble in the history of the world. The Soviets would be gambling, first of all, that their attack would succeed, that missile bias does not exist or is irrelevant, and that they can coordinate an attack of dazzling complexity. "A first-strike attempt on the U.S. fleet of 1,000 Minuteman ICBM silos is analogous to having 1,000 marksmen firing at 1,000 targets 500 meters away with the expectation that half of their shots will fall within a one-centimeter-diameter circle . . . ," J. Edward Anderson, a University of Minnesota engineer who has worked on missile guidance systems, has written. "The marksmen must wait 24 hours a day, 365 days a year, for years waiting to fire their one shot. If the expected precision is not realized, they, their families and most of their entire society will be destroyed." (To comments like these, Harold Brown replied, "It is equally important to acknowledge . . . that the coordination of a successful attack is not impossible, and that the 'rubbish heap of history' is filled with authorities who said something reckless could not or would not be done.")

The Soviets would also be gambling that the United States would not launch its entire Minuteman fleet as soon as the incoming attack was spotted and ask questions later. American officials have expressed discomfort with the launch-under-attack option, but they have always left it open (and in the midst of a crisis they could announce that it is in effect).

The Soviets would also be gambling that the American president, receiving reports of millions of Americans dead, would be able to restrain himself, and his military commanders, from firing back no matter what the cost.

The nightmare scenario also overlooks that the president does have nuclear options, that he could retaliate against a Soviet attack on our ICBMs by sending American weapons against unfired Soviet missiles and thus put the Russians in exactly the same bind in which they have put us. If the Soviet premier says, "We have so far spared your cities, but if you fire one shot at us we will destroy them," the American president can respond, "We are firing *many* shots at you but we are so far sparing *your* cities; if you fire one shot back at us we will destroy *them*." This option—the inverse of the nightmare scenario—is *already* the American nuclear war plan: the United States will seek (in the words of Harold Brown) to "leave the enemy with sufficient highly valued military, economic, and political resources still surviving but still clearly at risk, so that he has a strong incentive to seek an end to the conflict." Even if the president chooses not to respond to the Russian attack, he can still simply refuse to accede to whatever terms the Russians are demanding. If they don't like his refusal, they can proceed to bomb American cities, but they will know that Soviet cities will be attacked in return.

For that matter, the Soviets don't need to attack American ICBMs, or even to possess missiles capable of such an attack, in order to threaten an American president with the destruction of American cities if he does not accede to certain terms. The Soviets have had the capacity to destroy American cities for years; they could have made such a threat at any time. But they were deterred from doing so by the certainty of American retaliation (if not by common sense and decency), and nothing in the nightmare scenario makes such retaliation any less certain.

Finally, the nightmare scenario rests on the assumption that the Soviets—emboldened by their civil-defense program, or because they lost twenty million people in World War II and are used to such things, or because of their faith in the toiling masses as the determining force in history—will risk receiving that American retaliatory attack, the loss of their cities and their factories, and the chaos (and possible revolt) that will ensue even if not a single Russian life is lost, because they believe they can survive and win a nuclear war. "The improvements they have made in their ICBMs, their continued emphasis on anti-bomber, anti-missile, and strategic anti-submarine defenses, together with their ongoing civil defense program, can be seen as a concerted effort to take away the effectiveness of our second-strike forces . . . ," Harold Brown wrote in 1980. "If Soviet efforts persist, and we do not counter them, the Soviets may succumb to the illusion that a nuclear war could actually be won at acceptable, if large, cost."

The prime countermeasure supported by Brown was the MX missile. Many years and much ingenuity were devoted to devising a way to make the MX safe from a Russian missile attack, no matter how accurate, and thus eliminate the perceived problem of ICBM vulnerability. To this end, dozens of basing schemes were proposed and studied. Consideration was given to floating the missiles in a fleet of dirigibles, to scattering the missiles surreptitiously beneath the world's oceans (this could present a "hazard to navigation," the Air Force concluded), to carrying the missiles in large seaplanes that would fly about and park at random spots on the oceans, to shuttling the missiles among a large number of opaque pools, to burying

266

the missiles in silos at the feet of south-facing cliffs (which would shield the MX from Russian ICBMs arriving from the north), and to moving them about at random on highways, canals, or Western railways. All of these alternatives were rejected.

President Carter finally proposed a $33 billion plan to shuttle 200 MX missiles among 4,600 covered shelters in the Great Basin Desert of Utah and Nevada. Each missile would be based in a complex of twenty-three shelters, where a giant truck would move from one shelter to another, like a hand in a continuous shell game. The MX would sit in one of the shelters for weeks or months at a time; then it would be moved to another. At all times, the twenty-two empty shelters and the truck (when it was not carrying the missile) would be loaded with counterfeit missiles, emitting the same heat, sounds, radiation, magnetic field, even odors, as the actual missile in order to fool Soviet spies or sensors trying to figure out where the real missile was. To comply with arms control agreements, portholes in the shelter roofs would occasionally be opened so Soviet spy satellites could see that each complex contained just one real MX and twenty-two counterfeits (which would *look* different than the MX even though they smelled the same).

No MX shelter would be nearer than seven thousand feet to any other, so the Soviets would have to target all 4,600 shelters to be sure of destroying all 200 missiles, and that would require more weapons than the Soviet Union possessed. (To allow for error, two warheads are generally assigned to every target.) Administration spokesmen did acknowledge that the Soviets might deal with this problem by building more missiles; in that case, the spokesmen said, the United States would build more shelters.

And so the coming of the MX would close the "window of vulnerability," which was the name given to the period of several years between the deployment of Soviet missiles capable of destroying the Minuteman and the installation of the invulnerable MX. Those were the years, it was said, during which the Soviets might be emboldened to implement the nightmare scenario.

Ronald Reagan, of course, was as concerned about the window of vulnerability as anyone else. (He did not, however, understand what it was. Asked to explain it at a 1981 press conference, he said it referred to, among other things, "the imbalance of forces" in Europe and "the fact that right now they [sic] have a superiority at sea.") But Reagan threw out Carter's MX plan, which had encountered strong protests by ranchers, environmentalists, Indians, Mormons— and Reagan supporters—in Utah and Nevada. (They were distressed by the fantastic size of the project, which was to sprawl over a quarter of their states, and they were not calmed when the Air Force chief of staff explained that the purpose of the 4,400 decoy shelters was to act as "a great sponge to absorb" Soviet nuclear warheads.)

The Reagan administration announced it would consider plans to carry the missiles about in giant cargo airplanes or to bury them deep inside mountains. More studies proceeded. Consideration was given to a plan to launch MX missiles into orbit at the first sign of an attack; the president would later order them to descend on Russia or to land, without exploding, in some remote area. These plans were rejected.

In November 1982, the president announced that the MX (which he renamed "Peacekeeper," a name no one else ever used) would be deployed in a mode called "Dense Pack." Dense Pack was almost the exact opposite of the sprawling Carter plan. It involved placing one hundred missiles in an area of fourteen square miles. The missiles would be survivable, the White House explained, because of something called "fratricide." The first Soviet warheads to land amid the Dense Pack would indeed destroy their targets, but the radiation, heat, blast, and debris generated by their explosions would cause other incoming Soviet warheads to detonate, melt, erode, or go astray before they landed on *their* targets. There were many other subtleties involved in the Dense Pack scheme, including the possibility of a "pindown attack," in which the Soviets might explode warheads above the MX field to create a barrier through which the MX could not pass, and a "spike attack" or "slow walk attack," in which the Soviets might carefully space and time their incoming warheads to avoid fratricide. Some scientists also worried that the Soviets might someday be able to divert an asteroid to crash into the Dense Pack field, wiping it out in a single spectacular blow.

None of this mattered, however, because Dense Pack was almost immediately rejected by Congress. The president appointed a blue-ribbon commission to come up with something else.

In April 1983, the commission proposed that the MX be placed in existing Minuteman silos while development work began on a new, smaller, single-warhead missile (dubbed "Midgetman") to replace the MX. The recommendation to place the MX in Minuteman silos seemed somewhat perverse, since it was the alleged vulnerability of those silos that had spurred the development of the MX in the first place. Not to worry, said the commission. It was true that "the Soviets ... now probably possess the necessary combination of ICBM numbers, reliability, accuracy and warhead yield to destroy almost all of the 1,047 U.S. ICBM silos." But the Soviets would face "operational uncertainties" in launching such an attack, and they would in any case face the "mutual survivability shared by the ICBM force and the bomber force in view of the different types of attacks that would need to be launched at each." (The bombers could take off as soon as missiles were spotted heading for American ICBMs; if the Soviets tried to destroy the planes on the ground by launching an attack on bomber bases from missile-launching submarines offshore, *that* attack would alert the American ICBM force in time for it to be launched before it was destroyed.) In sum, the commission said, silo vulnerability was compensated for, at least for now, by America's other nuclear forces. The window of vulnerability was out the window.

Without embarrassment, Reagan endorsed the commission's recommendations and thus opened the way to the worst of all possible worlds. The *best* thing about the Carter MX plan had been its Rube Goldberg basing scheme. Despite environmental objections to digging up one-quarter of Utah and Nevada, the shell game scheme probably *would* have insured MX survivability (especially if coupled with SALT II limits on Soviet missile production), and the prospect of an invulnerable MX force would have discouraged a Russian first strike under any circumstances. The *worst* thing about the Carter MX plan was the MX itself. Its multiple warheads (it carries ten) and theoretical accuracy will threaten Russian ICBMs in exactly the same way Russian missiles threaten American ICBMs. "We plan to give the MX a high single-shot kill probability against hard targets:

269

including silos, submarine pens, nuclear storage sites, and command bunkers," wrote Harold Brown. "We see no reason to make these targets safe from U.S. ICBMs when comparable targets in the United States would be at risk from Soviet ICBMs."

The Soviets protested that the United States was building the MX so that it could launch a first strike against Russia; American critics of the MX, while ascribing no aggressive intentions to the United States, pointed out that the MX surely did *look* like a first-strike weapon. Defending the MX, Harold Brown acknowledged that it *could* "place a large percentage of the Soviet strategic force in jeopardy," but that did not make it a first-strike weapon, he said, because the MX could not wipe out the *entire* Soviet strategic force. "The Soviets would not be disarmed any more than we would by the loss of their ICBMs," he said. "At a minimum, hundreds of their SLBM [submarine-launched ballistic missile] warheads would survive." (By that argument, of course, there was no need to worry about American ICBM vulnerability in the first place, because thousands of American submarine-launched warheads would survive any attack. In fact, the Soviets have more to worry about than we do, because three-fourths of their strategic nuclear warheads are on ICBMs, while less than one-fourth of American strategic warheads are on ICBMs.)

If the Soviets didn't like the fact that their ICBMs were threatened, Carter administration spokesmen said, they could build their own version of the mobile MX, and that would be all to the good, because survivable mobile missiles on both sides would discourage a first strike by either side and thus make nuclear war less likely. "The primary advantage to the U.S. of having the same counter-silo capability as the Soviets, besides the obvious perception reasons, is that by giving the Soviets the same problem that they gave us, we motivate them to go to smaller, mobile survivable ICBMs as did we," said Under Secretary of Defense William Perry. "Smaller missiles are less threatening to the U.S., and stability will actually be *enhanced* if both sides move to survivable and verifiable ICBM basing." Asked if he would be troubled if the Soviet Union built a missile system like Carter's proposed MX, an Air Force general told a Senate committee, "I would be delighted."

Putting the MX in fixed silos, however, will eliminate every tendency toward stability. The strongest argument that the MX was not a first-strike weapon had been Carter's elaborate basing scheme. Why go to all the trouble of shuttling missiles around the desert if you're planning on launching them *before* any incoming attack? Reagan's proposal to put the MX in fixed silos, after the United States had often and loudly declared fixed silos to be non-survivable, laid the ground for "crisis instability"—arms control jargon for the prospect of World War III.

If fixed missile silos *are* vulnerable, and both sides have their ICBMs in fixed silos, then a premium is placed on being the first to strike in a nuclear war. The side that strikes first will be able to destroy many enemy missiles by firing a mere fraction of its own force (since the missiles have multiple warheads and each missile can destroy several). The side that holds back will lose most of its ICBMs before it strikes at all. Around the Pentagon, this incentive to go first is known as "use 'em or lose 'em."

It does not even matter if the silos really *are* vulnerable; all that matters is that Soviet and American leaders *believe* they are. Then, in any tense confrontation, if Side A begins to suspect that Side B is thinking of launching a first strike, there will be pressure on Side A to preempt. This pressure will grow even if Side A knows that Side B has no desire to start a war, but Side A fears that Side B may think that Side A thinks Side B *is* thinking of starting a war and thus that Side B may fear that Side A is planning to preempt and so Side B may decide it had better preempt first. And so on. Mutual ICBM vulnerability "may provide an incentive, in an extreme crisis, for one side or the other to strike first," acknowledged the U.S. Arms Control and Disarmament Agency in 1980. "This might occur in a situation in which war appeared to be virtually inevitable and in which one side believed that it would be better off, post-attack, if it struck first."

In 1983, Reagan said the Soviets had nothing to fear from an MX first strike because his plan called for deploying only one hundred missiles, and that would not be enough to destroy all Soviet ICBMs. But the MX was not the only "silo-buster" in development. The new D-5 missile scheduled to be deployed on Trident submarines in 1989 will be accurate enough "to attack any target in the Soviet Union, including their missile silos," the White House announced in 1981. New nuclear cruise missiles now being deployed on planes, ships, submarines, and trucks are also highly accurate, and all American missiles may soon benefit from in-course flight corrections dictated by Navstar navigational satellites. In the meantime, accuracy improvements in existing Minuteman missiles have already made *them* potential silo-busters.

First-strike fears are compounded when missile accuracy is combined with fast arrival times, a combination that will be in place when Trident submarines with D-5 missiles patrol off Soviet shores. And one of the main Soviet objections to American intermediate-range Pershing II missiles in Europe is that the Pershing II is theoretically accurate enough to destroy hardened Soviet missile sites and command centers, and near enough to Russian targets to hit them in less than ten minutes.

Ten minutes is not a lot of time to double-check warning signals—or to think about what to do. Both Soviet and American officials have hinted in recent years that they may respond to the other side's threatening new missiles by putting their own forces in a launch-under-attack or launch-on-warning posture, in which missiles would be fired at the first sign of enemy attack. With the survival of one's own forces threatened by accurate enemy missiles just minutes away, a new plateau has been reached in the nuclear stand-off, one where a first strike might well seem an attractive option.

ELEVEN

Open for Business

P reserving the little perquisites of rank, the desk reserved for the use of the chairman of the board of AT&T in the company's post-nuclear-war executive suite is a few inches larger than the postattack desk of the president of AT&T; the president's desk is a few inches larger than the desks for the vice presidents. None of the desks is luxurious—all are of spartan gray steel—and the surroundings as well are plain and unadorned. No one—not even the chairman—will have a window office.

AT&T's National Emergency Control Center is located forty feet beneath Netcong, New Jersey. All that is visible on the surface is a modest yellow-brick building the size of a large garage. Visitors are buzzed in through two doors, walk down four flights and then pass through two heavy vault doors that open one at a time (and could leave an unwelcome visitor stranded in the dead space between them). The two-story subterranean complex was constructed in the late 1960s by blasting through solid white granite to bedrock. Concrete was poured and reinforced for the walls and the roof, and four feet of earth was laid over the top. The entire structure was wrapped in sheet steel to shield its contents from the electromagnetic pulse of exploding nuclear bombs.

In peacetime, the Netcong center functions as a switching and relay station on the Boston-to-Miami cable. In a pre-nuclear-war crisis, the center's normal staff will be joined by workers from the AT&T Communications (formerly Long Lines) operations center at Bedminster, New Jersey, fifteen miles away. The workers at Bedminster oversee the nation's long-distance telephone network. When bottlenecks develop—on Mother's Day, for example—they reroute calls around cities where the circuits are jammed with people calling Mom. Following a nuclear attack, they will reroute calls around cities that have ceased to exist.

The AT&T Communications staff will work under fluorescent lights in a large open room in the Netcong center. Their desks and phones and computer terminals are ready and waiting for them. Bell System files are stored nearby and updated monthly, and a phone list of sixty people to be summoned to the center in a crisis is pinned to a bulletin board.

Elsewhere in the Netcong complex, bank after bank of eleven-foot-tall switching units are attached to the ceiling by heavy steel springs and anchored to the floor by thick elastic bands. If the building is struck by a massive blast wave, the elastic bands will snap and the switching units will swing, cushioned by the springs, from the ceiling. All of the mechanical equipment in the center is similarly shock-mounted. Storerooms are stocked with cots and dried food. Tanks hold drinking water and kerosene for emergency generators. The ventilation system is equipped with blast valves that will seal the air intakes if a blast wave hits. Sometimes the valves are activated by thunder. They slam shut, jolting the peacetime Netcong crew.

The desks for AT&T executives are in a large open area next to the operations center. While the AT&T Communications crew runs what is left of the long-distance network—with the help of crews at backup national centers in Kansas and Georgia and at seven regional underground centers—the corporate executives will run what is left of AT&T. There are twenty-three desks in the open area and a single semiprivate office for the desks of the president and the chairman of the board. The little office is decorated with a print of sailing ships, and nameplates identify the desks: "Chairman of the Board—Mr. Brown" and "President AT&T—Mr. Ellinghaus."

The nameplates are kept up to date.

A few months after the bombing of Hiroshima, the trade journal *American Banker* brought to its readers the good news that four large vaults manufactured by the Mosler Safe Company of Hamilton, Ohio, had survived the atomic bombing. "Many of the estimated 13,000,000 holders of safe deposit boxes [in the United States] have voiced their concern over the resistance of bank vaults to atomic explosion," the journal reported. Now they could relax. The Mosler safes, which had been sold before the war to the Teikoku Bank in Hiroshima, "were still in working order and the contents of the vaults completely intact."*

Trading on this experience, Mosler won the contract for the atomic-bomb-proof vault into which the Declaration of Independence and U.S. Constitution will descend during an attack. And Mosler refined its expertise in 1955 when the Federal Civil Defense Administration subjected the mock city dubbed "Doom Town" to a twenty-nine-kiloton atomic explosion at the Nevada test site. Several Mosler safes were there. "The safes had relatively small damage," a Mosler executive reported later. "I will admit, however, that the closest ones went around the world in a cloud of dust."

By then, both the government and American business were looking for ways to preserve corporate assets in a nuclear war. Following the passage of the Defense Production Act in 1950, it became official government policy "to encourage and, when appropriate, to require that new [industrial] facilities and major expansions of existing facilities important to national security" be located away from target areas. This policy, which was promoted by special tax breaks, was reevaluated following the development of the hydrogen bomb. The power of the new weapon made old safe-distance standards obsolete, and committees drawing up industrial dispersal plans in dozens of American cities had to start work all over again.†

---

* In 1950, Mosler received a formal testimonial letter from the Teikoku Bank. "As you know," it said, "in 1945 the Atomic Bomb fell on Hiroshima, and the whole city was destroyed and thousands of citizens lost their precious lives. And our building, the best artistic one in Hiroshima, was also destroyed. However it was our great luck to find that though the surface of the vault doors were heavily damaged, its contents were not affected at all and the cash and important documents were perfectly saved. ... Your products were admired for being stronger than the Atomic Bomb." Mosler reproduced the letter in its promotional literature.

† Business did, however, see a positive side to the hydrogen bomb. Increased military spending, the growth of new suburbs (as people fled the target cities), and the construction of new highways (for civil-defense evacuation) would all be good for busi-

Few companies actually moved their plants for reasons of nuclear safety, but a booming business did arise in building and leasing underground vaults in remote areas. Most major American corporations arranged atom-bomb-proof storage for their vital records. Eight Boston banks began shipping their records daily to an underground site in Pepperell, Massachusetts. "It is estimated that the Center would withstand the blast of any currently known bombs which struck anywhere outside a five-mile radius," boasted a brochure published by the First National Bank of Boston. U.S. Steel shipped to its underground site microfilm copies of all engineering drawings and financial and payroll records going back fifty years.

Vital records were only the beginning. Many corporations amended their bylaws to provide for emergency lines of succession to their boards of directors and top management positions after a nuclear attack. Air raid drills were conducted in corporate offices. (When IBM added air conditioning to its New York headquarters in 1959, it retested the building to make sure that exterior air raid sirens could still be heard.) J. Gordon Roberts, proprietor of a Nebraska dairy farm, built a $40,000 fallout shelter big enough to hold 217 Guernsey cows and two bulls.

In a worked-out iron mine (and former mushroom farm) in upstate New York, the Iron Mountain Atomic Storage Corporation offered well-guarded vaults for the preservation of corporate records—and larger vaults for the preservation of corporate executives. One of its tenants was the Shell Oil Company, which in 1965 leased a 4,400-square-foot cavern containing office space for forty-four people, a clinic, a lounge, a dining/conference room seating sixteen, sleeping accommodations, and what Shell literature described as a " 'home-like' kitchen." "If war or natural disaster prevented normal operations in New York the Executive Committee and representatives of head office departments would continue corporate activity from the new facilities," a notice enclosed with dividend checks informed company shareholders. "For alternate headquarters purposes, Iron Mountain offers an ideal situation," said a company magazine. "Although about 125 miles from mid-

---

ness, concluded an article in *U.S. News & World Report*. It quoted one analyst as saying, "The H-bomb has blown depression thinking out the window."

town Manhattan, it is easily accessible by automobile, railroad, helicopter or business plane, and if necessary, by boat up the Hudson River." Shell established other relocation sites for each of its major installations in the United States; employees not important enough to be relocated were issued yellow wallet cards listing the phone numbers of emergency reporting centers "established as a means for you to contact the Company in case of nuclear attack." (Space was left on the back of the cards for employees to fill in their supervisors' names and their own blood types.) In sum, the company magazine reported, "Shell is prepared to continue functioning as a Company under any foreseeable emergency circumstances."

Standard Oil of New Jersey was no less well prepared. *Its* emergency headquarters was a converted Westchester County rest home where fifty bedrooms were kept made up at all times and an emergency stash of Scotch was on hand. "The location is a bit too close for comfort [thirty miles] to targets in New York City," *Fortune* magazine reported, "but several rows of wooded hills between the relocation center and the city would help cushion the blast waves." Standard Oil maintained sixteen emergency reporting centers around New York for its four thousand employees in the area. Each center was stocked with a supply of preissued $25 and $100 checks for postattack payrolls. In this, Standard Oil was complying with federal civil-defense recommendations. "The checks," one civil-defense booklet advised, "should be marked 'good only after a nuclear attack,' or some similar wording to prevent their use in normal times."

Probably the greatest practitioner of corporate preparedness was AT&T, where the survival of company assets and the national interest in preserving a postattack communications system intermingled. The fortresslike AT&T buildings in many American cities were built with nuclear war in mind. "Windows were omitted to protect employes and equipment from fall-out radiation," *The New York Times* reported of a new AT&T building in Manhattan in 1961. All across the country, AT&T routed long-distance cables around target cities and buried the cables inside steel-and-concrete conduits to protect them from nuclear blast. "A $200 million blast-resistant cable . . . was opened for service today by the Bell Telephone System," AT&T announced in 1964. "The 4,000-mile transcontinental cable was built by the Bell System to withstand natural disasters ... and national crises, including nuclear blasts short of a direct hit. It can take on overall pressure of more than 100 pounds a square inch; an overall pressure of one-half pound per square inch could crush the average home. All communications equipment associated with the cable is shockmounted in underground concrete buildings. The cable itself is four to five feet underground. ... The cable runs from New York to California, skirting all major cities and potential target areas." Manned stations along the cable route were also built of concrete and buried. "Personnel enter the communications centers through an access vault sealed off by two lead-lined concrete doors, each weighing 3,600 pounds ... ," said AT&T. "In emergencies, each center can generate its own power and provide living quarters, food and water to operate in a 'buttoned-up' condition for at least three weeks."

All of this was paid for not by the government but by AT&T, which passed the cost on to its customers in their monthly telephone bills. It was a service the government relied on. The vast majority of long-distance military communications were—and still are—carried by the Bell System. "You are probably familiar with surveillance radars that are on the periphery of the United States," General William Hilsman, director of the Defense Communications Agency, said in 1982. "Those radars ... tie back to NORAD headquarters and SAC through the common carrier network. The information is picked up on the computers there and sent to the National Military Command Center on the commercial carrier network. Decisions are made and information goes back out again, back out to the forces, back to SAC, back to the Minuteman silos, the same way."

In 1979, President Jimmy Carter signed Presidential Directive 53, which spelled out America's reliance on telephone service that could survive nuclear war. "A survivable communications system is a necessary component of our deterrent posture for defense," it said. "In support of national security policy, the nation's telecommunications must provide for: Connectivity between the National Command Authority and strategic and other appropriate forces to support flexible execution of retaliatory strikes during and after an enemy nuclear attack; Responsive support for operational control of the armed forces, even during a protracted nuclear conflict ... ;

278

Continuity of government during and after a nuclear war . . . ; Recovery of the nation during and after a nuclear war."*

By 1979, however, the nation's telephone industry had changed. AT&T faced competitors offering cut-rate long-distance service, so AT&T could no longer comfortably pass nuclear war service charges along to a captive market. Meanwhile, the Justice Department had filed an antitrust suit to break up the Bell System. Military planners were not happy with these developments. "We want to make sure that despite divestiture, when [SAC Commander] General Bennie Davis has a problem [connecting] his command center to a Minuteman silo, he doesn't have to call AT&T Long Lines for one part of the solution and then go to a local telephone company for another, and then go to a third person who is going to deliver the end instruments, to try and figure out what's wrong with his circuit," said General Hilsman. Secretary of Defense Caspar Weinberger urged the Attorney General to drop the antitrust suit. Former secretary of defense Harold Brown testified as a defense witness at the trial that breaking up AT&T would weaken national security.

The suit was pressed nevertheless, and it resulted in a consent decree by which AT&T was separated from its local operating companies. The decree stipulated, however, that the newly independent companies would join a "centralized organization . . . to meet the requirements of national security and emergency preparedness." Meanwhile, defense communications planners had to begin looking for money to pay for nuclear hardening the phone companies were no longer willing to pay for on their own.

Elsewhere in corporate America, the civil-defense enthusiasm of the 1950s and 1960s had waned. Jones and Laughlin Steel, which once maintained an emergency headquarters in an abandoned coal mine, gave it up. "There are no longer plans for 30 percent of our staff to report to a mine shaft," said a Jones and Laughlin spokes-

---

* Federal Communications Commission regulations list the priorities for connecting postattack telephone calls. The highest priority category is designated "FLASH EMERGENCY." All other calls in progress will be interrupted to put through FLASH EMERGENCY calls, which will include those involving "command and control of military forces" and the "conduct of diplomatic negotiations critical to the arresting or limiting of hostilities."

man. In 1975, Shell Oil shut down its emergency headquarters inside Iron Mountain. "We don't feel it's practical to protect against something that can't be protected against," a Shell executive explained. Iron Mountain's management changed the company name from Iron Mountain Atomic Storage Corporation to the Iron Mountain Group, Inc., and changed the company's emphasis as well. "We no longer provide alternate management sites," said a company spokesman. "We're basically in the business of storing vital records crucial to disaster recovery planning—not so much nuclear holocaust as tornadoes, floods, or something like that."

But nuclear holocaust has not been forgotten. The underground records-storage business is still booming, run in many cases by companies like Iron Mountain that began with nuclear war in mind and then switched pitches. Their original orientation often still shows through. "Security in solid granite!" reads the headline in ads for Perpetual Storage Inc. in Utah. "Fireproof vault constructed of concrete and steel, drilled into a solid granite mountain with a 200' overburden to withstand any force known to man." Right to the point, the Inland Vital Records Center in Kansas advertises that it provides a "MAXIMUM SECURITY atomic blast proof vault." Companies utilizing such centers rarely cite nuclear war as their reason for being there today, but they do acknowledge that the centers might serve them well in a war. Don Baron, the Shell Oil executive who personally supervised the closing of Shell's Iron Mountain relocation center in 1975, says that the company continues to store vital records, including shareholder information and the titles to oil wells, in a remote location in Louisiana. "Records that will maintain the integrity of the company will be safeguarded in an area outside [nuclear] holocaust," he says. "The records can be reconstituted if someone survives." (So can the records of the Social Security Administration; microfilmed duplicates of all Social Security records are stored in a former limestone mine in Pennsylvania.)

Other companies retain their nuclear war emergency bylaws; IBM's provide for a special irregular committee to run the company "in the event of a major disaster or catastrophe or national emergency which renders the Board [of Directors] incapable of action by reason of the death, physical incapacity or inability to meet of some or all of its members." Bendix has oriented its emergency planning

280

toward natural disasters, but, says Jim Armstrong, the company's safety director, "The disaster control plans we have in effect, short of the total annihilation of everybody, would enable the corporation to survive."

And some companies continue to plan specifically for nuclear war. AT&T still works closely with the government and maintains its underground emergency operations centers. (It has also begun to replace its copper wire cables with optical fiber cables that are more efficient and also happen to be immune to nuclear electromagnetic pulse.) General Telephone and Electronics has established emergency lines of succession for its corporate officers and has begun to think about providing telephone service during a crisis evacuation. "In accordance with federal crisis relocation guidelines," GTE Vice President Bruce Carswell said in a 1982 speech, "probably 80 percent of our employees would move to host areas while 20 percent stay behind to man essential segments of the network. . . . They would also be involved in a continuation of hardening activities to try to increase survivability. . . . Our telephone employees would be a valuable work pool [in the host areas] to assist in local expansion of phone service." (If the crisis escalates, Carswell acknowledged, "although the bulk of our employees will feel a responsibility to their job, a few will undoubtedly disappear.")

"If a survivable nuclear exchange occurred," Carswell continued, "it would take years to recover any semblance of pre-war business as usual. However, if a crisis was resolved peacefully or with minimal damage, we would want to ensure a rapid and solvent recovery of business as usual. . . . If the world doesn't end, we would like people to pay their phone bills within a reasonable period of time."

The Federal Emergency Management Agency naturally encourages all such corporate planning. Emergency bylaws and alternate headquarters are endorsed in its 1978 *Disaster Planning Guide for Business and Industry*. (Alternate headquarters can serve as an economical and distraction-free alternative to hotels for peacetime company meetings, the guide points out.) FEMA has also suggested that corporations take part in crisis relocation planning as corporations, organizing things so that employees of a particular company will evacuate to a selected small town with their co-workers instead

281

of their neighbors. This will "provide badly needed, socially useful anchors for citizens enduring great stress," FEMA says, and will aid in preserving "as much as possible of the nation's economic organization through successive periods of crisis, attack, and recovery." The Boeing Aerospace Company studied the feasibility of corporate relocation (under a FEMA contract) and made a number of recommendations for improving FEMA guidelines in the area. More attention had to be given to the welfare of pets, Boeing found: "In a survey of Boeing employees concerning civil preparedness, more write-in comments were received concerning pets than any other subject." And the guidelines had to provide for including unions in the planning process: "Some employees will be more inclined to trust the union than the company." But Boeing concluded that corporate relocation could work and that companies could even continue some operations in host areas during the crisis.

Boeing itself, however, has not made plans for corporate evacuation. It *has* had a public relations employee record a tape that will be played over plant public address systems during a nuclear attack. "I'm trying to remember what it said," she recalled later. " 'Stay calm. We are in contact with federal authorities. Go immediately to your nearest fallout shelter. This is not a test. We will be in constant contact with you. If you cannot get to your nearest fallout shelter, go under a desk.' Something like that."

One company FEMA can be proud of is Exxon.

In the event of a nuclear attack upon the United States, or "the imminent threat of such attack," Exxon's board of directors is authorized (by Section 4 of Article II of the corporate bylaws) to operate with a reduced quorum. If even a reduced quorum of the preattack directors cannot be found, a quorum may be made up with predesignated stand-ins "who are known to be alive and available to act." The postattack directors are empowered to change the location of corporate headquarters and otherwise run the company as they see fit. None of them "shall be liable for any action taken . . . in good faith in such an emergency in furtherance of the ordinary business affairs of the corporation even though not authorized by the by-laws then in effect."

Exxon (formerly Standard Oil of New Jersey) no longer maintains the Westchester County rest home it once kept up as a corporate retreat, but it has made plans to keep its preattack directors alive for postattack board meetings. "Exxon has contingency plans that would relocate key executives at various locations some distance from New York City," a company spokesman says. "It's fair to assume the sites have communications equipment and supplies. *I* was not told where they are. Our security department is very cautious."

While the officers of Exxon, AT&T, and other well-prepared corporations are settling into their post-nuclear-attack quarters, the government of the United States will be doing its part to preserve the American economy. To that end, the order freezing all wages, prices and rents at preattack levels has been prepared and included as one of the Presidential Emergency Action Documents in Federal Emergency Plan D. The objectives of the freeze, according to a FEMA planning document, include the following:

- to maintain "market-place stability in undamaged areas."
- "to provide at least an interim basis of payment for foods, goods, or services which are requisitioned or allocated" by authorities.
- "to discourage hoarding, scare buying, and other harmful economic distortions that only add to inflation or produce inequities."*

The freeze order will apply to all attack survivors. (It "should be assumed to be in effect if a community or area is temporarily cut off" from communicating with the rest of the country, FEMA says.) While it is aimed primarily at preventing postattack inflation, it will also inhibit postattack *deflation*. ("There is a possibility of deflationary pressures on wages and salaries in undamaged areas where the influx of displaced persons from damaged areas could result in a manpower surplus," Labor Department guidelines point out.) Persons who feel they have been unfairly denied a raise because of the freeze will be able to petition the Wage and Salary Stabilization and

---

* Standby freeze plans were taken off the shelf and hurriedly applied in 1971 when President Nixon ordered a temporary wage and price freeze. "The order came on a Sunday and we implemented it Monday morning," says a postattack planner. "We were heroes. It showed the benefit of emergency planning."

Labor Disputes Administration, which will be set up by the Labor Department immediately following a nuclear attack and will set to work resolving disputes "as soon as conditions permit."

The nationwide freeze will be accompanied by nationwide rationing. As a first step, the freeze order includes a section banning (in undamaged areas) all retail sales "of food (except perishables), petroleum, and other essential survival items . . . for a period of five days or until otherwise determined by local authorities," according to a FEMA planning document. "This period would be designed to provide time for local authorities to initiate inventory control, assess supplies and possible resupply, register local consumers, to estimate local consumer demand, and to distribute rationing evidence [books and coupons]," FEMA explains. Until a full-scale postattack rationing system can be put in place, FEMA suggests that local authorities issue appeals for voluntary conservation, "suggesting such practicable measures as the use of perishable foods first, eliminating all waste, cutting needless driving, and so on." Meanwhile, uniformed guards might be placed "at a source of supply, with instructions to release goods only to certain authorized individuals or under specified conditions." Adds FEMA, "The *appearance* of an organized approach to the job may in itself help to control the initial situation and avoid panic, hoarding and other unmanageable responses."

On a larger scale, scarce resources will be allocated by the Office of Defense Resources, which will be created following a nuclear attack either by a presidential proclamation that is part of Federal Emergency Plan D or, if Congress can be found and assembled, by passage of a bill that has been prepared and included in the package of "Other Than D" documents. "The demand for military hardware might be so great that you couldn't build cars," explained FEMA executive William Baird. "The Office of Defense Resources would say, 'Don't build cars.' " Individual industries, meanwhile, will be regulated by specialized postattack agencies. The Emergency Solid Fuels Administration will be created in the Department of Energy to "estimate surviving capabilities for the production of solid fuels and coal chemicals in relation to direct attack effects and radioactive fallout hazards, and . . . issue instructions on the use of requisitioning powers." An Emergency Minerals Administration will be created in the Interior Department. The ODR, ESFA, EMA, and other postattack agencies will be staffed in part by members of the National Defense Executive Reserve, civilian executives who train a few days each year. The Reservists generally prepare for positions supervising the industries in which they work—mining company executives, for example, will join the Emergency Solid Fuels Administration—but conflict-of-interest laws will not apply if they quit their old jobs upon entering government service. As of 1982, about two thousand executives were active in the Reserve (down from three thousand in 1976) and FEMA was trying to recruit more.

All postattack economic planning will be guided by Defense Mobilization Order 4, issued pursuant to the Defense Production Act of 1950 and amended in 1980. DMO-4 establishes a list of "priority activities in [the] immediate postattack period" which will have priority "over all other claims for resources." The activities include "defense and retaliatory combat operations" (including the "production and distribution of . . . atomic weapons"), the "maintenance or reestablishment of Government authority and control," and the production and distribution of "essential survival items." Survival items are defined as those "without which large segments of the population would die or have their health so seriously impaired as to render them both burdensome and non-productive." The list includes anesthetics, rabies vaccine, surgical knives, fertilizers, sleeping bags, shoes, gloves, mittens, diapers, utility repair trucks, coal, radiological contamination warning signs, bulldozers, toilet paper, and rat poison.

The raw materials for some of these items have already been stashed away in the National Defense Stockpile. Stored at 122 locations around the country, the stockpile contains fifteen billion dollars' worth of sixty-one industrial metals and other "strategic and critical" materials, including 71,000 pounds of opium for postattack painkiller needs.* Stockpiled materials will be released as needed after a nuclear attack.

---

* Just over one thousand pounds of the opium was reported missing from a government warehouse at West Point in 1980, but stockpile officials attributed the shortage to evaporation rather than theft. In 1983, a routine proposal to add ten thousand pounds of morphine sulfate to the stockpile was rejected by the Reagan administration out of concern that the purchase might increase public fears that the United States was preparing for nuclear war.

Labor will also be funneled into priority areas. The Department of Labor has prepared forms to be filled out by state employment offices to report the status of the postattack workforce. There are blanks for "estimated number of civilian workers killed" and "estimated number of individuals age 16 and over not now in labor force who might be mobilized to meet area needs." "State employment offices have systems for identifying people's occupations and matching them up with employment needs," says Labor Department emergency planner Robert Covington. "That's the very same thing they'd do [after a nuclear attack]. People who survive will like to know that there's still an employment office and retraining programs, which might be drastic." Adds Jerry Smith, of the department's Employment and Training Administration: "An emergency itself creates a lot of jobs—clean-up crews, construction, health services. A nuclear scenario will really not be that different, except somebody would have to put people in those asbestos suits, or whatever kind of suits they use."

All federal efforts to get the postattack economy on its feet will be futile, planners recognize, without sound postattack fiscal, monetary, and credit policies. And so planners at FEMA, the Treasury Department, and the Federal Reserve System have been laboring for years on proposals for preserving this infrastructure of the economy. "The plans and programs [of] the Federal Reserve are a fundamental feature underlying all other [postattack] plans since the others assume a functioning monetary system," Federal Reserve System Governor Philip Coldwell told a congressional committee in 1976. Without a functioning monetary system and a generally accepted medium of exchange, Coldwell warned, widespread hoarding and a system of barter will develop, and "this would result in a rapid loss of economic momentum and a low probability of national survival."

Much attention has been given to devising plans for "the equitable sharing of war losses," *not* "to guarantee individuals against war losses but to assure the maintenance of a 'going concern' economy, [and] to assure the viability of financial institutions." This will cost the government money, so war-loss-sharing proposals are usually linked with postattack tax proposals. Neither tax nor war-loss policies have been firmly set. Instead, guidelines and selected proposals have been filed for postattack reference at government relocation sites. ("Policy choices should be left to be made intelligently by the survivors," an Internal Revenue Service official explained in 1977.) The issues are controversial. "Supply-side economics gives a different slant to emergency policies," a Treasury Department planner said in the first year of the Reagan administration. "But I think we'll wait to see how it works in peacetime before incorporating it into our postattack policies."

Current thinking favors a national sales tax, which will be easier to administer than an income tax, especially if records have been wiped out. An older tax proposal also filed at relocation sites suggests that the income tax not be abandoned but simplified. "Because of the necessity of maintaining the surviving labor force at maximum efficiency in a period of widespread illness, a complete or partial credit for medical expenses might be the only deduction allowed." If damage is "catastrophic" and widespread, the older proposal notes, the tax system might be temporarily abandoned altogether. "If the government simply confiscates available food supplies in order to supply free 'soup kitchens,' if it orders healthy survivors to work as needed in hospitals, food distribution, etc., its money payments could be suspended and tax collection could be suspended. Simply stated, everybody would be in the Army."

There will remain, however, strong reason to maintain a tax system even if the government doesn't need the money, a Treasury economist points out. "The only way to maintain the value of currency is if we maintain the tax system. If people need money to pay their taxes, that alone gives money value. And we must keep society monetized. We must keep it from breaking down to a barter system." If the printed dollar loses its value, the economist knows, then nobody will be reporting for work at the postattack AT&T headquarters or anywhere else. Everybody will be out scrambling for food and clothing if they have no confidence that their postattack paychecks will *buy* them food and clothing. It is unlikely that destroyed industries will be able to finance reconstruction if workers insist on being paid in potatoes.

The first step in maintaining a money economy is simply maintaining money, so the Federal Reserve System stores several billion dollars in cash at its main relocation site near Culpeper, Virginia. "Not too long ago," says Federal Reserve emergency planner Harry Guinter, "we sent over a large supply of two-dollar bills." Federal Reserve banks throughout the country have been instructed to suspend their normal practice of removing worn bills from circulation after a nuclear attack. Looking beyond immediate postattack needs, the Bureau of Engraving and Printing has stored obsolete presses outside Washington.

The next step in preserving the money economy will be preserving its major institutions—the banks. ("Victory in a nuclear war will belong to the country that recovers first, and the financial community will bear a heavy burden of responsibility in effecting rapid recovery," says a booklet distributed to banks by the Federal Reserve.) Since 1961, the Treasury Department has had in place a standby "Emergency Banking Regulation No. 1," to be "effective immediately after an attack upon the United States." To protect banks from postattack runs, the regulation will prohibit all cash withdrawals "except for those purposes, and not in excess of those amounts, for which cash is customarily used." Larger withdrawals and bank loans will be allowed only for paying taxes, payrolls, essential living expenses, or "expenses or reconstruction costs vital to the war effort." The regulation also requires all banks and branches, "without regard to whether or not the head office or any other branch or branches are functioning," to be open for business "during their regularly established hours," unless they are located in unsafe areas "or if essential personnel or physical facilities become unavailable." This will, presumably, bolster public confidence in the banking system.*

Established postattack federal policy specifies that provision will be made for "the clearance of checks, including those drawn on

* In 1979, in response to public concern generated by a report in a survivalist newsletter, the Treasury Department released a statement asserting that the restrictions on bank accounts in the emergency regulation are necessary "to guard against the misuse of the Nation's monetary resources." There is no truth, the Treasury said, to reports of "any existing or proposed measures which would permit the Government to confiscate bank accounts in any declared National Emergency, including nuclear attack upon the United States."

288

destroyed banks." The Federal Reserve will guarantee the payment of such checks (it will seek to recover the money later from the assets of the destroyed banks), and it has made arrangements for small-town banks to collect checks "in the event regular Federal Reserve banking facilities are rendered inoperable." "The mechanisms are set up to process checks and provide currency," says Marvin Mothersead, vice president of the Federal Reserve Bank of Kansas City, which has lined up banks in McCook, Nebraska; Altus, Oklahoma; and elsewhere to collect checks following a nuclear attack. "The basic functions to keep society moving are provided for."

The Federal Reserve Bank of Kansas City has sent all banks in its district a red loose-leaf binder labeled EMERGENCY OPERATING LETTERS AND BULLETINS. It includes instructions for postattack check clearing as well as the advice that banks finding themselves short of funds following a nuclear attack should borrow against securities they hold "rather than attempting to sell them in an unfavorable market." All banks, however, are encouraged to continue selling U.S. Savings Bonds.

In the headquarters of the Kansas City bank itself, huge basement vaults have been earmarked to serve as fallout shelters, and supplies of dehydrated food, water, medicines, cots, and gas masks have been laid in. If the headquarters is nonetheless "rendered inoperative by an enemy attack," an emergency bulletin says, the bank's Oklahoma City branch will take over. If that too is destroyed, the Omaha branch will take over. Next in line is Denver. And if Kansas City, Oklahoma City, Omaha, and Denver are all "rendered inoperative," a final backup "relocation office has been established near Hutchinson, Kansas."

That office "near" Hutchinson is actually within the city limits, but it is 650 feet straight down, inside the working Carey Salt Mine. Visitors to the bank's office there must don green hard hats and safety glasses and then wait until the miners' break to go down; during working hours the passenger elevator is occupied with four-ton loads of salt.

The ride down is long, silent, and totally dark. At the bottom, visitors reemerge into a low lighted cavern and walk along the little railway that carries salt to the elevator. A few yards on is a wall of solid salt, painted blue, that marks the entrance to Underground Vaults & Storage, a warehouse company that leases a worked-out section of the mine from Carey Salt and rents in turn two subterranean rooms to the Federal Reserve Bank of Kansas City.

One enters the UVS quarters to find a lobby decorated with a display case full of the company team's baseball trophies. The ceiling in the lobby, like that of the mine, is only six feet high. "We keep it that way on purpose," says a smiling UVS official as he ushers visitors into the warehouse offices, where the ceilings are higher, "to create an illusion of space in here for people who have claustrophobia."

The UVS offices do look almost normal, with bright shag rugs, drop ceilings, and artificial plants. The post-nuclear-attack headquarters of the Federal Reserve Bank of Kansas City is rather less cheerful. It's back in the warehouse proper, surrounded by partitioned rooms filled with stored Alaska pipeline weld X rays, old NCAA football game films, sacks of hybrid sorghum seed, and tons of corporate records, all coated with a fine layer of salt. The bank office is twenty-one feet wide by sixty-four feet long, and has an adjacent vault. Its walls, one of which is a solid slab of salt, are bare. The ceiling is salt and the floor is saltcrete (cement mixed with salt). The room is furnished with thirteen old desks and other old office equipment. The only amenity is the easy-listening music piped in on the UVS sound system.

"I feel kind of sheltered down here myself," said John Nolan, a tall and solemn former Air Force officer who showed visitors around the mine one day shortly before his recent retirement as the Federal Reserve Bank of Kansas City's emergency preparedness coordinator. "Our emergency operating center used to be in Topeka, but in 1961 the government ran a test exercise, and the results showed Topeka being hit pretty hard by the Russians. We went to the Department of Defense for targeting information and decided Hutchinson was a low-risk area. We could probably go to the surface here within two weeks after an attack."

Nolan was down in the mine that day to take part in a semiannual test of the emergency center's communications equipment. After a lunch of TV dinners in the UVS staff kitchen, he entered the bank's office to the strains of "Moon River" on the sound system and sat down at a telex machine to send and receive messages from the emergency relocation centers of the other eleven Federal Reserve Banks.

"Most centers just send some dumb thing," Nolan said while he waited. " 'The quick brown fox ...,' something like that." A firm believer in civil defense, Nolan was taking the opportunity of the test to send a more pointed message: "The British are advocating that enough food should be kept on hand for 28 days. Many experts are now advising even longer periods of shelter occupation—the battle could last intermittently for months. Is your relo site properly stocked?"

Nolan's is. The mine has its own water tank, and, in a gloomy mined-out area the size of a football field at the rear of the warehouse, the bank has stockpiled sleeping bags, pillows, clothing, and cartons full of freeze-dried chicken chop suey, spaghetti, chocolate pudding, granola, and other foods. The provisions will feed the 150 employees of the Kansas City bank and its branches who are under standing orders to rush to the salt mine upon receiving word of an "advanced alert," indicating the imminent possibility of nuclear attack. Notice of the alert will be flashed to bank headquarters from FEMA; members of the relocation team have been issued wallet cards with a phone tree showing to whom they are to relay the message after it is relayed to them. (The message shall be relayed *only* to the member of the staff being called and *not* to member's family," the card admonishes.)

"People are due to come here from every department," Nolan said, "check collection, auditing, all of them." So that bank employees will know just how things stand after a nuclear war, the vault in the mine is kept full of microfiche copies of current bank records. A fresh batch is brought down from Kansas City, 225 miles away, every day. "We used to have exercises down here where teams would come in and actually reconstruct the records," Nolan said. "We don't do it anymore, because of budget cutbacks. But the tests worked. The records could be reconstructed."

Nolan is confident that bank employees assigned to the mine will show up, as they will be allowed to bring their families in with them. (UVS officials express some concern, however, about the mine employee who must stay on the surface, operating the elevator. "If that were me," said one, "I'd say, 'The hell with you guys.' ")

"We're expecting about four hundred people," Nolan said, "and we can hold them in here for a month or more. We have enough food for four hundred people for fourteen days at twenty-eight hundred calories a day. We could cut the rations in half easily if we have to. I've been on a twelve-hundred-calorie-a-day diet for five months." He added that he'd lost forty-seven pounds.

The room where the four hundred people will sleep is dark now. It is an unimproved warehouse bay, fifty feet wide by three hundred feet long, exactly the way the salt miners left it. The cots are not set up but they are on hand, and so are the flashlights the re-locatees will use if the mine's generator, which is on the surface, is destroyed.

The bank options the space from the warehouse company for a nickel a foot a year, or $750 annually. "They'll pay a dollar a foot a year to exercise the option," said Michael Gingerich, UVS executive vice president. "But, if they ever need to use it, I don't think anybody will be too worried about the money."

Except, of course, the Federal Reserve Bank of Kansas City, or it wouldn't have optioned the space in the first place.

The bank office in the salt mine, the postattack corporate head-quarters, the planning for a postattack sales tax—all are dedicated not merely to preserving American lives and property in a nuclear war but to preserving as well the American way of life. "I would like to emphasize," said Maxwell McKnight, a Socony Mobil Oil Company emergency planner, back in 1963, "that our emergency planning is predicated on the idea that it is possible for our nation to survive, recover, and win, and that our way of life, including free enterprise, the oil industry, and the Socony Mobil Oil Company, can survive, recover, and win with it."

And so can Rembrandt and Grandma Moses.

Out of concern for the artistic and cultural side of our way of life, the General Services Administration established in 1979 a "Cultural Heritage Emergency Preparedness Group" dedicated to preserving museums, libraries, archives and historical monuments from "sabotage or wartime destruction." Inspired by Britain's success in moving the contents of its National Gallery to country houses and an underground slate quarry in Wales during World War II, the group set about identifying masterpieces in American museums and looking into ways to package and ship them to safe underground sites. "We made a list of the fifty most important paintings in the country," said Karel Yasko, the GSA's fine arts counsellor. "We're not publicizing it. We don't want to hurt people." Even so, he said, "the museum people are causing problems. Our idea is to use underground facilities for storage now. But the museums' attitude is that they want everything under their own roofs, so students and scholars can see them. Also, they don't want to risk robbery on the highway. . . . They can be prima donnas. They don't want to let go of their art, even if a nuclear bomb falls."*

While the art preservation effort is both limited and new, the free enterprise component of our way of life has had the government's attention for years. "Although the Government must and would take whatever action is required to insure national survival in times of great peril, this does not mean the end of personal and political freedoms . . . ," states the *National Plan for Emergency Preparedness*. "Consequently every effort should be made to . . . continue a basically free economy and private operation of industry." There have been some dissenters from this effort. "Capitalism, socialism and communism are all sophisticated social forms relevant only to the advanced world as it has now developed," John Kenneth Galbraith has written. "None would have existence or relevance in the wreckage and ashes . . . of a post-nuclear world." But government planners have recognized only that capitalism may need a few modifications following a nuclear war. "A post-attack private enterprise system could simply not be allowed to produce cake for some while many did not have sufficient bread," concluded a 1977 Treasury Department review of postattack economic proposals. A 1981

---

* Another element of American culture—television—is already being looked after. New York's Museum of Broadcasting has stored copies of its collection of thousands of old programs in facilities of the Iron Mountain Group. "If there were a nuclear war," museum president Robert Batscha said in 1983, "television might be the only cultural product that survived."

293

draft revision of the *National Plan*, sounding rather like the Republican Party platform, promised that "the Federal government shall not take over or operate privately owned enterprises except as required to protect the national security. . . . Every effort shall be made to channel resources to essential activities by using incentives and voluntary measures. Mandatory measures shall be used only as a last resort."

Even if some nationalization of industry does become necessary, says an economist cited in a report prepared for FEMA in 1979, the nationalized enterprises should be leased back to private operators. The economist "does not support the idea of direct government operation of this economy as is the practice in the Soviet Union."

After all, if we're going to run the United States like the Soviet Union, why have a nuclear war in the first place?

"If we don't care about the conditions under which we live, even if they are those of, say, a foreign or domestic totalitarian state," pointed out a 1980 consultant's report done for FEMA, "then 'better Red than dead' is a valid basis for strategy, and a strategy of preemptive surrender is a preferable alternative to war and a presumably effective way to prevent nuclear attack. . . .

"[The] linchpin for the preservation of our national values and objectives [is] saving not only people and assets but also the essence of our social, political and ethical system. Without this goal, there is no reason for fighting."

TWELVE

The Day After
World War III

The two men came together in the lobby of a conference center in the lush Virginia countryside and started to argue about the effects of nuclear war. One of the men—young, bearded, and earnest—was a doctor who had come to the center with a group called International Physicians for the Prevention of Nuclear War, a group that was drafting and would soon release to the press a declaration that a nuclear war "would ravage life on earth" and threaten "the very survival of civilization," and that civil defense would be useless. The young doctor agreed with this message wholeheartedly.

The second man, older and balder but equally earnest, was a public information officer with the Federal Emergency Management Agency, where a few months earlier he had written a press release critical of those who believe in "nuclear overkill" and who envision nuclear war as a scene "of endless destruction, of countless Hiroshimas." Much of the devastation produced by a nuclear attack, he had written, would depend "on the unpreparedness of the one attacked." FEMA's civil-defense plans for crisis evacuation and fallout shelters, he had written, echoing a stack of previous FEMA literature, could save 80 percent of the American population.

"You can *say* thirty million people will be saved by civil defense," the young doctor said scornfully to the civil servant, "but if there's any evidence for it you'd be able to get at least one physician to go on record and say so."

"Some have," replied the older man, "at least one or two."

The physician pounced. "Where was it published?"

The civil servant was prepared. "There was an article recently in the *Journal of Civil Defense*, a pro-civil-defense publication you may not have seen," he said, and handed the doctor a copy.

The doctor glanced at the magazine and then tossed it aside. "This article," he said dismissively, "doesn't have a single citation."

And so, for want of a footnote, the argument stalemated (although both men seemed to think they had won).

Certain facts concerning the effects of nuclear weapons are indisputable. Studies of Hiroshima and Nagasaki and of the hundreds of atmospheric nuclear tests conducted before the 1963 limited test-ban treaty have yielded volumes of data about what nuclear weapons do to people and buildings in the neighborhoods in which they explode. Much of that information is collected in a thick United States government publication called *The Effects of Nuclear Weapons*, which comes with a handy plastic "Nuclear Bomb Effects Computer." By twirling dials on the "computer" (a circular slide rule), one can quickly determine, for example, that a 165-pound man standing in the open one mile from a half-megaton nuclear explosion will absorb ten thousand rems of initial nuclear radiation (more than twice the dose required to kill him almost instantly), will be seared by heat amounting to five hundred calories per square centimeter (more than fifty times the amount required to give his fatally irradiated body third-degree burns), and will be sent flying through the air by the blast wave (in the unlikely event there is anything left of him) at a rate well over one hundred feet per second.

Other local, short-term effects of nuclear explosions are equally well documented. It is known that a one-megaton bomb exploding at ground level will blow apart brick houses 2.8 miles away and that the same bomb exploding at a height selected to maximize its blast effect will blow apart brick houses 4.4 miles away. (In a 1955 Nevada test, a brick house was actually built and then blown apart.) It is known that when a bomb explodes near enough to the ground to scoop up soil or water into its fireball, that debris will mix with radioactive elements created in the explosion and will begin immediately to drift back down to earth. The radioactivity of this fallout will drop off rapidly as the radioactive elements decay; if a given quantity of fallout is emitting 1,000 rads (similar to rems) per hour one hour after an explosion, it will be emitting 100 rads per hour six hours after the explosion, 10 rads per hour two days after the explosion, and 1 rad per hour two weeks after the explosion.* (Of course, even a small fraction of the radiation created by a large explosion may be formidable.) The greatest danger from the fallout will therefore be near the point of explosion, where the fallout will arrive promptly, but there will also be some immediate threat in all areas where the fallout comes down before it has had time to decay significantly. A person standing in the open ninety miles downwind from a one-megaton explosion (assuming the wind is blowing a steady fifteen miles per hour) will receive a dose of nine hundred rems in the first week. A person 250 miles downwind will receive ninety rems. Ninety rems will cause no immediate ill effects, but nine hundred rems will cause vomiting, diarrhea, hemorrhaging, infection, and death within days or weeks. A person ninety miles away who chooses not to stand in the open but instead goes into an ordinary basement and closes the door will receive one-tenth or less the radiation of a person outside and so will live. A person in a fallout shelter, as the civil defense people often point out, will receive even less radiation. The size of the area in which shelter will be necessary and the length of time it will be so depend on the size of the explosion, the speed and direction of the wind, and whether or not rain or snow happens to fall through the fallout cloud, carrying the radioactive particles to earth prematurely.

That much is known from experience and experiment with individual nuclear explosions. The long-term effects of individual explosions are less clear, because the cancers and other diseases caused by sublethal doses of radiation may take decades to appear.† And

---

* Another way to consider decay is to imagine a man standing amid a given quantity of fallout. Within one hour after the explosion he will have received more than half the radiation he will ever receive from that fallout. In one day he will have received 80 percent. It will take another seven days to reach the 90 percent level, another thirteen months to reach 99 percent, and another million years to approach 100 percent.
† Studies of Hiroshima and Nagasaki have found that atomic bomb survivors who received radiation doses exceeding one hundred rads died of leukemia between 1950

there have been no experiments under the conditions of a nuclear war, when not one but hundreds or thousands of nuclear weapons would be exploding at the same time. The short-term local effects of multiple explosions would presumably be additive. Individuals downwind from the explosions will be exposed to x rads from explosion number one plus y rads from explosion number two and so on; potentially lethal fallout areas would extend hundreds of miles downwind from multiple explosion sites. Individuals nearer the explosions will be burned or blown to death or fatally irradiated by explosion number one and explosion number two simultaneously.

The long-term global effects of multiple explosions are more difficult to calculate. The world experienced some 500 megatons of nuclear explosions in Japan and open-air tests between 1945 and 1963 (including 340 megatons in 1961 and 1962 alone) and there were no obvious catastrophic effects, although some number of cancers and genetic disorders were certainly created.* (And one scientist, University of Pittsburgh physicist Ernest Sternglass, even maintains that puzzling drops in SAT scores over the last two decades are explained by damage done to American schoolchildren by test fallout.) A nuclear war could involve twenty to thirty times as much megatonnage, and it would all be exploded within hours, days or weeks, not eighteen years. It is extremely difficult to predict what effects such explosions would have on the atmosphere and the environment, and on governments, economies, and the minds of human beings. Everybody agrees that such a war would be a horrible disaster. Nobody *knows* for certain exactly how horrible it would be.

---

and 1974 at more than ten times the normal rate and contracted other cancers at between 1.2 and 3.3 times the normal rate. More recent studies have indicated that the survivors' radiation doses were originally overestimated and that the incidence of radiation-induced cancer has been understated as a result. In any case, radiation-induced cancer has been a relatively minor cause of death among the survivors, because the normal cancer rate is modest to begin with and because many of those who were near enough to the bombs to receive large doses of initial nuclear radiation (the bombs were air-burst and created no local fallout) were also near enough to the bombs to be killed by blast and fire.

* A 1979 report by the Congressional Office of Technology Assessment estimated that a single one-megaton airburst will eventually cause between two hundred and two thousand cancer deaths and between 350 and 3,500 genetic effects.

But that hasn't prevented anyone from taking a position on the matter.

In his 1982 book, *The Fate of the Earth*, author Jonathan Schell acknowledged the uncertainty inherent in considering the global effects of a nuclear war: "When we proceed from the local effects of single explosions to the effects of thousands of them on societies and environments, the picture clouds considerably, because then we go beyond both the certainties of physics and our slender base of experience, and speculatively encounter the full complexity of human affairs and of the biosphere." Schell was undeterred, however, from launching himself into this speculative area. Following a graphic discussion of the local effects of nuclear weapons ("People in the street would immediately catch fire, and would shortly be reduced to heavily charred corpses") and his conclusion that the short-term local effects of a massive Soviet attack directed at American cities would kill almost everybody in the United States (civil defense notwithstanding) and leave little else alive save insects and grass, Schell proceeded to consider long-term global effects. He enumerated a variety of them, some certain, some probable, some just possible.

One of the effects upon which Schell dwelt at length was the "predicted partial destruction" of the layer of ozone in the stratosphere that shields the earth from dangerous ultraviolet radiation. Ozone depletion, Schell wrote, would lead to, among other things, "the temporary loss of sight through photophthalmia, or snow blindness, which can be contracted by exposure to heightened ultraviolet radiation. . . . One can avoid photophthalmia by wearing goggles whenever one goes outside, but so far the world has made no provision for each person on earth to have a pair of goggles in case the ozone is depleted." And, Schell noted, no such provision could ever be made for animals: "[T]he loss of sight would throw the environment into disarray as billions of blinded beasts, insects, and birds began to stumble through the world." Moreover, he wrote, "if the higher estimates of [ozone] depletion turn out to be correct," anyone venturing out of doors would receive an incapacitating sunburn in just a few minutes. "[A]nyone who crawls out of his shelter after radiation from fallout has declined to tolerable levels will have to crawl back in immediately. In the meantime, though, people would not have been able to go out to produce food, and they would starve."

Having sketched out all of this, and much else besides, Schell took a deep breath and laid out his main point:

Bearing in mind that the possible consequences of the detonations of thousands of megatons of nuclear explosives include the blinding of insects, birds, and beasts all over the world; the extinction of many ocean species, among them some at the base of the food chain; the temporary or permanent alteration of the climate of the globe, with the outside chance of "dramatic" and "major" alterations in the structure of the atmosphere; the pollution of the whole ecosphere with oxides of nitrogen; the incapacitation in ten minutes of unprotected people who go out into the sunlight; the blinding of people who go out into the sunlight; a significant decrease in photosynthesis in plants around the world; the scalding and killing of many crops; the increase in rates of cancer and mutation around the world, but especially in the targeted zones, and the attendant risk of global epidemics; the possible poisoning of all vertebrates by sharply increased levels of Vitamin D in their skin as a result of increased ultraviolet light; and the outright slaughter on all targeted continents of most human beings and other living things by the initial nuclear radiation, the fireballs, the thermal pulses, the blast waves, the mass fires, and the fallout from the explosions; and, considering that these consequences will all interact with one another in unguessable ways and, furthermore, are in all likelihood an incomplete list, which will be added to as our knowledge of the earth increases, *one must conclude that a full-scale nuclear holocaust could lead to the extinction of mankind.* [Italics added.]

Schell carefully hedged his prophecy of extinction with "could's" and "possible's." "To say that human extinction is a certainty would ... be a misrepresentation," he wrote. But, on the ground that any chance of such an irretrievable outcome must be taken as seriously as its certainty, the prospective extinction of the human race was the subject of, and the reason for, the rest of Schell's book. It concluded with an appeal to "save the world from extinction by eliminating nuclear weapons from the earth" (and to

300

accomplish *that* by first ridding the world of nation-states). *The Fate of the Earth* was a best-seller.

Schell has been joined in recent public discussion by others who present nuclear war as the end of the world. "Clearly, we are not so far from (and rapidly approaching) the situation depicted some 25 years ago by Nevil Shute," M.I.T. physicist Bernard Feld, editor of the *Bulletin of the Atomic Scientists*, wrote in 1981. In honor of *On the Beach* (which must be considered *The Fate of the Earth*'s precursor), Feld coined a new term of measurement—the "beach." One beach, he stipulates, is equal to one million megatons of fission, the amount required to fulfill Shute's prophecy and "guarantee our permanent extinction." (Feld's statement that we are "rapidly approaching" *On the Beach* is based on the fact that world nuclear stockpiles now contain somewhat more than 1 percent of a "beach.")

Meanwhile, antinuclear groups like Physicians for Social Responsibility and International Physicians for the Prevention of Nuclear War have been issuing statements and organizing public meetings to tell anyone who will listen how awful a nuclear war would be. "Recovery from nuclear war would be impossible," says PSR literature. "The economic, ecologic, and social fabric on which human life depends would be destroyed in the U.S., the USSR, and much of the rest of the world." Former PSR president Dr. Helen Caldicott, in her book *Nuclear Madness*, describes the aftermath of a nuclear war in science fiction terms: "Rendered intensely radioactive, the planet Earth would eventually become inhabited by bands of roving humanoids—mutants barely recognizable as members of our species."

Is this drumbeat of nuclear horror really necessary? A press release from International Physicians for the Prevention of Nuclear War says the group was founded to combat "the myth that people can survive a nuclear war." But don't people already believe that a nuclear war would be horrible beyond measure and possibly the end of the world? Popular literature, songs and movies, and statements by presidents and prime ministers have been telling them so for years. Polls conducted by predecessors of the Federal Emergency Management Agency consistently found that most Americans did not expect to survive a nuclear war. In a 1982 *Washington*

Post/ABC News poll, 79 percent of those surveyed said the United States and Soviet Union have more than enough nuclear weapons "to destroy each other no matter who attacks first." America's Catholic bishops declared in 1983, "We are the first generation since Genesis with the power to virtually destroy God's creation." Even Admiral Hyman Rickover, the man largely responsible for America's nuclear navy, including its fleet of missile-launching submarines, remarked (upon his retirement in 1982), "I think we will probably destroy ourselves. So what difference will it make? Some new species will come up that might be wiser."

Individuals and organizations that hold that a nuclear war would *not* be the end of the world complain that it is *they* and not the doomsayers who are bucking popular opinion. Witness the frustrated questions raised by a pro-civil-defense congressman during a 1976 congressional hearing: "Don't you think the majority of people believe you can't survive [a nuclear war]? Someone is teaching us this. Who is teaching that?" Dr. Conrad Chester, a federal civil-defense researcher, blamed the movie version of *On the Beach* for producing "in many, perhaps most, American minds the image of nuclear war in which every human in the world was doomed by worldwide fallout." And Chester blamed government officials as well: "The use of rhetoric at high government levels describing nuclear war as 'the end of mankind,' or 'the end of civilization' must be discontinued. In addition to being untrue, this misinformation of the American people undermines morale, and may discourage scores of millions from taking measures which can save their lives in a future crisis." (With risk-area evacuation and the construction of expedient fallout shelters, Chester testified, "it is theoretically possible to have a large nuclear war with no near-term civilian fatalities." In *practice*, he said, there would be deaths, because some people would be "too uninformed, lazy or stupid to evacuate and construct shelter," and some Soviet warheads would stray into evacuation areas.)

Chester and others have done their best to rebut this alleged misinformation. General Daniel Graham, retired director of the Defense Intelligence Agency and now head of an organization called the United States Defense Committee, asks people at his lectures: "Do you realize that you've brought a means of defense into this room with you? Your feet. Do you realize that if you had one hour's warning that a nuclear bomb was going to drop on this building and you used fifty-nine of those minutes to walk in a straight line and then popped behind a lilac bush, you would survive that blast?" (According to Graham, he recently delivered this lecture before an anti-nuclear audience and, "They ripped me apart. They stood on chairs and threw things.")*

Colin Gray, co-author of the 1980 article, "Victory Is Possible," and a consultant to the Departments of State and Defense, has written that, "with nationwide civil defense, plus some ballistic missile and air defense," the United States could lose no more than twenty million dead in a nuclear war. This "should not even come close to national destruction in its effect. . . . In fact, the United States suffered close to a nuclear war scale of casualties in the Civil War."

WOULD SURVIVORS OF NUCLEAR ATTACK ENVY THE DEAD? . . . EXPERTS SAY "NO" is the headline on a camera-ready newspaper column distributed to local civil-defense officials by the Federal Emergency Management Agency in 1981. The column, which is designed to be printed in newspapers during a pre-nuclear-war crisis, acknowledges that making accurate predictions about the aftermath of a nuclear war is "an enormously difficult task." Nevertheless, it asserts, "a close look at the facts shows with fair certainty that with reasonable protective measures, the United States could survive nuclear attack and go on to recovery within a relatively few years."

These are not the views of isolated cranks. The conviction that the post-nuclear-war world will contain recognizable people capable of engaging in complicated, coordinated activities is the basis upon which the American armed forces make plans for a drawn-out nuclear war that could last for weeks or months in round after round of strike and counterstrike. It is the basis of planning not only of the Federal Emergency Management Agency but also of the Treasury

---

* According to the Nuclear Bomb Effects Computer, four miles (an hour's walk) from a half-megaton ground burst, there will be a 68-mile-per-hour wind, enough blast pressure to send broken glass and other debris flying through the air, enough heat to instantaneously ignite blue jeans on the bodies of people in the open (and more than twice the heat required to cause third-degree burns on exposed skin), and, depending on which way the wind is blowing, perhaps a cloud of deadly fallout just minutes away. If the blast was a one-megaton airburst, conditions would be much worse.

Department, with its position papers on the post-nuclear-war tax system, and the Postal Service, with its plans to distribute emergency change of address cards and forward the mail after a nuclear war. "Hell, there'll be weeks of chaos," says Postal Service security manager David Madden. "We're talking about down the road."

It is this vision of a seminormal postattack world implicit in the nuclear war planning of the Pentagon and the rest of the American government that provokes the doomsaying campaign of the nuclear Jeremiahs. The people may believe that nuclear war will be the end of the world, but the government seems not to. So the anti-nuclear-war doctors recite over and over again the horrifying effects of a one-megaton bomb dropped on a major city, attempting to have some preattack effect on Washington.

Most arguments about the effects of nuclear war thus tend to be political arguments in the guise of scientific arguments. One generally finds that someone with a strong opinion about the likelihood of postattack ozone depletion will have an equally strong opinion about SALT II and the MX missile. Those preaching the dangers of ozone depletion are attempting to win converts not only to their theories of exo-atmospheric chemistry but also to their views about the best way to manage the arms race and arms control negotiations. Those who minimize the effects of nuclear war tend to have different views.

This is not to say that the beliefs of either side are insincere. Daniel Graham almost certainly believes that a lilac bush can save him and Helen Caldicott that mutant humanoids will roam the earth. This extreme disparity of views about the effects of nuclear war—views that are all derived from the same limited scientific evidence (opposing spokesmen often quote different paragraphs from the same documents)—has led to speculation about fundamental differences in the psyches of the two camps. "An underlying basis for . . . negative hypotheses [about the effects of nuclear war] may be psychological," said a report done for FEMA in 1979. "If everyone 'knew' that nuclear war would mean the end of the human species, somehow the world would appear more secure since no sane person would initiate a series of events that would lead to everyone's death, including his own." Another view was offered by Richard Pipes, an advisor to Reagan's National Security Council, in 1982: "As a rule, liberals tend to be more emotional than analytic; they seem to derive a great deal of satisfaction out of indignation and exhortation whether these activities have any bearing on reality or not. They love to exclaim, 'Stop this madness!' and to predict that mankind is doomed."

Looking at the question from the other side, Harvard psychiatrist John Mack, author of a Pulitzer Prize–winning psychobiography of Lawrence of Arabia, labeled the two camps the "thinkables" and the "unthinkables" in a 1981 essay. The thinkables, he wrote, are those who believe in planning for nuclear war and its aftermath, and they do so out of a sort of psychological inadequacy. "The thinkables appear unable to experience, or have found a way not to experience, the terror of the nuclear reality. . . . [T]he mentality of winning [a nuclear war] . . . can offset through denial and distortion the actuality of annihilation." The unthinkables are Mack's heroes. They believe nuclear war will be so awful and overwhelming that it is pointless to plan for it, and they have come to this position because they have been willing and able "to experience directly, or *hold* emotionally, the reality of the nuclear danger. . . . There are few willing so far to bear such fear, to experience the despair that accompanies the reality of confronting the arms race as it is . . . Group support is essential."

A few months later, Colin Gray replied that "we so-called 'nuclear use theorists,' or NUTs, tend not to be psychologically abnormal, moral pygmies, indifferent to suffering, etc."

This minor debate continues alongside the main event.

Of course, there are studies. There are studies, and then there are studies. FEMA alone has a roomful of studies about the long-term effects of nuclear war, including the study that reviewed 369 other studies and concluded, "In years of research, no insuperable barrier to recovery has been found."

Much of the early research by FEMA and its predecessors was compiled at a 1967 symposium at Fort Monroe, Virginia, where one scientist, a member of the staff of the Atomic Energy Commission, acknowledged that "the ecological aftermath of a nuclear attack is highly speculative" but expressed cautious optimism nonetheless.

(Rats and sea urchins, he noted, were reported doing well on Pacific islands where the United States had tested hydrogen bombs.) A scientist from the Public Health Service warned that nuclear-war survivors would face a major problem from rabies in pet dogs and wild animals, including skunks. "People don't realize how vicious a skunk can be," he said, "but a rabid skunk can easily bite six children in five minutes. The only solution during a recovery stage would be . . . to educate the public to be willing to sacrifice Fido, the household pet and the source of danger." Social scientists at the symposium agreed that it was difficult to predict the state of postattack American society, but one warned that nuclear war would create a large number of orphans and that "within the American value system . . . the existence of even a small number of socially dislocated orphans would constitute a severe emotional burden on the population at large. . . . A policy of desperation in the short run might be simply to let the orphans drift, and eventually to provide official subsidies for whomever they ultimately found to meet their needs for families."

The symposium thus addressed the two big questions of long-term postattack research: Will human beings, plants, and animals survive? Will human society survive? As far as recent FEMA-sponsored research is concerned, the first question has been answered yes. "Enough research and analysis has been done to provide confidence [that] the long term ecological consequences of nuclear attack would not be so severe as to prohibit or seriously delay recovery," reported *Recovery From Nuclear Attack and Research and Action Programs To Enhance Recovery Prospects*, the 1979 study co-authored by a former director of postattack research. Much attention has therefore been diverted to speculation about postattack social behavior. "Widespread panic probably would not occur . . . ," asserted the 1979 study. "By and large, people could be counted on to participate constructively if there is a recovery plan that seems to make sense. (This behavior pattern assumes that individuals could obtain the basic requisites for existence—food, water, shelter, etc.—for themselves and their families.)" A 1980 study confidently noted that previous catastrophes (it mentions the siege of Leningrad) "have been known to evoke incredible heroism, altruism and will to survive." It did acknowledge, however, that while "the physical requirements [for postattack recovery] may be understood . . . the soft behavioral variables have not yet been successfully modeled."

The difficulty of pinning down those "soft behavioral variables" was pointed out in a 1978 review study sponsored by the Defense Nuclear Agency, which is, like FEMA, a major consumer of postattack research. The DNA study reviewed ninety-four previous studies of the postattack economy, ranging from *Vulnerability of Natural Gas Systems*, conducted by the Interior Department in 1974, to *The Runout Production Evaluation Model: Structure and Methodology*, a 1973 "interindustry model of the U.S. economy in the first ninety days after a nuclear attack." The "overwhelming consensus" of those studies, the DNA report found, "is that sufficient economic capabilities will survive a full-scale nuclear attack so that viability of the nation can be achieved, and that if these capabilities are effectively managed, recovery will follow within five to ten years." The DNA report complained, however, that the studies "contain a bewildering array of conflicting results," that they are based upon "a myriad of implicit assumptions," and that many of them "have employed far more optimistic assumptions concerning the expected behavior of people than are warranted." Nevertheless, the report was itself optimistic about postattack economic recovery, provided the survivors could win the immediate postattack "race" to reestablish production of the necessities of life before they consumed existing stocks. If the race is lost, the report said, and inventories run out before new production can begin, there will be an "inevitable rise in [workplace] absenteeism as individuals attempt to meet their own and their family's needs by foraging, plundering, or selling their household goods. . . . It will become progressively more difficult to maintain order. Immediate threats of starvation, disease, and exposure will soon reappear. . . . The result will be a catastrophe, perhaps of the same order of magnitude as the war itself." This entire issue, the report recommended, "should be resolved in future studies."

At least as far as food is concerned, there should be no need for foraging or plundering, according to studies already conducted at the Oak Ridge National Laboratory, a center of postattack research for FEMA and its predecessors. While nuclear war survivors will quickly run out of food in many parts of the country, a 1976 Oak Ridge study found, large stocks of grain will survive in rural areas.

"[A] vigorous shipping program would have to be initiated within two or three weeks after the attack to avoid large-scale starvation in some areas," the study said, but it found that this would pose no problem:

> About 80 per cent of the U.S. crude refining capacity and nearly all oil pipelines would be either destroyed or inoperative. . . . However, a few billion gallons of diesel fuel and gasoline would survive in tank storage throughout the country, more than enough for trains and trucks to accomplish the grain shipments required for survival. Results of a computer program to minimize the ton-miles of shipments of grain . . . indicate that less than 2 per cent of the 1970 rail shipping capacity, or less than 6 per cent of the 1970 truck shipping capacity would be adequate to carry out the necessary grain shipments.

Who will climb into those trucks and trains and start driving grain across the country in the immediate aftermath of a nuclear attack? No computer program can answer that question, and the study's authors, who included Conrad Chester, apparently didn't believe it even needed to be raised. But their report did take note of some other touchy questions concerning human behavior:

> The major supply of grain in the postattack situation will be in the hands of farmers and owners of rural elevators. Surrender of grain by these people for federal promissory notes will require their confidence and trust in the federal government. It is unlikely that sufficient federal law enforcement or military personnel will be available to confiscate food in face of widespread opposition by local authorities.
>
>   Federal authority will depend on: (1) the existence of a functional national leadership with the appearance of self-confidence, and (2) the existence of a credible recovery program. . . . The President, or other emergent leaders, can make an enormous, almost indispensable, contribution to survival and recovery as well as national unity by frequent morale-building speeches broadcast on AM radio. The national resolve for recovery and unity could be increased by the existence of external threats, possibly from other than the Soviet Union. A strong feeling for revenge may arise, which may unite the nation toward a common goal even more intensely than the

spirit which pervaded the nation during World War II ("Remember Pearl Harbor").

Other studies prepared by or for federal agencies less institutionally dependent than FEMA on the conviction that nuclear war is survivable have been more pessimistic about both physical and societal survival. "Destruction of the transportation nodes would delay redistribution of supplies by two months or more . . . ," concluded a 1979 report by the Arms Control and Disarmament Agency. "Undoubtedly many survivors would have to leave shelters prematurely to search for food and water, and would be exposed to radiation." Another ACDA paper observed that many studies of individual nuclear-war effects underestimate the consequences of *combined* effects: "The destruction of buildings and housing, combined with radioactive contamination and severe ultraviolet radiation would make reconstruction activity very difficult and dangerous. . . . [W]hile some civil defense activities such as evacuation could increase the number of people who would survive the immediate effects of an attack, the long-term benefits have not been established." A 1979 study prepared for the Joint Congressional Committee on Defense Production found that most other studies were so narrowly focused that they "significantly understate" both the human casualties and the economic damage that would be caused by nuclear attack. Presidential radio broadcasts and the desire for revenge notwithstanding, it said, the aftermath of a nuclear war would see widespread antisocial behavior, heightened ethnic, racial, and regional antagonisms, and conflicts between refugees and local residents "over the possession and use of surviving resources."

Among the most thorough recent studies of the effects of nuclear war that have been prepared by agencies with no stake in the findings are a 1979 report by the Congressional Office of Technology Assessment and a 1975 study conducted under the auspices of the National Research Council. The OTA report, *The Effects of Nuclear War*, compiled previous estimates that between 20 and 165 million Americans would die within thirty days of a full-scale Soviet attack. (The highest estimate assumed that no civil-defense measures would be taken and that all incoming weapons were fallout-producing ground bursts; the lowest estimate was prepared by civil-defense officials and assumed excellent fallout protection.) These deaths would be accompanied, the report said, by "similar incomprehensible levels of injuries, and the physical destruction of a high percentage of U.S. economic and industrial capacity." Survivors, it said, might or might not win the "race" to reestablish industrial and agricultural production before existing stocks were exhausted. If they lose, it said, there would be many more deaths and the possible transformation of the United States into "the economic equivalent of the Middle Ages."

As for the physical survival of at least some Americans, the OTA report was optimistic: "Physical survival of some people is quite probable. . . . [R]ural people and those urban people who would survive are generally hardier than the American average." Between 1 million and 5.5 million of those who survive would die later of radiation-induced cancers, the report estimated, and there would be between 150,000 and 6 million abortions resulting from chromosomal damage and between 400,000 and 9 million other genetic effects. But, the report said, "it appears that cancer deaths and genetic effects . . . would be small relative to the number of immediate deaths."* Outside the United States, it estimated, drifting fallout would produce between 900,000 and 9 million cancer deaths, between 500,000 and 5 million abortions and between 1.5 and 15 million other genetic effects. "This would," it notes, "represent only a modest increase in the peacetime cancer death rate."

And so, it appeared, the world would survive. But the report warned that other potential but incalculable effects could invalidate all of its casualty and recovery estimates. "These include . . . the possibility of political disintegration (anarchy or regionalization), the possibility of major epidemics, and the possibility of irreversible ecological changes." And there might be additional synergistic effects, it said, such as that which could arise if fallout kills large numbers of birds at a time when insecticide factories have been

---

* Working with an older—and lower—estimate of postattack cancer deaths, the 1979 FEMA study, *Recovery From Nuclear Attack* . . . , characteristically put a good face on the matter. The risk of dying from radiation-induced cancer, it said, "corresponds to the additional risk faced today by the average individual who travels 80,000 miles by commercial air, or travels 12,000 miles by car, or spends 5 hours rock climbing, or lives about 3 days after his 60th birthday." Or smokes one pack of cigarettes a day for two years and then quits.

destroyed. The report concluded: "The effects of a nuclear war that cannot be calculated are at least as important as those for which calculations are attempted."

In sketching the potentially disastrous ecological consequences of a nuclear war, the OTA report relied on the 1975 report written by a committee organized by the National Research Council and published by the National Academy of Sciences. The report, *Long-Term Worldwide Effects of Multiple Nuclear-Weapons Detonations*, dealt specifically with the effects of a nuclear war that would show up far from the sites of the explosions and long after the war was over.

The most ominous of the report's findings was the ozone depletion later cited by Jonathan Schell. The nuclear explosions of a large war, the committee said, would create massive amounts of nitrogen oxides in the atmosphere, which in turn would reduce the layer of ozone that shields the earth from the sun's ultraviolet rays. Assuming the explosions were confined to the Northern Hemisphere, the report said that ozone reductions in that hemisphere "in the range of 30–70 percent are possible," along with reductions in the Southern Hemisphere of 20 to 40 percent. This could be fatal to some animal species and "could have serious implications for the ecosystem of which they are a part." Moreover, it would scald some crops (peas and onions but not soybeans or corn) and might cause "irreversible injury to sensitive aquatic species." In humans, there would be a significant increase in skin cancer and "snow blindness in northern regions." (And, as Schell would later relate, snow blindness would affect animals, too: "This is disabling and painful; there are no immune groups; there is no adaptation.") There would also be sunburn: "For a 70 percent decrease in ozone, which is at the upper range of what might be expected, a severe sunburn involving blistering of the skin could occur in 10 minutes."

(The OTA report, published four years after the National Research Council study, was less concerned about the ozone problem. New research indicated, the OTA said, that "ozone depletion is not believed to be likely" unless nuclear weapons are detonated at very high altitudes or a large number of very big nuclear weapons are detonated at lower altitudes. The development of multiple-warhead missiles, it pointed out, had led to a general reduction in the megatonnage of individual warheads, seemingly pointing the way toward some margin of safety on the ozone question. The OTA added, however, that "this is an area in which research continues, and further changes [in predictions about ozone depletion] should not be surprising.")

Other potential disasters foreseen by the committee included the possibility that radiation could cause mutations in disease-producing organisms, leading to virulent strains that might spread to produce worldwide disease epidemics among crops and farm animals, epidemics that would be especially disastrous because they would occur at a time when the United States had suddenly stopped exporting grain to hungry nations and important centers of agricultural research and technology in the Northern Hemisphere had been destroyed.

Despite all this, the report did not write off the earth or its inhabitants. In fact, it concluded that almost every nuclear war effect it investigated would be short-lived. Sixty percent of the depleted ozone would be restored in two to four years, it said. "Because of the resiliency of natural ecosystems, recovery [from all effects] during the subsequent 25 years could be expected to be fairly complete." Global radiation would produce only a 2 percent increase in the normal cancer death rate and a .2 to 2 percent increase in genetic disease; "no serious long-term damage to farm crops or animals would be expected." In a cover letter accompanying the report, National Academy of Sciences President Philip Handler summed up: "If I may restate [the] principal question as, 'Would the biosphere and the species, *Homo sapiens*, survive?,' the response by our committee is, 'yes.' "

Both the report and Handler's letter were immediately denounced by the Federation of American Scientists for drawing overly optimistic conclusions. "Modern science can not assess with much certainty the biological or ecological effects of 10,000 megatons," the FAS said. "A single scientist, tomorrow or next year, may suggest a mechanism—as yet unconsidered—by which the Academy would be flatly wrong."

Handler's letter *had* acknowledged that the report had not addressed "the utter horror which must befall the targeted areas," that the question of the recovery of targeted areas had likewise been beyond its scope, that the report's findings about the rest of the planet had "limited validity," that combinations of individual effects had not been considered, that the report had not addressed the war's "social, political, or economic consequences to the rest of the highly interdependent world civilization," and that, "although the principal findings of this report are encouraging in the sense that they indicate that *Homo sapiens*—but not necessarily his civilization— would survive a major nuclear exchange, this report further underscores the urgency of ... reducing the world's nuclear arsenal." Handler had emphasized that the world and the human species would survive, he explained after the FAS attack, only because he believed that the idea that a nuclear war would lead to human extinction had paralyzed public concern about the dangers of nuclear war.

None of this overcame the objections of the FAS, which has been lobbying against the nuclear arms race since 1945, to the letter's conclusion. The organization protested that "the uncertainties and dangers [cited in the report] could as easily have been highlighted as this possibility that the species would survive."

A new contribution to the end-of-the-world debate was made in late 1983 in a paper written by astrophysicist Carl Sagan and four other scientists (whose names were arranged on the paper to form the acronym TTAPS). They reported the "tentative conclusion" that clouds of dust thrown up by nuclear explosions and airborne soot from burning cities and forests could block sunlight from reaching the earth and thereby "have a major impact on climate—manifested by significant surface darkening over many weeks, subfreezing land temperatures persisting for up to several months, large perturbations in global circulation patterns, and dramatic changes in local weather and precipitation rates—a harsh 'nuclear winter' in any season." The 1975 National Research Council report had said major climatic changes were possible, but it—and other previous studies—had foreseen nothing as dramatic as the TTAPS conclusion. "The results of our calculations astonished us ... ," Sagan reported in an article in *Parade*. "There are severe and previously unanticipated global consequences of nuclear war."

"Relatively large climatic effects" (including two months of subfreezing temperatures) could result from a nuclear exchange of no more than one hundred megatons, the TTAPS paper reported, if the weapons were aimed at cities and produced large fires. The "nuclear winter" produced by a massive war, a companion paper by a committee of biologists said, could severely curtail photosynthesis, freeze water sources relied upon by animals, kill many plants and animals, lead to the extinction of many plant and animal species, and cause many human deaths from exposure, thirst, and starvation.

The biologists added, however, "It is likely that most ecosystem changes would be short term." And the TTAPS paper's prediction of "nuclear winter" was carefully qualified. "Our estimates of the physical and chemical impacts of nuclear war are necessarily uncertain because we have used one-dimensional models, because the data base is incomplete, and because the problem is not amenable to experimental investigation," the authors acknowledged.

Nevertheless, the biologists' report concluded that "the possibility of the extinction of *Homo sapiens* cannot be excluded." In *Parade*, Carl Sagan wrote that human extinction "seems to be a real possibility." These conclusions were embraced by the anti-nuclear camp. The *Journal of Civil Defense* protested that the TTAPS paper was based on "a number of highly questionable assumptions" (including the assumption that American cities would burn like Hiroshima and Nagasaki, "where most of the houses were constructed of bamboo and rice paper"). And the magazine complained once again about "the whole project to prove that any nuclear war would be the end of mankind."

The debate about exactly how horrible a nuclear war would be has cropped up once or twice a decade since the bombing of Hiroshima. Prophecies of doom have always been countered by promises of survival. And the debate has always worried those who want to feel free to threaten the use of America's nuclear weapons (for the sake of deterrence, they always explain). "A situation dangerous to our security could result from impressing on our own democratic peoples the horrors of future wars of mass destruction while the populations of the 'police' states remain unaware of the terrible implications," warned a memo from the Joint Chiefs of Staff in 1946, when the nuclear-effects debate was in its first round. "The decision to resist aggression by nuclear war requires a diplomacy which seeks to break down the atmosphere of special horror which now surrounds the use of nuclear weapons, an atmosphere which has been created in part by skillful Soviet 'ban-the-bomb' propaganda," wrote Henry Kissinger eleven years later.

In the early 1980s, the debate arose more sharply than ever for a variety of reasons, some obvious, some conjectural. Among the obvious ones were the words and actions of the administration of Ronald Reagan.

In its first two years, the Reagan administration:

- put forward a $180 billion program for nuclear weapons, including the MX missile and the revived B-1 bomber; this was a substantial increase over other recent administrations both in absolute spending and in spending on nuclear weapons as a percentage of the total military budget.
- ordered the production of seventeen thousand new nuclear warheads to supplement and replace the current stockpile; this was the largest expansion in warhead production in twenty years.
- established an Emergency Mobilization Preparedness Board to develop plans "for the maximum civilian contribution to the military operations which may be required to cope with the emergencies for which the Department of Defense is now preparing."
- made significant purchases, for the first time in twenty years, for the National Defense Stockpile of critical and strategic materials, the stockpile to be drawn upon if a war interrupts normal supply channels.
- abandoned negotiations with the Soviet Union for a comprehensive nuclear test ban, while increasing the number of underground nuclear weapons tests in Nevada. Observing one such test, Secretary of Energy James Edwards said he found it "exciting."

The president himself, meanwhile, casually remarked, "I could see where you could have the exchange of tactical [nuclear] weapons against troops in the field without it bringing either one of the major powers to pushing the button." Vice President George Bush, while a candidate for president in 1980, said he believed "you can have a winner" in a nuclear war. Secretary of Defense Caspar Weinberger said the United States was planning on "prevailing" in a nuclear war.

About civil defense, the president told a joke: "I feel a little bit like the old farm gentleman who was in a bar one day and two gentlemen with much more knowledge and sophistication than he had were discussing nuclear energy. And finally, aware of his presence and thinking they'd have a little joke, one of them said to the old farmer, 'Where would you like to be in the event of a nuclear explosion?' And the old boy said, 'Someplace where I could say, "What was that?" ' "

This is, of course, precisely the philosophy of the crisis relocation program developed by the Federal Emergency Management Agency. Reagan backed FEMA's plans with a National Security Decision Directive calling for civilian population relocation "during a period of international crisis" and directing that consideration be given to funding industrial protection and the construction of blast shelters "for key industrial workers in defense and population relocation support industries." Reagan also proposed substantial annual increases in the civil-defense budget (increases that, in accordance with all historical precedent, were substantially reduced by Congress).

Pleased with this White House support, General Louis Giuffrida, Reagan's appointee to head FEMA, told the American Civil Defense Association in 1981, "[T]his administration has categorically rejected ... the short-war, mutual-assured-destruction, it'll - all-be - over - in - twenty - minutes - so - why - the - hell - mess - around - spending - dollars - on - it [philosophy]. We're trying to inject long-war mentality." A few months later, Giuffrida told an interviewer on network television that "nuke war," as he calls it, "would be a mess. To suggest it wouldn't be a mess is ridiculous. It would be a terrible mess. But it wouldn't be unmanageable, to the extent that we had a plan."

To all of this, there arose a reaction.* A mass campaign for a

* "I would like to commend the administration for creating an arms control constituency," Senator Paul Tsongas said in 1982. "If you will remember, during the SALT process, you could not get a letter from a constituent on arms control or SALT. It was a non-issue. This administration comes in and talks about a winnable nuclear war, limited nuclear war, talked about a demonstration nuclear shot across the bow, and the average American has looked and listened and been horrified."

nuclear weapons freeze developed and gained strength. Senator Mark Hatfield proposed that Congress declare "that the United States should not base its policies or its weapons programs on the belief that the United States can limit, survive, or win a nuclear war"; the Federation of American Scientists backed the proposal with a petition drive. The news media were full of reports about nuclear weapons and warfare and accounts of the legal trials of people who got cancer after living or working near nuclear tests in the 1950s.* In June 1982, between 500,000 and one million people marched against nuclear weapons in New York City, including groups identifying themselves as "Australians for Nuclear Disarmament," "Tibetans for Peace," "P.S. 3 for Peace," "Animals for Peace," "Jugglers for a Friendly World," "Cyclistes du Québec pour le Désarmement," "Grandparents Opposed to Nuclear Expansion," "Dykes of Hoboken," and "1 Middle-Aged Middle-Class Member of the Silent Majority [Who] Has Had Enough." Star-studded antinuclear fundraising events were staged by groups like Performing Artists for Nuclear Disarmament and Dancers for Disarmament. Among professional organizations, Physicians for Social Responsibility was joined by Educators for Social Responsibility, Psychologists for Social Responsibility, Architects for Social Responsibility, the Lawyers Alliance for Nuclear Arms Control, Generals for Peace (a dozen retired NATO generals), Poets in Support of the June 12th Rally (who said they were concerned because "extinct species don't read books"), and the Life Insurance Industry Committee for a Nuclear Weapons Freeze, which dramatized its position by distributing copies of "The Last Life Insurance Policy."

In November 1982, voters in eight states and twenty-eight cities and counties approved nuclear freeze referenda, despite charges by President Reagan that the freeze movement "is inspired . . . by some who want the weakening of America and so are manipulating honest people and sincere people" and that "in the organization of some of the big demonstrations . . . there is no question about foreign agents that were sent to help instigate and help create and keep such a movement going." (The FBI looked into the matter and reported,

---

* One episode of a syndicated television series called *The Great Mysteries of Hollywood* reported that John Wayne, who died of cancer, had made a movie on location near a test fallout site in 1954. The episode was titled, "Did America Kill John Wayne?"

"[W]e do not believe the Soviets have achieved a dominant role in the U.S. peace and nuclear freeze movements, or that they directly control or manipulate the movement.") In 1983, the House of Representatives approved a freeze resolution. (No freeze ensued.)

Through all of this, the Reagan administration had its defenders; Phyllis Schlafly, having dispatched the Equal Rights Amendment, took up arms against the nuclear freeze movement, declaring, "The atomic bomb is a marvelous gift that was given to our country by a wise God." And the administration continued to get almost everything it wanted from Congress. (A few weeks after passing the freeze resolution, the House joined the Senate in approving construction of the MX missile.) But it felt compelled to retreat, if not in its policies, at least in its rhetoric. Administration officials began to protest that they did not really believe it was possible to win a nuclear war. (Some of the protests were a little weak: "I know of no one in the administration . . . who thinks that even after five years we would not bear terrible scars from that catastrophe of unimaginable proportions," Assistant Secretary of Defense Richard Perle told a Senate committee.) The annual Pentagon document that in its 1982 edition had spoken of "prevailing" in a "protracted" nuclear war appeared in 1983 with those words conspicuously absent.

One of the most battered outposts of the administration in the nuclear debate was the Federal Emergency Management Agency. At the White House and Pentagon, the assumption that the nation could survive a nuclear war was generally implicit in other plans and statements; at FEMA, nuclear war survivability is the explicit stock in trade. FEMA's assertions that crisis evacuation and fallout shelters could save 80 percent of the population were greeted with wide incredulity on their own account, and civil defense was also a convenient (and appropriate) target of attack for those who didn't really care if a tiny fraction of the federal budget was spent to identify evacuation routes but who were strongly opposed to other aspects of the Reagan nuclear program (which they feared might someday put those evacuation plans to the test). FEMA's plans were critiqued and lampooned, and dozens of cities and counties across the nation refused to participate in crisis relocation planning.

"There's a kind of almost blind revulsion against anything dealing with nuclear war," complained James Holton, FEMA's director of public affairs, in an interview at the height of the protest movement. "People who in the past would have been middle-of-the-road or would have favored increasing defenses are saying, 'Nuclear war is horrible. We must do everything to prevent nuclear war.' They won't take the next step and say, 'But if there is one [we ought to have plans].' *That's* our problem. . . . People are saying we shouldn't even think about it.

"As a result, although it's our responsibility to plan for civil defense for nuclear war, we have to go about it in a low-key way, at least for now. . . . I don't think we'll be able to swing public opinion away from fatalistic views until there is something on the horizon that is unmistakable. . . . If there's a surge situation, with an international crisis galvanizing everybody into action, I don't think we'd have much difficulty being heard. People would want to learn as much [about civil defense] as they could."

In the meantime, FEMA has sponsored a series of Gallup polls, looking for evidence that the Silent Majority supports civil defense.* FEMA officials have studied the statements of groups like Physicians for Social Responsibility and have practiced grilling each other in mock cross-examinations before going out for public appearances. And FEMA officials have occasionally gone on the offensive. Jonathan Schell, said FEMA Director Giuffrida in an interview with the *Journal of Civil Defense*, "wasn't completely accurate in the way he interpreted data and he was not in my judgment totally objective in the way he presented these data that he had misunderstood in the first place."

In general, however, FEMA has ducked direct debates with its critics, preferring to stay out the papers altogether than generate more public criticism and ridicule. But keeping a low profile, Holton said, created another problem. "What do we do for the poor guys

---

* Three polls conducted in 1982 in fact found between one-half and two-thirds of those surveyed supporting increased civil-defense spending and crisis relocation planning. Majorities also said they were likely to evacuate their homes in a crisis, even without being told to do so by civil-defense officials. At about the same time, in a survey conducted by the University of Massachusetts, 49 percent of those polled said they would rather fight an "all-out nuclear war" than "live under Communist rule." Thirty-three percent said they would prefer the war to Communism even if "it meant the death of everyone in the United States, our enemy's country and the population of some other countries" as well.

[local civil-defense officials and crisis relocation planners] who are out there being laughed at by their fellow citizens? I don't know. They're just going to have to be guys with thick skins and absolute faith in what they're doing."

The faith is there. And so are other elements. "At least we have a plan," says one postattack planner. "People can say the goddam plan isn't going to work, but they can't criticize us for not having one." Says a local crisis relocation planner: "I was laid off from my old job before I got this one. A friend asked me, 'Isn't working on civil defense depressing?' I said, 'No. Being laid off. *That's* depressing.' "

As part of its new low profile, FEMA in 1983 subsumed its civil defense planning (and budget requests) into a new concept called the Integrated Emergency Management System, which also includes planning for natural disasters. (The IEMS was adopted, FEMA announced officially, because of its "cost-effectiveness and practicality.") FEMA has continued to maintain, however, that civil defense preparations can save 80 percent of the population in a nuclear war (and that, even without crisis relocation planning, 40 percent would survive).* Such preparations, FEMA says, are prudent and humane. (Officials elsewhere in the government continue to stress the strategic aspects of the program. Effective American civil defense, Richard Perle said in 1982, "may help to dispel any possible delusions the Soviet leadership might harbor today or in the future that they can . . . intimidate the United States.")

In its public relations battles, FEMA has paid special attention to the physicians' anti-nuclear groups, groups that have had significant credibility with the press and public and have won considerable publicity for their contentions that the medical consequences of nuclear war would be so overwhelming as to render civil defense useless and that civil-defense planning is actually dangerous because it fosters the false illusion that nuclear war can be survived. The gov-

---

* The 1978 study from which FEMA derived these figures, *Candidate U.S. Civil Defense Programs*, counted as fatalities only people "killed directly by the attack or who [become] incapacitated or seriously ill as a direct result of the attack and [die] without recovering." The study did not count those who would die from fires started by exploding weapons, nor did it count those who would die of postattack epidemics and shortages. It assumed that crisis evacuees would have excellent fallout protection and that they would be able to stay in their shelters "as long as necessary."

ernment position on postattack medical care is, of course, more optimistic. "You wouldn't believe some of the meetings we have," says a Public Health Service planner. "People tell us health problems won't be so bad as in peacetime because radiation would kill the flies." This is not an argument FEMA has chosen to take to the public, but in 1981 two FEMA officials, William Chipman and Wayne Blanchard, did publish an article in a FEMA magazine that was specifically addressed as a reply to a series of public symposia organized by Physicians for Social Responsibility.*

One argument often made by the PSR is that very few doctors and hospitals would survive a nuclear attack, and that the millions of wounded would thus be left unattended to die painful and lingering deaths. This only proves, wrote Chipman and Blanchard, that crisis relocation planning is a necessity. They presented the results of a study which showed that, without evacuation, a nuclear war would leave seventy-nine thousand American physicians alive and uninjured and fourteen million Americans needing medical attention, for a patient-doctor ratio of 175 to 1. (There would be another eighteen million Americans suffering from radiation sickness, the study showed, but Chipman and Blanchard left them out of the patient-doctor ratio on the ground that "definitive treatment [that which makes a difference between living or dying] cannot be provided for . . . radiation sickness.") If the nuclear war were preceded by an evacuation of risk areas, the study showed, 315,000 physicians would survive uninjured and only eight million Americans would need their attention, for a much-improved ratio of 25 to 1. (This time, fourteen million seriously irradiated Americans were ignored.) "There would be great difficulties in moving many of the injured survivors to places where they could receive care," Chipman and Blanchard acknowledged. "There would be acute shortages of medical supplies and of facilities and hospital beds . . . But notwithstanding suffering and tragedy on a scale without precedent in U.S. experience, reasonable civil defense preparations could reduce this tragedy . . . It would, indeed, be a tragic irony if thousands, or perhaps millions, died needlessly because they failed to take those

---

* In a non-government publication, Blanchard wrote a less temperate article lambasting what he called the "Physicians for Social Irresponsibility."

actions which could save their lives, due to a belief that such measures would be useless."

Outside the government, free-lance civil-defense boosters have rallied around FEMA. A group called Doctors for Defense Preparedness was launched by the American Civil Defense Association to counter the anti-civil-defense doctors. Edward Teller, once more into the breach, published an article in the *Reader's Digest* exposing "dangerous myths about nuclear arms," including the myths that radioactive fallout or ozone depletion "would end life on earth." (This was support about which FEMA public relations chief Holton was not enthusiastic. "Who the hell wants the 'father of the hydrogen bomb' associated with civil defense?" he lamented.) Members of the grassroots movement known as "survivalism" have expressed their belief in nuclear-war survivability with both words and actions. They have stocked rural retreats with freeze-dried food, medical supplies, kerosene lamps—and weapons to defend their caches. (The Survival Books store in North Hollywood, California, sells a five-volume series titled *How To Kill*.) Survivalist writer Bruce Clayton, author of *Life After Doomsday* (and civil defense director of Mariposa County, California), has published long critiques of "Doomie myths" about the effects of nuclear war. The one "Doomie myth" that may be true, Clayton granted, is the one about ozone depletion. But even then, he wrote, "Remember that the high UV [ultraviolet] levels would be present only during the daylight hours. . . . Humans would wear protective clothing and would stay out of the sun during the middle of the day. Wild animals already confine their activities to the night, early morning and early evening. . . . Even animals as stupid as cows have a history of sleeping in the shade during the day and grazing at night when suffering from sunburn."

Criticism of those preaching nuclear doom has surfaced even among those who share their goals. "Beliefs in extinction through nuclear war are counterproductive for the peace movement," argued an article in the *Journal of Peace Research*; such exaggerated beliefs, it said, can justify inaction and defeatism now and inhibit the development of strategies to combat post-nuclear-war political repression. In the *Village Voice*, Alexander Cockburn and James Ridgeway questioned whether Jonathan Schell's "interminable vaporings" and Dr. Helen Caldicott's "hysterical and demobilizing preachments—liberalism's answer to the hellfire sermons of the Moral Majority" could nourish a sustained, politically cogent movement against the nuclear arms race.

As the debate has proceeded, some on the anti-nuclear side have concentrated on societal breakdown and not physical extinction as their ground for postattack gloom. "Simply to tally those who are still alive, or alive and uninjured, is to make a biological body-count that has little social meaning," writes Dr. H. Jack Geiger, who has been active in the physicians' anti-nuclear movement. Geiger suggests that the most useful survivors of a nuclear war will be medieval historians who know how life was lived in the ninth century. "The human race, unlike the dinosaurs, will survive over the next few millenniums, if only in the Southern Hemisphere . . . ," granted Dr. Herbert Abrams in an article in *The New York Times*. "Species survival, however, does not guarantee political or economic or social survival. . . . For the individual, what must be defined is acceptable survival: life with quality. Family. Friends. Home. Neighbors. Worshiping with acquaintances and family. 'Masterpiece Theatre,' '60 Minutes,' 'Nicholas Nickleby.' "

Abrams went too far in a new direction, of course; many Americans would find life perfectly acceptable without Andy Rooney. But, in concentrating on the end of the world as we have known it and not on the end of the world, Geiger, Abrams, and others have moved the argument to surer ground. Human extinction seems unlikely; chaos and misery beyond measure seem inevitable.

The anti-nuclear forces can in fact concede much to their opponents and still win the main point. What if FEMA were correct about the postattack doctor situation, for example? What if, despite the continuing protestations of the Physicians for Social Responsibility, there *would* be enough doctors surviving a nuclear war to treat the wounded? What if all doctors were given magical anti-nuclear amulets upon finishing school and so *every* doctor in the world would survive a nuclear war? Would nuclear war then be a good idea?

What if FEMA were right about *everything*? And only forty-five million Americans (FEMA's most optimistic estimate) would be vaporized or burned to death or buried under collapsed buildings or slashed by flying glass or condemned to a horrible lingering death from radiation sickness or otherwise killed or fatally injured in a nuclear attack? And only twenty or thirty million more would suffer sublethal radiation sickness or broken bones or disfiguring burns or other injuries? And everybody else would huddle for weeks in dark, makeshift shelters—overheated, short of supplies, not knowing if that little girl in the corner was vomiting and suffering from diarrhea because she was so upset that her parents were missing or because she was the first to show signs of the fatal radiation sickness that would soon afflict them all (because of an unexpected shift in the wind fifty miles away)? And those who survived their shelter stays would emerge to a more difficult world than any of them had ever faced, with epidemics and starvation and freezing to death and anarchy all real possibilities? And only a few million of those who survived those dangers would die of cancer later on? And the world did not end? And things were nearly normal in Argentina and New Zealand?

Would nuclear war be acceptable then?

But they're still getting ready for it.

It was a beautiful bright morning in the New Mexico desert in September 1981 when a small crowd gathered near the northern end of the vast White Sands Missile Range to watch the Defense Nuclear Agency set off a mock nuclear explosion. "White Sands Missile Range keeps a large complement of chaplains to get days like this," said the range commander, General Alan Nord, as he greeted the observers, who were seated in three sets of bleachers on a foothill of the Oscura Mountains. From where the bleachers were set up, the people could see Trinity Site in the distance. Trinity Site: where the world's first atomic bomb was exploded on July 16, 1945, startling Manhattan Project scientists with its power, setting the stage for Hiroshima and the modern history of the world. A few of the people in the bleachers trained their binoculars in that direction, but most turned toward the south, toward a barely visible haystack-shaped pile six miles away on the desert floor. The pile, thirty-seven feet high and thirty feet across, was made up of almost 25,000 fifty-pound sacks of ammonium nitrate. Ammonium nitrate is generally used as a fertilizer; *this* ammonium nitrate had been doused with diesel fuel oil. When ignited, the pile would explode with the blast pressure of a one-kiloton atomic bomb.

The explosion, designated "Mill Race," had been planned for more than a year. The crowd in the bleachers included military officers (foreign and domestic), FEMA engineers, and civilian contractors and technicians. They had come to New Mexico not just to watch 25,000 bags of fertilizer explode but to use that explosion to test equipment and structures they had designed to function during a nuclear war. More than one hundred experiments were laid out at carefully measured distances around the explosive pile. The U.S. Army had parked two brand-new M-1 tanks, each inhabited by five anthropomorphic dummies, at the thousand-foot mark and elsewhere had set up an armored personnel carrier, several mobile shelters, antennas, and a battery of ground-to-air missiles. The U.S. Navy had constructed a model deckhouse. FEMA had honeycombed the area with prototype blast and fallout shelters. A delegation from the United Kingdom had erected a Sea Wolf missile launcher (a missile that would later distinguish itself by shooting down several Argentinian planes in the Falklands War) and had dressed three dummies in nuclear war protective clothing and set them out in the open facing ground zero. Sweden had installed a portable shelter and peopled it with a new breed of dummy with simulated internal organs. Offstage, two F-86 drones were waiting to take off and fly through the blast wave. A B-52 bomber would fly over the site two hours after the explosion on a mock damage-assessment run. "We're all working," said General Nord, "to gain knowledge to keep the free world free."

"We call it nuclear survivability testing," explained Armando De La Paz, an engineer from the Army's Nuclear Weapons Effects Laboratory, as the crowd on the hillside milled about, drinking coffee and waiting for the blast. De La Paz was on hand to monitor the effects of the explosion on the M-1 tanks, which had been designed, he said, to meet "nuclear survivability criteria" for blast pressure, radiation, and heat. "We don't expect damage to the basic tank structures today," he said. "We're interested in the ancillary systems, like the gun sights. ... The probability that the M-1 would be involved in the tactical nuclear environment is significant, so it's important to insure that it can carry out its functions—to move at high speed and fire with great accuracy—in that environment."

Before 1963, when the limited test-ban treaty drove nuclear testing underground, military equipment—and personnel—were tested in "the nuclear environment" by running exercises near exploding nuclear bombs. The underground tests conducted since 1963 have proved perfectly adequate for developing new nuclear weapons, but testing the effects of those weapons on other objects has been difficult. Relatively small pieces of equipment, including MX missile components and communications satellites, have been suspended underground near exploding nuclear warheads to test their resistance to electromagnetic pulse and other nuclear effects. But much of the equipment designed by military and civil-defense planners in recent years for use during a nuclear war has had to be tested with simulated nuclear explosions.

Prototype MX missile silos have been tested by detonating conventional explosives designed to mimic the effects of incoming Soviet warheads. Blast and fallout shelters were tested in explosions similar to Mill Race in 1973, 1976, and 1978. The 1978 blast also tested two mock factories constructed by a Boeing Corporation team seeking to counter the popular "impression that nothing can be protected from a nuclear onslaught." The Boeing team erected two identical steel-frame-and-concrete factory buildings at the blast site, stocked them with identical industrial equipment, including lathes, drill presses, and oscilloscopes, and then blew them up. Before the blast, the machinery in one of the buildings was packed in Styrofoam, metal shavings and other protective material, wrapped in plastic, and then covered with dirt. A front-end loader piled up more dirt around the sides of that building, and then the front-end loader was buried. The second building was left entirely unprotected. After the explosion, which was equivalent to a one-fifth-kiloton atomic bomb, not much was left of the unprotected building or the equipment it had housed. The protected building was also badly damaged, but most of the equipment buried inside it (and the buried front-end loader) survived in working condition. "Within four days," the Boeing team reported, "the protected facility was sufficiently restored to permit full production."*

The Mill Race blast, officials of the Defense Nuclear Agency said, would be the best nuclear simulation yet. Like its predecessors, it would create neither the radiation nor the multimillion-degree heat of an actual nuclear explosion, but the Mill Race site had been rigged with "thermal radiation simulators." They would spew forth flaming liquid oxygen and aluminum powder to create temperatures of 3,500 degrees and lend some extra realism to the experiments.

There was, however, a problem with the drones. They were supposed to take off from a landing strip ninety miles away, fly up from the south through Mockingbird Gap, and pass over the stack of ammonium nitrate as it exploded. Instruments would measure the effects of a one-kiloton blast on low-flying aircraft. But at T minus twelve minutes (9:48 a.m.), the countdown stopped and the expectant crowd in the bleachers was told that one of the drones had faulty brakes. The blast would be postponed until 11:30.

The generals put down their binoculars, and the bleachers emptied. Four bemedaled officers of the Swedish Army; observers from Israel, France, Norway, and Britain; a couple of hundred GIs who had come up to see the show; and delegations from the Alamagordo, Socorro, and Truth and Consequences chambers of commerce that had been invited to view the blast as part of the White Sand Missile Range's good neighbor program, all moved toward the lunchwagon. Donald Bettge, a FEMA engineer, stood to one side, waiting patiently for the test to proceed. He hoped, he said, that the blast shelter experiments dug in around ground zero would con-

---

* Boeing and civil-defense officials cited this and similar tests to argue that it is both possible and economical to protect American industry during a nuclear war. "If executed along with population protection, industrial protective measures would have a significant impact on the credibility of our strategic deterrent as well as on the survival of our society in the event that deterrence should fail," Boeing said. The Boeing and civil defense officials also warned that the Soviet Union had a substantial headstart in this kind of industrial protection. (Many of the techniques used to protect equipment in the Boeing tests were copied from Soviet civil-defense manuals.) These arguments were rejected by critics of civil defense. "There is a broad gulf between demonstrating the feasibility of making certain kinds of plant equipment more or less survivable and ... protecting a significant proportion of the complex economic infrastructure that is the fundamental underpinning of a major power," said a 1977 congressional report. You cannot, it pointed out, wrap a dam or an oil refinery in plastic and bury it.

vince his superiors to publicize blast shelters' life-saving benefits. "If we can get this information into our literature and convince people this is what they should do," he said, "we've achieved a lot."

Cresson Kearny, also calmly waiting for the blast, had already done *his* best to spread the word that a nuclear war can be survived. Kearny is a retired federal civil-defense researcher and the author of *Nuclear War Survival Skills*, a volume chock-full of information on post-nuclear-war first aid, sanitation, and recipes. It also includes detailed instructions for make-it-yourself blast and fallout shelters, for a make-it-yourself shelter ventilation aid known as the Kearny Air Pump (some of the shelters illustrated in FEMA literature, Kearny says, are insufficiently ventilated "death traps"), and for the Kearny Fallout Meter, a surprisingly effective device that can be made of rubber bands, an empty soup can, and other objects commonly found around the house "even after fallout arrives." Kearny was also the designer of an "expedient key worker blast shelter" being tested at Mill Race. "It was a Russian shelter," he said. "I give credit to the Russians. But I greatly improved the blast doors."

Kearny said he was working to oppose the "myth" that nuclear war is not survivable, a myth that is propagated, he said, by American intellectuals and policymakers who tend to be in their middle years or beyond and so do not have small children to arouse their "natural animal instinct to protect the young." They also tend to be wealthy, Kearny said, "so they have the farthest to fall, even if they survive," and they tend to live in big cities, which makes them especially vulnerable to being caught in an attack. "So the people in Kansas, say, who *could* survive and who have a good healthy animal instinct to try to survive, don't have the leadership or information they need, because these three factors militate against their leaders' taking it seriously. . . .

"I saw the Chinese up against death in World War II. They really struggle. I saw refugees in the cold, on the road, a hundred miles from food. The road was slimy with excrement . . . Dogs were eating corpses. But the people struggled on. In India, I saw people just sit and die. They're Hindus. American intellectuals are like Hindus." Kearny wandered off to have lunch.

As 11:30 approached, the blast was postponed another hour. Spontaneous picnics spread out around the bleachers. Lieutenant

Colonel Robert Flory, the Mill Race project officer, assured some reporters that, although safety and security considerations would prevent their being allowed a close look at the experiments after the blast, they would be allowed a good look at the crater. "You're going to be able to walk right up to it, look over the lip, and say, 'Gee whiz!' "

Finally, at 12:17, the drones appeared, two specks flying low over the desert in the distance. They swung to the north, then circled back toward the explosive pile. Binoculars went up all around. At T minus 13 seconds, four brilliant plumes erupted from the thermal radiation simulators. The countdown proceeded to zero.

The first visible sign of the explosion was the shock wave. It burst out from the stack like a clear soap bubble expanding impossibly fast. In an instant the wave disappeared inside a puff of white smoke, followed by a brown cloud of dirt blown out of the desert floor. It gradually rose into the shape of a mushroom.

All this was silent. Not until T plus 24 seconds did the sound reach the bleachers. Then it hit like thunder, rolling into the mountains beyond and echoing back. The spectators' shirts ruffled in remnant of the blast wave.

The spectators applauded.

Ninety minutes later, when a bus loaded with reporters reached the blast site, one experimental result was obvious: the British nuclear-war protective clothing had not been a total success. Two of the dummies wearing it were wrapped in white shrouds. The third, charred black, was still smoldering.

The crater, as promised, was impressive—30 feet deep and 130 feet across. Not much was visible around it. Many of the military experiments had been covered up, and the FEMA shelters had not yet been excavated. A few months later, a FEMA report would say the shelter tests had been "eminently successful." In one of them, a concrete basement blast shelter, of the type that might be fled to by key workers left behind in a target area during crisis relocation, had been constructed at a point where it was subjected to 40 pounds per square inch of blast pressure (equivalent to being about a mile from a one-megaton explosion). The shelter was divided into several sections with different kinds of ceiling construction and reinforcement techniques. A section where the ceiling was not reinforced at all collapsed; a dummy in that section was found with its left arm ripped off and a 500-pound concrete fragment lying on its leg. In sections where the ceiling was shored up with telephone poles every four feet, dummies emerged unscathed. The blast shelter designed by Kearny also stood up well, but the report noted that it had taken sixty man-hours to construct, using power tools and not counting the excavation of the deep ditch where it was buried, and that it had required as much lumber as six small houses. It was designed to be an "expedient" shelter, meaning one that can be built in forty-eight hours with materials at hand; the report concluded that it did not appear to be expedient.

None of this was apparent immediately after the blast. The objects that *were* visible around the crater bore evidence of mixed results. The M-1 tanks looked all right. So did the Sea Wolf missile launcher. But a few antennas were bent at crazy angles, and big chunks of concrete that had anchored instruments to the desert floor lay smashed and haphazard where the explosion had blown them.

"The worst thing that can happen is when one of those concrete blocks goes flying into one of your experiments," said Tom Kennedy of the Defense Nuclear Agency as he surveyed the scene from the lip of the crater. "We try to avoid too many surprises. . . . Now *that* may be a surprise." He pointed to a trailer designed to carry launch equipment for the nuclear-armed Pershing II missile then being readied for deployment in Europe. The trailer had a nasty crease in its side. A missile relying on that trailer's nuclear survivability might have trouble getting off the ground.

Technicians looked it over. Others were dousing the smoldering British dummy with a fire extinguisher. One FEMA consultant asked another, "Are you going to the party tonight?" And a worker stood at the lip of the crater, occupied with a living survivor of the mock nuclear battlefield. It was a horned toad. The worker held it in his palm. "He was probably underground and came up to see what happened," the man said. "He was at five p.s.i. [five pounds per square inch, enough blast pressure to blow apart a brick house]. But he's okay. I had to chase him to catch him." He stroked the toad and looked into its eyes. "He's saying, 'I could eat some Cheerios right now.'"

THIRTEEN

The Day Before
World War IV

The experts agree it will be difficult to know when a nuclear war is over.

After the initial attacks and counterattacks, some number of unfired nuclear weapons will survive on airplanes, ships, and submarines scattered around the world. Communications will be disrupted. Commanders will be dead. New orders and information may be getting through, or they may not. Submarine captains and bomber pilots, far from home, wondering what has happened at home, wondering what is happening there now, pondering orders that may be outmoded, may elect to let fly their remaining missiles and bombs. Or they may not.

Stunned survivors of the war's first rounds will never know for sure that one more weapon is not coming their way. They may not even know if attacks are continuing, at any given moment, in neighboring cities or states. If, two months after the first attack, and weeks after the first feeble efforts at reconstruction have begun, listeners in Michigan suddenly stop hearing a Cleveland radio station, does that mean that the station's batteries have finally worn down or that a new round in the war has just begun with an attack on Cleveland? " 'Recovery' may not be synonymous with 'peacetime,' " warned a former director of the Federal Preparedness Agency at a 1979 seminar. "A recovery period may be just another phase of the war, giving new targets." Survivors, he said, should put their efforts into building facilities appropriate for "an extended attack period" instead of creating "new targets."

Most studies of the effects of nuclear war are based on some assumed single-volley war. This might be misleading, acknowledged *The Effects of Nuclear War*, the 1979 report of the Office of Technology Assessment, which was itself based on a single-volley war. "How much worse would the situation of the survivors be if, just as they were attempting to restore some kind of economy following a massive attack, a few additional weapons destroyed the new centers of population and of government?"

To terminate a nuclear war—to terminate it rapidly, completely, officially, and favorably—is the goal of America's nuclear war-fighting strategy.* American forces are designed, as Caspar Weinberger explained in 1982, "to impose termination of a major war—on terms favorable to the United States—even if nuclear weapons have been used—and in particular to deter escalation in the level of hostilities." Exactly how this is to be accomplished was explained in greater detail by Harold Brown in 1981:

> Plans for the controlled use of nuclear weapons, along with other appropriate military and political actions, should enable us to provide leverage for a negotiated termination of the fighting. At an early stage in the conflict, we must convince the enemy that further escalation will not result in achievement of his objectives, that it will not mean "success," but rather additional costs. To do this, we must leave the enemy with sufficient highly valued military, economic, and political resources still surviving but still clearly at risk, so that he has a strong incentive to seek an end to the conflict.†

---

* Any official consideration of ways in which a nuclear war might be terminated unfavorably is illegal in the United States. In 1958, a RAND Corporation analyst named Paul Kecskemeti, working on an Air Force contract, published a mostly historical study called *Strategic Surrender*, which pointed out that it might be counterproductive to press on for unconditional surrender against an enemy armed with nuclear weapons. Enraged senators, reacting to misleading newspaper accounts of the book, immediately passed, by a vote of 88–2, an amendment to a military appropriations bill forbidding the expenditure of any federal funds "to conduct any studies concerning the circumstances under which the United States would surrender to any aggressor."
† Brown's strategy statement was heavily indebted to President Richard Nixon's 1974 National Security Decision Memorandum 242, which called for the development of "limited [nuclear] employment options" so that even after the outbreak of nuclear war, the United States could "hold some vital enemy targets hostage to subsequent destruction by survivable nuclear forces" and control "the timing and pace of attack execu-

332

This "strong incentive" to quit the war will be provided by un-fired American nuclear weapons aimed at those "highly valued mili-tary, economic, and political resources still surviving." So there must *be* some American nuclear weapons still unfired. Every option in the Single Integrated Operational Plan (SIOP), the American blueprint for nuclear war, now provides for holding some weapons in reserve. And some American nuclear weapons—a "secure reserve force"—are not available to SIOP planners at all. They are reserved exclusively for the "post-SIOP" period.

Things didn't used to be this way. "In a 1974 study, we talked about an NCA [National Command Authority] reserve force," re-calls Daniel Payton of the Air Force Weapons Laboratory. "We were called heretics in those days. If you went to SAC headquarters and talked about putting missiles on reserve that weren't part of SIOP, they'd throw you out. They'd say, 'You don't understand war. War is SIOP.' " Now, Payton says, "The emphasis has really shifted. Now at SAC they talk about post-SIOP plans and enduring capa-bility."

The old plans were a legacy of the 1950s, when America's nu-clear strategy was to drop every single available weapon on the So-viet Union and its allies as soon as possible after the outbreak of war. The new plans have evolved from changes introduced by Sec-retary of Defense Robert McNamara in the early 1960s, when strat-egists began to envision a limited and protracted nuclear war and developed the concept of "intrawar deterrence." The idea of a nu-clear reserve force "for protection and coercion during and after major nuclear conflict" was institutionalized by President Nixon's National Security Decision Memorandum 242, and it has been reemphasized by every succeeding administration. The idea, as it is explained by Colonel Robert Gifford of SAC's 90th Strategic Mis-sile Wing, is simple. Firing all your weapons right off isn't "a very good way to fight a war nowadays," he says. "It's like two kids fighting with rocks. The kid with the last rock is likely to become the winner."

tion, in order to provide the enemy opportunities to reconsider his actions." Explained then-Secretary of Defense James Schlesinger: "To the extent that we have selective response options . . . we may be able to bring all but the largest nuclear conflicts to a *rapid* conclusion before cities are struck."

Operating on this "last rock" theory, Pentagon documents of recent years have been filled with charts illustrating "post-exchange residuals." That is, they illustrate the U.S.-Soviet balance of nuclear forces as it is expected to look *after* a nuclear exchange. No longer is it considered important only to have more or better weapons than the Soviets right now; it is considered at least as important to have more or better nuclear weapons than the Soviets midway through a nuclear war. "The state of the strategic balance after an initial exchange . . . could be an important factor in the decision by one side to initiate a nuclear exchange," wrote Harold Brown. "Thus, it is important—for the sake of deterrence—to be able to deny to the potential aggressor a fundamental and favorable shift in the strategic balance as a result of a nuclear exchange."

To this end, all American nuclear weapons have been "hardened" against nuclear weapons effects. "Survivability" has been a driving force behind the development of new weapons like the MX missile. New American counterforce weapons (such as the MX), which are capable of destroying Soviet missiles in their silos and so will put the Russians in a dangerously provocative "use 'em or lose 'em" situation in a crisis, have been justified on the ground that they will be able to destroy Soviet reserve forces after a first strike and so help preserve a favorable intrawar strategic balance.

Special attention has been given to America's own reserve forces. Ballistic-missile-launching submarines, with their ability to hide beneath the oceans for months at a time, have always been a *de facto* reserve. Now a certain percentage of America's nuclear bombers has also been assigned a reserve role. When they scramble off their runways during an enemy attack, they will head not to Russia but into holding orbits, to await further orders and developments. Land-based missiles, with their fixed locations, do not lend themselves to a reserve role, but the Pentagon is working (with $20 million appropriated by Congress in 1983) on schemes to base some MX missiles deep underground, where they will be safe from enemy attacks until they are called on to be brought to the surface for firing.

Another, brand-new nuclear reserve force is just now being created. Beginning in 1984, some 750 nuclear cruise missiles are scheduled to be deployed on American surface ships and subma-

334

rines—not on the ballistic-missile submarines that have always carried long-range nuclear weapons but on attack submarines, whose role until now has been to hunt and sink enemy ships. With the cruise missiles, which carry 200-kiloton warheads and have a range of 1,500 miles, the attack submarines will be a formidable new nuclear force. "The SLCM [sea-launched cruise missile] has the accuracy, yield, range, and penetration capability to threaten a very significant variety of strategic and theater targets," says the Navy. But it will be assigned no SIOP role. "Nuclear SLCMs will be part of the strategic reserve force and will be available for reconstitution and targeting, if necessary, during the post-SIOP periods," according to Admiral Frank Kelso, director of the Navy's Strategic Submarine Division. This will help the United States "retain a measure of coercive power in the post-exchange environment," he said. "Surviving SLCM ships could make an important contribution during the war termination phase following a massive exchange of strategic nuclear weapons," another Navy statement explained.

Neither the SLCM ships nor other elements of the reserve force will be of any use during "the war termination phase" unless American commanders can talk to them and tell them what to do. So billions of dollars are being spent now to develop survivable communications for the "post-SIOP period." The goal, the Reagan White House explained in 1981, is "a communications and control system that would endure for an extended period beyond the first nuclear attack." Research and construction is proceeding on redundant radio and satellite links designed to resist enemy jamming and to survive the electromagnetic pulse effects of exploding nuclear weapons.

If the weapons do survive, and if the communications systems do work, American reserve forces will be ready after the initial innings of a nuclear war to play the coercive rule envisioned by the strategists.

"If we are attacked by strategic nuclear forces," General Jasper Welch, assistant chief of staff of the Air Force, told Congress a few years ago, "our primary objective will be to survive sufficient forces to terminate the conflict on terms that are favorable to the United States. To accomplish this objective, our strategic forces must ... have the capability to continue operating in an extended conflict environment and to provide the necessary strength to allow the U.S. to influence postwar negotiations."

And so, if all goes according to plan, the president of the United States, safe above the battle in his National Emergency Airborne Command Post, will get in touch with the Soviet leadership, point out that Russia has already taken an impressive—but limited—beating, mention that surviving American forces are poised to deliver much worse blows, and suggest that the time has come for the Soviet Union to quit the war. The Soviets, knowing what the president says to be true, will conclude that it is indeed time to quit. And World War III will be over. Unless negotiations are derailed by one of several possible problems.

The first trick will be to find somebody alive for the president to call. The current American target list places special emphasis on Soviet military and political command posts. This raises the question: If Soviet leaders are all killed, who will surrender? This question is sufficiently obvious to have occurred to American strategists. "We recognize the role that a surviving supreme command could and would play in the termination of hostilities," Harold Brown noted in 1981, "and can envisage many scenarios in which destruction of them would be inadvisable and contrary to our own best interests." So supreme command centers will presumably be spared in the early rounds of a nuclear war. "The President might want to launch a crippling retaliation, and then call Brezhnev on the hot line to say that, unless he stops the war, some further strike will land on his personal bunker," an American official told *The Wall Street Journal* in 1980.

That call may not be easy to make. "Strategic C^3 must . . . facilitate termination of nuclear conflict, and thus includes the capacity to communicate with adversaries," Harold Brown wrote in 1981. But who will be manning the switchboard? The "hot line" (actually a teleprinter, not a voice circuit) between the White House and Kremlin is not well-hardened against nuclear effects. President Reagan proposed in 1983 that the system be improved by adding equipment to transmit photocopies of long messages and graphic material, and that a second hot line be established between the

American and Soviet military commands. There is no guarantee that any of this will survive a nuclear attack.

And even if it does, and enemy leaders are alive, located, and on the line with the president, how will they be convinced that it is time to end the war? The Soviet Union may have taken a beating, and American reserve forces may have surviving Soviet forces outgunned, but how will the Soviet leaders *know* that? Communications between their bunkers and the rest of their country and the world may be intact and delivering an accurate picture of the status of the war. Or they may not.

And if enemy leaders are alive, located, talking, and well-informed, are they likely to be in a reasonable mood? In 1974, James Schlesinger told a Senate committee he believed a limited nuclear war could lead to rational negotiations and a quick cease-fire.

> I believe . . . if we were to maintain continued communications with the Soviet leaders during the war, and if we were to describe precisely and meticulously the limited nature of our actions, including the desire to avoid attacking their urban industrial base, that in spite of whatever one says historically in advance that everything must go all out, when the existential circumstances arise, political leaders on both sides will be under powerful pressure to continue to be sensible. Both sides under those circumstances will continue to have the capacity at any time to destroy the urban industrial base of the others. The leaders on both sides will know that. Those are circumstances in which I believe that leaders will be rational and prudent. I hope I am not being too optimistic.

Leaders *might* be rational and prudent. But in the midst of a nuclear war, with millions of their countrymen dead, they may indeed prove Schlesinger to have been too optimistic.

And if none of these problems arises—enemy leaders are alive, in communication, well-informed, rational, and willing, even eager, to declare a cease-fire—what then?* How do you turn off a nuclear

---

* Anything more complicated than a simple cease-fire is unlikely, as in the time it would take to negotiate over any contested territory, that territory could be totally destroyed. To speed up the termination process, Harvard law professor Roger Fisher has suggested that the United States and Soviet Union sit down now and draft some stand-by cease-fire terms. "Simply having on hand a set of jointly prepared drafts with which each side was familiar would facilitate the task of ending a conflict.... An

war? The order to cease firing must reach forces spread over the globe, from Soviet submarines lurking in the Caribbean to American B-52s flying low over Siberia. Communications systems must be capable of providing for an "orderly and controlled termination of conflict," an assistant secretary of defense told Congress in 1981. And so the communications systems being developed to manage reserve forces in the "post-SIOP period" are also intended to be capable of telling those forces to stop firing and come home.* The message to cease fire will go out over every available channel, from the Bell telephone system to the Emergency Rocket Communications System (ERCS), the Minuteman missiles that carry tape recorders and radio transmitters instead of nuclear warheads. American commanders, including the stand-by team on the Looking Glass plane, can send messages into those recorders and launch the missiles, which will then broadcast the messages as they fly. "Certain messages are considered so important that ERCS must be launched . . . ," says Major Norwood Jennings of the Looking Glass battle staff. "It would be to order some kind of retaliation or to terminate the war. The president may have negotiated resolution and immediately want to terminate."

There will be little room for error here. If a single ship or plane fails to get the message—or to believe it—and proceeds with an attack, any truce could be wrecked. The side attacked might suspect treachery. The war might begin all over again.

If the message gets out, the cease-fire holds, and the nuclear war is over, the last difficult strategic question will be to decide who won.

---

urgent hot-line message might then propose that both sides accept 'the 1980 Warsaw Pact/NATO standard cease-fire terms, Draft B, effective 0100 hours tomorrow.' "
* For this reason, Bob O'Brien, the civil-defense director of Omaha, Nebraska, says he does not think Omaha will be attacked, even though Strategic Air Command headquarters are at nearby Offutt Air Force Base. "I don't think Offutt will be a target," says O'Brien (who *does* think the United States lags behind Russia in the nuclear arms race). "We don't need Offutt to run the war, but they [the Soviets] will need Offutt to run the peace. Offutt knows where every missile and bomber is, and it can send out orders to every one: 'Don't ping away for the next month. We have surrendered. You will surrender to Ivan So-and-So. He'll be landing there tomorrow morning. Be sure to give him a list of all weapons and personnel under your control.' "

If the war began over some particular issue, say, control of the Persian Gulf, then one way to determine the victor will be to send someone to the Persian Gulf to look around and see who, if anyone, is in control there now, and what, if anything, there is still worth controlling.

Another, more general way of determining the winner will be to calculate which side can recover first. For more than twenty years, American weapons have been aimed at Soviet "recovery targets," such as oil refineries and fertilizer plants, and nuclear war scenarios have paid careful attention to postattack resources. "Assessments made in exercises of food capability become very strategic . . . ," says Keith Peterson, of FEMA's division of exercises and tests. "The conclusion that enough grain is left in silos in Nebraska to feed the nation for thirty days becomes classified. If the Soviet Union finds that out, and they know they can survive for thirty-one days, they've won the war."

More sophisticated analyses of the Soviet economy have been conducted by the Pentagon to discover where missiles might most profitably be aimed to retard postattack recovery. "The present planning objective of the Defense Department is clear," Secretary of Defense Donald Rumsfeld wrote in 1977. "We believe that . . . an important objective of the assured retaliation mission should be to retard significantly the ability of the USSR to recover from a nuclear exchange and regain the status of a 20th-century military and industrial power more rapidly than the United States."

American targeting changes ushered in by Jimmy Carter's Presidential Directive 59 have reduced the emphasis on recovery targeting (while increasing the emphasis on targeting war-supporting industry). And Rumsfeld acknowledged that recovery targeting was both complicated and possibly irrelevant to crisis decisions. "The techniques currently used to assess the post-attack powers of recuperation of the two sides are analytically weak and plagued with uncertainties," he wrote. "Key decision-makers, in any event, are not likely to be very interested in the possibility that the Soviet Union could restore its prewar Gross National Product in 10 years, while it would take the United States twice as long to achieve the same result."

A more immediate indicator of victory will be the capacity of the United States and Soviet Union, after a nuclear war, to continue fighting. "We are very worried about Soviet armed reconnaissance aircraft ... having the freedom to roam around and wipe out whatever surviving mobile assets you have, which you've used for reconstitution, endurance, and survival," Deputy Undersecretary of Defense Donald Latham said in 1982, in support of plans to improve American air defenses. "Some way to counter the air-breathing [aircraft] post-strike threat is very critical." But more than simple postattack mop-up operations are at stake. Entire new campaigns might be launched after a nuclear war. "General-purpose forces will have high utility for taking U.S. presence and control into areas destroyed and disrupted by nuclear war," Commander Robert Powers of the U.S. Navy observed in a 1980 article. "Surviving naval forces could prevent the import of recovery assistance and have a substantial impact," said a study conducted for FEMA in 1981. "Either side might also feel compelled to annex adjacent territory useful to its own recovery, particularly if it could not 'buy' help." Past studies of American postattack recovery have been optimistic about the nation's ability to fight a post-nuclear-war war. Enough young American males will survive even a heavy attack to supply a large post-nuclear-war draft and provide "considerable potential for subsequent military actions," a 1967 report by Lloyd Addington of the Army Corps of Engineers concluded. "Will our postattack economy support the military operations necessary to maintain the United States as a world power?" Addington asked. The answer, he said, was yes; a lot of industrial capacity will be freed to manufacture military supplies because the postattack civilian economy will have "about 100 million fewer people to support." More recently, PONAST [Post-Nuclear Attack Study] II, conducted for the Joint Chiefs of Staff, concluded that after a major nuclear war both the United States and Soviet Union could survive, recover, and "continue the conflict."

The ultimate measure of victory in nuclear war—for those who care—will be the shape of the postwar world. "The victor will be in a position to issue orders to the loser and the loser will have to obey them or face complete chaos or extinction," Paul Nitze (the Reagan administration's negotiator on theater nuclear weapons) wrote in a famous 1956 article. "The victor will then go on to organize what remains of the world as best he can." In 1977, the Joint Chiefs of Staff reaffirmed this goal: "To the extent that escalation cannot be controlled, the U.S. objective is to maximize the resultant political, economic, and military power of the United States relative to the enemy in the post-war period."

The postwar balance of power, however, may be complicated by formerly second-rate powers that emerge from the war relatively intact. "Could either [former] superpower protect its pre-war boundaries against predators and opportunists?" wondered the study conducted for FEMA in 1981. "Would Mexico, Cuba, or even Canada try to improve their own posture by encroaching on surviving U.S. resources, assets, and productive territory? . . . Would Vietnam seek to take over all of Southeast Asia? Would the Koreans attempt to subjugate the Japanese?" For postattack reference, the study included a list of the twenty "strongest post-nuclear survivor nations," as determined by the "Sullivanov" method for scoring military capabilities.*

But strong survivor nations need not be troublesome. They might instead be saviors, sources of aid and trade. "Many countries now produce the principal products required for economic recovery . . . ," observed a study prepared for FEMA by the Hudson Institute in 1980. "For example, generators, switches, transformers, etc., needed to rebuild critical power networks, could be purchased from Korea, Mexico, Japan, Western Europe or many others, without having to wait for reconstruction of those industries in the United States." The report acknowledged that "the value of the dollar . . . would fall relative to currencies of countries not attacked," so it suggested that the United States begin accumulating foreign currency reserves now for postattack purchases.

The report noted also that this fruitful postattack trade will be inhibited if the Soviet Union wins the war. "If the USSR dominated the conflict . . . they could probably enforce a sharp reduction in oil shipments, thus seriously restraining recovery of economic activity in the U.S." To keep the trade flowing, the experts agree, the United States must not be a post-nuclear-war weakling. "A postwar world

---

* The list (in order): China, Israel, North Korea, South Korea, India, Egypt, Taiwan, Japan, Vietnam, Iraq, Spain, Syria, Pakistan, Cuba, Sweden, South Africa, Brazil, Switzerland, Australia, and Thailand.

compatible with U.S. interests and values" can only be guaranteed, a study conducted for the Defense Department in 1978 concluded, if the United States emerges from a nuclear war in a position of relative strength. And the most important strength it can have will be a surviving stockpile of nuclear weapons.

This *is* the American goal. The United States intends to "maintain in reserve, under all circumstances, nuclear offensive capabilities so that the United States would never emerge from a nuclear war without nuclear weapons while still threatened by enemy nuclear forces," said the classified "Fiscal Year 1984–1988 Defense Guidance" leaked to the press in 1982. Such a reserve, Admiral William A. Williams explained to Congress, "could be pivotal in the postwar balance and struggle for recovery."

The weapons will not necessarily be fired, of course. They will shore up the postwar balance of power just by their existence. They will keep our postwar enemies from stepping out of line by the implied threat to use them. They will preserve the postwar peace by being a deterrent force.

Just as nuclear weapons preserve the peace today.

Sources and Acknowledgments

Major sources of information for this book were personal interviews, government planning documents, visits to bases of the Strategic Air Command, congressional hearing transcripts, the military trade press, and previously published articles and books. Specific sources are listed by chapter. No attempt is made to link each bit of information in the text to its source; that would have been impossibly cumbersome. Many important sources are, however, sufficiently identified in the text to lead the careful reader to their full descriptions in this section.

I would like to thank all of the scientists, military officers, corporate officials, and government workers, past and present, who granted me interviews and provided me with documents. Some of my research was conducted in the libraries of the Federal Emergency Management Agency, the U.S. Army, the Center for Defense Information, the Arms Control Association, the Los Alamos Scientific Laboratory, and the American Institute of Physics, as well as at the National Archives, the John F. Kennedy Library, the New York Public Library, and the Brooklyn Public Library. I thank all those who opened those institutions to me and aided me in my work. I am grateful for the existence of the Freedom of Information Act, which I used to obtain certain documents from the U.S. Postal Service and the Department of the Treasury (and the mere existence of which made its use unnecessary in other cases).

An Alicia Patterson Foundation fellowship helped support me during my research. Alicia Patterson fellowships are probably the most generous and useful awards being given to American journalists today. I thank the Foundation once again.

I thank Amanda Urban and Bill Strachan, my agent and editor, for their efforts on behalf of the book, and I thank, for various favors and services, the following: Maria Casale, Tom Downey, Ken Emerson, Gerald Feinberg, Mary L. Gwynn, Bart Reppert, Judy Richland and Kevin Shea, Michael Rosenbaum, Raphael Sagalyn, Fred Solowey, and Spencer Weart.

Edward Zuckerman
New York City
December 1983

ONE: "Present Address: Mortuary #10"

Interviews

Harold Gay
Harold Gracey
Gary Robbins

Additional interviews were conducted with officials of the following government agencies:

Department of Agriculture
Department of Commerce
Department of Health and Human Services
Department of Housing and Urban Development
Department of Labor
Department of the Treasury
Federal Emergency Management Agency
United States Postal Service

Articles

Haley, Peter J., "In the Event of a National Emergency . . . ," *Federal Register Update*, August 1979.

Rothchild, John H., "Civil Defense: The Case for Nuclear War," *Washington Monthly*, October 1970.

Documents and Reports

Defense Civil Preparedness Agency, "Post-Nuclear Attack Study (PONAST II)," unclassified briefing charts, 1973.

———, *What the Planner Needs To Know About the Post-Shelter Environment*, Chapter 8 of *DCPA Attack Environment Manual*, June 1973.

Department of Housing and Urban Development, Office of Administration, *Emergency Repair of Damaged Housing*, Operating Instruction Number 2, July 1980.

———, *Emergency Housing Management Manual*, Operating Instruction Number 6, July 1980.

Department of Labor, Employment and Training Administration, *Civil Emergency Preparedness*, Chapter 7110 of *Employment and Training Manual*, January 1978.

———, Employment Standards Administration, *Wage and Salary Stabilization Programs in a Postattack Emergency*, March 1981.

Department of the Treasury, "Design of an Emergency Tax System," [1981].

———, "Emergency Tax Proposal for a Post-Attack Economy," 1966–67.

———, "Review of Treasury Emergency Planning Documents," Memorandum to William J. Beckham, Jr., from Daniel H. Brill, November 14, 1977.

———, "Treasury Emergency Planning Documents," Memorandum from Frank H. MacDonald to Assistant Secretary Beckham, December 20, 1977.

———, untitled report on REX-80 Alpha by Gary Robbins, Jim Ukockis, Ted Langolis, and David Brennan, [1980].

———, "War-Loss Sharing," January 1963.

Federal Civil Defense Administration, *Mortuary Services in Civil Defense*, TM-11-12, April 1956.

Federal Emergency Management Agency, "National Plan for Civil Emergency Management," draft, April 1981.

———, "Preparedness Program and Training Guide for Emergency Economic Measures (Stabilization) for National Security Emergencies," [1980].

———, *Stockpile Report to the Congress, October 1980–March 1981*, November 1981.

Greene, Jack C., Robert W. Stokley, and John K. Christian, *Recovery From Nuclear Attack and Research and Action Programs To Enhance Recovery Prospects*, prepared for Federal Emergency Management Agency, contract DCPA01-78-C-0270, Washington, International Center for Emergency Preparedness, 1979.

Internal Revenue Service, "Review of Treasury Emergency Planning Documents," Memorandum from Commissioner to Deputy Secretary, Department of the Treasury, October 31, 1977.

Office of Emergency Planning, *Ration Board Instructions for Postattack Consumer Rationing*, June 1965.

Office of the Federal Register, *Code of Emergency Federal Regulations*, 1965–1981.

Peskin, Henry M., "The Problem of Evaluating and Distributing Surviving Postattack Assets," in *Postattack Recovery From Nuclear War*, Proceedings of the Symposium held at Fort Monroe, Virginia, Office of Civil Defense, 1967.

Shinn, A. F., "Food Crops and Postattack Recovery," in *Postattack Recovery From Nuclear War*, Proceedings of the Symposium held at Fort Monroe, Virginia, Office of Civil Defense, 1967.

U.S. Congress, *Defense Industrial Base: New Stockpile Objectives*, Hearings before the Joint Committee on Defense Production, Part III, 94th Congress, 2nd session, 1976

———, *Federal, State, and Local Emergency Preparedness*, Hearings before the Joint Committee on Defense Production, 94th Congress, 2nd session, 1976.

———, House, *Civil Defense Review*, Hearings by the Civil Defense Panel of the Subcommittee on Investigations of the Committee on Armed Services, 94th Congress, 2nd session, 1976.

U.S. Postal Service, *Postal and Health and Human Services Registration and Information Program*, Part 1, Chapter 14 of *Emergency Planning Manual*, December 1981.

———, *Standby Emergency Actions*, Part II of *Emergency Planning Manual*, September 1975.

Other

Giuffrida, Louis, General, testimony before Subcommittee on HUD/Independent Agencies, Appropriations Committee, U.S. Senate, April 1, 1982.

Leahy, Patrick, Senator, remarks before Subcommittee on HUD/Independent Agencies, Appropriations Committee, U.S. Senate, April 1, 1982.

TWO: **Fermi's Bet**

Interviews

Hans Bethe
Emil Konopinski
Philip Morrison
Edward Teller

Books

Aston, F. W., *Isotopes*, London, Edward Arnold & Co., 1924.

Bernstein, Jeremy, *Einstein*, New York, Penguin Books, 1976.

Blumberg, Stanley A., and Gwinn Owens, *Energy & Conflict: The Life and Times of Edward Teller*, New York, G.P. Putnam's Sons, 1976.

Clark, Ronald W., *The Greatest Power on Earth*, New York, Harper & Row, 1980.

Compton, Arthur Holly, *Atomic Quest*, New York, Oxford University Press, 1956.

Eisenhower, Dwight D., *Mandate for Change, 1953-1956*, Garden City (New York), Doubleday & Co., 1963.

Groves, Leslie R., *Now It Can Be Told: The Story of the Manhattan Project*, New York, Harper & Row, 1962.

Jungk, Robert, *Brighter Than a Thousand Suns: a Personal History of the Atomic Scientists*, New York, Harvest/Harcourt Brace Jovanovich, 1958.

Kunetka, James W., *City of Fire: Los Alamos and the Birth of the Atomic Age, 1943-1945*, Englewood Cliffs (New Jersey), Prentice-Hall, 1978.

Lamont, Lansing, *Day of Trinity*, New York, Atheneum, 1965.

Leahy, William D., *I Was There*, New York, Whittlesey House, 1950.

Sherwin, Martin J., *A World Destroyed: The Atomic Bomb and the Grand Alliance*, New York, Vintage Books/Random House, 1977.

Soddy, Frederick, *The Interpretation of Radium*, London, John Murray, 1912.

Stimson, Henry L., "The Decision To Use the Atomic Bomb," in Bernstein, Barton J., ed., *The Atomic Bomb: The Critical Issues*, Boston, Little, Brown, 1976.

Truman, Harry S., *Memoirs, Volume One—Year of Decisions*, Garden City (New York), Doubleday & Co., 1955.

Weart, Spencer R., and Gertrud Weiss Szilard, eds., *Leo Szilard: His Version of the Facts*, Cambridge (Massachusetts), M.I.T. Press, 1980.

Wells, H. G., *The World Set Free: A Story of Mankind*, London, Macmillan and Co., 1914.

Wilson, Jane, ed., *All in Our Time: The Reminiscences of Twelve Nuclear Pioneers*, Chicago, Bulletin of the Atomic Scientists, 1975.

Articles

"Atomic Energy," *Science*, October 24, 1919.

"Atomic Power Again," *New York Times*, May 7, 1940.

"Freeing Atomic Energy," *Literary Digest*, October 16, 1920.

"German Savants Awed by a Fake," *New York Times*, December 28, 1920.

Harrington, Jean, "Don't Worry—It Can't Happen," *Scientific American*, May 1940.

"Infinite Energy Just Out of Reach," *Literary Digest*, November 15, 1924.

"Is the Universe Committing Suicide?", *Review of Reviews*, August 1930.

Kaempffert, Waldemar, "Atomic Energy—Is It Nearer?", *Scientific American*, August 1932.

Laurence, William L., "Vast Power Source in Atomic Energy Opened by Science," *New York Times*, May 5, 1940.

"Might-Have-Been," *Time*, February 12, 1940.

"New Force Predicted by Sir Oliver Lodge," *New York Times*, September 18, 1919.

Parsons, Floyd, "The Stupendous Possibilities of the Atom," *The World's Work*, May 1921.

"Perhaps the Ghosts Warned Him," *New York Times*, September 19, 1919.

"Radio Uses Split Atom," *New York Times*, July 29, 1940.

"Shall We Ever Use This Power in the Industrial World?", *Current Opinion*, June 1920.

"Talking Moonshine," *Scientific American*, November 1933.

"Tapping Atomic Energy," *Newsweek*, March 27, 1939.

"U-235 Held of No War Use Now," *New York Times*, May 6, 1940.

"Vision Earth Rocked by Isotope Blast," *New York Times*, April 30, 1939.

Weaver, Thomas A., and Lowell Wood, "Necessary Conditions for the Initiation and Propagation of Nuclear-Detonation Waves in Plane Atmospheres," *Physical Review*, July 1979.

Williams, Henry Smyth, "Six Ways To Make a Billion Dollars," *The American Magazine*, July 1927.

Documents and Reports

Konopinski, E. J., C. Marvin, and E. Teller, "Ignition of the Atmosphere With Nuclear Bombs," Los Alamos Scientific Laboratory, LA-602, 1946.

Norstad, Lauris, Major General, "Memorandum for Major General L. R. Groves: Subject: Atomic Bomb Production," September 15, 1945, Manhattan Engineering District files, National Archives, Modern Military Branch, Washington, D.C.

THREE: "The Good News Is You'll Be President"

Interviews

William Baird
Daniel Payton
Keith Peterson

Additional interviews were conducted with officials of the following government agencies:

Federal Emergency Management Agency
U.S. Air Force

Books

Fisher, Roger, "Preventing Nuclear War," in *The Final Epidemic: Physicians and Scientists on Nuclear War*, eds. Ruth Adams and Susan Cullen, Chicago, Educational Foundation for Nuclear Science, 1981.

Gulley, Bill, with Mary Ellen Reese, *Breaking Cover*, New York, Simon and Schuster, 1980.

McPhee, John, *The Curve of Binding Energy*, New York, Farrar, Straus and Giroux, 1974.

ter Horst, J. F., and Colonel Ralph Abertazzie, *The Flying White House: The Story of Air Force One*, New York, Coward, McCann & Geoghegan, 1979.

Articles

"An Education for Bell," *New York Times*, February 23, 1981.

Arkin, William M., "Nuclear New Math," *The Nation*, August 8, 1981.

349

Babyak, Blythe, "The Plane: Cruising to Armageddon," *Washington Monthly*, December 1978.

Bundy, McGeorge, George F. Kennan, Robert S. McNamara, and Gerard Smith, "Nuclear Weapons and the Atlantic Alliance," *Foreign Affairs*, Spring 1982.

"The Doomsday Exercise," *Newsweek*, April 5, 1982.

Fialka, John J., "Nuclear Reaction: U.S. Tests Response to an Atomic Attack," *Wall Street Journal*, March 26, 1982.

Gelb, Leslie, "Reagan Reported To Order Building of Neutron Arms for Stockpiling in the U.S.," *New York Times*, August 9, 1981.

Getler, Michael, "Pentagon Trumpets 'Tripwire,' A-Arms," *Washington Post*, February 2, 1980.

Gwertzman, Bernard, "Pentagon Kept Tight Rein in Last Days of Nixon Rule," *New York Times*, August 25, 1974

————, "Reagan Clarifies His Statements on Nuclear War," *New York Times*, October 22, 1981.

————, "U.S. Refuses To Bar Possible First Use of Nuclear Arms," *New York Times*, April 7, 1982.

"He Was Checked, O'Neill Says," *New York Times*, April 1, 1981.

Meehan, Mary, "The Flying Fuhrerbunker," *Washington Monthly*, April 1974.

"NATO Commander Opposes U.S. Troop Cut," *New York Times*, October 14, 1982.

"NATO Plans To Scrap 1,400 Warheads," *New York Times*, October 28, 1983.

Nossiter, Bernard D., "Soviet Forswears Using A-Arms First," *New York Times*, June 16, 1982.

Raines, Howell, "Reagan, Facing Allen Issue, Returns to the Capital," *New York Times*, November 16, 1981.

Tyler, Patrick E., and Bob Woodward, "FBI Got Reagan's Code Card After Shooting," *Washington Post*, December 13, 1982.

Wilson, George C., "Air Command Post," *Washington Post*, February 12, 1977.

Documents and Reports

Congressional Research Service, Library of Congress, *Authority To Order the Use of Nuclear Weapons*, 1975.

————, "Strategic Command and Control," by Kenneth L. Moll, May 15, 1980.

————, *U.S. Policy on the Use of Nuclear Weapons, 1945–1975*, November 14, 1975.

Department of Defense, Joint Chiefs of Staff, *Dictionary of Military and Associated Terms*, June 1979.

———, Joint Chiefs of Staff, *Military Posture for FY 1983*, 1982.

Foster, Richard B., with Francis Hoeber, *Survival, Reconstitution and Recovery: U.S.-Soviet Asymmetries and U.S. Policy Options*, prepared for Federal Emergency Management Agency, contract DCPA01-78-C-0308, Arlington, Virginia, SRI International Strategic Studies Center, February 1980.

Hart, Gary, Senator, and Senator Barry Goldwater, *Recent False Alerts From the Nation's Missile Attack Warning System*, Report to the Committee on Armed Services, U.S. Senate, October 9, 1980.

U.S. Air Force, Strategic Air Command, "Positive Control," fact sheet, August 1981.

U.S. Army, *Staff Officers' Field Manual: Nuclear Weapons Employment Doctrine and Practices*, FM 101-31-1, March 1977.

———, *Staff Officers' Field Manual: Operations*, FM 100-5, 1976.

———, *Staff Officers' Field Manual: Operations for Nuclear Capable Units*, FM 100-50, March 1980.

U.S. Congress, Congressional Budget Office, *Strategic Command, Control, and Communications: Alternative Approaches for Modernization*, October 1981.

———, House, *First Use of Nuclear Weapons: Preserving Responsible Control*, Hearings before the Subcommittee on International Security and Scientific Affairs of the Committee on International Relations, 94th Congress, 2nd session, 1976.

———, House, *Strategic Warning System False Alerts*, Hearing before the Committee on Armed Services, 96th Congress, 2nd session, 1980.

———, Senate, *Department of Defense Authorization for Appropriations for Fiscal Year 1982*, Hearings before the Committee on Armed Services, Part 7, 97th Congress, 1st session, 1981.

———, Senate, *Nuclear War Strategy*, Hearing before the Committee on Foreign Relations on Presidential Directive 59, 96th Congress, 2nd session, 1981.

Weinberger, Caspar W., Secretary of Defense, *Annual Report to the Congress, Fiscal Year 1983*, February 1982.

Other

CBS, "The Defense of the United States: Part I: Ground Zero," June 14, 1981.

Giuffrida, Louis, General, address to American Civil Defense Association, Arlington, Virginia, October 9, 1981.

FOUR: "All This From One Bomb"

Interviews

Jack Greene
Emil Konopinski
Philip Morrison

Books

Blumberg, Stanley A., and Gwinn Owens, *Energy & Conflict: The Life and Times of Edward Teller*, New York, G.P. Putnam's Sons, 1976.

Deitz, David, *Atomic Energy in the Coming Era*, New York, Dodd, Mead, and Co., 1945.

Divine, Robert A., *Blowing on the Wind: The Nuclear Test Ban Debate 1954–1960*, New York, Oxford University Press, 1978.

Glasstone, Samuel, and Philip J. Dolan, eds., *The Effects of Nuclear Weapons*, Washington, U.S. Department of Defense and the Energy Research and Development Administration, 1977.

Gofman, John W., *Radiation and Human Health*, San Francisco, Sierra Club Books, 1981.

Hilgartner, Stephen, Richard C. Bell, and Rory O'Connor, *Nukespeak: Nuclear Language, Visions, and Mindset*, San Francisco, Sierra Club Books, 1982.

Lang, Daniel, *From Hiroshima to the Moon: Chronicles of Life in the Atomic Age*, New York, Simon and Schuster, 1959.

Pringle, Peter, and James Spigelman, *The Nuclear Barons*, New York, Holt, Rinehart and Winston, 1981.

Shepley, James, and Clay Blair, Jr., *The Hydrogen Bomb: The Men, the Menace, the Mechanism*, New York, David McKay Co., 1954.

Shute, Nevil, *On the Beach*, New York, William Morrow and Co., 1957. (Reprint ed., New York, Ballantine Books, 1979.)

Smith, Alice Kimball, *A Peril and a Hope: The Scientists' Movement in America 1945-47*, Cambridge (Massachusetts), M.I.T. Press, 1971.

Teller, Edward, with Allen Brown, *The Legacy of Hiroshima*, Garden City (New York), Doubleday & Co., 1962.

Articles

"A-Bombs on Your Doorstep Next?," *U.S. News & World Report*, April 2, 1954.

"Anatomic Bomb," *Life*, September 3, 1945.

"Atom Fallout . . . How Bad It Is . . . What We Can Do About It Now," *Newsweek*, April 6, 1959.

"Ban Is Put on Song About the Atom," *New York Times*, September 1, 1950.

"Bikini: Breath-Holding Before a Blast—Could It Split the Earth?", *Newsweek*, July 1, 1946.

"Bill Urges Cash for Atomic Tips," *New York Times*, July 31, 1954.

"Bradley's Slumber Belies 'Insomnia' at Soviet Atom," *New York Times*, October 25, 1949.

"Cabbages vs. Fall-Out," *New York Times*, May 13, 1958.

Callender, Harold, "Early Use of Atom as Fuel Predicted," *New York Times*, August 8, 1945.

"Cobalt Bomb Use in War Scouted," *New York Times*, April 12, 1954.

Cummings, Judith, "Three Decades After Bomb Tests, Utah Sheep Ranchers Feel Little Bitterness," *New York Times*, August 15, 1982.

Curry, Bill, "Retrial Ordered in Fallout Case," *Los Angeles Times*, August 5, 1982.

de Seversky, Alexander P., "Atomic Bomb Hysteria," *Reader's Digest*, February 1946.

"Eisenhower Urges Brighter Outlook," *New York Times*, March 12, 1950.

Finney, John W., "U.S. Eliminates 95% of Fall-Out From the H-Bomb," *New York Times*, June 25, 1957.

"Gags Away," *The New Yorker*, August 18, 1945.

Gruson, Sydney, "Khrushchev Says Eisenhower Talks Bomb 'Stupidities,' " *New York Times*, July 12, 1957.

Grutzner, Charles, "City Folks Fear of Bomb Aids Boom in Rural Realty," *New York Times*, August 27, 1950.

"H-Bomb 'Fouling Air,' British Scientist Says," *New York Times*, March 21, 1955.

"Helen Caldicott," *Life*, June 1982.

"House Bill Seeks Atomic Defenses," *New York Times*, September 26, 1945.

Laurence, William L., "U.S. Atom Bomb Site Belies Tokyo Tales," *New York Times*, September 12, 1945.

———, "Ending of All Life by Hydrogen Bomb Held a Possibility," *New York Times*, February 27, 1950.

———, "H-Bomb Can Wipe Out Any City, Strauss Reports After Tests; U.S. Restudies Plant Dispersal," *New York Times*, April 1, 1954.

Lawrence, W. H., "No Radioactivity in Hiroshima Ruins," *New York Times*, September 13, 1945.

"Lilienthal Hits Sad Talk," *New York Times*, March 7, 1950.

Littell, Robert, "What the Atom Bomb Would Do to *Us*," *Reader's Digest*, May 1946.

"The Mathematics of Doom," *Scientific American*, December 1950.

"New York Bomber Built in Germany," *New York Times*, June 8, 1945.

Nordyke, Lewis, "Atoms in the Home," *New York Times Magazine*, October 14, 1945.

Pauling, Linus, "Fact and Fable of Fallout," *The Nation*, June 14, 1958.

"Pig Declines Texas Bid," *New York Times*, August 8, 1946.

"Political Fallout," *Newsweek*, June 17, 1954.

"Second Capital Urged in Atom Era; Underground Plan To Be Broached," *New York Times*, February 20, 1950.

"70-Year Effect of Bombs Denied," *New York Times*, August 9, 1945.

Shalett, Sidney, "Arnold Reveals Secret Weapons, Bomber Surpassing All Others," *New York Times*, August 18, 1945.

Sontheimer, Morton, "Memories of a Small Bomb," *Newsweek*, June 29, 1981.

Sullivan, Walter, "Film Spots Trace Vast A-Bomb Range," *New York Times*, May 23, 1946.

"Survive the H-Bomb!", *Newsweek*, August 31, 1953.

Teller, Edward, and Albert Latter, "The Compelling Need for Nuclear Tests," *Life*, February 10, 1958.

"Tennesseans Near a Reactor Receive Anti-Radiation Pills," *New York Times*, November 29, 1981.

"Tokyo Puts Toll of Atomic Bombs at 190,000 Killed and Wounded," *New York Times*, August 23, 1945.

"Truman Is Urged To Bar Atom Bomb," *New York Times*, August 20, 1945.

Uhler, H. S., "Bomb Site Discussed: Bikini Explosions Might Produce Disastrous Repercussions," *New York Times*, April 7, 1946.

"Vatican Deplores Use of Atom Bomb," *New York Times*, August 8, 1945.

"Washington Real Estate Ads Stress Atomic Safety," *New York Times*, July 30, 1950.

Weisgall, Jonathan M., "The Nuclear Nomads of Bikini Atoll," *Foreign Policy*, Summer 1980.

354

"What's Back of the Fallout Scare?", *U.S. News & World Report*, June 7, 1957.

Wyant, William K., Jr., "50,000 Baby Teeth," *The Nation*, June 13, 1959.

Documents and Reports

Groves, L. R., Major General, "Memorandum for the Chief of Staff," August 24, 1945, Manhattan Engineering District files, National Archives, Modern Military Branch, Washington, D.C.

U.S. Congress, House, *Civil Defense Review*, Hearings by the Civil Defense Panel of the Subcommittee on Investigations of the Committee on Armed Services, 94th Congress, 2nd session, 1976.

————, House, *The Forgotten Guinea Pigs: A Report on Health Effects of Low-Level Radiation Sustained as a Result of the Nuclear Weapons Testing Program Conducted by the United States Government*, Report prepared for the use of the Committee on Interstate and Foreign Commerce, 96th Congress, 2nd session, August 1980.

————, Senate, *Atomic Energy*, Hearings before the Special Committee on Atomic Energy, Part 2, 79th Congress, 1st session, 1945.

Other

"Atomic Cafe: Radioactive Rock 'n' Roll, Blues, Country & Gospel," Somerville (Massachusetts), Rounder Records, 1982.

FIVE: **"This Area *Will* Be Evacuated"**

INTERVIEWS

Ed Baez
Russell Clanahan
Richard Herskowitz
Russ Lawler
Joseph Mealy
Bill Reiling

Additional interviews were conducted with officials of the following government agencies:

Federal Emergency Management Agency
Greenfield (Massachusetts) Civil Defense
New York City Office of Civil Preparedness
New York State Office of Disaster Preparedness
Plattsburgh (New York) Office of Civil Defense

Books

Kahn, Herman, *On Thermonuclear War*, Princeton (New Jersey), Princeton University Press, 1960.

Kearny, Cresson H., *Nuclear War Survival Skills*, Oak Ridge (Tennessee), Oak Ridge National Laboratory, 1979. (Reprint ed., Boston (Virginia), American Security Council Education Foundation, undated.)

Articles

Bennetts, Leslie, "City Says No to 'Crisis Relocation,'" *New York Times*, June 10, 1982.

"City Transit Unit Drops Plan on Nuclear Safety," *New York Times*, March 24, 1981.

Gant, K. S., and C. V. Chester, "Minimizing Excess Radiogenic Cancer Deaths After a Nuclear Attack," *Health Physics*, September 1981.

"Gun Thy Neighbor?", *Time*, August 18, 1961.

Hudson, Edward, "Bus Drivers Take a Course on Nuclear Radiation," *New York Times*, May 24, 1983.

Miniclier, Kit, "Sub Missile Attack? Just Time 'to Get All Tensed Up,'" *Denver Post*, April 26, 1981.

Phelps, Timothy M., "Nuclear Attack and Subways: Ways Sought to Guard Power," *New York Times*, March 23, 1981.

Wald, Matthew, "Plans for Safety at Indian Point Faulted by U.S.," *New York Times*, December 18, 1982.

Weinraub, Bernard, "Civil Defense Agency: 'Trying To Do Something,'" *New York Times*, April 8, 1982.

Zuckerman, Edward, "Hiding From the Bomb—Again," *Harper's*, August 1979.

Documents and Reports

Defense Civil Preparedness Agency, *Guide for Crisis Relocation Contingency Planning: Overview of Nuclear Civil Protection Planning for Crisis Relocation*, CPG 2-8-A, January 1979.

———, "Memorandum for NSS-CRP Report Users: CRP Host Area Facility Listing," April 20, 1978.

———, "News Conference—Mr. Tirana," November 13, 1978.

———, *The Nuclear Crisis of 1979*, CPG 2-8-5, February 1976.

———, *Protection in the Nuclear Age*, H-20, February 1977.

356

————, "Questions and Answers on Crisis Relocation Planning," August 9, 1978.

————, *What the Planner Needs To Know About Blast and Shock*, Chapter 2 of *DCPA Attack Environment Manual*, June 1973.

————, *What the Planner Needs To Know About the Shelter Environment*, Chapter 7 of *DCPA Attack Environment Manual*, June 1973.

Department of Defense, Office of Civil Defense, *Highlights: Decision Information Distribution System*, MP-57, November 1971.

Federal Emergency Management Agency, *Camera-Ready Newspaper Columns*, P&P-5, December 1980.

————, *Civil Defense and the Public: An Overview of Public Attitude Studies*, MP-62, September 1979.

————, *Emergency Management Instruction: Grades K-3*, Draft IG 1.2, April 1981.

————, "FEMA-Produced Radiation Detection Device Flying Aboard Space Shuttle Columbia," Release 82-54, June 26, 1982.

————, *Guide for Increasing Local Government Civil Defense Readiness During Periods of International Crisis*, CPG 1-7, May 1981.

————, "Highlights of FY 1983 Civil Defense Program," 1982.

————, *How To Manage Congregate Lodging Facilities and Fallout Shelters*, SM-11, June 1981.

————, *Materials for Presentation on Nuclear Civil Protection*, P&P-2, September 1980.

————, *Motion Picture Catalog*, FEMA-2, June 1980.

————, "Preparedness Program and Training Guide for Economic and Financial Measures During Crisis Relocation," [1980].

————, "President Reagan Directs Implementation of Seven-Year Civil Defense Program," Release 82-26, March 30, 1982.

————, *Principles of Warning and Criteria Governing Eligibility of National Warning Systems (NAWAS) Terminals*, CPG 1-14, November 1981.

————, *Procedures Manual for National & Regional Warning Centers*, Manual 1550.2, January 1981.

————, "Questions and Answers on Crisis Relocation Planning," P&P-4, October 1980.

————, *Shelter Management Handbook*, P&P-8, February 1981.

————, "Statement by Lee M. Thomas," Release 82-34, April 22, 1982.

357

————, "Statement by Louis O. Giuffrida," Release 82-17, March 12, 1982.

————, "U.S. Civil Defense Program," September 11, 1981.

————, *U.S. Crisis Relocation Planning*, P&P-7, February 1981.

Greenfield (Massachusetts) Civil Defense Agency, "Nuclear Civil Protection Plan," September 2, 1980.

Henderson, Clark, and Walmer E. Strope, *Crisis Relocation of the Population at Risk in the New York Metropolitan Area*, prepared for Defense Civil Preparedness Agency, contract 01-76-C-0308, Menlo Park (California), SRI International, 1978.

Massachusetts Civil Defense, *Relocation Instructions: Greater Boston Risk Area, Suburban West*, undated.

National Capitol Systems, *Special Problems of Blacks and Other Minorities in Large Scale Population Relocation*, prepared for Federal Emergency Management Agency, contract 01-79-C-0293, January 1981.

Plattsburgh [New York] Office of Civil Defense, *Evacuation Instructions: Plattsburgh Risk Area*, undated.

Sullivan, Roger J., Winder M. Heller, and E. C. Aldridge, Jr., *Candidate U.S. Civil Defense Programs*, prepared for Defense Civil Preparedness Agency, contract 01-77-C-0219, Arlington (Va.), System Planning Corporation, March 1978.

Sullivan, Roger J., Jeffrey M. Ranney, and Richard S. Soll, *The Potential Effect of Crisis Relocation on Crisis Stability*, prepared for Defense Civil Preparedness Agency, contract 01-77-C-0237, Arlington (Virginia), System Planning Corporation, September 1978.

U.S. Congress, *Federal, State and Local Emergency Preparedness*, Hearings Before the Joint Committee on Defense Production, 94th Congress, 2nd session, 1976.

University of Colorado at Denver, *Field Testing and Evaluation of Expedient Shelters*, prepared for Defense Civil Preparedness Agency, contract 01-76-0-0388, February 1978.

Wyoming Disaster and Civil Defense Division, "Host Area Information," undated.

Other

Dickey, John, remarks to Newport Institute, Newport, Rhode Island, November 6, 1982.

Federal Emergency Management Agency, "Protection in the Nuclear Age," Film, 1978.

SIX: "The Number-One Myth of the Nuclear Age"

Interviews

Harold Goodwin
Donald Mitchell
Walmer Strope
Bardyl Tirana

Additional interviews were conducted with officials of the following agencies and organizations:

The American Civil Defense Association
Defense Civil Preparedness Agency
Federal Emergency Management Agency
New York City Office of Civil Preparedness

Books

Britannica Book of the Year 1956, Chicago, Encyclopaedia Britannica, Inc., 1957.

Kramer, Michael, and Sam Roberts, "I Never Wanted To Be Vice-President of Anything!" An Investigative Biography of Nelson Rockefeller, New York, Basic Books, 1976.

Lehrer, Tom, Too Many Songs by Tom Lehrer, New York, Pantheon Books, 1981.

Pringle, Peter, and James Spigelman, The Nuclear Barons, New York, Holt, Rinehart and Winston, 1981.

Smith, Alice Kimball, A Peril and a Hope: The Scientists' Movement in America 1945-47, Cambridge (Massachusetts), M.I.T. Press, 1971.

Teller, Edward, with Allen Brown, The Legacy of Hiroshima, Garden City (New York), Doubleday & Co., 1962.

Uhl, Michael, and Tod Ensign, GI Guinea Pigs, New York, Playboy Press, 1980.

Weart, Spencer R., and Gertrud Weiss Szilard, eds., Leo Szilard: His Version of the Facts, Cambridge (Massachusetts), M.I.T. Press, 1980.

Wigner, Eugene P., ed., Who Speaks for Civil Defense?, New York, Charles Scribner's Sons, 1968.

Articles

Bird, Caroline, "Nine Places To Hide," Esquire, January 1962.

"Bomb Shelters Away," Time, September 3, 1951.

"Boom to Bust," Time, May 18, 1962.

Burt, Richard, "Ex-U.S. Aides Assail Soviet Arms Treaty," *New York Times*, April 12, 1979.

"Churches and Civil Defense," *Christian Century*, July 11, 1951.

"Cult of Death: People's Temple," *Newsweek*, December 4, 1978.

Evans, Rowland, and Robert Novak, "The Civil-Defense Snafu," *Washington Post*, January 5, 1979.

"Excerpts From President's Speech in Japan," *New York Times*, November 11, 1983.

"Fallout Shelters," *Life*, September 15, 1961.

"For New Yorkers: Compulsory Shelters," *Newsweek*, July 20, 1959.

"Gun Thy Neighbor?", *Time*, August 18, 1961.

Hill, Gladwin, " 'Town' Does Well in Atomic Blast," *New York Times*, May 7, 1955.

Lanouette, William J., "The Best Civil Defense May Be the Best—or Worst—Offense," *National Journal*, September 9, 1978.

Lawrence, W. H., "President To Use 'Copter in Test," *New York Times*, July 12, 1957.

Leviero, Anthony, " 'H-Bombs' Test U.S. Civil Defense; Government Is Moved to Hide-Outs; City Raid Alert Termed a Success," *New York Times*, June 16, 1955.

"No to Civil Defense," *Washington Post*, December 15, 1978.

Power, Jonathan, "A Conversation With Brzezinski," *Washington Post*, October 9, 1977.

Reagan, Ronald, "Civil Defense," *Santa Rosa* (California) *Press Democrat*, November 21, 1978.

"Rocky's Fight on Fallout," *Life*, April 11, 1960.

Strope, Jerry, "The 'Bad-Cold' War Syndrome," *Journal of Civil Defense*, June 1982.

"Survival: Are Shelters the Answer?", *Newsweek*, November 6, 1961.

"Survive the H-Bomb!", *Newsweek*, August 31, 1953.

"Text of Truman's Address on Measures for Defense," *New York Times*, May 8, 1951.

"Traders in the Suburbs," *New York Times*, April 16, 1946.

"U.S. Defense Moves on Atom Proposed," *New York Times*, June 30, 1946.

Walsh, John, "Civil Defense: Congress Refuses Funds To Complete Shelter Survey and Stocking Program This Year," *Science*, April 19, 1963.

Weinraub, Bernard, "Brown Says Stronger Air Defense Is Needed To Face Soviet Bomber," *New York Times*, April 7, 1978.

———, "Carter Plans To Limit Civil Defense Budget," *New York Times*, December 28, 1978.

Additional material consulted included wirephotos of United Press International.

Documents and Reports

Berger, Howard M., *A Critical Review of Studies of Survival and Recovery After a Large-Scale Nuclear Attack*, prepared for Defense Nuclear Agency, contract DNA001-78-C-0009, Marina del Rey (California), R&D Associates, December 1978.

Bundy, McGeorge, "Memorandum to the President," December 16, 1961, National Security Files, Box #295, John F. Kennedy Library, Boston, Massachusetts.

Defense Civil Preparedness Agency, "News Conference—Mr. Tirana," November 13, 1978.

———, *Significant Events in United States Civil Defense History*, July 1, 1975.

———, *What the Planner Needs To Know About the Post-Shelter Environment*, Chapter 8 of *DCPA Attack Environment Manual*, June 1973.

Federal Emergency Management Agency, *Civil Defense and the Public: An Overview of Public Attitude Studies*, MP-62, September 1979.

———, "Fact Sheet on Nuclear Civil Protection (NCP) Planning," May 1980.

———, "Material for the Record, Senate Committee on Labor and Human Resources, Subcommittee on Health and Scientific Research, Hearings June 19, 1980, on Short- and Long-Term Effects on the Surviving Population of a Nuclear War."

———, *Research Summaries, FY 1971–FY 1980* (10 volumes).

Foster, Richard B., with Francis Hoeber, *Survival, Reconstitution and Recovery: U.S.-Soviet Asymmetries and U.S. Policy Options*, prepared for Federal Emergency Management Agency, contract DCPA01-78-C-0308, Arlington (Virginia), SRI International Strategic Studies Center, February 1980.

Greene, Jack C., Robert W. Stokley, and John K. Christian, *Recovery From Nuclear Attack and Research and Action Programs To Enhance Recovery Prospects*, prepared for Federal Emergency Management Agency, contract DCPA01-78-C-0270, Washington, International Center for Emergency Preparedness, 1979.

361

Huntington, Samuel, "Civil Defense for the 1980s," testimony before the Committee on Banking, Housing and Urban Affairs, U.S. Senate, January 8, 1979.

Kennedy, John F., "Memorandum for Mr. Bundy," July 5, 1961, National Security Files, Box #295, John F. Kennedy Library, Boston, Massachusetts.

——, "Memorandum for Secretary of Defense," August 29, 1961, National Security Files, Box #291-296, John F. Kennedy Library, Boston, Massachusetts.

National Security Council, "Presidential Directive/NSC-41," September 29, 1978.

Pittman, Steuart, "Civil Defense and Congressional Acceptance," February 23, 1978.

Sullivan, Roger J., Winder M. Heller, and E. C. Aldridge, Jr., *Candidate U.S. Civil Defense Programs*, prepared for Defense Civil Preparedness Agency, contract 01-77-C-0219, Arlington (Virginia), System Planning Corporation, March 1978.

U.S. Arms Control and Disarmament Agency, "An Analysis of Civil Defense in a Nuclear War," December 1978.

U.S. Congress, *Deterrence and Survival in the Nuclear Age (The "Gaither Report" of 1957)*, printed for the use of the Joint Committee on Defense Production, 94th Congress, 2nd session, 1976.

——, House, *Civil Defense Review*, Hearings by the Civil Defense Panel of the Subcommittee on Investigations of the Committee on Armed Services, 94th Congress, 2nd session, 1976.

——, Senate, *Oversight Hearing on Civil Defense*, Committee on Banking, Housing and Urban Affairs, January 8, 1979.

Warnke, Paul C., "The Role of Civil Defense in the U.S./Soviet Strategic Balance," testimony before the Committee on Banking, Housing and Urban Affairs, U.S. Senate, January 8, 1979.

SEVEN: **The Long Nuclear War**

Interviews

Lieutenant Colonel James Davis
Colonel Robert Gifford
Captain Frank Grindel
Sergeant Gary Hunt
Major Norwood Jennings

Lieutenant Colonel Paul Murphy
Major William Stalcup

Additional interviews were conducted with officers and enlisted personnel at the following United States Air Force bases:

Kirtland AFB, New Mexico
Loring AFB, Maine
Offutt AFB, Nebraska
F. E. Warren AFB, Wyoming

Articles

Albright, Joseph, "Plane Serves as Ultimate Switchboard in Wartime," *Atlanta Constitution*, September 22, 1980.

Ball, Desmond, "Counterforce Targeting: How New? How Viable?", *Arms Control Today*, February 1981.

Broad, William J., "Nuclear Pulse (I): Awakening to the Chaos Factor," *Science*, May 29, 1981.

Covault, Craig, "FB-111's Effectiveness Increased," *Aviation Week & Space Technology*, May 10, 1976.

"Crew Flexibility Tied to War Order Familiarity," *Aviation Week & Space Technology*, May 10, 1976.

Gottlieb, Irving, "Meteoric Bursts Could Keep Post-Attack Communications Open," *Defense Electronics*, November 1981.

Halloran, Richard, "Reagan Arms Policy Said To Rely Heavily on Communications," *New York Times*, October 12, 1981.

————, "Weinberger Denies U.S. Plans for 'Protracted' War," *New York Times*, June 21, 1982.

Klass, Philip J., "Studies Weigh Approaches in Blue-Green Laser Use," *Aviation Week & Space Technology*, June 21, 1982.

" 'Looking Glass' Capabilities Improved," *Aviation Week & Space Technology*, May 10, 1976.

McNamara, Robert S., "No Second Use—Until," *New York Times*, February 2, 1983.

Miller, Barry, "ICBMs Get Major Modernization," *Aviation Week & Space Technology*, May 10, 1976.

"Preparing for Nuclear War: President Reagan's Program," *Defense Monitor*, Vol. X, no. 8, 1982.

Prochnau, Bill, "Night Flight to Armageddon," *Washington Post Magazine*, September 20, 1981.

Robinson, Clarence A., Jr., "Survivability, Accuracy, Yield Pressed for Minuteman," *Aviation Week & Space Technology*, October 22, 1979.

Scott, William B., "Radiation Hardening Found Effective," *Aviation Week & Space Technology*, March 15, 1982.

Stanford, Phil, "Who Pushes the Button?", *Parade*, March 28, 1976.

Stein, Kenneth J., "E-4B Boosts SAC's Communications Net," *Aviation Week & Space Technology*, June 16, 1980.

Sullivan, Walter, "How Huge Antennas Can Broadcast Into the Silence of the Sea," *New York Times*, October 13, 1981.

Talbot, Stephen, and Jonathan Dann, "Broken Arrows: How America (oops!) Drops the Bomb on America," *Rolling Stone*, October 1, 1981.

"Targeting Flexibility Emphasized by SAC," *Aviation Week & Space Technology*, May 10, 1976.

Documents and Reports

Brown, Harold, Secretary of Defense, *Department of Defense Annual Report, Fiscal Year 1982*, January 1981.

Department of Defense, Joint Chiefs of Staff, *United States Military Posture for FY 1982*, [1981].

————, Joint Chiefs of Staff, *United States Military Posture for FY 1983*, [1982].

U.S. Air Force, Strategic Air Command, "Communications," fact sheet, August 1981.

————, Strategic Air Command, "Global Shield 82 Briefing," [1982].

————, Strategic Air Command, "FB-111," fact sheet, August 1981.

————, Strategic Air Command, "Modernization of the SAC Force," fact sheet, December 1981.

————, Strategic Air Command, "Positive Control," fact sheet, August 1981.

————, Strategic Air Command, "SAC Alert Force," fact sheet, August 1981.

U.S. Arms Control and Disarmament Agency, *Fiscal Year 1983 Arms Control Impact Statements*, March 1982.

U.S. Congress, Senate, *Department of Defense Authorization for Appropriations for Fiscal Year 1980*, Hearings before the Committee on Armed Services, Part 6, 96th Congress, 1st session, 1979.

————, Senate, *Department of Defense Authorization for Appropriations for Fiscal Year 1982*, Hearings before the Committee on Armed Services, Part 7, 97th Congress, 1st session, 1981.

————, Senate, *Nuclear War Strategy*, Hearing before the Committee on Foreign Relations, 96th Congress, 2nd session, Top Secret hearing held on September 16, 1980, Sanitized and printed on February 18, 1981.

————, Senate, *Strategic Weapons Proposals*, Hearings before the Committee on Foreign Relations, Part 1, 97th Congress, 1st session, 1981.

U.S. General Accounting Office, *Countervailing Strategy Demands Revision of Strategic Force Acquisition Plans*, August 5, 1981.

Weinberger, Caspar W., Secretary of Defense, *Annual Report to Congress, Fiscal Year 1983*, February 1982.

Other

Ball, Desmond, *Can Nuclear War Be Controlled?*, Adelphi Papers, no. 169, London, International Institute for Strategic Studies, 1981.

EIGHT: "We Sound a Little Crazy"

Interview

Edward Teller

Books

Ball, Desmond, *Deja Vu: The Return to Counterforce in the Nixon Administration*, Los Angeles, California Seminar on Arms Control and Foreign Policy, 1974.

Brown, Anthony Cave, ed., *Dropshot: The American Plan for World War III Against Russia in 1957*, New York, Dial Press, 1978.

Eisenhower, Dwight D., *Mandate for Change, 1953-1956*, Garden City (New York), Doubleday & Co., 1963.

Freedman, Lawrence, *The Evolution of Nuclear Strategy*, New York, St. Martin's Press, 1981.

Haldeman, H. R., *The Ends of Power*, New York, Times Books, 1978.

Herken, Gregg, *The Winning Weapon: The Atomic Bomb in the Cold War 1945-1950*, New York, Alfred A. Knopf, 1980.

Kahan, Jerome H., *Security in the Nuclear Age*, Washington, Brookings Institution, 1975.

Kahn, Herman, *On Escalation*, New York, Frederick A. Praeger, 1965.

Kaplan, Fred, *The Wizards of Armageddon*, New York, Simon & Schuster, 1983.

Kissinger, Henry A., *Nuclear Weapons and Foreign Policy*, New York, Harper & Brothers (for the Council on Foreign Relations), 1957.

Mandelbaum, Michael, *The Nuclear Question: The United States and Nuclear Weapons 1946–1976*, New York, Cambridge University Press, 1979.

McPhee, John, *The Curve of Binding Energy*, New York, Farrar, Straus and Giroux, 1974.

Schlafly, Phyllis, and Chester Ward, *The Gravediggers*, Alton (Illinois), Pere Marquette Press, 1964.

Weart, Spencer R., and Gertrud Weiss Szilard, eds., *Leo Szilard: His Version of the Facts*, Cambridge (Massachusetts), M.I.T. Press, 1980.

Articles

"Agent Says Spy Suspect Told of Secrets Sale," *New York Times*, September 27, 1981.

Anderson, Jack, "Not-So-New Nuclear Strategy," *Washington Post*, October 12, 1980.

Ball, Desmond, "Counterforce Targeting: How New? How Viable?", *Arms Control Today*, February 1981.

———, "U.S. Strategic Forces: How Would They Be Used?", *International Security*, Winter 1982–83.

Broad, William J., "Nuclear Pulse (III): Playing a Wild Card," *Science*, June 12, 1981.

Freedman, Lawrence, "NATO Myths," *Foreign Policy*, Winter 1981–82.

Friedberg, Aaron L., "A History of the U.S. Strategic 'Doctrine' —1945 to 1980," *Journal of Strategic Studies*, December 1980.

Gray, Colin S., "Chacun à son gout," letter, *Bulletin of the Atomic Scientists*, June/July 1981.

———, "Nuclear Strategy: the Case for a Theory of Victory," *International Security*, Summer 1979.

Gray, Colin S., and Keith Payne, "Victory Is Possible," *Foreign Policy*, Summer 1980.

Halloran, Richard, "Pentagon Draws Up First Strategy for Fighting a Long Nuclear War," *New York Times*, May 30, 1982.

———, "Weinberger Angered by Reports on War Strategy," *New York Times*, August 23, 1982.

———, "Weinberger Confirms New Strategy on Atom War," *New York Times*, June 4, 1982.

Keeny, Spurgeon M., Jr., and Wolfgang K. H. Panofsky, "MAD Versus NUTS," *Foreign Affairs*, Winter 1981/82.

Paine, Christopher, "Nuclear Combat: the Five-Year Defense Plan," *Bulletin of the Atomic Scientists*, November 1982.

"Pentagon Details $7.8 Billion Air Defense Plan," *New York Times*, March 6, 1983.

Powers, Thomas, "Choosing a Strategy for World War III," *Atlantic Monthly*, November 1982.

"Private Shelter: Option for the Wary," *Protect and Survive Monthly*, May 1981 (reprinted from *Journal of Civil Defense*, August 1980).

Rosenberg, David Alan, "American Atomic Strategy and the Hydrogen Bomb Decision," *Journal of American History*, June 1979.

———, " 'A Smoking Radiating Ruin at the End of Two Hours': Documents on American Plans for Nuclear War with the Soviet Union, 1954-55," *International Security*, Winter 1981–82.

———, "U.S. Nuclear Stockpile, 1945 to 1950," *Bulletin of the Atomic Scientists*, May 1982.

Shalett, Sidney, "Arnold Reveals Secret Weapons, Bomber Surpassing All Others," *New York Times*, August 18, 1945.

Sherry, Michael, "The Slide to Total Air War," *New Republic*, December 16, 1981.

"The 36-Hour War," *Life*, November 19, 1945.

Wells, Samuel F., Jr., "The Origins of Massive Retaliation," *Political Science Quarterly*, Spring 1981.

Weinberger, Caspar W., "Where We Must Build—And Where We Must Cut," *Defense 81* (publication of the Department of Defense), December 1981.

Documents and Reports

Brown, Harold, *Department of Defense Annual Report, Fiscal Year 1980*, January 25, 1979.

————, *Department of Defense Annual Report, Fiscal Year 1981*, January 29, 1980.

————, *Department of Defense Annual Report, Fiscal Year 1982*, January 19, 1981.

Congressional Budget Office, *Counterforce Issues for the U.S. Strategic Nuclear Forces*, January 1978.

Congressional Research Service, *U.S. Policy on the Use of Nuclear Weapons, 1945-1975*, November 14, 1975.

Defense Atomic Support Agency, *A Study of Morals and the Nuclear Program*, presented at the Fifth Military Chaplains Nuclear Symposium held at Sandia Base, Albuquerque, New Mexico, 10–11 March 1965.

————, *A Study of Morals and the Nuclear Program*, presented at the Eighth Military Chaplains Nuclear Symposium held at Sandia Base, Albuquerque, New Mexico, 12–15 March 1968.

Defense Civil Preparedness Agency, "Civil Defense for the 1980's—Current Issues," July 13, 1979.

————, "Recent Documents Relating to Civil Defense Issues," [1977].

Department of Defense, "Remarks Prepared for Delivery by the Honorable Harold Brown, Secretary of Defense, at the Convocation Ceremonies for the 97th Naval War College Class, Naval War College, Newport, Rhode Island, August 20, 1980."

————, *Russian Language Guide*, TM 30-344, 1974.

Foster, Richard B., *The Soviet Concept of National Entity Survival*, prepared for Office of the Assistant Secretary of Defense, International Security Affairs, contract MDA903-78-M-3207, Arlington (Virginia), SRI International Strategic Studies Center, March 1978.

National Security Council, "Presidential Directive/NSC-53," November 15, 1979.

Norstad, Lauris, Major General, "Memorandum for Major General L. R. Groves: Subject: Atomic Bomb Production," September 15, 1945, Manhattan Engineering District files, National Archives, Modern Military Branch, Washington D.C.

U.S. Congress, Senate, *Briefing on Counterforce Attacks*, Hearing before the Subcommittee on Arms Control, International Law and Organization of the Committee on Foreign Relations, 93rd Congress, 2nd session, secret hearing held on September 11, 1974, sanitized and made public on January 10, 1975.

————, *Department of Defense Authorization for Appropriations for Fiscal Year 1982*, Hearings before the Committee on Armed Services, Part 7, 97th Congress, 1st session, 1981.

———, *Department of Defense Authorization for Appropriations for Fiscal Year 1983*, Hearings before the Committee on Armed Services, Part 7, 97th Congress, 2nd session, 1982.

———, *Effects of Limited Nuclear Warfare*, Hearings before the Subcommittee on Arms Control, International Organization and Security Agreements of the Committee on Foreign Relations, 94th Congress, 1st session, September 18, 1975.

———, *Nuclear War Strategy*, Hearing before the Committee on Foreign Relations, 96th Congress, 2nd session, September 16, 1980.

———, *U.S.-USSR Strategic Policies*, Hearing before the Subcommittee on Arms Control, International Law and Organization of the Committee on Foreign Relations, 93rd Congress, 2nd session, March 4, 1974.

NINE: Continuity of Government

Interviews

William Baird
William Fehlberg
Harold Gracey
Harry Guinter
Buford Macklin
David Madden
Joseph Mealy
Robert Merchant
Larry Oberg
Richard Pidgeon
John Policastro

Additional interviews were conducted with officials of the following government agencies:

Department of Agriculture
Department of Health and Human Services
Department of Housing and Urban Development
Department of Labor
Federal Emergency Management Agency
Greenfield (Massachusetts) Civil Defense
National Archives
National Oceanic and Atmospheric Administration
New York State Office of Disaster Preparedness

Office of the Federal Register
Office of Personnel Management
Plattsburgh (New York) Office of Civil Defense

Books

Glasstone, Samuel, and Philip J. Dolan, eds., *The Effects of Nuclear Weapons*, Washington, U.S. Department of Defense and the Energy Research and Development Administration, 1977.

Wigner, Eugene P., ed., *Who Speaks for Civil Defense?*, New York, Charles Scribner's Sons, 1968.

Articles

Burt, Richard, "Better Protection of Leaders in War Ordered by Carter," *New York Times*, August 12, 1980.

"The Declaration of Independence and the Constitution of the United States," *Mpulse* (publication of the Mosler Corporation), February 1975.

Haley, Peter J., "In the Event of a National Emergency . . . ," *Federal Register Update*, August 1979.

Lawrence, W. H., "Eisenhower Goes to Secret Center," *New York Times*, June 16, 1955.

Leviero, Anthony, "Mock Martial Law Invoked in Bombing Test Aftermath," *New York Times*, June 17, 1955.

"Mock Crop Order Arouses Farmers," *New York Times*, June 17, 1955.

"New FEMA Symbol," *Emergency Management Newsletter* (FEMA publication), June 25, 1981.

"Second Capital Urged in Atom Era; Underground Plan To Be Broached," *New York Times*, February 20, 1950.

Walters, Robert, "Going Underground," *Inquiry*, February 2, 1981.

Weil, Martin, and Tom Zito, "92 Killed in Virginia Jet Crash," *Washington Post*, December 2, 1974.

Williams, Frank, "Let There Be Truth . . . ," *Journal of Civil Defense*, January-February 1978.

Documents and Reports

Department of Agriculture, "USDA Essential Uninterruptible (Category A) Functions To Be Carried Out by Three Emergency Executive Teams in the Immediate Preattack, Transattack, and Immediate Postattack Periods by Agencies," undated.

370

Department of Health and Human Services, Division of Emergency Coordination, *Emergency Management Team Member's Handbook*, July 1980.

———, "Emergency Preparedness Report, Telephone Alerting Tests, November 3 and 6, 1980," [1980].

Department of Labor, *National Office Alerting Plan*, January 1977.

———, Employment and Training Administration, *Civil Emergency Preparedness*, January 1978.

Department of the Treasury, "A Proposed Presidential Proclamation To Authorize the Secretary To Waive Import Requirements," undated.

———, Bureau of Government Financial Operations, Division of Disbursement, *Emergency Disbursing Plan*, January 1979.

Emergency Planning Committee, *Report to the President: On a Re-examination of Federal Policy With Respect to Emergency Plans and Continuity of Government in the Event of Nuclear Attack on the United States*, June 11, 1962, National Security Files, John F. Kennedy Library, Boston, Massachusetts.

Federal Emergency Management Agency, *Civil Defense Emergency Operations Reporting System*, CPG 2-10/1-8 (eight volumes), June 1978.

———, "Federal Employee Emergency Identification Card Issued," Release 80-47, October 14, 1980.

———, *How To Manage Congregate Lodging Facilities and Fallout Shelters*, SM-11, June 1981.

———, "National Plan for Civil Emergency Management," Draft, 1981.

———, *React User's Guide*, TM-251, September 1980.

———, "Introduction to Nuclear Emergency Operations," Chapter 1 of *FEMA Attack Environment Manual*, June 1980.

———, Region I, "Vital Statistics for Federal Regional Center, Maynard, Massachusetts," undated.

Federal Preparedness Agency, "Federal Preparedness Circular FPC-14: Emergency Succession to Key Positions of Federal Departments and Agencies," December 3, 1976.

———, *Resource Data Catalog*, TM-258, February 1976.

———, *Unclassified Nuclear Case-Lesson Example of 1973 (UNCLEX-73), Volume II, National Survival After UNCLEX-73*, TR-112, November 1978.

General Accounting Office, *Continuity of the Federal Government in a Critical National Emergency—A Neglected Necessity*, April 27, 1978.

Office of Emergency Planning, *The National Plan for Emergency Preparedness*, December 1964.

Office of the Federal Register, *Code of Emergency Federal Regulations*, 1965–1981.

U.S. Congress, *Federal, State, and Local Emergency Preparedness*, Hearings before the Joint Committee on Defense Production, 94th Congress, 2nd session, 1976.

———, Senate, Senator Roth speaking for a bill on Transportation of Certain Persons, S. 1729, *Congressional Record*, October 7, 1981.

U.S. Postal Service, *Emergency Planning Manual*, undated.

Weather Bureau, "Fallout Winds," Part I, Chapter 4 of *Operations Manual*, 1970.

Other

ABC, "Life After Doomsday" segment of "20/20," April 15, 1982.

Giuffrida, Louis, General, address to American Civil Defense Association, Arlington, Virginia, October 9, 1981.

Hilsman, William J., General, "National Security Emergency Preparedness—Joint Planning With Industry," address to Armed Forces Communications and Electronics Association, Washington, June 16, 1982.

TEN: "Comrade, What Is This?"

Interviews

Les Aspin
Leon Gouré

Additional interviews were conducted with officials of the following government agencies:

Arms Control and Disarmament Agency
Defense Civil Preparedness Agency

Books

Freedman, Lawrence, *The Evolution of Nuclear Strategy*, New York, St. Martin's Press, 1981.

Gouré, Leon, *War Survival in Soviet Strategy: USSR Civil Defense*, Monographs in International Affairs, Coral Gables (Florida), Center for Advanced International Studies, University of Miami, 1976.

372

Kahan, Jerome H., *Security in the Nuclear Age*, Washington, Brookings Institution, 1975.

Kaplan, Fred, *Dubious Specter: A Skeptical Look at the Soviet Nuclear Threat*, Washington, Institute for Policy Studies, 1980.

————, *The Wizards of Armageddon*, New York, Simon and Schuster, 1983.

Milovidov, A. S., General-Major, and Colonel V. G. Kozlov, eds., *The Philosophical Heritage of V.I. Lenin and Problems of Contemporary War*, Soviet Military Thought, no. 5, Washington, U.S. Government Printing Office, undated.

Prados, John, *The Soviet Estimate: U.S. Intelligence Analysis and Russian Military Strength*, New York, Dial Press, 1982.

Semyonov, Sergei Nikolayevich, *Meropriyatiya po Grazhdanskoi Oboronye v Pionerskom Lagere*, Moscow, Izdatel'stvo Dosaaf SSSR, 1980.

Shepley, James, and Clay Blair, Jr., *The Hydrogen Bomb: The Men, the Menace, the Mechanism*, New York, David MacKay Co., 1954.

Skirdo, M. P., Colonel, *The People, the Army, the Commander* (translated by Translation Bureau, Secretary of State Department, Ottawa, Canada), Soviet Military Thought, no. 14, Washington, U.S. Government Printing Office, undated.

Soviet Committee for European Security and Cooperation, *The Threat to Europe*, Moscow, Progress Publishers, 1981.

USSR Ministry of Defense, *Whence the Threat to Peace*, Moscow, Military Publishing House, 1982.

U.S. Department of Defense, *Soviet Military Power*, Washington, U.S. Government Printing Office, 1981.

Yegorov, P. T., I. A. Shlyakhov, and N. I. Alabin, *Civil Defense* (translated by Oak Ridge National Laboratory and U.S. Air Force), Soviet Military Thought, no. 10, Washington, U.S. Government Printing Office, undated.

Articles

Alter, Jonathan, "Reagan's Dr. Strangelove," *Washington Monthly*, June 1981.

Altunin, A., General, "The Valuable and Advanced—Into Practice," *Voyennyye Znaniya* (Moscow), October 1978.

Bergmann, David, "PBS Airs Web-Rejected Program on Medical Effects of N-War," *Variety*, October 15, 1982.

Biddle, Wayne, "The Silo Busters," *Harper's*, December 1979.

Burns, John F., "Russians, Too, Joke Sadly on Atom-War Survival," *New York Times*, June 11, 1982.

Burt, Richard, "Brown Admits Aides Distorted MX Issue," *New York Times*, October 5, 1980.

Cockburn, Andrew, "Graphic Evidence ... of Nuclear Confusion," *Columbia Journalism Review*, May/June 1983.

———, "Sure, But What About the Russkies?", *Mother Jones*, September/October 1982.

"Could U.S. Survive First Strike by Soviets?: Exclusive Interview With General George Keegan," *Human Events*, September 24, 1977.

"Do the Russians Ponder Nuclear Victory?", *Public Interest Report* (publication of Federation of American Scientists), October 1980.

Doder, Dusko, "Euromissile May Spur New Soviet Retaliatory Plan," *Washington Post*, November 30, 1982.

Downey, Thomas J., "Against Trident II," *New York Times*, February 11, 1982.

Finney, John W., "Congressional Study Discounts Usefulness of Soviet Civil Defense," *New York Times*, May 17, 1977.

Getler, Michael, "Pershing II Missile: Why It Alarms Soviets," *Washington Post*, March 17, 1982.

Gouré, Leon, and Michael J. Deane, eds., "The Soviet Strategic View," *Strategic Review*, Summer 1981.

Greenfield, Marc, "Life Among the Russians," *New York Times Magazine*, October 24, 1982.

Gwertzman, Bernard, "Reagan Clarifies His Statements on Nuclear War," *New York Times*, October 22, 1981.

Halloran, Richard, "Reagan Drops Mobile MX Plan, Urges Basing Missiles in Silos; Proposes Building B-1 Bomber," *New York Times*, October 3, 1981.

———, "Shift of Strategy on Missile Attack Hinted by Weinberger and Vessey," *New York Times*, May 6, 1983.

———, "Soviet Has Edge, U.S. General Says," *New York Times*, May 12, 1982.

Halloran, Richard, and Leslie Gelb, "CIA Analysts Now Said To Find U.S. Overstated Soviet Arms Rise," *New York Times*, March 3, 1983.

Kaplan, Fred, "The Soviet Civil Defense Myth," *Bulletin of the Atomic Scientists*, March 1978.

Pipes, Richard, "Why the Soviet Union Thinks It Could Fight and Win a Nuclear War," *Commentary*, July 1977.

Rhea, John, "General George Keegan," *Oui*, May 1978.

Roberts, Steven V., "Administration Opens a Drive in Congress for MX," *New York Times*, April 21, 1983.

Robinson, Clarence A., Jr., "Administration Refines MX Basing Plan," *Aviation Week & Space Technology*, May 3, 1982.

————, "USAF Restudies Orbital Basing of MX," *Aviation Week & Space Technology*, April 12, 1982.

Schemmer, Benjamin F., "Pentagon Labors Overtime to Brief President Reagan with Cartoons," *Armed Forces Journal International*, October 1981.

Scott, Harriet Fast, "Civil Defense in the USSR," *Air Force Magazine*, October 1975.

Scott, Robert, and Wendy Silverman, " 'Soviet Military Power'—A Review," *Arms Control Today*, November 1981.

Smith, Hedrick, "MX Panel Proposes Basing 100 Missiles in Minuteman Silos," *New York Times*, April 12, 1983.

Sullivan, Walter, "Scientists Ponder Forcing Asteroids Into Safe Orbits," *New York Times*, January 4, 1983.

"U.S.-Soviet Military Facts," *Defense Monitor*, Vol. XI, no. 6, 1982.

Weisman, Steven R., "Reagan Proposes 'Dense Pack' of 100 MX Missiles in Wyoming; Seeks Arms Pacts With Soviets," *New York Times*, November 23, 1982.

Zuckerman, Edward, "Krieg aus dem Keller," *Playboy Deutschland*, April 1981.

Documents and Reports

Brown, Harold, *Department of Defense Annual Report, Fiscal Year 1980*, January 25, 1979.

————, *Department of Defense Annual Report, Fiscal Year 1981*, January 29, 1980.

————, *Department of Defense Annual Report, Fiscal Year 1982*, January 19, 1981.

Defense Civil Preparedness Agency, "Civil Defense for the 1980's—Current Issues," July 13, 1979.

————, "Recent Documents Relating to Civil Defense Issues," [1977].

Department of Defense, "Major Alternate M-X Basing Concepts," poster, 1981.

————, "Statement on MX and Strategic Force Modernization by the Honorable William J. Perry, Under Secretary of Defense for Research and Engineering, Before the Committee on Foreign Relations of the U.S. Senate," September 12, 1979.

————, Joint Chiefs of Staff, *United States Military Posture for FY 1981*, [1980].

Department of State, "President Reagan: Paths Toward Peace: Deterrence and Arms Control," Current Policy No. 435, November 22, 1982.

————, "Secretary Haig: Arms Control and Strategic Nuclear Forces," Current Policy No. 339, November 4, 1981.

————, "Secretary Shultz: Modernizing U.S. Strategic Forces," Current Policy No. 480, April 20, 1983.

Director of Central Intelligence, *Soviet Civil Defense*, July 1978.

Huntington, Samuel, "Civil Defense for the 1980s," testimony before the Committee on Banking, Housing and Urban Affairs, U.S. Senate, January 8, 1979.

International Physicians for the Prevention of Nuclear War, "The Soviet Response to Medical Efforts for the Prevention of Nuclear War," July 10, 1981.

National Security Council, "Presidential Directive/NSC-41," September 29, 1978.

U.S. Arms Control and Disarmament Agency, *An Analysis of Civil Defense in Nuclear War*, December 1978.

————, *Fiscal Year 1980 Arms Control Impact Statements*, March 1979.

U.S. Congress, House, *Civil Defense Review*, Hearings by the Civil Defense Panel of the Subcommittee on Investigations of the Committee on Armed Services, 94th Congress, 2nd session, 1976.

————, House, Congressman Aspin speaking on civil defense, *Congressional Record*, 96th Congress, 1st session, January 15, 1979.

————, Joint Committee on Defense Production, *Civil Preparedness Review, Part II: Industrial Defense and Nuclear Attack*, 95th Congress, 1st session, April 1977.

————, Senate, *Briefing on Counterforce Attacks*, Hearing before the Subcommittee on Arms Control, International Law and Organization of the Committee on Foreign Relations, 93rd Congress, 2nd session, secret hearing held on September 11, 1974, sanitized and made public on January 10, 1975.

————, *Department of Defense Authorization for Appropriations for Fiscal Year 1980*, Hearings before the Committee on Armed Services, Part 6, 96th Congress, 1st session, 1979.

————, *Nuclear War Strategy*, Hearing before the Committee on Foreign Relations, 96th Congress, 2nd session, September 16, 1980.

————, Senate, *Strategic Weapons Proposals*, Hearings before the Committee on Foreign Relations, Part 1, 97th Congress, 1st session, 1981.

376

———, *U.S.-USSR Strategic Policies*, Hearing before the Subcommittee on Arms Control, International Law and Organization of the Committee on Foreign Relations, 93rd Congress, 2nd session, March 4, 1974.

ELEVEN: **Open for Business**

Interviews

Jim Armstrong
Don Baron
William Baird
Robert Covington
Michael Gingerich
Harry Guinter
Marvin Mothersead
John Nolan
Jerry Smith
Karel Yasko

Additional interviews were conducted with officials of the following corporations and government agencies:

AT&T
Boeing Aerospace Company
Department of Commerce
Department of the Treasury
Exxon Corporation
Federal Emergency Management Agency
Federal Reserve Bank of Kansas City
First National Bank of Boston
Iron Mountain Group, Inc.
Jones & Laughlin Steel Corporation
Roberts Dairy
Shell Oil Company
Underground Vaults & Storage, Inc.

Book

Galbraith, John Kenneth, "Economics of the Arms Race—and After," in *The Final Epidemic: Physicians and Scientists on Nuclear War*, eds. Ruth Adams and Susan Cullen, Chicago, Educational Foundation for Nuclear Science, 1981.

Articles

"A Windowless Building To Cut Fall-Out Hazard," *New York Times*, April 19, 1961.

"Better Security Urged for West Point Opium Depot," *New York Times*, May 18, 1980.

Broad, William J., "Nuclear Pulse (II): Ensuring Delivery of the Doomsday Signal," *Science*, June 5, 1981.

"The Corporation and the Bomb," *Fortune*, December 1958.

"Fed Keeps Hillside Vault," *Washington Post*, February 26, 1976.

"The Government Finds Security Underground," *Information and Records Management*, March 1981.

"H-Bomb Can Wipe Out Any City, Strauss Reports After Tests; U.S. Restudies Plant Dispersal," *New York Times*, April 1, 1954.

Lacayo, Richard, "Preserving the Best of Today's Programming for Tomorrow's Viewers," *New York Times*, October 30, 1983.

Miller, Judith, "U.S. Delays Buying Morphine To Avoid War-Ready Image," *New York Times*, February 14, 1983.

Morris, John D., "U.S. Plans To Freeze Debts and Ration Cash in a Raid," *New York Times*, June 17, 1955.

"Mountain Shields Bomb-Proof Town," *New York Times*, November 10, 1963.

Pear, Robert, "Pentagon Studies Phone Pact's Security Provision," *New York Times*, January 10, 1982.

Rothchild, John H., "Civil Defense: The Case for Nuclear War," *Washington Monthly*, October 1970.

"Weinberger Defends AT&T," *New York Times*, April 9, 1981.

"What H-Bomb Means to Business," *U.S. News & World Report*, April 23, 1954.

"Will U.S. Bank Vaults Resist Atom Bombs? Hiroshima Experience Proves They Do," *American Banker*, July 13, 1946.

Documents and Reports

AT&T, "Netcong: A Vital Communications Link With the World," press release, undated.

———, untitled press release, December 2, 1964.

Board of Governors of the Federal Reserve System, *Preparedness Programs for Emergency Operations in Banking*, undated.

Code of Federal Regulations, Title 44, Chapter 1, Part 320, "Dispersion and Protective Construction: Policy, Criteria, Responsibilities (DMO-1)," 1980.

————, Title 44, Chapter 1, Part 323, "Guidance on Priority Use of Resources in Immediate Post Attack Period (DMO-4)," 1980.

————, Title 47, Chapter 1, Appendix B, "Precedence System for Public Correspondence Services Provided by the Communications Carriers."

Department of Labor, Employment and Training Administration, *Civil Emergency Preparedness*, January 1978.

————, Employment Standards Administration, *Wage and Salary Stabilization Programs in a Postattack Emergency*, March 1981.

Department of the Treasury, "Emergency Tax Proposal for a Post-Attack Economy," 1966–67.

————, "Information Concerning Department of the Treasury Emergency Banking Regulation No. 1," August 27, 1979.

————, "Review of Treasury Emergency Planning Documents," Memorandum to William J. Beckham, Jr., from Daniel H. Brill, November 14, 1977.

————, "Standby Instructions and Authorizations Issued to Federal Reserve Banks and the Board of Governors of the Federal Reserve System To Perform Essential Fiscal Functions," May 13, 1977.

Exxon Corporation, *Bylaws*, May 17, 1979.

Federal Emergency Management Agency, *Disaster Planning Guide for Business and Industry*, CPG 2-5, July 1978.

————, "FEMA Seeks Candidates for National Defense Executive Reserve Program," Release 82-24, March 31, 1982.

————, *Implications of Organizational Relocation to FEMA Programs and to the Preservation of United States Industrial Capability*, M&R-5, vol. 2, April 1981.

————, "National Plan for Civil Emergency Management," draft, April 1981.

————, "Preparedness Program and Training Guide for Emergency Economic Measures (Stabilization) for National Security Emergencies," [1980].

————, *Stockpile Report to the Congress, October 1980 - March 1981*, November 1981.

Federal Reserve Bank of Kansas City, *Emergency Operating Letters and Bulletins*, December 16, 1974.

First National Bank of Boston, "Underground Records Storage Center," undated.

Foster, Richard B., with Francis Hoeber, *Survival, Reconstitution and Recovery: U.S.-Soviet Asymmetries and U.S. Policy Options*, prepared for Federal Emergency Management Agency, contract DCPA01-78-C-0308, Arlington (Virginia), SRI International Strategic Studies Center, February 1980.

Greene, Jack C., Robert W. Stokley, and John K. Christian, *Recovery from Nuclear Attack and Research and Action Programs to Enhance Recovery Prospects*, prepared for Federal Emergency Management Agency, contract DCPA01-78-C-0270, Washington, International Center for Emergency Preparedness, December 1979.

IBM, *Bylaws*, April 27, 1981.

Miller, John M., I. James Carney, Paul J. Parham, and George R. Pederson, *Prepare and Evaluate an Organizational Relocation Plan*, prepared for Federal Emergency Management Agency, contract DCPA01-79-C-0218, Seattle, Boeing Aerospace Company, April 1980.

Mosler Safe Co., "History of Mosler," special issue of *Mpulse*, [1973].

National Security Council, "Presidential Directive/NSC-53," November 15, 1979.

Office of Emergency Planning, *The National Plan for Emergency Preparedness*, December 1964.

————, *Ration Board Instructions for Postattack Consumer Rationing*, June 1965.

Shell Oil Company, "Emergency Head Office To Be Developed," Head Office Management Letter, no. 625, March 3, 1965.

U.S. Congress, *Defense Industrial Base: New Stockpile Objectives*, Hearings before the Joint Committee on Defense Production, Part III, 94th Congress, 2nd session, November 24, 1976.

————, *Federal, State, and Local Emergency Preparedness*, Hearings before the Joint Committee on Defense Production, 94th Congress, 2nd session, 1976.

Other

Carswell, Bruce, "Communications for Emergency Mobilization From a Human Resources Point of View," address to Armed Forces Communications and Electronics Association, Washington, June 16, 1982.

Hilsman, William J., General, "National Security Emergency Preparedness—Joint Planning With Industry," address to Armed Forces Communications and Electronics Association, Washington, June 16, 1982.

TWELVE: **The Day After World War III**

Interviews

Donald Bettge
Cresson Kearny
Tom Kennedy
Armando De La Paz
James Holton
David Madden

Additional interviews were conducted with officials of the following agencies and organizations:

Defense Nuclear Agency
Federal Emergency Management Agency
International Physicians for the Prevention of Nuclear War
Performing Artists for Nuclear Disarmament
Public Health Service
White Sands Missile Range

Books

Caldicott, Helen, *Nuclear Madness*, New York, Bantam Books, 1980.

Feld, Bernard T., "Mechanics of Fallout," in *The Final Epidemic: Physicians and Scientists on Nuclear War*, eds. Ruth Adams and Susan Cullen, Chicago, Educational Foundation for Nuclear Science, 1981.

Finch, Stuart C., "Occurrence of Cancer in Atomic Bomb Survivors," in *The Final Epidemic*.

Geiger, H. Jack, "Illusion of Survival," in *The Final Epidemic*.

Glasstone, Samuel, and Philip J. Dolan, eds., *The Effects of Nuclear Weapons*, Washington, U.S. Department of Defense and the Energy Research and Development Administration, 1977.

Herken, Gregg, *The Winning Weapon: The Atomic Bomb in the Cold War 1945-1950*, New York, Alfred A. Knopf, 1980.

Kearny, Cresson H., *Nuclear War Survival Skills*, Oak Ridge (Tennessee), Oak Ridge National Laboratory, 1979. (Reprint ed., Boston (Virginia), American Security Council Education Foundation, undated.)

Kissinger, Henry A., *Nuclear Weapons and Foreign Policy*, New York, Harper & Brothers (for the Council on Foreign Relations), 1957.

Scheer, Robert, *With Enough Shovels: Reagan, Bush & Nuclear War*, New York, Random House, 1982.

381

Schell, Jonathan, *The Fate of the Earth*, New York, Alfred A. Knopf, 1982.

Sternglass, Ernest, *Secret Fallout: Low-Level Radiation From Hiroshima to Three-Mile Island*, New York, McGraw-Hill, 1981.

Articles

Abrams, Herbert L., "Surviving a Nuclear War Is Hardly Surviving," *New York Times*, February 27, 1983.

"Better Dead Than Red?", *Nuclear Times*, June 1983.

"Blast Tests Missile Components," *New York Times*, November 1, 1980.

Boffey, Philip M., "Nuclear War: Federation Disputes Academy on How Bad Effects Would Be," *Science*, October 17, 1975.

————, "Radiation Risk May Be Higher Than Thought," *New York Times*, July 26, 1983.

Briggs, Kenneth A., "Bishops Endorse Stand Opposed to Nuclear War," *New York Times*, May 4, 1983.

"British Prove Capability of New Missile," *Aviation Week & Space Technology*, May 17, 1982.

Butterfield, Fox, "Professional Groups Flocking to Antinuclear Drive," *New York Times*, March 27, 1982.

Chipman, William K., and B. Wayne Blanchard, "Civil Defense and the Medical Consequences of Nuclear War," *Emergency Management* (publication of the Federal Emergency Management Agency), Spring 1981.

Clayton, Bruce, "Nuclear Nonsense: Dispelling 'Doomie' Myths," *Survive*, fall 1981 and winter 1981.

Cockburn, Alexander, and James Ridgeway, "Bomb Porn and the Apocalypse: Will the Freeze Movement Be More Than a Fad?", *Village Voice*, April 13, 1982.

"DDP Activities on Upswing," *Journal of Civil Defense*, June 1983.

Dyke, Peter D., "Integrated Emergency Management System—Deceit or Incompetence?", *The Front Line*, September 1983.

Ehrlich, Paul R., *et al.*, "Long-Term Biological Consequences of Nuclear War, *Science*, December 23, 1983.

"Excerpts From Farewell Testimony by Rickover to Congress," *New York Times*, January 30, 1982.

"FAS Petition Campaign," *Bulletin of the Atomic Scientists*, June 1982.

382

Fenyvesi, Charles, "The Man Not Worried by the Bomb," *Washington Post*, April 11, 1982.

Flora, Whitt, "Congress Okays Strategic Weapon Plan," *Aviation Week & Space Technology*, November 28, 1983.

"FY 1983: A CD Liftoff? Interview With FEMA Director General Louis O. Giuffrida," *Journal of Civil Defense*, April 1982.

" 'Generals for Peace' Push Case at U.N.," *New York Times*, June 27, 1982.

Giuffrida, Louis O., "Building a Strong National System for Emergency Management," *Emergency Management Newsletter* (publication of the Federal Emergency Management Agency), July 1983.

Gray, Colin S., "Chacun à son gout," *Bulletin of the Atomic Scientists*, June/July 1981.

———, "Issues and Non-Issues in the Nuclear Policy Debate," *Bulletin of the Atomic Scientists*, December 1981.

Haaland, Carsten M., "Nuclear Winter and National Security," *Journal of Civil Defense,* February 1984.

Halloran, Richard, "Reagan Reported Seeking a Big Rise in Nuclear Funds," *New York Times*, January 9, 1983.

Herman, Robin, "Anti-Nuclear Groups Are Using Professions as Rallying Points," *New York Times*, June 5, 1982.

Kendall, John, "Opposition to Nuclear Evacuation Plan Grows," *Los Angeles Times*, August 9, 1982.

Mack, John E., "Psychosocial Effects of the Nuclear Arms Race," *Bulletin of the Atomic Scientists*, April 1981.

Maitland, Leslie, "FBI Rules Out Russian Control of Freeze Drive," *New York Times*, March 26, 1983.

Martin, Brian, "Critique of Nuclear Extinction," *Journal of Peace Research*, Vol. XIX, no. 4, 1982.

Miller, Judith, "Reagan Endorses Rise in Atomic Warheads by 380 Over Carter Goal," *New York Times*, March 21, 1982.

———, "U.S. Confirms a Plan To Halt Talks on a Nuclear Test Ban," *New York Times*, July 21, 1982.

"The Nuclear Joke," *New York Times*, April 26, 1983.

Oberdorfer, Don, "Plan Approved To Move Citizens in War Threat," *Washington Post*, March 30, 1982.

Pear, Robert, "Foreign Agents Linked to Freeze, Reagan Says," *New York Times*, November 12, 1982.

"President Says Foes of U.S. Have Duped Arms Freeze Group," *New York Times*, October 5, 1982.

Prochnau, Bill, "Doomsday Fears, Once Submerged, Rise to a Renewed Crest," *Washington Post*, April 26, 1982.

"Reagan Budget Request for 1983 Calls for Revitalized Civil Defense Program," *Emergency Management Newsletter* (publication of the Federal Emergency Management Agency), March 29, 1982.

Rosellini, Lynn, "Victory Is Bittersweet for Architect of Amendment's Defeat," *New York Times*, July 1, 1982.

Sagan, Carl, "The Nuclear Winter," *Parade*, October 30, 1983.

Shribman, David, "House Approves Altered Version of Arms Freeze," *New York Times*, May 5, 1983.

Silberner, Joanne, "Hiroshima & Nagasaki," *Science News*, October 31, 1981.

Strope, Jerry, "Capital Commentary," *Journal of Civil Defense*, December 1983.

Sullivan, Walter, "New Atom Bomb Data Hint Greater Radiation Risk," *New York Times*, May 16, 1981.

Sussman, Barry, and Robert G. Kaiser, "Survey Finds 3-to-1 Backing for A-Freeze," *Washington Post*, April 29, 1982.

Teller, Edward, "Dangerous Myths About Nuclear Arms," *Reader's Digest*, November 1982.

Turco, R. P., O. B. Toon, T. P. Ackerman, J. B. Pollack, and Carl Sagan, "Nuclear Winter: Global Consequences of Multiple Nuclear Explosions," *Science*, December 23, 1983.

Turner, Wallace, "Atom Arms Testing Will Be Continued, Cabinet Officer Says," *New York Times*, August 6, 1982.

"U.S. Atom Arms Tests at a Post-1970 Record," *New York Times*, October 24, 1982.

"Weinberger Drops Disputed Words in Revision of '82 Arms Proposal," *New York Times*, March 18, 1983.

" '82: The Freeze," *The Nation*, November 13, 1982.

Documents and Reports

Berger, Howard M., *A Critical Review of Studies of Survival and Recovery After a Large-Scale Nuclear Attack*, prepared for Defense Nuclear Agency, contract DNA001-78-C-0009, Marina del Rey (California), R&D Associates, December 1978.

Committee To Study the Long-Term Worldwide Effects of Multiple Nuclear-Weapons Detonations, *Long-Term Worldwide Effects of Multiple Nuclear-Weapons Detonations*, Washington, National Academy of Sciences, 1975.

Defense Civil Preparedness Agency, "Research Report on Recovery From Nuclear Attack," Information Bulletin No. 307, May 10, 1979.

Defense Nuclear Agency, "Mill Race Information Brochure," 1981.

Federal Emergency Management Agency, "Backgrounder: Civil Defense Surveys," Release 82-64, July 21, 1982.

———, "Backgrounder: Results of Second Gallup Civil Defense Survey," Release 82-88, October 18, 1982.

———, "Backgrounder: Results of Third Gallup Civil Defense Survey," Release 82-100, December 28, 1982.

———, *Camera-Ready Newspaper Columns*, P&P-5, December 1980.

———, "Can America's Industry Survive a Nuclear Attack?", by Russell B. Clanahan, For the Record No. 2, December 1980.

———, *Civil Defense and the Public: An Overview of Public Attitude Studies*, MP-62, September 1979.

———, " 'For Want of a Nail . . .': The Vital Role of Scarce Materials in America's Future," by Paul K. Krueger, For the Record No. 4, May 1981.

———, "President Reagan Directs Implementation of Seven-Year Civil Defense Program," Release 82-26, March 30, 1982.

Foster, Richard B., with Francis Hoeber, *Survival, Reconstitution and Recovery: U.S.-Soviet Asymmetries and U.S. Policy Options*, prepared for Federal Emergency Management Agency, contract DCPA01-78-C-0308, Arlington (Virginia), SRI International Strategic Studies Center, February 1980.

Greene, Jack C., Robert W. Stokley, and John K. Christian, *Recovery From Nuclear Attack and Research and Action Programs To Enhance Recovery Prospects*, prepared for Federal Emergency Management Agency, contract DCPA01-78-C-0270, Washington, International Center for Emergency Preparedness, 1979.

Haaland, Carsten M., Conrad V. Chester and Eugene P. Wigner, *Survival of the Relocated Population of the U.S. After a Nuclear Attack*, prepared for Defense Civil Preparedness Agency, contract 01-74-C-0227, Oak Ridge (Tennessee), Oak Ridge National Laboratory, 1976.

International Physicians for the Prevention of Nuclear War, "Media Notice: Organizational Principles," undated.

———, "Proceedings of the First Congress of the International Physicians for the Prevention of Nuclear War, Airlie, Virginia, March 20-25, 1981."

Kearny, Cresson H., and Conrad V. Chester, *Blast Tests of Expedient Shelters in the Dice Throw Event*, Oak Ridge (Tennessee), Oak Ridge National Laboratory, 1978.

Kearny, Cresson H., Conrad V. Chester and Edwin N. York, *Blast Tests of Expedient Shelters in the Miser's Bluff Event*, Oak Ridge (Tennessee), Oak Ridge National Laboratory, 1980.

Office of Civil Defense, *Postattack Recovery From Nuclear War*, Proceedings of the Symposium Held at Fort Monroe, Virginia, 1967.

Physicians for Social Responsibility, "The Medical Aspects of Nuclear War," undated.

Reagan, Ronald, "Memorandum for the Vice President [and thirty-three other officials], Subject: Emergency Mobilization Preparedness Board," December 17, 1981.

Russel, J. W., and E. N. York, *Expedient Industrial Protection Against Nuclear Attack*, Washington, Federal Emergency Management Agency, 1981.

Sullivan, Roger J., Winder M. Heller, and E. C. Aldridge, Jr., *Candidate U.S. Civil Defense Programs*, prepared for Defense Civil Preparedness Agency, contract 01-77-C-0219, Arlington (Virginia), System Planning Corporation, March 1978.

Tansley, R. S., and J. V. Zaccor, *Testing of Shelter Design and Industrial Hardening Concepts at the Mill Race Event*, prepared for Federal Emergency Management Agency, contract EMW-C-0611, Redwood City (California), Scientific Service Inc., 1982.

U.S. Arms Control and Disarmament Agency, "An Assessment of Frequently Neglected Effects in Nuclear Attacks," ACDA Civil Defense Study Report No. 5, April 19, 1978.

———, "Effects of Nuclear War," April 1979.

———, *Worldwide Effects of Nuclear War . . . Some Perspectives*, [1975].

U.S. Congress, House, *Civil Defense Review*, Hearings by the Civil Defense Panel of the Subcommittee on Investigations of the Committee on Armed Services, 94th Congress, 2nd session, 1976.

———, Joint Committee on Defense Production, *Civil Preparedness Review, Part II: Industrial Defense and Nuclear Attack*, 95th Congress, 1st session, April 1977.

———, Office of Technology Assessment, *The Effects of Nuclear War*, 1979.

———, Senate, Committee on Banking, Housing and Urban Affairs, *Economic and Social Consequences of Nuclear Attacks on the United States*, 96th Congress, 1st session, March 1979.

Other

ABC, "Life After Doomsday" segment of "20/20," April 15, 1982.

Giuffrida, Louis, General, address to American Civil Defense Association, Arlington, Virginia, October 9, 1981.

Graham, Daniel, General, address to American Civil Defense Association, Arlington, Virginia, October 9, 1981.

Perle, Richard, testimony before Subcommittee on Arms Control, Foreign Relations Committee, U.S. Senate, March 31, 1982.

Tsongas, Paul, Senator, remarks before Subcommittee on Arms Control, Foreign Relations Committee, U.S. Senate, March 16, 1982.

THIRTEEN: The Day Before World War IV

Interviews

Colonel Robert Gifford
Major Norwood Jennings
Bob O'Brien
Daniel Payton
Keith Peterson

Additional interviews were conducted with officers of the Strategic Air Command.

Book

Freedman, Lawrence, *The Evolution of Nuclear Strategy*, New York, St. Martin's Press, 1981.

Articles

Anderson, Jack, "Not-So-New Nuclear Strategy," *Washington Post*, October 12, 1980.

Ball, Desmond, "U.S. Strategic Forces: How Would They Be Used?", *International Security*, Winter 1982/83.

Clines, Francis X., "Reagan Backs Better Emergency Links with Soviet," *New York Times*, May 25, 1983.

Fisher, Roger, "Thinking About War," *New York Times*, May 7, 1980.

Flora, Whitt, "Congress Okays Strategic Weapon Plan," *Aviation Week & Space Technology*, November 28, 1983.

Halloran, Richard, "New Weinberger Directive Refines Military Policy," *New York Times*, March 22, 1983.

———, "Weinberger Angered by Reports on War Strategy," *New York Times*, August 23, 1982.

Kaplan, Mark, "U.S. Cruise Missile Programs," *Arms Control Today*, May 1983.

Mossberg, Walter S., "Fighting a Nuclear War," *Wall Street Journal*, August 27, 1980.

Nitze, Paul, "Atoms, Strategy and Policy," *Foreign Affairs*, January 1956.

Nunn, Jack H., "Termination: The Myth of the Short, Decisive Nuclear War," *Parameters* (journal of the U.S. Army War College), December 1980.

Paine, Christopher, "Nuclear Combat: the Five-Year Defense Plan," *Bulletin of the Atomic Scientists*, November 1982.

———, "Reagatomics, or How To 'Prevail,'" *Nation*, April 9, 1983.

Powers, Commander Robert C., "Escalation Control," *U.S. Naval Institute Proceedings*, January 1980.

Rosenbaum, Ron, "The Subterranean World of the Bomb," *Harper's*, March 1978.

"Senate Rejects Surrender Fund," *New York Times*, August 16, 1958.

Documents and Reports

Addington, Lloyd B., "Postattack Viability of the United States—1975," in *Postattack Recovery From Nuclear War*, Proceedings of the Symposium held at Fort Monroe, Virginia, Office of Civil Defense, 1967.

Brown, Harold, *Department of Defense Annual Report, Fiscal Year 1982*, January 19, 1981.

Brown, William M., and Doris Yokelson, *Postattack Recovery Strategies*, prepared for Federal Emergency Management Agency, contract DCPA01-79-C-0217, Croton-on-Hudson (New York), Hudson Institute, November 1980.

Center for Defense Information, "Recent Reagan Administration References to Nuclear War-Fighting and Winning," January 21, 1982.

Congressional Budget Office, *Counterforce Issues for the U.S. Strategic Nuclear Forces*, January 1978.

Defense Civil Preparedness Agency, "Post-Nuclear Attack Study (PONAST II)," unclassified briefing charts, 1973.

Department of Defense, Joint Chiefs of Staff, *United States Military Posture for FY 1983*, [1982].

Foster, Richard B., *The Soviet Concept of National Entity Survival*, prepared for Office of the Assistant Secretary of Defense, International Security Affairs, contract MDA903-78-M-3207, Arlington (Virginia), SRI International Strategic Studies Center, March 1978.

Foster, Richard B., with Francis Hoeber, *Survival, Reconstitution and Recovery: U.S.-Soviet Asymmetries and U.S. Policy Options*, prepared for Federal Emergency Management Agency, contract DCPA01-78-C-0308, Arlington (Virginia), SRI International Strategic Studies Center, February 1980.

Joint Chiefs of Staff to Senator William Proxmire, letter, January 28, 1977, in *Congressional Record* (Senate), January 31, 1977.

Rumsfeld, Donald H., *Department of Defense Annual Report, Fiscal Year 1978*, January 1977.

Sullivan, Leonard, Jr., and W. Scott Payne, *Conceptual Framework for FEMA Mobilization and Resource Management Research*, prepared for Federal Emergency Management Agency, contract DCPA01-78-C-0274, Arlington (Virginia), System Planning Corporation, March 1981.

U.S. Congress, Office of Technology Assessment, *The Effects of Nuclear War*, 1979.

————, Senate, *Department of Defense Authorization for Appropriations for Fiscal Year 1980*, Hearings before the Committee on Armed Services, Part 6, 96th Congress, 1st session, 1979.

————, *Department of Defense Authorization for Appropriations for Fiscal Year 1982*, Hearings before the Committee on Armed Services, Part 7, 97th Congress, 1st session, 1981.

————, *U.S.-USSR Strategic Policies*, Hearing before the Subcommittee on Arms Control, International Organizations and Security Agreements of the Committee on Foreign Relations, 93rd Congress, 2nd session, March 4, 1974.

Weinberger, Caspar W., *Annual Report to the Congress, Fiscal Year 1983*, February 1982.

Other

Ball, Desmond, *Can Nuclear War Be Controlled?*, Adelphi Papers, no. 169, London, International Institute for Strategic Studies, 1981.

Index

ABC News, 302
abortions, incidence of, 310
Abrams, Herbert, 323
accidents, 151*n*, 155
Addington, Lloyd, 340
Afghanistan, Soviet invasion of, 50, 261
Agriculture, Department of:
  emergency management, 221–22, 236
  food supply and rationing, 9–12
  labor management, 11–12
Airborne Launch Control Center, 150, 160
aircraft shielding, 156–57, 162
Alaska warning systems, 45, 61
alert operation, 215
Allied Forces Central Europe, 52
Alternate National Military Command Center, 44
Alternate National Warning System, 112–13, 212
Alternate Reconstitution Base, 55
Altunin, A., 254–55
American Banker, 274
American Telephone & Telegraph Corporation (AT&T), 273–74, 277–81
Anderson, J. Edward, 264–65
Andrews Air Force Base, Maryland, 57

animals:
  fallout effects on, 78, 89, 299–300, 306, 311, 330
  food allowances, 10–11
  safeguarding, 282
antimissile systems, 194, 205–206, 262–72
antinuclear movement, 71, 95, 126, 245, 295, 301, 304–305, 313–24
Armed Forces Journal International, 259*n*
Arms Control Association, 261
Arms Control and Disarmament Agency (ACDA), 145, 252–53, 271, 309
Armstrong, Jim, 280–81
Army, United States:
  atomic bomb, attitude toward, 35, 73, 183
  civil defense mission, 140
  on fallout hazard, 91
  on radioactivity effects, 68–69
Army Air Forces, United States, 43, 181–82
Arnold, Henry, H., 72, 177, 181
Arnold, James, 81*n*
artillery, nuclear, 48–49, 52–53, 151
art collections. *See* cultural resources
Aspin, Les, 253–54
assured destruction concept, 195–96, 202–204

Aston, F. W., 28
atomic bomb (*see also* hydrogen
    bomb; nuclear war; nuclear
    weapons; radioactivity):
  casualties from, 43, 78, 128
  chain reaction in, 1, 27–34, 41–42
  control proposed, 76–77
  development, 15–16, 27, 30–31
  explosive power, 42
  fallout from. *See* fallout effects
  first explosion, 15, 41–42, 324
  implications foreseen, 21–23
  jokes about, 70–71
  public attitude toward, 78
  radioactivity from. *See* radioac-
    tivity
  security measures on, 16, 34, 36
  size limits, 79
  songs about, 72
  stockpile needs estimates, 43,
    181–83
  tests, 77–78
  warfare revolutionized by, 72–73
atomic energy:
  peacetime uses foreseen, 72–73
  research in, 16–29
Atomic Energy Commission, 79–80,
    88–91
attack, detection and response to,
    44–48, 55–65, 149–75, 213–14,
    248, 265, 272, 278

B-1 bomber, 315
B-29 bomber, 35, 42–43
B-52 bomber, 154, 156–57, 161–62,
    325
Baez, Ed, 108
Bainbridge, Kenneth, 41–42
Baird, William:
  on government continuity, 215
  on mail service, 221
  and president's safety, 63
  on presidential succession, 217
  on resources control, 284
  on warning system failure, 63
Baker, Charlie, 33n
Baker, James, 56

Baker, Russell, 233n
Baldrige, Malcolm, 64
Ball, Desmond, 196
Ballistic Missile Early Warning Sys-
    tem, 45, 61
banking services, 109, 275–77, 288
Barksdale Air Force Base, Louisi-
    ana, 156
"barn" defined, 33n
Baron, Don, 280
Batscha, Robert, 293n
"beach" defined, 301
Belgium, and uranium supply,
    26–27
Ball, T. H., 56
Bedminster, New Jersey, 273–74
Bendix Corporation, 280
Berlin crisis, 137
Bethe, Hans, 30, 81, 85, 93
Bettge, Donald, 327
Bikini atoll tests, 77–78, 84, 181
blackmail, potential for, 264–66
Blanchard, Wayne, 321
Boeing Aerospace Company, 282,
    326–27
Bohr, Niels, 29
Bradley, Omar, 78
Brezhnev, Leonid, 242–45
Britain. *See* United Kingdom
Brown, Harold:
  on antimissile missiles, 263
  on civil defense funding, 146
  on communications, 279
  on deterrence, 199–200, 203
  on escalation, 163, 168
  on government continuity, 217
  on lay strategists, 208
  on MX missile, 266, 269–70
  on limited attack, 180, 200, 207,
    243, 265
  on Soviet view, 240, 246–47, 266
  on strategic superiority, 261
  on tactical missiles, 152
  on target selection, 165–66
  on terminating war, 332, 334, 336
  on time factor in response, 61
Brzezinski, Zbigniew, 63, 127

Bulletin of the Atomic Scientists, 128
Bundy, McGeorge, 136
Bush, George, 315
Butler family, 6–7, 9
Byrnes, James, 36, 38–39

Caldicott, Helen, 95, 126, 301, 304, 323
cancer, incidence of, 11, 297–98, 310–11
Carey Salt Mine, 289–90
Caswell, Bruce, 281
Carte Blanche exercise, 189–90
Carter, Jimmy:
    on cities evacuation, 144, 147, 257
    and civil defense, 145–46, 257
    code security, 58
    and communications, 201, 278
    deterrence policy, 200, 240
    on E-4 aircraft, 62
    on government continuity, 233
    and limited attacks, 164, 201, 207
    and missiles deployment, 60
    on MX missile, 267, 269–71
    on nuclear submarines, 153
    on survival, 128
    and targets in Soviet, 339
    and weapons modernization, 202
Carter, Powell, 202
Case, Clifford, 199
casualties, reported and estimated, 43, 78, 128, 131, 133, 145, 181, 186*n*, 190, 195, 199–200, 214, 251, 264, 303, 309–10
Cavendish Laboratory, 20–21
Central Army Group, 52
Central Locator System, 55–57, 64, 217
Chadwick, James, 20
chaplains, training of, 196
Chazov, Yevgeny, 245*n*
Chester, Conrad, 11, 127–28, 302
Cheyenne Mountain, Colorado, 44, 112
Chicago civil defense, 131
China, liaison with proposed, 40

Chipman, William, 321
Christian, Linda, 71
Churchill, Winston, 178
cigarette industry, 11
cities:
    communal dispersion, 130
    evacuating, 8–9, 97–115, 130, 133–34, 144–47, 257
Civil Defense (Soviet textbook), 249–50
civil defense:
    decline in interest, 279
    as deterrent, 98–99, 103–104
    funding, 131, 134, 141, 147, 206
    local government missions, 229
    national organization, 131–32, 134
    parody on, 141
    polls on, 319
Civil Defense Corps, 131
civil liberties, assuring, 216
Clanahan, Russell, 102
Clausewitz, Karl von, 244
Clayton, Bruce, 322
clergymen, 71, 138
climate, effect of nuclear weapons on, 313
Coalition for Peace Through Strength, 145
Coast Guard, United States, 113
cobalt bomb development, 86, 95
Cockburn, Alexander, 322
Cockroft, John, 20
Code of Emergency Federal Regulation, 236
Coldwell, Philip, 286
Columbia Records, 82
Columbia University, 28–29
Command, Control, and Communications (C^3), 4–5, 38–40, 46, 62, 144, 156, 158–60, 170–74, 193–94, 196, 201, 206, 274–79, 290–91, 331, 335–38
command post, airborne. *See* National Emergency Airborne Command Post

communications systems. *See* Command, Control, and Communications

Compton, Arthur Holly, 29–30, 40

computer failures, 4

Concrete, North Dakota, 45, 61

Congress, safety of, 217

Congressional Budget Office, 203

Continental Airborne Reconnaissance and Damage Assessment, 170

corporations. *See* industry

Covington, Robert, 286

Crisis Relocation Planning (CRP), 98, 103, 110

Cronkite, Walter, 217n

Cuban missile crisis (1962), 139, 258

cultural resources, preservation of, 292–94

currency supply and control, 286–89, 341

damage assessment and control, 170, 172–75, 206, 211–13

Davis, Bennie, 206–207

Davis, James, 167–69, 175

Davy Crockett bazooka, 48

De la Paz, Armando, 325

de Seversky, Alexander P., 75

dead, identification and disposal of, 7–8, 122–23, 142, 228

deception measures, 47

Decision Information Distribution System, 114

decoy missiles, 267–68

Defense, Department of:
  on antimissile missiles, 263
  casualties estimates, 199
  civil defense budget, 147
  civil defense missions, 139
  dispersal proposed, 78–79
  on economic recovery, 342
  emergency management team, 226
  missiles design policy, 60
  response timing policy, 61
  and shelters, 139–40

  on Soviet armed forces strength, 260
  on weapons purpose, 202

Defense Civil Preparedness Agency (DCPA), 102, 104–105, 142–43, 147, 252, 255

Defense Nuclear Agency, 307, 324–30

Defense Production Act (1950), 275, 285

dentists. *See* medical services

Dickey, John, 108–109

Dinneen, Gerald, 57

Disaster Planning Guide for Business and Industry, 281

displaced persons, relocating, 8–9, 106–12, 144–47, 226–27

Doctors for Defense Preparedness, 322

dose effectiveness, 51–52

drills, 276

Dropshot Plan, 183–84

Dulles, John Foster, 71, 135, 146, 187–88

E-4 aircraft, 62

Eastman Kodak Company, 90n

ecology, effects on, 310–11, 313–14. *See also* animals

economy, recovery of, 13, 283–92, 293n, 307, 340–42

Effects of Nuclear War, 332

Effects of Nuclear Weapons, 296

Einstein, Albert:
  and atomic bomb development, 27
  energy formula, 18
  and hydrogen bomb development, 81
  on inducing radioactivity, 24–25
  and uranium supply, 26–27

Eisenhower, Dwight, D.:
  on atomic bomb smuggling, 83
  and bomb-drop decision, 37
  in civil-defense test, 133–34
  on conventional forces, 183
  on deterrence value, 178

and fallout threat, 83–84
and government continuity, 215–16
and hydrogen bomb development, 81–82
on limited attacks, 192–93
and neutron bomb, 93–94
and nuclear war threat, 186–88
on shelters, 134–35
on survival, 128
on tactical missiles, 48, 188–89
and tests ban, 87–88
electromagnetic pulse (EMP), 106n, 169, 171, 273, 281, 335
Ellsberg, Daniel, 192
Ellis, Richard, 168, 170, 175
Elugelab hydrogen bomb test, 82
Emergency Broadcast System, 5, 59, 113
Emergency Federal Register, 237
Emergency Management Team Member's Handbook, 218, 222, 232–33
Emergency Minerals Administration, 284–85
Emergency Operating Centers (EOCs), 228–30
Board, 315
Emergency Rocket Communications System, 159, 170, 338
Emergency Solid Fuels Administration, 284–85
enemy aliens internment, 234
Energy, Department of, 284
England. See United Kingdom
escalation control concept, 163–64
Esquire, 139
Evans, Melvin, 57
Exxon Company, 282–83

F-86 aircraft, 325
fallout effects, 83–86, 88–91, 118
false alerts, 45–46, 60
farmers:
equipment replacement, 10

loans to, 236
seed and fertilizers supply, 10–11
Farrell, Thomas, 42, 75
Fate of the Earth (Schell), 299–301
FB-111 aircraft, 154, 161
Federal Aviation Adminstration, 113
Federal Bureau of Investigation, 58, 83, 205
Federal Civil Defense Act (1950), 131
Federal Civil Defense Administration (FCDA), 131–33, 275
Federal Communication Commission, 279n
Federal Council of Churches of Christ in America, 71
Federal Emergency Management Agency (FEMA) (see also Central Locator System; Giuffrida, Louis):
and antinuclear movement, 318–21
basic operating situations, 231–32
computer services, 211–14
on corporate planning, 281–82
on displaced persons, 107–11
on economy restoration, 286
and emergency centers, 224
and emergency orders, 1–2
evacuation plans, 98–102, 104, 106
food supply and control, 108–109, 284
and freeze program, 283
identification cards, 225
on nuclear weapons effects, 295, 305, 310n
planning guidance, 220
radioactivity detection, 118–19
and resources control, 284
on shelters construction and management, 117, 119–24
on survival, 143–44, 301–304, 320
and traffic control, 110
warning system, 112–15

Federal Preparedness Agency, 220, 331
Federal Regional Center, 212
Federal Reserve Bank of Kansas City, 289–92
Federal Reserve System, 226, 286, 288–89
Federal Trade Commission, 138n
Federal of (Atomic) American Scientists, 75, 77, 312–13, 317
Fehlberg, William, 212, 214
Feld Bernard, 301
Fermi, Enrico:
  and allies, liaison with, 40
  in atomic energy research, 24–25, 27
  chain reaction, concern over, 15–16, 42
  and hydrogen bomb development, 80
fertilizers, supply of, 11
films on civil defense, 100–104, 129
First National Bank of Boston, 276
first-strike fears, 60, 145–46, 264–65, 271–72
Fisher, Roger, 59n, 337n
flexible response concept, 49–50, 192–94
Flory, Robert, 329
food:
  for farm animals, 11
  supply and control, 12, 108–10, 121–22, 140, 213, 215, 221, 228, 236, 284, 287, 307–309
Ford, Gerald, 58, 169
Fort Ritchie, Maryland, 44
Fortune, 277
France, 24, 26, 40, 52
Franck (James) Report, 38, 40, 126
free enterprise preservation, 293n
freeze orders, 1, 110, 234, 283–84
Freedman, Lawrence, 208
Fuchs, Klaus, 195n
fuels supply and control, 284–85

Fukuryu Maru (Lucky Dragon) incident, 84, 86–88
Fulbright, J. William, 64, 198

Gaither Committee, 134
Gallup Poll on tests ban, 94
Galbraith, John Kenneth, 293
Gallery, Daniel, 186
Gavin, James, 85
Gay, Harold, 9–10
Geiger, H. Jack, 323
Geiger counter, 70, 84
General Accounting Office, 155, 175, 226
General Services Administration, 292–93
General Telephone & Electronics, 281
Germany, atomic research in, 15, 21–22, 24–26, 31, 35, 37
Gifford, Robert, 166–67, 174, 333
Gingerich, Michael, 292
Giuffrida, Louis (see also Federal Emergency Management Agency):
  on cities evacuation, 105, 316
  on government continuity, 234
  and identification cards, 225
  on nuclear weapons effects, 319
  on presidential succession, 65
  and war plans, 13–14
  on warning systems, 114–15
Glenn, John, 179–80
Global Shield exercise, 156–57
Gofman, John, 92n
gold transmutation, 19–20, 22
Goodwin, Harold, 133
Goudsmit, Samuel, 76n
Gouré, Leon, 239–40, 250–51, 255
government, United States. See United States government
Gracey, Harold, 8, 222n
Graham, Daniel, 302–304
Gray, Colin, 208–10, 303, 305
Greene, Jack, 83
Greenfield, Massachusetts, 229

Greenland warning systems, 45, 61
Grindel, Frank, 155–56
Grissom Air Force Base, Indiana, 57
Gromyko, Andrei, 245
Groves, Leslie:
  in atomic bomb development, 30, 35
  on bomb stockpile estimates, 182–83
  and first bomb test, 15–16
  and radioactivity effects, 67, 69–70
  Szilard, relations with, 38
guidance systems, 201
Guinter, Harry, 226, 290
Gulley, Bill, 58–59, 63

Haig, Alexander, 49, 151, 152n, 261
Haldeman, H. R., 191n
Hale, Barbara, 138
Hammacher Schlemmer, 138
Handler, Philip, 312–13
Harmon Committee, 184–85
Hatfield, Mark, 317
Health and Human Services, Department of (HHS), 7–9, 218n, 222–23, 227
Hein, Joseph, 97
helium, experiments with, 20
Helms, Richard, 64
Herskowitz, Richard, 105
Hilsman, William, 233, 278–79
Hinton, Sam, 82
Hiroshima, 41, 43, 67–70, 74–75, 78, 85, 128, 275, 297n, 314
Ho Chi Minh, 191n
Hoegh, Leo A., 135
Holton, James, 318–19
housing, management, 8–9, 225. See also shelters
Hudson Institute, 207, 341
Hunt, Gary, 156–57
Huntington, Samuel, 145
hydrogen, experiments with, 20, 32–33

hydrogen bomb (see also atomic bomb; nuclear war; nuclear weapons):
  explosive power, 35, 80–84
  fallout effects. See fallout
  first explosions, 82, 84
  power derivation, 79
  production costs, 81n
  research and development, 27–30, 32–33, 79–83, 91, 93, 176–78, 186
  size unlimited, 79
  songs about, 82

IBM Corporation, 276, 280
Indian Point, New York, 110n
industry:
  executives lines of succession, 276, 281
  relocation plans, 130, 275–77, 281–83
  resources and records preservation, 275–76, 280–81
inflation control, 1, 283
Inland Vital Records Center, 280
Integrated Emergency Management System, 320
Integrated Operational Nuclear Detonation Detection System (IONDS), 47, 170
intelligence reports, 257
intercontinental ballistic missiles (ICBMs). See nuclear weapons
Interior, Department of the, 285
intermediate-range missiles defined, 48n
Internal Revenue Service, 2–4, 287
International Physicians for the Prevention of Nuclear War, 245, 295, 301
Interstate Commerce Commission, 236–37
Iron Mountain Atomic Storage Corporation, 276–77, 279–80, 293n
Italy, atomic research in, 24

"Ivy League" exercise, 64, 65, 151

Jackson, Henry, 93
Jacobson, Harold, 68–69
Japan (*see also* Hiroshima; Nagasaki):
    air assaults on, 43, 69–70, 78, 185
    as atomic bomb target, 36–41, 43
    fallout scare in, 84–85
Jennings, Norwood, 150, 172, 338
Johnson, Lyndon, 140
Joint Chiefs of Staff (JCS):
    on Afghanistan invasion, 261
    Alerting Network, 158
    and antimissile systems, 206n
    on antinuclear movement, 314
    attack, reaction to, 45
    conventional-war plans, 183–84
    on economic recovery, 13, 340–41
    and flexible response, 193
    on missile-launching submarines, 173
    on Soviet win policy, 248
Joint Committee Against Communism, 82
Joint Committee on Defense Production, 252–53, 309
Joint Strategic Target Planning Staff, 164
Joliot, Frédéric, 27
Jones, Jim, 139
Jones, T. K., 74–75, 127, 251–52
Jones & Laughlin Steel Corporation, 279
Journal of Civil Defense, 204, 233n, 296, 314
Journal of Peace Research, 322
Justice, Department of, 220, 279

Kahn, Herman, 104, 118n, 138, 190–91
KC-135 aircraft, 155–57
Kearny, Cresson, 122n, 328, 330
Kecskemeti, Paul, 332n
Keegan, George, 251
Keeny, Spurgeon, Jr., 204–205

Kefauver, Estes, 87
Kelso, Frank, 335
Kennedy, John F.:
    and antimissile systems, 194
    on civil defense as deterrent, 136–37, 139–40, 146, 194
    on government continuity, 216
    on limited attacks, 192
    on nuclear weapons effects, 330
    on shelters, 136–38
    on survival, 128
    and underground tests, 96
Khrushchev, Nikita, 94, 257–58
Kirby, Fred, 71–72
Kissinger, Henry, 178–79, 189–90, 261, 314–15
Kistiakowsky, George, 42
Kōbe, air assaults on, 70
Kokura as target, 41, 43
Konopinski, Emil, 30–34, 42, 79
Korean War, missiles in, 50, 187
Kuboyana, Aikichi, 84–85
Kuril Islands, 45
Kyoto as target, 41

Labor, Department of:
    emergency management, 230, 234
    executives succession plan, 220
    and deflation effect, 283
    labor management, 11–13, 284, 286
    and medical services, 12
    on records safety, 225
labor force:
    in bomb development, 15
    management, 11–13, 284, 286–87
labor unions, 282
Laird, Melvin, 62
Lang, Daniel, 69
language guides, 196
Las Vegas, Nevada, 87, 107
Las Vegas Review Journal, 132
laser weapons, 46
Latham, Donald, 340
Laurence, William, 41, 78
Lawler, Russ, 113

Lawrence, Ernest, 40, 79, 93–94
Leahy, Patrick, 13–14
Leahy, William, 37
Legacy of Hiroshima (Teller), 91, 95
Lehrer, Tom, 129
LeMay, Curtis, 183
Lenin, V. I., 242, 244
Leningrad, 80, 306
Leonardo da Vinci, 71
Libby, Willard, 90, 138
Life, 71, 137, 180–81
Lilienthal, David, 81–82
limited war concept, 163–65, 168, 172, 179, 189–94, 196–201, 206, 208–10, 243, 248, 265
lithium, experiments with, 20
Literary Digest, 18
living conditions. *See* housing; shelters
local governments, emergency management, 227–32
Lodge, Oliver, 17–18, 22
Looking Glass aircraft, 149–51, 155, 158, 160, 170–73, 193–94, 338
Loring Air Force Base, Maine, 156–57
Los Alamos Scientific Laboratory, 15–16, 31, 39–40
Lucky Dragon (Fukuryo Maru) incident, 84, 86–88

MacArthur, Douglas, 43
Mack, John, 305
Macklin, Buford, 223
Madden, David, 225, 304
mail service. *See* postal service
Marshall Islands, fallout on, 84–85
martial law, 216
Marvin, Cloyd, Jr., 31, 33
Massachusetts civil defense, 103
massive retaliation concept, 134–35, 166, 181, 187–88, 195, 199, 243–44
Mayaguez incident, 169
Maynard, Massachusetts, 227–28
McKnight, Maxwell, 292

McNamara, Robert:
  on assured destruction, 195–96, 202
  on Command, Control, and Communications, 193–94, 196
  on flexible response, 192–94
  on limited attacks, 164, 200
  on tactical missiles, 49
Mealy, Joseph, 113–15, 228–29, 232
medical services, 321
medical supples control, 12, 140, 285, 321
Merchant, Robert, 226–27
metals:
  supply and control, 12, 285
  transmutation experiments, 18–20, 22
Metro-Goldwyn-Mayer studio, 71
Military Strategy, 245
Mill Race exercise, 324–30
minerals supply and control, 284–85
mines, nuclear, 49
Mininson family, 141
minorities relocation, 106–107
missiles. *See* nuclear weapons
Mitchell, Donald, 127, 129
Mitchell, William, 185–86
morale maintenance, 122–23, 308–309
Morrison, Philip:
  on atomic bomb effect on war, 73
  and bomb-drop decision, 39–40
  and concern over chain reaction, 31
  on protection against radioactivity, 73–74
  on radioactivity effects, 67–70, 74–77
  on underground testing, 96
Moscow as target, 80
Mosler Safe Company, 275
Mothershead, Marvin, 289
Mount Hebo, Washington, 45
Mount Weather, 223–25, 232, 234
municipal governments. *See* local governments

Murphy, Paul, 166
Museum of Broadcasting, 293*n*

Nagasaki, 41, 43, 67–68, 70–72, 75, 85, 128, 297*n*, 314
Nagoya, air assaults on, 70
Namu hydrogen bomb test, 84
National Archives, 238
National Command Authority (NCA), 64, 158, 162–63, 201
National Committee for a Sane Nuclear Policy, 89
National Defense Executive Reserve, 285
National Emergency Airborne Command Post (NEACP), 57, 63–64, 65, 150, 171, 217
National Emergency Alarm Repeater, 114
National Fallout Shelter Survey, 139
National Military Command Center, 44–45, 58, 278
National Oceanic and Atmospheric Administration, 113
National Plan for Emergency Preparedness, 216, 293–94
National Research Council, 311, 313
National Security Council, 189, 233
National Strategic Target List, 164–66
National Weather Service, 157, 206–12
navigation systems, 271
Navy, United States, 185–86, 263. *See also* submarines, missile-launching
Nehru, Jawaharlal, 135
Netcong, New Jersey, 273
neutron, experiments with, 20–21, 25–26
neutron bomb, 49, 93–94
New Look, the, 188
New York City civil defense, 107, 115–16, 131, 133

New York State emergency center, 228
New York Times, The:
on atomic-bomb jokes, 71
on atomic energy use, 20, 22, 72
on AT&T construction, 277
on chain reaction, 34
on communal dispersion, 130–31
on escalation control, 166
on public attitude toward bomb, 78
on radioactivity effects, 70
on Soviet civil defense, 254
on submarines vulnerability, 263
on targets in Soviet, 210
on uranium production, 29, 35
New Yorker, The, 70
Newsweek, 28, 89, 138
Niigata as target, 41
Nimitz, Chester, 78
nitrogen, experiments with, 18–19, 32–33
Nitze, Paul, 129, 264, 340–41
Nixon, Richard M.:
and authorizing use of nuclear weapons, 59–60*n*
China visit, 58
on government continuity, 220
on limited attacks, 196–97, 332*n*
on massive retaliation, 187, 191*n*
on reserve missiles, 333
and test bans, 87–88
wage and price freeze, 283*n*
Nogales, Arizona, civil defense, 108–109
Nolan, John, 290–92
Nord, Alan, 324–25
North American Aeorspace Defense Command (NORAD):
attack, reaction to, 44–45, 55, 112, 115
detonations estimates, 213–14
false alerts by, 60
on tactical missiles, 48, 50, 151
Nuclear Madness (Caldicott), 301
nuclear-power plants shutdown, 110*n*

Nuclear Regulatory Commission, 110n
nuclear war (see also atomic bomb; hydrogen bomb; nuclear weapons):
  deterrence value, 181, 192, 203–204
  forces reconstitution, 174–75
  opposition to. See antinuclear movement
  political implications, 244–45, 261
  post-attack plans, 1–13
  preemptive strike risks, 203, 264–66, 270–72
  scenarios production, 207–10
  stalemate produced by, 177–78
  strategy criticized, 208–10
  survival in, 126–31, 138–40, 142–45, 147, 213, 295, 301–13, 322–23, 328, 331, 334, 340
  termination phase, 331–42
  victory indications, 339–42
nuclear weapons (see also atomic bomb; hydrogen bomb; nuclear war):
  approval for use, 52, 54, 59, 158
  blast effects, 101, 126, 132
  classification, 48n
  D-5, 271–72
  defined, 48n
  Dense Pack plan, 268
  deployment plans, 60, 188, 198
  doctrine on use, 48–55
  effects of, 67–70, 74–78, 295–314, 329–30, 332. See also fallout; radioactivity
  freeze on. See antinuclear movement
  Honest John, 49
  intercontinental missiles, 262–66
  Lance, 60
  Midgetman, 269
  Minuteman, 60, 152, 154, 159–61, 164, 166, 173, 193, 263, 265, 338
  modernization program, 202
  multiple warheads, 166–67, 269

MX, 60, 166, 202, 266–72, 318, 326, 334
  neutralizing, 173
  new generations development, 202
  Pershing, 202, 272, 330
  radioactivity from. See radioactivity
  reserve stocks, 333–35, 342
  safety risks in firing, 53–54
  Sea Wolf, 325, 330
  strike planning and pattern, 4, 51–55
  tactical weapons use, 48–55, 151–52, 186n, 189, 198
  tests, 15, 41–42, 82, 84, 125–26, 132, 183, 275, 324–30
  test ban agreements, 87–89, 91–96, 139
  test moratorium, 95–96
  time factor in use, 54–56, 60–61
  Titan, 152n
  Trident, 153, 202
  underground tests agreement, 96
  unused missiles disposition, 174
  warning systems. See warning systems
Nuclear Weapons and Foreign Policy (Kissinger), 178
Nunn, Sam, 46–47

Oak Ridge National Laboratory, 307
Oberg, Larry, 238
O'Brien, Bob, 338n
Office of Defense Resources, 284
Office of Emergency Planning, 220
Office of Emergency Preparedness, 216
Office of the Federal Register, 237
Office of Personnel Management, 235
Office of Technology Assessment (OTA), 199, 309–12
Ogarkov, Nikolai, 246–47
oil supply and control, 308

Olney, Maryland, 112, 212
Omaha World-Herald, 245*n*
On the Beach (Shute), 94–95,
    125–27, 129
On Thermonuclear War (Kahn),
    118*n*
One World or None, 76
O'Neill, Thomas, 56, 217
Oppenheimer, J. Robert:
    on allies, liaison with, 40
    chain reaction, concern over,
        29–30, 42
    heads Los Alamos, 31
    and hydrogen bomb, 29–30,
        79–80, 82
    on radioactivity effects, 69
    security risk alleged, 80
    on tactical weapons, 186*n*
oxygen, experiments with, 18–19
ozone depletion, 299, 304, 311–12,
    322

Panofsky, Wolfgang, 204–205
Pauling, Linus, 88–89
Payton, Daniel, 61, 333
Pentagon. *See* Defense, Department
    of
People, the Army, the Commander,
    242
Pepperell, Massachusetts, 276
Percy, Charles, 60
Perimeter Acquisition Radio Attack
    Characterization System, 45
Perle, Richard, 318, 320
Perpetual Storage Inc., 280
Perry, William, 270
Peterson, Keith, 56, 339
Peterson, Val, 82–83, 132
*Philosophical Heritage of V. I.
    Lenin, The,* 241–42
physicians. *See* medical services
Physicians for Social Responsibility,
    95, 126, 321
Pidgeon, Richard, 223–24, 226
pigs in Bikini tests, 78
Pipes, Richard:
    on Soviet civil defense, 248

    on Soviet damage acceptance,
        252
    on Soviet mentality, 246
    on Soviet strategic bombing, 241
    on Soviet win concept, 240, 245
    on survival, 304–305
    on U.S. no-win concept, 246
Pittman, Steuart, 139–40
Plattsburgh, New York, civil de-
    fense, 97–102, 105, 107, 229
plutonium production, 30–31
Policastro, John, 233
Portland, Oregon, civil defense,
    133
Post Attack Command Control
    System (PACCS), 150, 158
postal service, 5–7, 221
Powers, Robert, 340
Pravda, 78, 245*n*
president of the United States (*see
    also by name*):
    and civilian evacuations, 103
    and damage assessment, 170
    emergency orders, 1
    missiles use approval, 52, 158
    role during crisis, 57–65, 113, 150,
        308, 336
    safety of, 63, 65, 217
    successors' safety and installation,
        55–57, 64–65, 216–17, 230
prices control, 1, 109, 234
Primary Alerting System, 170
property requisitioning, 237
Protection in the Nuclear Age,
    100–101, 116
Proxmire, William, 248
Public Health Service, 222*n*, 224

Quarles, Donald, 86

Rabi, Isidor, 25–26, 80
Rabideau, George, 97–98
"rad" defined, 51
radar in missiles detection, 45–46,
    61, 169, 213, 278
radio and television, 100–104, 106,
    113, 115, 134, 156

radioactivity (*see also* atomic bomb; atomic energy; hydrogen bomb; nuclear weapons):
  in cobalt bomb, 86
  detecting and measuring, 118–19
  fallout effects, 83–86, 88–91, 118, 178, 211, 297–98, 310–12
  inducing, 16–20, 24–25
  protection from, 6, 9, 72–73, 115–16, 132–33, 162, 212. *See also* shelters
radium, experiments with, 16, 18
Railroad Retirement Board, 220
RAND Corporation, 142, 192, 207
rationing plans, 10–11, 213, 236, 284
RCA Victor, 82
REACT computer program, 214
READY damage-estimation program, 212–13
Reagan, Ronald:
  and antimissile systems, 205–207
  on antinuclear movement, 317
  assassination attempt on, 58
  on assured destruction concept, 205
  and B-1 bomber, 315
  on civil defense, 98, 136, 147–48, 206, 316
  code security, 58
  on Command, Control, and Communications, 206
  on command post functions, 171, 335
  and damage control, 206
  deterrence policy, 203, 207, 210
  on E-4 aircraft, 62
  on first-strike risks, 271
  on government continuity, 234
  on hot-line improvement, 336–37
  on limited attacks, 166, 206
  on medical stockpiling, 285n
  nuclear weapons program, 267–68, 271, 315
  on Soviet missiles stocks, 258–60
  on Soviet win concept, 240
  successors' safety, 56
  on survival, 128

on tactical weapons, 50, 244, 315
  and test ban, 315
Recovery from Nuclear Attack, 306
refueling systems, airborne, 156–57
religious groups, 71. *See also* clergymen
Reiling, Bill, 108
rent controls, 1, 8
research agencies scenarios, 207–10
resources supply and control, 11–12, 284–85
Rickover, Hyman, 302
Ridgeway, James, 322
risk area defined, 98n
Robbins, Gary, 3–5
Roberts, J. Gordon, 276
Rockefeller, Nelson, 135, 228
rockets, antisatellite, 46
Rogers, Bernard, 49
Rogers, William, 64
Roosevelt, Franklin D., 27, 38
Rosenberg, David Alan, 183
Rumsfeld, Donald, 58, 252, 339
Russia. *See* Soviet Union
Rutherford, Ernest, 16–19, 21, 23–24

saboteurs. *See* terrorists
Sagan, Carl, 313–14
Sagebrush exercise, 189
Sales taxes, 4–5, 287
SALT II. *See* Strategic Arms Limitation Talks
sanitation facilities, 122, 142
satellites:
  decoys, 46
  killer systems, 46
  laser weapons against, 46
  missiles detection by, 44–46, 169, 201
  navigational, 271
  rockets against, 46
Schell, Jonathan, 299–301, 311, 319, 322–23
Schlafly, Phyllis, 195n, 318
Schlesinger, James, 50, 60n, 197–200, 205n, 262

Scientific American, 21, 29
scientists:
  and atomic bomb control, 76–77
  hydrogen bomb, opposition to, 81
Scott, Harriet Fast, 250
Scripps-Howard newspapers, 72–73
Securities and Exchange Commission, 220
security measures and systems, 16, 34, 36, 46, 58, 152–53, 156–57, 212, 238, 267
seed distribution, 10
sheep, fallout effect on, 89
Shell Oil Company, 276–77, 280
shelters, construction and management of, 111, 116–24, 131–32, 134–42, 276, 289–92, 329–30
Shultz, George, 263–64
Shute, Nevil, 94–95
Single Integrated Operational Plan (SIOP), 164–67, 189, 193, 195, 333
Slobodenko, A., 243
Smith, Jerry, 286
Social Security Administration, 280
Soddy, Frederick, 17–19, 22, 89
Sokolovskii, V. D., 245
Sons of the Pioneers, 82
Soviet Military Power, 259–62
Soviet Union:
  antimissile systems, 262–72
  in antinuclear movement, 318
  armed forces strength, 260
  atomic bomb acquisition, 76, 78–79, 131, 186, 241
  atomic bomb, attitude toward, 241–42
  attack by, detection and reaction to, 44–48, 55–65, 149–75, 213–14, 248, 265, 272, 278
  attack by, predicted, 85–86, 145
  blackmail potential, 264–66
  bomber strength estimates, 257
  casualties estimates, 251–53, 256
  civil defense, 144–46, 239, 248–57
  Command, Control, and Communications (C³), 169

  conventional war against planned, 183–84
  deterrence capability, 205*n*
  evacuation plans, 147, 249, 251, 253, 256
  fallout from tests by, 87–88
  false attack alerts, 45–46
  hydrogen bomb acquistion, 82, 132
  intelligence operations, 194*n*
  killer satellites, 46
  liaison with proposed, 40
  limited attacks on, 164, 172, 189–94, 209–10
  limited attacks, view on, 243, 265
  and massive retaliation, 243–44
  missiles stocks, 257–58, 261
  morale assessed, 186*n*
  and nuclear threat political use, 244–45, 261
  nuclear war, views on, 242–47
  preemptive strikes by, 203
  shelters program, 239, 249–51, 256
  strategic bombing doctrine, 241
  surveillance by, 156
  targets in, 80, 164–68, 182, 184, 188–89, 192–93, 201, 209, 336, 339
  and termination phase, 336–37, 338*n*
  and tests ban, 92–93, 139
  tests moratorium agreement, 95–96
  underground tests agreement, 96
  vulnerability estimates, 261–63, 266
  war plans against, 184–85, 188
  weapon stocks growth, 197–98
  win concept, 240–42, 244, 247–48
Sputnik launch, 134
Stalcup, William, 149–50, 170, 172
Standard Oil of New Jersey, 277
State, Department of, 26
state governments. *See* local governments
Sternglass, Ernest, 298

Stevenson, Adlai, 87
Stimson, Henry, 35–38, 40–41
Stockman, David, 259n
Strategic Air Command (SAC):
  attack, response to, 44, 55–57, 59,
    149–175, 183, 278
  Soviet, plans against, 188
Strategic Arms Limitation Talks,
    145
strategic bombing debate, 185–86
Strategic Bombing Survey, 78,
    130–31, 185
strategic missile defined, 48n
Strauss, Lewis, 82, 85, 90–91
Strope, Walmer E., 125–27, 141–42,
    144
submarines:
  communications systems, 171, 173
  detecting, 154
  missile-launching, 44–45, 55–57,
    153–54, 161, 173–74, 263,
    271–72, 334–35
  survivability, 173
Supreme Court justices safety, 217
Supreme Headquarters Allied
    Powers in Europe, 52
survival kits, 162
Symington, Stuart, 199
Szilard, Leo:
  atomic energy research, 23–27
  and bomb-drop decision, 39
  and end-of-wars concept, 177
  on evacuation, 130
  on fallout hazard, 85–86
  Groves, relations with, 38–39
  and hydrogen bomb, 81–82
  and nuclear arms control, 38–40
  on shelters, 138
  and uranium supply, 26–27

tactical missiles. See nuclear weap-
    ons
target selection and location, 40–41,
    51–52, 164–68, 182, 201, 209,
    336, 339
TASS, 233n
taxes, post-attack, 2–5, 7, 287

Taylor, Theodore, 177
Teikoko Bank, 275
telephone service, 159, 218–19, 274,
    277–79, 281, 338. See also
    Command, Control, and Com-
    munications
television programs, preserving,
    293n
Teller, Edward:
  and bomb-drop decision, 39
  chain reaction, concern over, 16,
    30–33
  and end-of-wars concept, 177
  on fallout hazard, 91–92
  hydrogen bomb development,
    27–28, 32, 79, 91, 176
  and neutron bomb, 93–94
  and On the Beach, 95
  on shelters, 135–36
  on survival, 322
  and test ban issue, 91–96
terrorists, atomic bomb acquisition
    by, 83, 205
theater missiles defined, 48n
thermonuclear bomb. See hydrogen
    bomb
thorium, experiments with, 16
Time, 28
Tinian, as staging area, 41, 66
Tirana, Bardyl, 107, 146–47
Tokyo, air assaults on, 43, 69, 78
traffic control, 97–98, 110, 133
Trans-Siberian Railway, 44
transportation systems, 4, 13,
    236–37
Treasury, Department of the:
  banking regulations, 288
  currency supply and control, 2, 4,
    235
  and economic recovery, 286
  and families relocation, 226–27
  and free enterprise preservation,
    293–94
  functions continuity, 221
  import duties waiver, 236
  indemnification policies, 2–4
  tax policies, 2–5, 7, 287

Trojan plan, 184–85
Truman, Harry S.:
  on archives preservation, 238
  and atomic bomb development,
    36
  on atomic bomb effect on war, 72
  and bomb-drop decision, 36–41,
    43, 71–72
  and bomb stocks estimates, 183
  on civil defense, 131
  on communal dispersion, 130
  and hydrogen bomb develop-
    ment, 80
  and nuclear arms control, 38
  on Soviet bomb acquisition, 78
Tsongas, Paul, 165, 316n
Tsuzuki, Masao, 67
TTAPS, 313–14

U-2 aircraft, 257
Underground Vaults & Storage
  (UVS), 290, 292
United Kingdom:
  atomic energy research, 16–19,
    21–26, 35
  cultural resources preservation,
    293
  fallout from tests, 87
  missiles use approval, 52
  tests moratorium agreement, 95,
    139
  underground tests agreement, 96
  warning systems in, 45, 61
United States government (see also
    president; agencies by name):
  alternate capital, 79, 215, 223
  atomic energy research in, 24, 26
  archives preservation, 237–38,
    275
  continuity, preserving, 215–17,
    220, 225–27, 232–34
  deterrence policy, 181
  emergency centers, 222–25
  emergency management teams,
    219–26, 230
  emergency notifications, 217–19
  emergency regulations code, 237

  employees relocation, 234–35
  evacuation plans, 8–9, 97–115,
    130, 133–34, 144–47, 257
  executives relocation, 230, 233–34
  executives succession, 220
  fallout from tests, 87, 89
  funds disbursement plans, 235
  identification cards, 225, 235
  nepotism ban suspension, 236
  planning guidance, 220–21
  records safety, 225, 237–38, 275
  tests moratorium agreement,
    95–96, 139
  underground tests agreement, 96
  warnings to officials, 217–19
United States Steel Corporation,
  276
Unruh, Willi von, 20
uranium:
  chain reaction established,
    28–30
  experiments with, 16–17, 24–26
  fissionability, 29
  supply and production, 26–27,
    29–31, 34–35
U.S. News & World Report, 83, 89,
  276n
Ustinov, Dmitri, 243

Vandenberg, Hoyt, 241
Vatican City, 71
vaults, underground, 274–76, 280,
  289–90
Vessey, John, Jr., 258
vice president, role of, in crisis,
  63–64, 150
Village Voice, 322–23
Vista Project, 186n

Wage and Salary Stabilization and
  Labor Disputes Administration, 283–84
wages, control of, 1, 232, 283–84
Walton, E. T. S., 20–21
war-loss policies, 286–87
Warning Attack Assessment Study,
  61

warning systems:
   in attack detection, 44–45,
      112–16, 213
   failures in, 62–63
   neutralizing, 46–47
Warnke, Paul, 145–46
Warren Air Force Base, Wyoming,
      166, 173
Washington evacuation drill, 133
Washington Post, The, 113, 147,
      301–302
Watson, Edwin, 27
Watt, James, 64
Wayne, John, 317n
weather service, 157–58, 211–12,
      214
Weinberger, Caspar:
   on attack detection, 47
   budget estimates, 259n
   on command post functions, 65,
      171–72
   on communications, 279
   and deterrence policy, 207, 210

   on first-strike risks, 60
   on limited attacks, 163, 206
   on tactical missiles, 152n
   on time factor in response, 61
   on win concept, 240, 247, 315–16,
      332
Weizmann, Chaim, 24
Welch, Jasper, 335–36
Wells, H. G., 22–23, 25
Westinghouse Corporation, 138
Whence the Threat to Peace, 260
White Sands Missile Range, 324
Whitten, Jamie, 131
Who Speaks for Civil Defense, 217n
Wigner, Eugene, 26
Williams, Henry Smyth, 19–20
Williams, William A., 342
win concept, 163, 240, 247–48,
      315–16, 332
World Set Free, The (Wells), 22–23,
      25

Yasko, Karel, 293

```
UA      Zuckerman, Edward.
23
Z83     The day after World
1984    War III
```

DATE			